Once a Thief

Once a Thief
Suzann Ledbetter

MIRA®

MIRA

ISBN 0-7783-2300-5

ONCE A THIEF

Copyright © 2006 by Suzann Ledbetter.

All rights reserved. Except for use in any review, the reproduction or utilization of this work in whole or in part in any form by any electronic, mechanical or other means, now known or hereafter invented, including xerography, photocopying and recording, or in any information storage or retrieval system, is forbidden without the written permission of the publisher, MIRA Books, 225 Duncan Mill Road, Don Mills, Ontario, Canada M3B 3K9.

All characters in this book have no existence outside the imagination of the author and have no relation whatsoever to anyone bearing the same name or names. They are not even distantly inspired by any individual known or unknown to the author, and all incidents are pure invention.

MIRA and the Star Colophon are trademarks used under license and registered in Australia, New Zealand, Philippines, United States Patent and Trademark Office and in other countries.

www.MIRABooks.com

Printed in U.S.A.

For Pat Fortune, a beloved, loyal, always-there friend who should have had a book dedicated to her eons ago. As the Sister Hazel song says, "I will not take these things for granted."

ACKNOWLEDGMENTS

Once a Thief may have germinated from my ongoing and probably Hollywood-inspired fascination with Depression-era gangsters, but my seed of an idea didn't grow into a book-length caper without lots of folks helping with the spadework.

Dave Ellingsworth, my husband and love of my life, should lead seminars on the care and feeding of writer spouses. He keeps me reasonably sane, reads and rereads every line, brainstorms and catches errors. Any still present are mine, not his.

As usual, the crew of nonspousal helpers who answered my questions and then some are: Corporal Todd Revell, Springfield Police Department; Ms. Nicole Lebeda, former U.S. Parole Officer; Darrell Moore, Green County, Missouri, Prosecuting Attorney; Crystal Cobb, Kelly King and Jim Lightner, People's Bank, Nixa, Missouri; Susan Fawcett, dear friend, published writer and United States Postal Service consultant.

A big thank-you also goes to Al Livingston, a onetime city patrolman in Boonville, Missouri, who shared the legend of John Dillinger's cruise through town and the story attached to the single Thompson machine gun housed in the department's evidence room, and to Bob Skaggs, my husband's dear and eternal friend and mentor, for whom life was a game, but darts were serious business.

Sasha Bogin, my new and absolutely fabulous editor, deserves kudos, as do the ever-wonderful dolls and guys at MIRA and my agent and business partner, Robin Rue.

1

Morning events will give you a boost toward an
aim that you once believed was completely
impossible.

Oh really? Ramey Burke rolled her eyes.

Horoscopes were like fortune cookies—silly, yet
strangely intriguing. Reading hers every day in the
Plainfield News-Messenger was as much a ritual as
reading Dear Abby's advice column and Heloise's
household hints. A transition, as it were and was intended, between downer national news and journalism's dessert course, otherwise known as the comic
page.

Ramey poured a glass of freshly squeezed Florida
orange juice made from frozen concentrate, then
swigged it thoughtfully. Her list of erstwhile aims included the long-awaited call from NASA inviting her
aboard the next mission to the moon. That mutual love-

at-first-sight encounter with Robert Redford hadn't happened yet, either. It was his fault, of course, for neglecting Missouri's cinematic potential. It even had a Hollywood, down east in the Bootheel, midway between Arbyrd and Leachville Junction.

Nor had the thirty extra pounds she carried metamorphosed into sleek, sinuous muscle. Reminders that at under five foot six and maxing out at one hundred and forty pounds, Marilyn Monroe was an inch-and-a-half shorter than she was, didn't soothe the self-image as it used to.

The April sunshine streaming through the breakfast nook's windows glared off the newspaper splayed on the banquette table. A less frivolous list of goals slithered up from the recesses of Ramey's mind. Funny how something as innocuous as a horoscope could compromise the defenses she'd gradually built, armor plated and welded shut.

She blinked, concentrating her filmy gaze on the cartoon doldrums of Dilbert, then Snoopy, crouched on his doghouse, banging out the Great American Novel on a typewriter.

Cute, but what she wouldn't give for a *Calvin and Hobbes* revival, or *The Far Side*. They'd been her husband's favorites, too. Every Christmas she and Stan stuffed each other's stocking with a new Gary Larson desk calendar.

For the past two years, she'd bought her own.

He'd been riding a motorcycle he'd just repaired. "A spin around the block," Stan's boss had said. "Same as a hundred other times." Except that day, he didn't come back to the shop.

Whether he blew through a red light, or the tractor-trailer he hit was at fault couldn't be established. Several people heard the collision. Nobody aside from the truck driver actually witnessed it.

Impossible was believing you could survive the loss of your mother to cancer, then your father to a massive coronary, then your husband to a freak traffic accident, all in a three-year span.

But somehow, Ramey had. One day at a time, as the platitude went. Going on eight hundred of them since her husband's funeral. She knew she was healing when she couldn't recall the precise number.

Telling herself the emptiness deep in her belly was hunger, she forced herself up from the cushioned bench. An archway trimmed in fluted oak separated the breakfast nook from a kitchen larger than the average living room. To the right of the sink, the frosted glass cupboard doors creaked wide on seventy-year-old hinges.

Moving back to this rambling house her grandparents built had grounded her. Memories attached to the house where she and her older sister grew up weren't emotional minefields, unlike the duplex she and Stan had leased. It had been his place, then theirs. But this house would always be her home.

Ramey hooked her fingers on the cabinet's nickel-plated catches and peered into the cavernous shelves. Apparently the Muffin Fairy had again failed to deliver a single, frosted apple chunk confection during the night.

There was no bread left for toast, either. The last two reduced carb, wafer-thin slices had anchored the tuna sandwich she'd eaten for lunch yesterday. Peanut butter and crackers would be great, if she had any crackers.

A trip to the supermarket was well overdue, except food shopping when you're starved was like an ex-smoker bumming a cigarette for old times' sake. One whiff of the bakery at Trantham's IGA would induce a doughnut binge of epic proportions. Just thinking about it made Ramey's mouth water.

Losing weight was easy. Don't eat or drink anything worth swallowing for the rest of your life and *allakazam*. Goodbye fat and jolly. Hello lean and mean.

Would the bathroom scale ever top out again at a hundred and twenty? Sure, if she lay across it instead of standing on it. On the other hand, tearing hell-bent to the grocery store for maple bars probably wasn't the type of "morning event" Madame Astrid's horoscope implied.

Besides, it'd be noon in a mere four hours and fifty-seven minutes. The reward for breakfast deprivation would be a justifiable deluxe cheeseburger, fries and a diet soda for lunch. If she held out till one-thirty or so, there could be onion rings.

Armed with a bowl of baby carrots, black coffee and the *News-Messenger*'s Wednesday classified section, Ramey started up the stairs to her home office.

Some people choose a career; sometimes careers choose them. Ramey's older sister, Portia, was so enamored of Gerald O'Hara's declaration, "Land is the only thing in the world that amounts to anything" in *Gone With the Wind,* she'd decided at the tender age of twelve to become a real estate agent.

How her identification with a fictional, Irish plantation owner translated to listing properties and schlepping prospective buyers to them defied explanation. Ramey admired her, though, for knowing what she wanted to be when she grew up before she actually did.

Ramey's own childhood dreams of interplanetary exploration and a fleeting interest in dinosaurs deadended at a series of retail sales and secretarial jobs, until the fateful day she'd tagged along with Portia to view another agent's listing. The house was a threebedroom, single bath horror. Saggy foam-backed drapes covered every window, trapping the stench of fried fish, cigar smoke and dust. In the galley kitchen, stencils of somewhat menacing teapots cavorted on the bulkheads and walls. The bathroom's leaky sink was frothed in lime deposits. Mildew crept up the tub surround.

"Sad," Portia said. "The asking price is right for the neighborhood, but if the old man who owns it even gets an offer, it'll be thousands below what it's worth."

"Why?" Ramey asked. "All it needs is a lot of scrubbing, a plumber, nice curtains and a few gallons of paint."

"From your lips to the seller's ear. His real estate agent hinted that it needed a good cleaning, but there's a fine line between a good cleaning and a miracle. The poor guy tried, but his eyesight is failing."

"Okay," Ramey allowed, "but if I can visualize its potential, you'd think a buyer would."

"Potential, as in money pit, is the problem." Portia ticked off on her fingers. "Most prospects want a home, not a mortgaged renovation list. They can't see the bay windows for the dirt and grandma's god-awful drapes. The floors are cluttered and that paneled hallway looks like the tunnel of doom. Deferred maintenance, like drippy faucets, sound a warning that the plumbing is shot."

Portia gave the murky living room a final, dejected appraisal. "Every agent in town has mutts like this one. If I had the talent and the tact, I'd make as much money grooming these ugly dogs as I do trying to sell them."

For days, her comments nagged at Ramey. Her mind

regrouped furniture, repainted walls, envisioned inexpensive white sheers billowing in the breeze.

Interior design wasn't her thing, yet she did have an affinity for decorating on the cheap. Where Portia loved perfectly coordinated rooms, Ramey's taste leaned toward shabby chic years before the nicked and slightly threadbare was fashionable.

On something between a whim and a dare, she revisited the grungy house with an array of paint chips, a tape measure and a notebook, then made the owner a deal he didn't refuse. If her cosmetic improvements brought an acceptable offer within two weeks, he'd pay her two-hundred-and-fifty dollars for labor and materials. If his ugly dog still didn't hunt, he wouldn't owe her a penny.

From a hallucinogenic paint-fumed fog emerged the idea to host an open house and invite all the local real estate agents. Life being a persistent font of humility, a steady rain began to fall at dawn that Sunday. By noon, the front lawn resembled a rice paddy.

Perhaps not coincidentally, Portia had her own open house to tend to that day. The majority of her peers were no-shows, as well, but the listing agent arrived with a young couple who'd toured the house at its worst. Within an hour, the trio waded off with homemade cookies and a signed contract—for the full asking price.

The grateful seller paid Ramey's fee, plus a hundred-dollar bonus. Minus expenses, she figured she'd cleared a dollar and seventeen cents an hour.

Live and learn. Trial and lots of error. After several years of both, the profits of accidental self-employment were still far below Portia's commissions, but Ramey loved being an independent contractor of sorts.

These days, her style of sweat equity even had a name—home-stager. Cable TV popularized the term and concept, but seriously skewed the expense and labor involved.

Although four stagers' boxed ads had joined Ramey's in the Plainfield phone book, she still received more referrals than she could handle.

The luxury of working out of her own home was the biggest perk. No commute. No frantic search for a parking spot. No anal-lovelorn-manically cheerful-gropey-mopey-busybody coworkers to avoid. Overtime, yes. Deadlines, ditto. But coffee breaks at will and theoretically, time off for no particular reason.

The doorbell rang just as Ramey reached the second-floor landing. Assuming it was Chad, the UPS guy, making his almost daily rounds, she surveyed the humongous St. Louis Rams T-shirt she'd slept in. Below the frayed hem were a pair of chartreuse, high-water sweatpants. Argyle wool socks sufficed as house shoes.

Oh well. Chad had seen her look worse. The question was, had he ever seen her look any better?

"No one looks good before eight freakin' o'clock in the morning," she grumbled, setting down the carrot bowl coffee mug and newspaper. "He's got his uniform, I've got mine. You want gorgeous, go ring Portia's chimes."

A row of square glass panes near the top of the door let in sunlight, but they were too high to work as peepholes, unless Frankenstein's monster was on the porch. Reminding herself again to buy a fish-eye thing the next time she went to the hardware store, Ramey twisted the dead bolt's brass swivel.

Her fake smile wouldn't distract UPS guy from her embarrassing ensemble, but years of orthodontia during high school hadn't been a total waste.

"Surprise!" yodeled a buxom woman dressed in a floral muumuu, support hose and sneakers. The purplish-gray frizz that haloed her head smacked of a recent home perm and dye job gone horribly wrong.

Behind her stood two grinning, wiry men of approximately the same age, somewhere between seventy and graveside services. Their shirt collars were dingy, but starched as stiff as polyester nooses. Their respective black and brown double-breasted suits were the same vintage as their tablecloth neckties.

The taller codger held a bouquet of jonquils, their

scalloped yellow petals adrip with dew. In the other man's knob-knuckled hands were a pair of battered suitcases sealed with duct tape.

All three gazed upon Ramey with the requited joy usually reserved for religious conversions and Elvis sightings.

The woman gasped and clapped a hand to her chest. "Heavenly days, child! The last time I saw you, you were no bigger'n a minute."

The flower bearer sucked his teeth. "Now here you are, all grown-up. Prettier than peaches, too."

"Ah, I'da recognized her anywhere," said the one with the suitcase. "Look at them big ol' brown eyes."

"And that chin." The woman angled her head, her lips pursed like a coquette's. "See the little dimple? She's Sylvie's daughter, all right."

Ramey started. Her mother's name was Sylvia. Nobody had ever called her Sylvie, not even Ramey's father. Which was odd, now that Ramey thought about it. Her mother's personality and wicked sense of humor better fit the nickname.

On guard, but curious, Ramey asked, "Who are you? How did you know my mother?"

Suitcase Man's laugh was a cross between a wheeze and the hiccups. "Wish I had me a sawbuck for every time I changed Sylvie's diapers."

"Like hell." Flower-bearer flinched and hastily

begged Ramey's pardon for his language. "What I meant to say was, my brother's a mite confused about who did the changin' and who went runnin' when that sweet baby girl messed her britches."

A rumble akin to a suddenly undormant volcano resonated beneath Ramey's breastbone. Her eyes darted from one geezer to the other, then to the geriatric Shirley Temple beaming up at her. A whimper accompanied a silent prayer for deliverance.

"N-n-no," she said. "You can't be...."

"Lookee there, Ed," the flower-bearer chuckled. "The girl's so tickled to see her long-lost kinfolk, the cat done snatched her tongue."

Ramey's tongue was still attached, but momentarily consonant-challenged.

Shirley Temple advised, "Breathe in through your nose, hon, then out your mouth."

"What are you—How did you—" Ramey cleared her throat. "You're supposed to be in prison. All three of you. For *life*."

"That's what we thought, too," the man with the suitcase drawled. "Interesting story, how we got sprung." Stepping closer, he added, "Scootch over, so's I can lug these bags inside and we'll give you the lowdown."

The woman pinched Ramey's cheek as she passed by. "I'll put on the coffee."

"While you're at it," Flower-Bearer said, "rustle up a vase for these posies. Seeing as how that banshee down to the corner chased after me for picking 'em, it'd be a crying shame to let 'em wilt."

2

The Other Dillinger Gang.

That's what a Nixon-era newspaper reporter dubbed Ramey's maternal uncles Ed and Archie, and Archie's wife, Melba Jane. As though Plainfield, Missouri's branch of the Dillinger clan might be confused with the gat-happy thieves and killers led by that notorious son of an Indiana preacher, John Dillinger.

True enough, the Other Dillinger Gang *did* rob banks. They'd even fled with some cash in their loot bags. Despite the cops' best efforts to catch them, they'd gotten away with grand larceny for quite a while, too.

Thankfully the differences between the Dillinger Gang and the Other Dillinger gang were numerous. Ramey derived enormous comfort from that, considering they were seated on her living room sofa, sipping coffee like church elders.

First off, her Dillingers hadn't registered a blip on

J. Edgar Hoover's radar, whereas back in '34, Johnnie became the FBI's first Public Enemy Number One.

Ed, Archie and Melba Jane never hurt anybody, either. Nor had they associated with anyone nicknamed "Baby Face," as in Nelson, John Dillinger's right-hand sociopath.

Lastly, Ramey's mother had adored her older brothers. Forever the realist, Sylvia hadn't minced words when she spoke of their crimes and misdemeanors, but she'd loved Ed and Archie without shame, or cease.

"The jonquils look real pretty on the coffee table, don't they?" Melba Jane said to no one in particular. "Smell nice, too."

Yes, they did, Ramey thought, but if her mother had lived long enough for this bizarre reunion, she'd have pitched a fit about Archie's raid of the neighbor's flower bed.

"Your heart was in the right place," she'd say, as she had when Ramey once presented her with a bouquet of prize roses from a neighbor's garden. "But it's a sin to take things that don't belong to you."

When Sylvia then arranged the roses in a vase and displayed them on the dining room table, it confused Ramey to no end. Eventually she'd decided that one person's violation of the Ten Commandments must be another person's Finders-Keepers.

Archie whistled. "Lord-a-mercy, this coffee's

mighty stout. I told Melba Jane she was dumping the grinds too heavy into the machine."

"It's fine," Ramey lied. "I like it strong." She'd never been wider awake in her life. The residual caffeine buzz should wear off in a week or so.

Ed's shrewd hazel eyes surveyed the room's textured plaster walls. Nodding slowly, he cased the red-brick fireplace flanked by windows, the window seats, then the oak-boxed beams that spanned the ceiling like a giant tic-tac-toe board. "I like what you've done with the place."

Ramey looked around. "Thanks, but I haven't done anything to it."

Reaching behind his back, Ed adjusted a beaded sofa pillow, then wormed against it. Judging by his scowl, he'd gladly chuck it on the floor, but resisted to be polite.

"Well, the furniture's different. So's the little stuff— lamps and knickknacks and such. Near as I can remember, though, it's mostly the same as it was when me and Archie were kids."

Their father, "Chicken" Charlie Dillinger, sank to a foolhardy recklessness after the death of his wife, Lauraleen, and their stillborn daughter. From the money he made raising and shipping live poultry by the flatbed truckload, he graduated to numbers running, then amassed a fortune during Prohibition.

On occasion, Federal agents stopped the trucks, suspecting illegal whiskey was stashed in crates under the slimy straw that was weighted by agitated, incontinent fowl with beaks and no compunction against using them. Anyone who's trailed a live poultry truck on the highway for a mile or so can understand the agents' reluctance to investigate further.

Prohibition was repealed nationally, but Chicken Charlie continued supplying counties in Missouri, Arkansas and Kansas that voted to stay dry. The house he built for his second wife, Ava, was large and practical, in keeping with architect Gustav Stickley's devotion to form and function.

When Sylvia Dillinger Patterson inherited the property, she sold off all but an acre of the original farm in order to finance new plumbing and wiring, central heat and air-conditioning, and a touch of remodeling.

Portia still made noise about selling what she considered a four-bedroom, two-and-a-half-bath white elephant. Ramey bought ten bucks' worth of lottery tickets every week hoping to hit the jackpot and buy out her sister's share.

Melba Jane's sugar spoon clanked inside her cup, drawing Ramey's attention back to the problem at hand. "Aside from the house," she said, "everything else around here is pure strange. I guess it shouldn't have befuddled us, but when the bus pulled into the depot this morning, Archie asked the driver if he was sure this was Plainfield."

Archie grunted. "I half expected to see our old stomping grounds paved over and one of them new-fangled shopping malls smack-dab in the middle of it."

Newfangled? Shopping malls had been around since, well, forever it seemed. Plainfield, Missouri wasn't the epicenter of progress, but developers had bulldozed the trees and leveled the ground for Sycamore Hills Mall when Ramey was in the first grade.

Trying not to regard her visitors as though they had just beamed down from Mars, she said, "How long have you been, uh, away?"

"Thirty-four years, five months and seventeen days," Ed said.

"That's counting time served in the county jail," Archie clarified. "Before we went to trial and all."

"Except we didn't," Ed said. "The shyster lawyer we got told us to plead guilty and ask for the court's mercy, on account of it's easier to persuade one old boy than twelve of 'em sitting on a jury."

"If these two'd listened to me…" Melba Jane cut a scathing look at her husband and brother-in-law. "The judge gave them twenty-five-to-life for being habitual criminals. Me, I got fifteen years for being an accomplice."

"And for that dadblasted gun in your pocketbook."
Archie sighed. "How many times did we tell you, *no
guns*. We didn't need 'em and you couldn't hit the
broad side of a barn with a Buick, anyhow. But would
you listen?"

"Oh, for pity's sake. How many times do I have to
tell you. The dang thing wasn't loaded. Nobody'd ever
known it was there if that sheriff hadn't jostled me so
rough that I dropped my purse on his sore toe."

Ed grinned. "I swear, that county mountie wasn't a
tick over five-one in his cowboy boots and must've
weighed three-hunnert pounds. When he went to jumping up and down bellowing like a gored ox, me and
Archie couldn't run for laughing."

Ramey couldn't stifle her laughter, either. Picturing
a short, tubby sheriff howling and hopping on one foot
with the Dillingers staggering around in hysterics was
a hoot.

Except, apparently, to Archie. "If you think that's
bad, would you care to hear the second dumbest thing
my darlin' bride ever did?"

Ed muttered, "Not especially."

"Now understand, I was having a high ol' time being
a bachelor when I fell for Melba Jane hook, line and
till death do us part. Without her, we couldn't have
pulled a bank job for squat, but there's a reason me and
Ed's always been the brains of this outfit."

"Uh-huh." Melba Jane shot him a look. "It takes both of yours to make a whole one."

"Is that so? Well, who was it that took a notion to make a break for it and got another twenty years tacked on for her trouble?"

Melba Jane's jaw thrust forward. "I'da been free as a bird all this time, too, if that investigator had picked a different day to poke through the garbage bins."

To Ramey, she implored, "How was I to know the Bureau of Prisons got a tip that the warden was skimming the food budget every chance he could? They checked all the trash for evidence and found me instead."

Archie allowed, "For what he billed the taxpayers, Melba Jane and the other gals should've been up to their ears in steaks 'n strawberry shortcake."

Ramey's empty stomach growled. The calculator in her head added up calories for a six-ounce filet and a medium baked potato. If she went easy on the butter, sour cream, cheddar cheese and bacon bits, a luscious bowl of strawberry shortcake was doable for dessert. Then she'd join a gym and rack up three or four thousand miles on a treadmill.

"Beans and weenies." Melba Jane's lips curled as if she were retasting both. "That's all we got, lunch and supper, and scant little of it for nigh onto two years."

With the emphasis on beans, Ramey assumed, and

not the yummy, tomato-saucy kind she'd spooned straight from the can on family camping trips.

Slow starvation being an affliction any serial dieter could identify with, Ramey asked, "Is that why you tried to escape? Because the food was so awful?"

Melba Jane fiddled with the rickrack trim of her dress. "Well, er, no...not entirely."

"It's like this, hon." Ed deposited his coffee cup on the lamp table, then leaned forward, his forearms resting on his thighs. "When you're in our line of work, you spend a lion's share of your time trying to stay out of prison. Once you're locked up, you spend even more time divining how to get out again."

"Oh." Ramey's smile felt feeble, even to her. Scenes from *The Desperate Hours* scrolled behind her eyes. The classic prison-break flick starred Humphrey Bogart as a vicious escaped convict who took a family hostage in their home to elude a manhunt.

Any second now, squad cars would squeal to a halt on the street. Flashing red, white and blue lights would reflect off her window panes. Broderick Crawford would shout into a bullhorn, *You—in the house. This is the police. We've got you surrounded. Come out with your hands up and nobody'll get hurt.*

Ramey wasn't sure he was in that movie, but once upon a time, Broderick Crawford and bullhorns were as inseparable as Bogart and fedoras.

"What you mentioned when you came in," Ramey said, "you know, about how you, 'got sprung'? It wouldn't have anything to do with tunnels or bedsheet ropes, would it?"

Archie elbowed his brother. "Is she thinking we went over the wall?"

"Uh-huh. Or under it."

"You gotta be kidding." Archie laughed. "At our age?".

"Like they say, just 'cause there's snow on the roof, don't mean the fire's out in the stove." Ed joked.

Archie hesitated, then said, "I don't think it's a jail-break she's talking about."

Ed shrugged. "Nah, the parole board released us nice and legal. Seems every prison in the country is short on vacancies. With us being senior citizens, they reckoned we'd paid our debt to society and turned us loose."

"That's the heartstrings reason," Archie said. "Truth is, it's cheaper to toss graybeards out into the world to croak than it is to build geriatric wards and bigger hospital units."

Melba Jane added, "Me, I don't much care about the hows and whys." Laying a hand atop Archie's, she wriggled her fingers between his thicker, liver-spotted ones. "'Twas the happiest day of my life when I heard the feds weren't just giving me my walking papers. Bless 'em, they signed off on the boys, too."

Archie's eyes moistened at the corners. "The happiest day of mine is when you said I do."

Gagging noises erupted from Ed's throat, as though a brick had wedged in his windpipe. "Hope you ain't fresh out of Maalox, Ramey girl. All this billin' and cooin's enough to urp a hog."

Melba Jane sniffed. "You're just jealous."

"And you've lost what excuse for a mind you had left."

"Put a sock in it, the both of you," Archie snapped. "We didn't come here to squabble."

Which begged the question, why *had* they come? A sentimental journey to the town and home they'd grown up in was part of it. Books had been written and documentaries filmed portraying the primordial urge to return to one's roots.

Childhood memories weren't exclusive to them, but Ramey's were faint and lacked context. Quite possibly, hers were the product of her mother's stories about her brothers. Kids often superimpose themselves on family history they've heard about, but didn't actually witness. Except the hazy recollection of playing Cootie on the rug with her young, dark-haired Uncle Ed seemed real. Had she only imagined watching her mother and Archie laughing themselves silly trying to jitterbug to a Beatles' song?

Forcing herself back to the present, Ramey made a

point of consulting the mantel clock. "Listen, it's been wonderful talking with you, but I really have to get to work. I know Portia would love to see you, too, while you're in town. Unless you have other plans, I'll call her and we can pick you up later at your hotel for dinner."

The phrase "deafening silence" is not a conflict in terms to those who've experienced one.

Melba Jane's fingernail traced the fuchsia hibiscus petals abloom on her muumuu. Archie fidgeted, as if plagued by an itch in need of a private scratch. The tip of Ed's tongue probed teeth yellowed by age and nicotine. "Us being close to strangers," he said, "that's mighty sweet of you to offer to take us out for supper and all."

Ramey motioned, Don't mention it.

"And the last thing we want to do is make you late for work…"

"Well, my office is just up—" Ramey caught herself. "It's not far from here."

Squinting at the ceiling, Ed went on, "But that ring over yonder, above the windows? I suspect the gutters are clogged and rainwater's backed up under the shingles."

Ramey twisted around to look for herself. Darned if there wasn't a ragged mark a few inches from the crown molding.

"When we came up the sidewalk," Archie said, "I spied a bunch of dead limbs hanging from the old walnut tree. Could be they'll gouge the roof, first spring storm that kicks up."

Ramey's friend, Don Blevins, had noticed the droopy branches, too. He'd also volunteered to saw them off, but she wasn't sure what month, year, perhaps decade, he might get the job done.

Archie added, "And from what I saw, the bushes could sure use a trim."

Last spring they needed a trim. Now it'd take major surgery to tame the banked evergreens, hedges and shrubs planted from one end of the acre lot to the other and along both sides.

"No offense," Melba Jane said, "but give me a mop and a bucket and before you can say 'Boo' I'll have the inside sparkling like brand-new."

Archie prompted, "How many blue ribbons was it you won at the prison cafeteria's bake-offs?"

"Ten. I got four in a row for my Goozly Pie, before they said I couldn't enter it anymore so's somebody else could have a crack at the dessert category."

"Gooseberry pie? In prison?" Ramey said incredulously.

"Not gooseberry, hon. *Goozly.* There's frozen berries in it—strawberries, blackberries, even cherries, if you can lay hands on 'em. Where the name came from, I dunno, but cover that fruit with a big glob of sour cream mixture and it'll bring tears of joy to a tater's eyes."

Ramey could have wept just thinking about it.

"Hey, hey, hey." Ed slapped his knee. "I just had me one heck of an idea. How 'bout if Melba Jane cooks up an extra-special homecoming dinner, whilst me and Archie see about that leaky roof and the shrubs and whatever else needs fixing?"

Melba Jane giggled and rubbed her hands together. "Oh I *do* so love a party. I'll fix a platter of fried chicken, mashed potatoes and gravy, some hot rolls and…oh, a pineapple upside-down cake."

Archie teased, "That ought to hold me till it's time for you to rustle us up some breakfast."

Words usually didn't fail Ramey. Assorted X-rated nouns, verbs and adjectives swirled in her mind like sludge in a centrifuge.

"I know what you're thinking," Ed said, "but we won't be a bother or a burden. All we're asking is for a few days to get on our feet."

"A few *days?*"

"No more'n a week," Archie said. "Two at the outside."

Ed added, "It'll take us that long to get the house shipshape again."

"Of all the—" Ramey paused for a moment to let her tone relax from shriek to civilized. "The house isn't the issue. I'm sorry, but there's plenty of nice motels all over town. Staying here is absolutely out of the question."

Melba Jane looked from her husband to her brother-in-law, then scooted forward on the sofa cushion. "I'll get myself sideways with both of them for telling you this—"

"Then don't," Ed warned.

"But the truth is, we don't have anyplace else to go and not a nickel between us to take us there."

Nostalgia be damned. It was a handout they were after. They'd probably whiled away the bus ride from their respective prisons and on to Plainfield rehearsing their bait-and-switch. Assuming their mode of transportation wasn't as fabricated as their charm.

"You and Portia's all the family we've got," Melba Jane said. "We're not asking for charity. Wouldn't take it, if it was offered."

Sarcasm laced Ramey's chuckle. "Ah, but a check from your nieces wouldn't be charity, now would it?"

"No." Ed blew out a sigh. His head bowed, as though he'd exhaled what remained of his pride. "It'd be worse than charity."

Was he the greatest actor since Brando, or a thoroughly humiliated old man? Beside him, Archie's steady, unfocused stare intimated desperation and the kind of sorrow it inflicts.

"A second chance to go straight is all we're asking," Ed said. "No different than what your daddy gave Sylvie."

"Bill Patterson was a fine man," Melba Jane offered.

"For a cop," Archie allowed.

Ed slanted him a glare. "*Especially* for a cop. He caught Sylvie burgling that drugstore red-handed. If Cupid hadn't gotten the drop on Bill before he slapped the cuffs on her, she'd have been a gone goose."

Lukewarm coffee splashed from Ramey's cup onto her sweatpants. "Are you insinuating that my mother robbed a drugstore?"

It was Ed's turn to recoil. "She never told you how her and Bill met?"

"Yeah, about a thousand times. She was thirsty from shopping and went into the Rexall store for a soda. Daddy walked in, took one look at her and swept her off her feet."

"That's so romantic," Melba Jane cooed.

"Bill did the sweeping, sure as the world," Archie said, laughing. "Except when he scooped her up, Sylvie was wiggling out the drugstore's back window with a pocketful of greenbacks from the cash register."

"Why you lyin' old—"

Ed's hand shot up. "Fetch me a Bible and I'll swear on it."

"Aw, now it's nothing to get upset about," Archie told her. "Sylvie just did it the once, and only 'cause she was mad at me and Ed."

Ramey didn't want to believe it, yet she sensed they were telling the truth. Her mother's version had always sounded too Disney meets *Days of Our Lives*. But as curled black and white snapshots of Corporal Bill Patterson in uniform had shown, he'd been a handsome man in his prime.

Rising up the ranks to Chief of Police had aged him prematurely, as had the weight he'd put on from being parked behind a desk. His easy grin and sense of humor remained, but dimmed when Ramey's mother passed away.

Archie said, "Sylvie knew me and Ed were boosting grocery stores and gas stations pretty regular. She begged to tag along, like she did when she was a kid."

"I nixed that idea," Ed said. "I reminded her that she was a young lady, and we weren't going out nights to play sandlot baseball." He chuffed. "Your mama being your mama, what she heard was, 'I dare you to beat us at our own game.'"

"And if she'd cleared that windowsill a couple of seconds faster, she might've done it, too," Archie said. "We knew when and where every cop in town drove or walked his beat."

Ramey's eyebrows arched. "So that was the secret of your success."

Snide remarks were wasted on Ed. "And Sylvie's big mistake. Bill saw her clamber through that window, cooled his heels awhile, then snagged her on her way out."

"Did Dad arrest her?"

Ed shook his head. "Would have put a crimp in courtin' her, don'tcha think? Nah, Bill just hoisted her up again, so's she could put the money back, then took her home to Papa."

Melba Jane sighed and patted her bosom. "Now that *is* romantic."

It was, Ramey supposed. It also typified her parents' diametric, yet complementary personalities. Sylvia's impulsiveness had mellowed over the years, but she'd been the fun mom that Ramey and her sister's friends loved being around. Bill Patterson, ten years Sylvia's senior, was a teddy bear disguised as General Patton— tough, but fair.

His daughters—Ramey in particular—had learned early on that if they got caught in a lie, they were toast. Honesty wasn't the best policy. It was the only policy.

The ring of Ramey's office phone echoed from upstairs. Archie and Melba Jane swiveled their heads as people do at an unfamiliar sound. Ed's gaze remained leveled at Ramey. "The second chance Bill gave Sylvie is all we're asking of their daughter. If you can find it in your heart to let us earn our keep, we'll do anything and everything you ask, and then some."

I'm sorry, I can't. My heart and my life are just beginning to mend hadn't made the transition from thought to assertion, when the front door swung open.

"Ramey Jo, you'd better be up and—"

Portia Carruthers, nee Patterson, halted in the broad doorway between the vestibule and living room. Four-inch stilettos accessorized a tailored plum suit and lengthened a perfect pair of legs by approximately nine miles. Amber, silken curls brushed her shoulders like a model's in a shampoo commercial.

She took in the ratty suitcases on the floor. The senior citizens perched on one sofa. Her frumpy younger sister slouched on the other. She then eyed the front door, as if reconciling the absence of a vehicle outside with the presence of three strangers gawking at her from the living room.

Ed and Archie bounced up off the cushions. "Portia!" they exclaimed in unison, then Archie tacked on, "I'da recognized you anywhere. Look at them big ol' green eyes."

"And that square chin," Melba Jane said. "She's Bill Patterson's daughter, all right."

Ramey proceeded with the formal introductions. Her sister, who wouldn't chip a nail in an F-5 tornado, said, "Please excuse us for a moment," then blasted Ramey with the visual code for *your butt, in the kitchen, now.*

It was a tribute to the durability of the brick pavers used to floor the vestibule and corridor that Portia's heels didn't reduce them to dust as she marched to the kitchen. She whirled around the instant she cleared the doorway. "What in the *hell* are they doing here?"

A reasonable question. It was the unpleasant delivery that Ramey objected to. "They were granted parole because of their age."

"That explains why they aren't locked up, not the tea party underway in my living room."

"*Your* living room?" Ramey struggled to keep her temper in check. As cool as Portia always seemed on the outside, her defenses were as subject to failure as Ramey's.

"Fine. In *my* half of *our* living room." Portia growled and knuckled a hip. "I didn't haul you in here to argue joint ownership of the family mausoleum."

Ramey leaned against the counter. Crossing her arms, she reminded herself that other than being bossy, stuck-up, overbearing and beautiful, she really couldn't ask for a better sister. "Look, if anybody understands the shock value in the Dillingers appearing out of nowhere, it's me. How about we both count to ten and start this conversation over."

She'd made it to six before her alpha sibling said, "Okay. I'm sorry. I overreacted."

"Apology accepted. In fact, if I were in your shoes—" Ramey glanced down and winced. "I'd be crippled for life, but that's beside the point."

"If they weren't comfortable, I wouldn't wear them."

Oh yes, you would, Ramey thought. Goddesses don't wear flats.

Portia stated the obvious. "After all these years, the family jailbirds are on the loose again."

"Yep."

"You didn't know they were coming?"

"They wanted it to be a surprise."

"And it was one, wasn't it?" Portia snickered. "I'd give anything to have seen your face when you opened the door."

"The expression on yours when you walked in was pretty good. Like the witch in *The Wizard of Oz* when Dorothy grabbed that bucket of water."

Portia's mouth tucked into a wistful smile. "If Mom were here, she'd be thrilled to pieces to see them again."

Ramey nodded.

"Dad, too, I think. He didn't like what they did, but he liked them. Called them overgrown juvenile delinquents."

"To hear them talk, nothing's changed much." Ramey flapped a hand. "Which reminds me, they told me that Mom fibbed about falling in love at first sight with Daddy at the drugstore's soda fountain. Get this— he caught her burglarizing the joint."

Her sister motioned, So what?

"You mean you already knew that?"

"Sure. Didn't you?"

"Not until about three minutes ago."

"Hmm." Portia hiked a shoulder. "Funny, I just always assumed you did. Mom told me ages ago, around the time we had that little talk about the birds and bees."

"Well, she never told me." Come to think of it, she never mentioned anything about the birds and bees, either. Ramey'd found out the hard way, in a manner of speaking.

The trouble with family secrets was, if one was revealed, you had to wonder how many more lurked under the rocks somewhere, if only you knew which one to kick. Ed, Archie and Melba Jane weren't just ripe for prospecting family secrets—they were the last remaining quarry for Ramey to mine.

A shrill facsimile of Crosby, Stills, Nash and Young's "Our House" teedled from the cell phone in her sister's pocket. She gave the caller ID a myopic squint, then answered, "Portia Carruthers, Boulevard Realty."

A wink, then, "Yes, Mrs. Chopin. It certainly is a beautiful morning. A half hour?" A wide smile accompanied a thumbs-up. "Of course I can meet you there. See you in a few."

Portia closed the phone and did a little dance. "Gotta go. Wish me luck. I think I've unloaded the Scanlon house." Starting from the kitchen, her heels screed to a halt on the bricks. "Aw, crap. I forgot all about your company."

Your company. *My* living room. Ramey raked her fingers through hair that was as corkscrewed and babyfine as her mother's. "The Dillingers aren't company. Like it or not, they're family."

It was a status more meaningful to Ramey than to her sister. Portia's husband was a dickhead, but alive, and they had two, almost-grown sons. Fate had demolished Ramey's nest before she and Stan had a chance to fill it.

What's the rush, they'd said countless times. Let's have fun, just the two of us, then one of these days, when we're ready, we'll settle down, start a family and do the whole white picket fence and minivan thing.

Portia said, "Hey, Rame. I know how awful it's been for you, since Stan died…"

No, you don't.

"…but you're not thinking about letting the Dillingers stay, are you?"

As she moved closer, Portia's tone resembled an empathetic talk-radio psychologist's. "They're ex-cons, hon, not three sweet old folks visiting from the retirement home."

One more 'hon,' and Ramey'd come out swinging. "Go meet your client. I'll call you later."

"After they're gone, right?"

No, Ramey decided. After Melba Jane sets a time for tonight's homecoming dinner.

3

One viciously cold winter night back in 1998, Herb Trantham sat at the bar at Sinatra's Place nursing a lukewarm draft Budweiser. Herb wasn't much of a drinker, but a man didn't wrap his hand around a virgin Bloody Mary to contemplate which type of financial suicide to commit.

Earlier that afternoon, a CPA confirmed what Herb already knew. In Plainfield's commercial scheme of things, Trantham's IGA, the town's lone surviving independent grocery store, was a fly and two national supermarket chains were the swatters.

Herb's options were clear and depressing. He could file for Chapter 11 and watch the third-generation business leak assets until the well ran dry. Option two was cut his losses, declare standard bankruptcy, lock the doors and throw away the keys.

As was his custom, Frank, the bar's owner, whose surname was Wallencheskie, not Sinatra, hummed along with Ol' Blue Eyes belting "My Way" on the jukebox. In hindsight, the song might seem prescient, except the machine's repertoire was exclusive to Sinatra, Dean Martin and Sammy Davis, Jr. tunes. In its heyday, three-fifths of the renowned Rat Pack recorded dozens of them, but Wallencheskie had rigged the juke to play "My Way" at least twice an hour.

For regulars, the song faded to white noise. For Herb, it was musical Chinese water torture. The harder he tried to ignore it, the more it picked at his already frayed nerves.

Thankfully, he wasn't a violent man. Rather than spin around on the bar stool and hurl his pilsner glass at the Rock-Ola, Herb just mopped his sweaty brow with a napkin and prayed for a power outage.

"You're quieter than usual tonight," Frank said.

A gulp of flat, warm beer exchanged one bitter taste in the grocer's mouth for another.

"My accountant's got me by the balls."

Frank chuckled. "Yeah, and his other hand's on your wallet. What else is new?"

"Man, you don't know the half of it." In the manner of a crack in a dam, of one straw too many bringing a camel to its knees, the veritable flood of grievances, frustrations and failures that had given Herb's ulcers ulcers spewed forth.

"Bottom line," he concluded, "the big dogs' retail

is cheaper than I can buy wholesale. There's no way in hell I can compete."

"Then don't." Frank dumped Herb's stale beer in the sink and drew a fresh one. The barkeep's beefy thumb pronged upward at the speakers embedded in the ceiling tiles. "If you can't win, before you blame the game, look at how you're playing it."

If there was a point to the remark, it was lost on Herb Trantham.

"Sinatra was a scrawny punk from Hoboken," Frank went on. "Sure, he had style and could carry a tune, but better than anybody else? Hardly. He wasn't tall, dark and handsome, either, so how'd he beat out crooners with everything going for them?"

Herb didn't know and didn't care, but Wallencheskie had let him vent, and for that he was grateful. "Caught a big break, I guess."

"Uh-huh. That's what 'My Way' is all about. Pure dumb luck." The bar owner grunted in disgust. "There's a lesson in that song, if you're smart enough to listen."

Later, Herb left the bar no happier than when he'd gone in. Actually, he was even more depressed. That damned song droned on in his skull, like the soundtrack of a nervous breakdown.

"Mr. Trantham?"

Herb started. The past snapped to the present in the form of the supermarket's customer service clerk. She stared at him from the doorway to his office. "Are you okay, sir?"

Embarrassed at letting his mind drift to a bygone time, Herb switched off the *Sinatra's Greatest Hits* CD that must have triggered it.

"Showing my age, is all." He smiled. "Dad used to say, you know you're getting old when folks catch you daydreaming before the noon whistle blows."

Liz Newkirk didn't laugh, but she did retreat a step. She'd been in diapers when the city disconnected the noon whistle, for fear newcomers would confuse it with a tornado siren. "Sorry I bothered you," she said. "I'll just, uh, wait and ask the manager about this when he comes back from the bank."

Herb's tone balanced diplomacy with *don't forget who signs your paychecks.* "You're here, I'm listening. What's the problem?"

"It's probably nothing." Liz scanned the triplicate phone-order sheet in her hand. "Ramey Burke called in this delivery order a few minutes ago." She laid it on Herb's desk. "Actually, she called the store and gave me her account number and ID code, then turned the phone over to her aunt for the order."

The columnar form, divided by departments, such as produce, dairy, meat and frozen, listed all food and nonfood items available via Trantham's My Way Express Delivery.

To Herb's everlasting amazement, the service's popularity was immediate and had grown with each succeeding year. "Innovative," the newspaper called it. "A money pit," his competitors had snickered. "We're phasing in automated checkstands and Trantham's acting like it's 1947 all over again."

Delivered groceries did harken back to the good old days, but although the reasons had changed, meeting a need wasn't a new idea. The elderly and infirm, families too busy to devote hours to cruising grocery aisles, and those who simply appreciated the convenience hadn't balked at the thirty-dollar minimum order requirement, or surcharges.

Shelf stockers who doubled as delivery drivers earned tips in addition to hourly wages, thus employee turnover had dropped. As the store's profit margin steadily climbed, complaints and refunds for subpar or damaged merchandise remained fewer than from in-house customers.

Herb knew a My Way van could steer itself to Portia Carruther's house. Her sister, Ramey, didn't avail herself of the service more than five or six times a year.

"I make myself shop," she once told him. "It's like aerobics, only I don't break a sweat and there's a rack of candy bars at the finish line."

Liz Newkirk shook her head. "Maybe I should have

given this to an order picker, but gosh, it's quadruple what Ms. Burke usually calls in. I didn't think that old lady on the phone was ever going to stop."

The order's total and fees would warm any grocer's heart. "You're sure it was Ramey Burke who authorized the charge?"

"Oh yes, sir. She has a really deep voice for a woman—like the deejay on KSYK. And I double-checked her account number and code in the computer."

Herb handed back the form. "Then tell the picker to take extraspecial care filling this and get it to Ramey's house, pronto."

The background racket outside Ramey's office should be driving her nuts. Besides the freedom to dress like a laundry hamper with feet, the other advantages to working at home were the unrelieved peace, quiet and solitude.

None of the above had applied since the Dillinger invasion several hours ago. Once she agreed to let them stay, they'd deployed in three different directions to make good on their work-for-board promises. True, they'd left her alone in her office, but their presence was as intrusive as the garage band that used to practice next door.

Above her, Ed clomped through the attic. Outside,

Archie cussed Ramey's chain saw, the branches that
bonked him on the head and the Amazonian shrubs re-
plete with sticker vines. From the kitchen came the
symphonic bangs and bongs of cupboard doors, drawers, pots, pans and utensils.

Despite the clamor, she'd managed to get some work
done. Phone calls had been made and returned, the callees
probably assuming she was on a cell phone in traffic. The
morning newspaper's real estate section had also netted
two new For Sale By Owner classifieds to capitalize on.

The one slugged "Reduced for Quick Sale" indicated the owners had probably closed on a new house.
Losing equity on the old one was more cost-effective
than making double mortgage payments.

The photo of the second house showed a neat saltbox
with a snowy roof and two new cars in the shoveled
driveway. The only snowfall of that magnitude had fallen
the week before Christmas. It was now April. The photo
indicated the sellers were too cheap to rework the ad, and
told prospective buyers the property had been on the
market for months, so something must be wrong with it.

Ramey also guessed its interior was as cluttered as
the garage. As a general rule, people with seventy-
some thousand dollars invested in transportation didn't
leave the cars in the driveway to brave the elements.
And those who used a garage as a storage facility often
had as much or more stuff piled inside their house.

Each homeowner would receive a promotional packet in tomorrow's mail. Letters to their respective real estate agents were printed and stamped, as well. A nudge from that direction never hurt.

She was in the process of double-checking the materials list for staging Marvin and Gladys Leonardo's dated split-level, when a wave of heavenly aromas undulated upstairs from the kitchen. Like cartoon waftaroms, they hooked Ramey's nose and levitated her up from the drafting table.

The kitchen was accessible from the elled hallway off the vestibule or the breakfast nook, which was converted from a butler's pantry. Melba Jane must have heard Ramey's footfalls on the stairs. She intercepted Ramey on the bottom step. Scowling like a bouncer, she said, "I'll tell you, same as I did the boys. No free samples. I'm not working like a Trojan for y'all to spoil your supper before it's on the table."

Aside from her breakfast carrots, Ramey hadn't eaten all day, as though unspent calories were deposited in an interest-bearing account earmarked for luxuries, such as homemade fried chicken.

The burn-to-earn concept always left her a little woozy, but she reasoned the fat grams she'd inhaled earlier ought to hold her until dinnertime.

"Did Trantham's deliver everything you ordered?" she asked.

"Yes'm. They threw in a couple of loaves of French bread for a thank-you, too. Dang things are as hard as truncheons, but they'll do for French toast in the morning."

Ramey's eyelids fluttered. French toast for breakfast, oh my. Forget joining a gym. She'd move into one and only come home for meals.

"I didn't want to bother you while you were working," Melba Jane said, "so I went ahead and signed the bill." She grimaced. "I hope that's okay."

It was better than okay. At the moment, Ramey would sign over her half of the house to Herb Trantham for bringing the groceries to her door.

The logistics involved in food shopping arose soon after Portia left that morning. To provide the raw materials for a family dinner, Ramey could either haul all three Dillingers to the supermarket with her, or take Melba Jane and leave the uncles behind unsupervised, or trust in the rehabilitative capabilities of long-term incarceration and go by herself.

The safest choice was to take them with her. Ramey was swallowing two preemptive aspirin tablets when a refrigerator magnet advertising My Way Delivery Service hove into view. In under a minute, she authorized the credit card charge, lobbed the telephone receiver at Melba Jane and scurried back upstairs to her office.

"It made more sense for you to sign for the groceries than me," Ramey said. "I wouldn't have known whether they left anything out or not."

"Yes, but being fresh out of cash money, I added on a tip, too." Melba Jane's expression turned wistful. "I remember when Chester Trantham used to bring Mama's order to the house. Truth is, I remember Chet's bicycle clearer than him. Redheaded and skinny as a fence post he was, but lo, how I coveted that wheel— that's what we called 'em in those days. Lightning blue and chrome it was, with whitewall balloon tires and baskets on the handlebars and fenders.

"Mama always tipped Chet a shiny silver dime, but that was a long time ago. A dollar didn't seem enough, either, seeing as how a van costs more to run than a bi-cycle. I wrote in five dollars, then fretted ever since that three would have been plenty."

Five sounded a little chintzy to Ramey, but she didn't want to hurt her aunt's feelings. "Perfect," she said. "All I need is the receipt to check against my next credit card statement."

"Oh. Yes. The receipt." Melba Jane's eyes swept left, then right, then her lips pursed. "Umm, well, can't say I got one."

Ramey didn't use the service often, but the driver usually tore off the customer copy as soon as it was signed.

No problem. If it didn't turn up, she'd drop by the store later for a duplicate.

"There's a pitcher of sweet tea cooling in the kitchen," Melba Jane said. "Want me to fix you a glass and bring it upstairs for you?"

"No thanks, but are you sure you don't need any help? Cooking a meal for eight is a lot of work. It doesn't seem fair for you to do it all by yourself."

"Nice of you to offer, hon, but it's wonderful to have an entire kitchen to myself. Between sifting this and stirring that, I take myself out to the porch and rest a spell. When Archie's not fawnching too loud, I can hear the birds singing."

She paused, as though testing a remark before making it, then said softly, "I'm glad you invited your *boyfriend* to eat with us. When I heard your husband passed away so quick after your folks, it like to broke my heart."

Ramey looked away. "Mine did."

"Oh, honey. I knew I should've kept—"

"No, no, it's okay. Time really is an amazing healer." Ramey's smile reinforced her words. "I'll admit, for a while, I was barely functional. Much as I didn't believe it could, or wasn't sure I wanted it to, life does go on."

"That it does. You've gotta squint to see it sometimes, but there's always enough good mixed in with the terrible to keep you going."

"Working helped. It forced me out of the house and around people again, when what I most wanted to do was mope and feel sorry for myself."

"You had every right to."

Ramey pushed back the hair flopping in her face. "Not really. I mean, I started feeling pretty ashamed of myself when I focused on what I'd *had* instead of what I'd lost. For starters, I had the best parents anybody could ask for. And a great, funny, overgrown kid for a husband who loved me more than anything in the world. That's why it hurt so much when they were gone. But I'm lucky. Way luckier than a lot of people to have been Bill and Sylvia's daughter and Stan Burke's wife."

Melba Jane searched Ramey's face, then cocked her head. "So, this fella of yours, does he make you happy?"

Now there was an intriguing question. Don Blevins didn't make her unhappy. But happy?

"Don's a nice guy. Loyal, dependable…" Ramey's voice trailed off into a laugh. "I suppose that's why we're just *friends*. It sounds like I'm describing a Labrador retriever."

"Lawsy, how I'd love to have a dog, but Archie's allergic to pet dander." The oven timer buzzed. Turning to answer it, Melba Jane added, "I reckon having Ed underfoot is as close to having a dog as I'm likely to get."

* * *

Dinner was at six. Not six-oh-five, or five-of. Melba Jane Dillinger was a Swiss watch in sneakers and elastic hosiery.

The necessary introductions were barely made when she hustled everyone into the dining room. The table was laid with Grandma Dillinger's prized Irish lace cloth, silver, bone china and crystal.

Portia whispered to Ramey, "After dessert, you wash, I'll dry, and we'll count the heirlooms."

Ramey gave her sister the evil eye. "Gee, and everybody says I'm the funny one."

While Ed asked the Lord's blessing, Ramey assumed He'd forgive her a peek at the assembled multitude. It had, after all, been years since three generations had broken bread together.

By virtue of seniority, Ed had taken the chair at the head of the table, with Archie at the foot. Ramey sat to Ed's right, then Don Blevins, then Melba Jane to Archie's left.

Opposite them were Portia, her attorney husband Preston, and their sixteen-year-old son, Chase. His older brother, Preston Hitchcock Carruthers III, nicknamed Tripp, was a sophomore at Yale, and was thus spared from the rare privilege of dining with three convicted felons.

Before the Amens, Ramey lowered her eyes. Her

mom and dad and Stan were there, too. Not as shim-
mery vapor trails from a three-hankie chick-flick. She
felt their presence and knew if she looked up precisely
at the right fraction of an instant, Stan would be beside
her, Bill Patterson at the head of the table and Sylvia
at the foot, just as they had all those times Ramey took
for granted and never imagined could end.

A sadness welled up inside her. As brilliant as it
sounds on a bumper sticker, nobody can live each day
as though it's the last.

God, she missed Stan. He wasn't the prince of ambition and cared less than she did for material things,
but no matter what befell them, he'd always made her
laugh.

Under the table, Don Blevins's knee nudged hers,
just as Ed said, "Girl, you gonna help yourself to a
chicken leg, or are you gonna wait for it to stump over
to your plate?"

Melba Jane made scooping motions. "Dig in, all of
you. There's plenty of everything."

Archie reached for a tureen heaped with green
beans. "While me and Ed puttered around the house,
she cooked up forty pounds of mashed potatoes, a gallon of gravy, ten whole fryers and five dozen hot rolls."

Melba Jane shrugged. "I fixed vittles for a cell block
for most of my life. It might could take a day or two to
whittle the portions down to size."

No wonder the grocery receipt had disappeared and she'd banned Ramey from the kitchen. The room measured eleven by sixteen, but after Trantham's van was unloaded, Melba Jane must have needed pitons and spikes to climb over all the chicken parts and potato peelings.

Ramey envisioned the decimal point in her credit card balance skipping two digits to the right, the numbers spinning like a race car's odometer. Channeling her inner optimist, which was a bit rusty from disuse, she told herself that her aunt meant well. And dinner for eighty, instead of eight, guaranteed leftovers. Oodles and gobs of leftovers, whereas of this morning, the refrigerator contained raw veggies, fossilized take-out containers, beer, diet soda, assorted condiments and orange juice.

Positive thinking was starting to work its magic when Don leaned sideward and said, "Did she say, 'cell block'?"

Uh-oh. The look Ramey returned promised, *I'll explain later.*

Yes, she should have explained sooner. She planned to, in fact, when canceling their movie and pizza nondate weaseled him a place at the dinner table. Was it her fault that his cell phone signal died before she got the chance?

Being forewarned wasn't always a good thing, she'd decided. Let Don get acquainted with and hopefully charmed by the Dillingers, then minor biographical details about bank robberies and prison and escape attempts wouldn't be as apt to shock him out of his crepe-soled shoes.

Ed smushed a crater in his potatoes, waiting for the gravy boat to dock. To Portia, he said, "The last time we gathered round this table, you had to sit on a stack of Sears Roebuck Wishbooks to reach your milk glass."

"You looked like an angel," Melba Jane gushed, "with all those blond curls done up in pink ribbons."

Preston beamed at his wife. "She still does, if you ask me."

Gag me with a spatula, Ramey thought. If the three-stone diamond ring sparkling on Portia's right hand was a clue, Preston the dickhead was worming his way back into her sister's heart, again, and Portia was letting him. Again.

Her statute of limitations on adultery was considerably higher than Ramey's. Ramey's rule of one strike, you're out, was quite different from Portia's acceptance of several suspected and one verified fling before she consulted a divorce attorney.

Archie chuckled and said, "What I remember about that last dinner was Ramey's big, ol' brown beagle eyes peeking around the door."

Ah, yes. The angel child and the beagle. Some

things you never outgrow because some people wouldn't let you.

Archie went on, "'Bout the time we sat down to eat, Sylvie caught Ramey making mud pies in her new Easter dress. Poor kid got her legs switched good 'n' plenty and sent to her room without a bite."

Melba Jane provided Scene Two. "Ramey snuck down again, but I shooed her upstairs before her mama saw her. If Sylvie had, that child would've eaten off the mantel for a week."

Everyone laughed. The crime and punishment she didn't recall. Whether it was that incident or another, memories of Uncle Ed tiptoeing into her room with a ham sandwich, a slab of cherry pie and a jelly glass of Kool-Aid was as clear as his sly wink was now.

"Ramey always was a corker," Ed said, as though she wasn't seated at his elbow. "Still is, isn't she, Don?"

"Not really." He glanced at Ramey. "I, uh—well, you are, but in a mature, adult way." As if the ditch he'd dug was too shallow, he added, "We aren't kids, anymore, you know."

Ed snorted. "You're only as old as you feel, bub."

"Darn right." Archie tapped his temple, then pointed at Chase. "Up here, me and him's 'bout the same age."

Assent murmured around the table. By Melba Jane's expression, a zinger was burning the tip of her tongue, but she restrained herself.

Into the conversational lag bounded Archie's intellectual peer. "You guys are bank robbers, huh?" Chase seemed skeptical yet intrigued by the prospect of adding felons to an otherwise boring gene pool.

Don's fork halted in midair. As did Ramey's ability to breathe.

"Ex-bank robbers," Ed corrected.

"Retired," Archie said.

Chase was undeterred. "How many banks did you rob altogether?"

"Three," answered Ed and Archie, not completely drumming out Melba's "Seven."

The brothers glared at her. She sniffed and plucked a hot roll from the breadbasket. "Three, seven, what's the difference?"

Preston, who'd worked in the county prosecutor's office before opting for personal injury law, said, "You were suspected of more robberies, but were only convicted on three counts, right?"

Portia chirped, "I wrote a contract on the Scanlon house this afternoon. A full-price offer."

"Congratulations!" Ramey turned to Don. "Did you hear that? Portia sold a house. Isn't that terrific?"

His nod possessed the dazed quality of a postsurgery patient's. "She's a real estate agent."

"Oh, but not just any real estate agent. The best in town. Why the stories she could tell…" Ramey telegraphed an all-points SOS to her sister. "Like now, for instance."

"Did you guys ever shoot anybody?" Chase asked.

Ed waved dismissively. "You watch too much TV, boy. Guns are for amateurs and nut-jobs. What you do is take your time, case the joint for a week, maybe two. Then when you hit it, keep a hand in your coat pocket and let 'em think you'll cap 'em if they squawk. Do it smart and you'll be in and out before anybody knows what happened."

Portia chimed in, "Speaking of stories, there was this couple from Germany that wanted a—"

"What, I'm not allowed to talk?"

Preston said, "Of course, you are, son."

Portia's eyes threatened spousal homicide. To Chase, she minced, "I'm sure everyone would love to hear about your speech and debate tournament—"

"Gimme a break, Mom, okay? Just because I ask a couple of questions doesn't mean I'm going to cut school tomorrow and knock off Metropolitan National."

"The Bank of Plainfield's still an easier mark," Archie said.

"It is? How come?"

Portia moaned, her head dropping into her hand.

"Well, for one, it's smaller and still locally owned. This article in *American Banker* said the big chains have security up the wazoo and they're more prone to chuck in dye packets with the cash."

Ed added, "The hell with laws against defacing government property being a felony. Banks get by with it every day of the week."

"*American Banker* is a professional trade journal," Don sputtered, his mouth full of sliced beets. "A sub-scription-only trade journal. I deliver it to the banks on my route."

"Don's a mail carrier," Ramey said. "He's—"

"That rag costs the danged moon, too," Ed grumbled, as if the representative employee of the U.S. Postal Service were to blame. "I s'pose it's a tax write-off for everybody else, but a man's gotta keep up."

"Cry me a river," Melba Jane said. "You had Archie to split the tab with. If I hadn't quit smoking way back when, I couldn't've kept taking the *News-Messenger*."

Chase beat everyone else to the same punch. "What's smoking have to do with the newspaper?"

"Well, hon, in stir, cigs are like baseball cards. You can sell 'em, trade 'em, or bargain for special privileges, long as you don't strike a match to your profits."

"And of all things," Preston said, "you used what money you had to get the *News-Messenger* by mail?"

So that's how she knew about Stan, Ramey thought.

From the obituary. And how Archie knew the Bank of Plainfield hadn't merged with a national chain.

Melba Jane's cheeks ripened a shade. She entreated Archie, then Ed, who finally said, "What's peculiar about taking the paper? Lots of folks do after they move off elsewheres." His gaze shifted to Don. "Don't they?"

Don agreed. "Some people start subscriptions before they move here to get a feel for the town."

"I've taken the *Wall Street Journal* by mail for years," Preston told them, as though anyone cared. "And I pick up the Sunday *New York Times* now and then from the newsstand."

"You don't read them," Chase said. "You just put them on your desk to impress your clients."

There was a reason Chase was Ramey's favorite nephew. He was a beagle, too, compared to Golden Boy Tripp. Chase also had a mouth as snarky as her own, particularly when it came to bursting his pompous ass of a father's bubble.

Ramey asked Melba Jane, "If you've read the newspaper all these years, why were you so surprised the town had grown so much?"

Portia, who could have been the cover girl for *Stressed and Miserable Daily,* sneered, "She wasn't. She just wanted you to think she was. It was research, in case they got the chance to rob another bank. Or three. Or seven."

She glowered at Ed. "So what if you're old and out of practice. It's all you people know how to do, isn't it? Steal the town blind and drag our family name through the dirt."

A stunned silence stretched several beats before Archie forced out a laugh. Melba Jane joined in and finally, Ed. "Hooeee, now that's a good 'un."

What the appropriate reaction should have been, Ramey didn't know. Portia's outburst was mean-spirited and she'd embarrassed herself in the process. Laughing at her was the same as branding her a fool.

Portia whipped the napkin from her lap. "Preston, Chase." She scooted back her chair and stood. "Come on. We're going home."

"Oh, no you're not, missy." Ed commanded. "Sit down and hush, and I don't mean maybe."

Portia's face flushed. Lips compressed into a tight oval, she glared at her immobile husband, then at Ed. "How dare you tell me—"

"I shouldn't have to. I happen to know you were raised with better manners than you're showing. It's past time you started actin' like it."

Ed's voice dropped as deep as doom. "My daddy wasn't nothin' but a chicken farmer and a bootlegger, but when you sit at his table, you stay put, till *you're* excused."

Nobody moved for a long moment. Then, without

a word, Portia plopped down as if her legs had been pulled out from under her. In a manner of speaking, they had.

Ed pushed aside his plate. Forearms crossed on the table, he said, "I ain't gonna tell you this but once. We came here 'cause it's our home and the only one we've ever had, save the kind with bars on the windows."

Portia stared past Ramey at the massive china cabinet built into the wall. She was listening, maybe even absorbing, but God forbid she let on.

"We'll move on, by and by," Ed said. "When we do, we won't be looking over our shoulders for the cops." He paused, then quietly demanded, "Look at me, Portia."

Always the obedient one, her eyes shifted to his.

"I don't blame you for being angry and skittish about why we're here," he said. "I wish you'd have just asked instead of pitching a hissy, but I swear to you on Sylvie's and Bill's graves, we robbed our last bank thirty-five years ago."

The breath Ramey hadn't realized she'd been holding wheezed through her lips. Promises were breakable. What Ed had given her sister, given them all, was an ironclad vow.

Portia sat stone still for a moment longer, then eased her napkin off the table and smoothed it in her lap. One by one, smiles replaced anxious expressions. It seemed as if a truce had been successfully negotiated. For now, anyway.

Chase, who'd reacted to the drama by ignoring it, kept chewing and swallowing and forking food into his mouth. At his age, tuning out the entire adult population was an art form.

"Well," Portia cleared her throat. "I don't know about the rest of you, but I'd love a piece of Melba Jane's pineapple upside-down cake."

Dessert being a course she seldom acknowledged the existence of elevated her request to a bygones-be-bygones apology. A breakthrough, as it were, even if Ramey and maybe Preston were the only ones aware of it.

Ramey winked at her sister. "Then, if you'll excuse me, Uncle Ed, I'll put on the coffee."

"Best make a gallon, hon," Archie warned. "The wife didn't bake just one cake. There's five to pick amongst and a batch of chocolate cupcakes to boot."

4

Staging a house for resale is an art, a science and a helluva lot of work.

The art involves persuading homeowners to finance repairs and cosmetic changes without insulting their taste or housekeeping abilities. While the science aspect isn't exact, stagers must have the objectivity to decide which features to showcase, which to edit, delete or camouflage and the creativity to work magic on a limited budget.

As for the labor intensity…

Ramey switched off the floor buffer. Three coats of paste wax and a slow polish had restored the hardwoods time-capsuled beneath a sea of harvest-gold carpet. Wiping a sleeve across her brow, she flinched a little as the fabric brushed her skin. Earlier that morning, she'd twisted the valves to their usual settings for the perfect shower temperature.

Mentally ticking off the day's work schedule, she

failed to register the scalding water jetting from the showerhead. The entire left side of her body received a painful scalding.

Melba Jane had been similarly burned at the kitchen sink, before Ed discovered the cold water valve had been shut off in the cellar.

Mr. Fix-it swore he hadn't touched the "damned spigot." The problem was easily rectified, but Ramey's skin was still tender and pink.

Adventures in personal hygiene aside, she was pleased with the work in progress. A grueling, two-and-a-half-day facelift had subtracted a couple of decades off Gladys and Marvin Leonardo's '79 split-level rancher.

On Thursday, Ramey and her crew jettisoned contractor bags full of dusty fake plants, broken blinds and yards of pouffy valances and limp lace panels. After they prepacked Mrs. Leonardo's thousand-piece thimble collection, Mr. Leonardo's antique toys and a kazillion knickknacks, the popcorn texture was scraped off the living room's vaulted ceiling. Drywall mud was troweled over cracks and blemishes, then they primed the paneled walls and the hideous yellow brick fireplace.

Friday's task list had included sanding the ceiling smooth, priming it and then painting over the main bathroom's pink walls and cabinets, the kitchen cabinets, and the utility room's aqua walls. Today being Saturday, Ramey needed all hands on deck to get to the finish line. A new, coordinated color scheme of antique white, sage-green and warm, buttercream-yellow had neutralized and visually expanded each room. *The Brady Bunch* Revisited was becoming a retrocontemporary space anyone would be proud to call home.

As soon as the general contractor, Jill Antoine, installed the kitchen hardware, the fun part of Ramey's job would commence. Accessorizing was the key. Decluttering, painting and making repairs helped set the scene, but it was the little things that scored signatures on contracts.

Early Dawes, the electrician, tapped Ramey's shoulder. "The new lights are up in the john and the dining room." The toothpick forever clamped in Early's teeth rolled to the other side of his mouth. "Whatcha want me to do with the old junk?"

"The bathroom fixtures should go straight to the Dumpster," Ramey said. "The dining room chandelier needs to be packed for the move."

He made a face. "Are you sure about that? It's all plastic, top to bottom. Even the little dangly doodads are plastic."

"I know, but it has sentimental value to the Leonardos."

"Whatever you say, boss." Striding toward the garage for a packing carton, Early muttered, "I wouldn't hang that thing in an outhouse."

Neither would she, but replacing the tacky fixture was a triumph. It wouldn't have prevented a sale, but it would have clashed with the redesign like a candelabra on a card table.

Which reminded her, she'd forgotten to unload the box of pillar candles from the van. If they'd melted to wax mushrooms, replacing them would be at her expense. The money was negligible. She didn't have a minute to spare for a shopping trip.

The old saying that the more things change, the more they remain the same didn't apply to downtown Plainfield. Melba Jane's happy memories of Saturday's hustle and bustle, slurping cherry Cokes at Woolworth's horseshoe counter after the picture show let out, then listening to the new 45s in the booths at Bergmeyer's Music Store seemed like a dream, not a recollection.

Woolworth's and lots of the dignified old buildings were gone, replaced by parking lots as vacant as the windows that overlooked them. They'd outlived their usefulness, she supposed. Just as people do eventually.

As if that wasn't enough to get her down, the corn on her left pinky toe was killing her. Soaks in epsom salts and sawing off a chunk of her tennis shoe to give it room to breathe had helped for a while.

Melba Jane looked down at the throbbing appendage that stuck out like a sore thumb in a dirty mitten. If the thing didn't fall off of its own accord before they made it to Mexico, she'd buy a pair of those fancy leather huaraches and never wear proper shoes again.

Hobbling along, favoring her foot for all the good that did, had allowed a half block gap of littered sidewalk to open between her and her husband and brother-in-law. Poor Archie. The wagonful of food that was his turn to pull surely played hell with his sciatica, too.

Trading sides of the bed after he'd complained about the lumpy mattress had soothed his aching back a mite. The complaining, that is, not the cause. Which was, in Melba Jane's estimation, the skinny, know-it-all-strolling beside him, whistling, "When the Saints Come Marching In."

Hah. Not in this neighborhood, they wouldn't. Melba Jane's eyes locked on a grease spot on Archie's coat. Ignoring the bums loitering in boarded-up doorways didn't keep her from smelling them.

Oh, there but for the grace of Ramey, go us, she thought.

The lap of luxury Ed had delivered them to evoked a shiver of gratitude. By right of inheritance, the Dillinger family home should have been two-thirds his and Archie's, not entirely Sylvie's to pass down to her daughters.

Portia always was full of herself. At least she acted that way, fearing somebody would think less of her for not being perfect. Ramey's heart was pure gold, and God love her, she was as gullible as the walk to the Samaritan Mission was long.

The wagon slowed. Archie glanced back at Melba Jane, who was now lagging nearly a block behind. His gimlet eyes fired a machine gun glare at the vagrant slouched against a beater Pontiac.

"Take your time," he said, as much to Ed, as his gimpy wife. "I'll wait for you." The smile reserved exclusively for her added, *I did for thirty-four years, five months and seventeen days. What's another couple of minutes?*

When she huffed up alongside them, Ed said, "I hoped we'd make better time, but it doesn't appear that the parole officer's here yet."

They'd regrouped two doors down from the corner of Fifth and Main Street. Samaritan Mission was on Main, two doors to the west. Melba Jane said, "Oh, so now you can see around corners, huh? Would've come in handy back in '69 when we hit the First National over yonder."

Ed pointed at an abandoned clothing store's soaped windows on the opposite side of Main. Reflected in the glass was the mission's entrance. Above it was a logo of St. Christopher clutching a staff and bearing the Christ child across a stream. "See any blue pickup trucks parked out front?" he asked.

No, she didn't. Last Tuesday, when they cabbed from the bus depot to the mission and met Gordon Sweeney, the district parole officer assigned to them, Melba Jane hadn't noticed what type of vehicle he drove, either. Frogs would fly before she'd admit it to Ed.

"When we go inside, it's best if you two leave the gabbing to me," Ed told them.

Archie nodded.

"Then why'd the three of us have to come all the way down here? My foot hurts like blue blazes and it'll be twice worse by the time we hoof it back home."

Ed patted his coat pocket to remind her of the six hundred and fourteen dollars inside it. "I already told you, since the wagon'll be empty, we'll snag a taxi back to that coffee shop a couple of blocks from the house, same as we did Wednesday morning."

Archie said, "Ramey isn't supposed to be home until five or after. How 'bout we skip the walk home for Melba Jane's sake and have the driver take us straight home?"

"Great idea." Ed poked a Camel between his lips and struck a match on his thumbnail. "Then if Portia or Preston happen by, or a neighbor gets nosy, *you* can explain to Ramey where the money for cab fare came from."

Technically speaking, the dollars in his pocket were of the honest kind. They'd pooled their respective earnings from various prison jobs that remained in their accounts. Ed appointed himself banker. Archie didn't mind. Melba Jane did, but who ever listened to her?

"Let's just get this over with and get back to business," she said with a resigned sigh. "I was supposed to be drinking Tequila Sunrises with teensy little umbrellas in 'em by now."

Archie kissed her cheek. "You will be, before you know it."

She had her doubts, but kept them to herself.

The stench of poverty and cleaning solvents that were advertised to dispel it permeated the mission's lobby. The building, originally a grand hotel for railway travelers, had slumped to fleabag status, then abandoned. It was in danger of being imploded when Lucy Curtis bought it cheap and turned it into a halfway house and soup kitchen for the indigent.

Lucy received equal parts praise and castigation for sheltering, if not catering to criminals, drunkards, junkies, prostitutes, perverts and welfare cheats.

In truth, she ran a tight ship. At six foot two and a solid three hundred pounds, Lucy could catapult rule breakers out the door without mussing a hair on her shaggy, hennaed head.

Tears rimmed her eyes when Ed presented her with the wagon-size donation of food for the soup kitchen. "Lord forgive me." A meaty thumb and forefinger pinched a whisker apart. "I was this close—to reporting you AWOL to officer Sweeney, and here you are with enough groceries to feed an army."

"It's a bribe," Ed said.

Lucy's laugh sounded like a duck caught in a wind sock. "Fair enough. So what am I being bribed to do?"

"To keep Gordon Sweeney from finding out that our niece took us in." Ed raised a hand to stave off a rebuttal. "I know what you're thinking, but last we saw her, she was just a tyke. If we'd put her on the release plan for the parole board, she'd have refused and we'd have wound up here, anyhow."

"So what's wrong with telling Sweeney now?" Lucy arched an eyebrow. "Let me guess. This niece of yours won't exactly ace a background check."

Melba Jane bristled. "She'd better'n ace it. Folks don't come any squeakier clean than her."

"That's the problem," Archie chimed in, also acting in direct violation of Ed's gag order. "If anyone fears a cop digging for dirt more'n somebody that's up to his neck in it, it's somebody cleaner than a tin whistle."

Lucy's grin exposed teeth as pearly white as a dentist's mistress. "Especially a girl related to three federal parolees."

"With a lawyer for a brother-in-law," Archie said.

"And a gentleman caller that doesn't like us being there," Melba Jane added.

Ed handed a slip of paper to Lucy. "Here's a phone number where you can reach us, in case of an emergency."

"Like an unannounced visit from Sweeney?" She fingered the paper. Her head shook slowly from side to side. "This is an awful lot to ask, Mr. Dillinger. If something goes wrong and I can't take in those without a friend or relative in the world offering them a home anymore…"

Ed looked the woman straight in the eye. His voice quavering, he said, "Our lives, or what little's left of them, are in your hands, Ms. Curtis. Whatever you decide, we're beholden to you for helping us when we needed a welcome, a hot meal and a bed to rest our tired old bones for the night."

Melba Jane had to admit, Ed was many things—a slew of derogatory labels came to mind—but that man could hornswoggle a penguin out of his tuxedo.

Mark Mason and Beatty Frick, Ramey's hired muscle and all-around helpers, stood arms akimbo as they watched Ramey rearrange furniture. To protect the freshly buffed floors, the college football stars were sock-footed. So was Ramey and the sofa she'd repositioned four times.

"How about putting it on an angle," Mark suggested. "The fireplace will be the focal point without blocking the sliders or messing up the flow."

"I dunno." Beatty curried his goatee. "What about that area rug Ramey bought? As much as the room needs a punch of color, it might jump out too much if the couch is on the slant."

Ramey looked from one to the other. "Focal point? Punch of color?" She laughed. "You guys are really getting good at this."

A voice behind her said, "Good enough to give the boss a break?"

Ramey whirled around. Don Blevins leaned against the doorway, one hand thrust in his trousers pocket. "My route was light, even for a Saturday, so I figured I'd come by and take you to lunch."

She glanced at her watch to mask her annoyance. Don knew that she and the crew always brought sandwiches and chips to wolf down between projects. Progress came to a halt when they left the premises for lunch. Her hired help preferred getting in, getting done and going home.

Besides, in four hours the Leonardos were due back from visiting their grandchildren in Kansas City. Their real estate agent would also be dropping by for a walk-through in preparation for tomorrow's open house.

"I'm sorry, Don, but I can't. Not with so much stuff left to do."

"Okay." Pushing himself upright, he nodded toward the dining room. "Can you spare a minute to talk?" His tone inferred, "Or is that too much to ask, too?"

"You're due for a break," Mark said. "It'll give me and Beatty a chance to throw the furniture around and see where it lands."

Don's arm draped Ramey's shoulders—companionable, but cumbersome. "I guess it's me that ought to apologize," he said. "I know you don't like it when I bug you when you're working."

Then why do you keep doing it?

He went on, as though he'd read her mind but was oblivious to the nuance. "You've been a mighty busy gal the last couple of weeks. I just figured, with all the hours you've put in here, you might finish up early."

Had she ever finished early? Westheimer's Rule stated that to estimate the time necessary to complete a task, gauge the time you think it'll take, multiply it by two, then change the unit of measure to the next highest unit. It'll take longer than that, regardless, but you won't be as surprised when it does.

In the dining room, Jill Antoine was admiring the final length of white crown molding she'd nail-gunned in place. In baggy overalls and her hair tucked up in a baseball cap, the journeyman carpenter could be mistaken for a junior high school kid.

"Nice touch, eh?"

"Perfect." Ramey surveyed the matching chair rail, sage walls and wrought iron, monterrey rust chandelier. She could hardly wait to see the new toile curtains hung and the Leonardo's oval mahogany table, chairs and sideboard in place and accessorized.

Jill must have detected something besides approval in Ramey's expression. "I believe I hear the Roman shades for the bathroom calling me."

The instant she was out of sight, Don pulled Ramey to him and kissed her on the lips. "There now. How's that for an apology?"

Schoolboyish and inappropriate, but she forced a smile. They'd met last October at Preston's fortieth birthday party—it was a setup, although neither of them knew it. The following Saturday was their first date. By the third, Ramey realized that friends were all they were destined to be.

Don admitted that he wished it could be more, but what was the harm in hanging out together, until one or both of them found somebody else.

Ramey'd supposed he was right, as long as she paid her half of the tab. Going out with Don was better, *healthier,* than roaming the ancestral home she'd moved into after Stan died, pigging out on cheese puffs and peanut butter cups and contemplating adopting a cat, then reminding herself that pets die, too.

But lately—when exactly she wasn't sure—Don had begun to wear on her like a turtleneck sweater accidentally washed in hot water. Too nice and warm to throw away, yet increasingly itchy and uncomfortable.

A cordless drill whined in the main bathroom. The living room's vaulted ceiling echoed Early Dawes's exasperated, "Where in Sam Hill did Ramey go off to now?" and Mark's, "Keep your shorts on, dude. She'll be back in a sec."

"Hey, you." Don stroked the side of Ramey's face. "Of all people, don't you think I know how tired you are?"

Of course, he did. He'd seen her in every kind of mood. He'd helped her chip away the shell she'd retreated inside. Ye gods, one night, he even went to the store for Tampax when she'd been so busy with a staging that she'd neglected to check the calendar.

"What you need," he said, "is a quiet evening at my place, away from everything and everybody. Pop the cork on a bottle of merlot, toss a salad and throw some steaks on the grill." He tapped the tip of her nose with his finger. "I already rented that new Julia Roberts flick you've been dying to see."

Yeah, she thought, months ago, at the theater.

Heaven forbid we see a first-run anything that doesn't feature Bruce Willis bleeding, natural or unnatural disasters, or aliens attacking major metropolitan areas.

Don caught her hand and held it. "So, what time should I pick you up. Six o'clock? Six-fifteen?"

Ramey sagged, in body and in spirit. All she wanted was a bubble bath, a book and a bed to doze off in while reading it.

"Hey, boss, I—" Mark stopped short in the archway. "Oops. Bad timing."

If only he knew. "No, it isn't. Don was just leaving." Ramey sidestepped, pulling her hand from his. "I might not be home until after six. I'll call you."

Don's eyes narrowed. "I thought you had to be finished by four."

"The *owners* are due back at four. I can't just tear out the door the minute they walk through it."

"All right, but—" Whatever else Don intended to say, he stifled. Turning on a heel, he tossed a curt, "See ya" at Mark and strode away.

The front door closed with a *whump*. Mark observed. "You don't look like the happiest camper in the park."

"Nope." Ramey toed a wrinkle in the paint-crusted tarp protecting the floor. "Just tired, I guess. Of a lot of things."

"Not that you asked for it, but my diagnosis is separation anxiety anxiety." The psychology grad student sobered when Ramey didn't laugh.

"You tell me, Dr. Freud. Why would any handsome, heterosexual guy with a civil service job and benefits package spend platonic time with a chubby, middle-aged widow, when he could be out with a genuine, sex-having, possible future-making girlfriend?"

Not that, with the slightest encouragement, Don wouldn't bed Ramey in a Missouri minute. Honestly, the thought had occurred to her a few times. The regrettable morning after-effects perished them. Chemistry couldn't be forced or feigned. For Ramey, it wasn't there.

Mark was wise enough not to field a rhetorical question. There'd have been bonus points for arguing that Ramey wasn't quite middle-aged and for downgrading "chubby" to pleasingly plump. Or better, Monroe-esque, as in Marilyn, not James, the homely fifth president.

Alas, instead of taking the bait, Mark changed the subject. "Me and Beatty have gotten used to chowing down on your aunt's coffee cakes these past couple of days." He smacked his lips. "Edible fringe benefits."

"Spoiled you, huh?" Ramey moved to the chandelier and adjusted a small, parchment shade. "After tackling the first-floor closets yesterday, Melba Jane was too pooped to bake one for today."

"She's still on a cleaning binge?"

Ramey recalled an earlier, psychoanalytical comment Mark had made. "Melba Jane's accustomed to a six-by-nine prison cell. She's a neatnik, not acting out her hostilities toward society for punishing her."

"I said that?" He massaged his shaven pate, as the purposely bald are wont to do. "Maybe I'm hitting the books too hard."

She resisted the urge to tease him about the dangers of disassociating himself from reality. Instead she said she'd meet him in the living room posthaste, after checking on Jill's Roman shade installation.

The main bath no longer made her feel trapped inside a Pepto-Bismol bottle. The pink ceramic wall tiles had receded to an accent color, thanks to three coats of white wall paint. The four-globe chrome fixture above the vanity matched the tub and sink fixtures and cabinet hardware. Completing the transformation from awful to awesome was the pastel shade, shower curtain and overdrape and leftover crown molding framed around the vanity's sheet glass mirror.

Jill rapped on the door. "I added today's hours to the time sheet, so I'm outta here."

"You outdid yourself on this one," Ramey said. "I really appreciate it, especially on such short notice."

"If I'm available, I'm yours." Starting away, Jill snapped her fingers. "Oh—I picked up that toilet-tank lid at the home center this morning and put it in your van. The receipt's with the time sheet."

"Thanks, Jill." Ramey rolled her eyes. And thank heavens for contractor discounts. Uncle Ed's handyman skills weren't proportional to the stuff he'd broken, warped, bent, cracked, or in the case of the tank lid, shattered to smithereens.

From daylight to dinnertime, he and his trusty tool belt clanked from cellar to attic eking out things to fix—many of which were in greater need of repair afterward, than before. Brother Archie had dug innumerable holes and trenches in the backyard in preparation for dividing and transplanting shrubs, bulbs, groundcover and saplings. Nothing had actually been replanted, but the man was a human bulldozer in secondhand dungarees.

Now cooking meals for twenty-five—a rapid descent from eighty, all things considered—Melba Jane sang along to an oldies station on the radio while tearing through cupboards and closets like a one-woman Mongol horde.

Ramey gnawed her lower lip as she arranged fluffy white towels and facecloths on the vanity and towel bars. Right or wrong, she'd rather eat whatever was on Melba Jane's menu tonight and listen to three reformed bank robbers bicker than hang out with an evermore touchy-feely Don Blevins.

Unlike sexual chemistry and orgasms, a headache could be easily faked. Especially over the phone.

"This doesn't even look like my house." Gladys Leonardo's tone implied that wasn't a good thing. "It's so empty. And plain. And tomorrow, the sunlight coming through those flimsy curtains, why, it'll be enough to blind somebody." Her hands fluttered to her mouth. "Oh, Marvin, look—just *look* what they did to our *beautiful* fireplace."

Ramey had dubbed such reactions as staging remorse. The plan was always approved in advance, but owners were often shocked to see rooms devoid of things that made the house their home. Which was the whole point. One couple's lovely was another's handyman special.

Upward of two hours and an assist from the real estate agent were required before the Leonardos' complaints changed to compliments. They hated it still, but if buyers wanted airy, spacious, neutral rooms in move-in condition, Ramey and her crew had granted their wishes and then some.

It was well past six before she turned onto her peaceful, tree-canopied street and saw Preston's hardtop convertible Mercedes parked at the curb.

"The freakin' fun just never ends," she told the windshield, gunning her van up the sloped driveway.

She'd seen more of her brother-in-law since Wednesday's reunion dinner than she had since Thanksgiving. In the meantime, due to the finite number of hours in a day, it must've been a bitch for him to find enough time to chase ambulances, screw a competitor's junior law partner's brains out and feign a sudden onset of familial helpfulness.

A little harsh, Ramey thought, but so were his remarks about the house falling apart around her ears, followed by a low-ball offer to buy her out, then unload it before it flunked a mandatory loan inspection.

Other than that, Preston's drop-ins had been quite more the merrier, particularly with her working at the Leonardos most of the time. Oh, he still looked down his aquiline nose at her, but he seemed fascinated by the Dillingers. Perhaps scofflaws held more cachet than a sister-in-law with paint under her fingernails instead of polish on them.

She parked a few yards back from the detached garage Chicken Charlie had built for his prized '31 Duesenberg Phaeton. The doors were wide enough for her van, but the ladder racks bolted on top wouldn't clear the header. Thoughts of raising the garage's roof were dashed by her savings account balance.

Life insurance was one of those things she and Stan had discussed when brochures arrived in the day's junk mail, or when has-been actors touted it on TV commercials. They'd just neglected to call any of the toll-free 800-numbers *right now* that Ramey dutifully copied down on magazine covers.

Her finances were nothing to brag about, nothing to cry over; ergo, not worth dwelling on. The thing that was heaviest on Ramsey's mind was the "Not tonight, dear" call to Don Blevins. She shouldn't have chickened out to spare a scene—odd, the connection between poultry and cowardice—but a no-strings friendship shouldn't feel like a noose.

On the back veranda, a lump shrouded in a chenille throw in one of the Adirondack chairs turned out to be her sister. Portia motioned toward the other chair and the thermal mugs on the table between them. "Take a load off, kiddo. Melba Jane's hot chocolate is almost as good as Mom's was."

Ramey's head tipped. The blonde braving the gloaming hour's descent to forty-eight degrees was a dead ringer for Portia, but definitely an imposter. Her real sister didn't expose herself to the elements, unless there was a Greek god employed as a ski instructor nearby, or a white sand beach lapped by ocean waves.

Adding to Ramey's disorientation was the man dressed in grimy jeans, muddy tennis shoes and a shrunken Plainfield High School sweatshirt helping Archie rake away leaves banked against the toolshed.

For Preston Hitchcock Carruthers, Jr., attorney-at-law and adulterer-at-will to turn over a new leaf was astonishing. Doing it manually boggled the mind.

"Where's the pixie dust?" Lowering herself into her chair punished Ramey's sore thigh muscles. "I want to be ready when Snow White and Mr. Goodwrench dance outside singing Bibbeldy-bobbledy-boo."

"The way this week's gone, anything's possible." Portia watched her sweaty husband and uncle ring the ever-growing brush pile with twigs and soggy leaves. "Wednesday night, after Chase went to bed, Preston and I talked until four in the morning."

Ramey sifted numerous responses and settled for a quasi supportive, "Worked some things out, huh?"

"It wasn't that kind of talking. Just, you know, *stuff*. Like we did a thousand years ago when we were dating."

Portia reached for her cocoa and took a sip, then balanced the mug on the chair's broad arm. "Among other things, Preston said that losing Mom and Dad, then Stan shook him up more than he realized. It was especially hard for him to deal with Stan's death, since he was a couple of years younger than Preston."

Catching the look in Ramey's eye, she went on, "I'm not an idiot for wanting to keep my family intact."

"I never said you were." Ramey noted, however, that her sister hadn't said she loved Preston, in spite of his faults, for a very long time.

"He might have slept with the latest Ms. Silicone, even if Stan hadn't died, but—"

"I know. Men grow up believing they're invincible. It scares the shit out of them to find out they aren't."

Ramey scratched at a blob of spackle dried on her jeans. It's terrifying to acknowledge your and everyone else's mortality. Preston's confession still sounded awfully close to blaming unfaithfulness on fate, instead of taking responsibility for it.

Darkness was reducing her uncle and brother-in-law to poltergeists with gardening implements. "Just don't forgive him too fast, okay?" Ramey said. "Let him prove he deserves to be trusted."

Portia made a noise in her throat, then a face, then blew a raspberry. "Stunning insight, Dear Abby. It took what, an hour, an hour-and-a-half for you to trust three ex-cons?"

She didn't exactly trust them. Ramey simply enjoyed having them around, just as her mother had and Portia would never appreciate.

"A husband versus visiting relatives," she said. "Totally different things."

"Only if a promise on Mom and Dad's graves has more wiggle room than wedding vows."

Given a moment's thought, Ramey decided she must be either too tired or too rational to make that leap and said so.

"A little while after Preston and I got here this afternoon, Ed and Archie started arguing. Archie insisted that both of Guaranty Federal's entry doors had automatic locks. Ed called him a chowderhead and bet five bucks that just the main one does."

Eyes widening, Ramey gasped in horror at the implications. "You don't mean—" She nearly got a hand clapped to her mouth before she cracked up laughing.

"Funny?" Portia screeched, like a bluejay in labor. "You think them planning to rob again is funny?"

Archie looked back from the toolshed where he and Preston were wrestling a wheelbarrow atop a heap of junk. "Did you say supper's ready?"

"Not yet, Uncle Archie." Ramey lowered her voice. "They aren't planning anything, Portia. It's a game to them. Kind of like fantasy football."

Older sisters needn't say a word to express complete and utter disbelief, while reducing a younger sibling to a bubble-brained twelve-year-old. The younger sibling usually reacts like a bubble-brained twelve-year-old, but once that trigger is tripped, there's no turning back.

"Go ahead, Professor Know-It-All," Ramey said. "Tell me how they'll pull a heist when they haven't left the house once since they got here Wednesday morning."

"Haven't left *yet*."

"None of them have a driver's license, or a car."

Portia countered, "Driver's license, big whoop. Cars can be stolen. Driving is like riding a bike."

"Fine. You win. After thirty-five years behind bars, they have no qualms whatsoever about discussing the robbery they're planning in front of you and Preston, even though they'll have to commit grand theft auto five or six times in broad daylight to case the bank, then steal another car to pull it off and make their getaway."

Portia's mouth opened, then shut. She frowned. She mulled. Then she said, "Well, when you put it like that."

A tepid concession, but Ramey grinned, as though victory had been declared and the parade was about to start.

Archie and Preston walked up and slouched on the porch railing. Neither smelled fresh as a daisy. "Dadblasted shame that setting them leaves afire tomorrow ain't gonna hurt them half as much as raking 'em did me," Archie drawled.

Preston clapped the older man's shoulder. "That's why you're going to relax on the porch and watch them burn while I tackle that mess of a toolshed." He waggled a finger at Ramey. "If somebody whose name I won't mention didn't come from such a long line of pack rats, the shed wouldn't be such a disaster."

Archie shook off Preston's hand. "Boy, I already

done told you umpteen times. You tend to your knittin' and me and Ed'll tend ours. If'n we need your help, we'll ask for it."

"You won't have to. Tomorrow's Sunday. I'll be here by eight."

"It's not as if *you're* working for food. They made a deal with Ramey. Butt out, already," Portia told her husband.

"Yes, *honey*," Preston replied. "Why don't you do that."

The door off the mudroom swung open. Melba Jane said, "Ramey isn't home from work, is she?"

Detecting a worried tone, Ramey called, "Here I am," and levered her numbed posterior off the chair. "Sorry. Portia and I started talking and I guess I lost track of time."

"Oh, that's all right. I didn't think a thing about it, till Don came looking for you."

He slid out from behind Melba Jane and stepped out onto the porch. The light at his back obscured his face. A gunfighter stance projected anger, loud and clear. "I thought we had a date."

5

Archie sniffed the air. "Whew, boy. Whatever kind of aftershave you slapped on, it ain't Old Spice."

Ed stomped around the corner of the house. "What's going on? Why's everybody huddled up out here?"

"Come on, Don," Preston said. "I'll get you a cup of Melba Jane's coffee while Ramey hops in the shower."

"I'm not hopping anywhere." Ramey started forward, primed to tell Don to perform a sex act on himself.

Portia grabbed her wrist and yanked down hard. "What's the matter with you," she whispered. "Don's a great guy. At your age and the way you... well, if you think anybody better's going to come along, you're fooling yourself."

Not at your age and as fat as you are, Ramey finished to herself. *So what if I'm a solid—okay, an extra-solid—five on a ten-point scale?*

Portia was a born nine. And what did she have to show for it? A shallow, philandering snob for a husband that sues people for a living. Ramey'd rather French-kiss frogs for the rest of her life.

She jerked her arm free, motioned at Don to follow her and stormed into the house. Keeping her tongue and temper in check, she blew through the kitchen, the breakfast nook's short corridor, then the dining room.

The pocket door dividing it from the living room balked from years of disuse. As if being seriously pissed at her sister and Don weren't enough, the door's reluctance to roll on its track provided Ramey with an inanimate enemy.

Strangely, muscling its cooperation had somewhat the same effect as primal scream therapy. Ramey's tone was subzero but civil when she turned to Don and said, "You have to be dating to have a date. We aren't."

"Aw, now. Calm down, babe."

Without exception, *calm down* were two words that virtually guaranteed to induce the opposite reaction.

"There's no reason to be mad at me," he went on, his voice as soothing as an amateur hypnotist's. "Mrs. Leonardo told me what time you left her house. I figured you'd cleaned up when you got home and would be ready to go when I came by."

Ramey clenched her teeth, conceivably fracturing a

molar's aged filling. "You called my clients to check up on me?"

He flashed a Brad Pitt grin she suspected he practiced in front of a mirror. "Hey, it's true what they say. You really are pretty when you're mad."

Observant enough to perceive that his pathetic attempt at flattery hadn't flown, he shifted to the time-honored injured party ploy. "Look, I spent all afternoon putting together a night we'd remember forever and I'm not gonna let that stubborn streak of yours ruin it."

"Remember forever? What in the world are you talking about?"

"I'd planned to wait until after dinner, but now that you've got your back up, I guess this is as good a time as any."

He knelt in front of her, bringing to mind a medieval warrior about to be knighted, or perhaps, beheaded. A jewelry box materialized in his hand. Resting in its velvet niche was a huge, pear-cut diamond solitaire set on a wide, gold band.

"I bought us a Las Vegas wedding package online for like, ninety-nine bucks, airfare included. The plane leaves at 3 a.m.—plenty of time for you to pack. On Monday afternoon, we fly to Maui for a two-week honeymoon. Free Continental breakfast, hourly shuttles to the beach and buy one, get one free Mai Tais every night at Happy Hour. From the photos, the hors d'oeuvres spread they lay out ought to hold us till breakfast."

Don removed the solitaire from the box and took her hand. "All you have to do is say yes."

There was a perverse, unnerving insolence in his out-of-the-blue proposal. It was designed not to sweep her off her feet, but to *knock* her off them.

"Why are you doing this?" Ramey's voice pitched so high, it sounded like wind shear. "I don't want to hurt you. We're friends." Or were, she amended. "That's all we've ever been. All we're ever going to be."

"You need me." Don pushed up to his feet, the ring still pinched between his fingertips. "You love me— or would, if you'd let yourself."

"No, Don. How you got the idea that I do, or could, I don't know. Unless it's because you only hear what you want to hear."

"Oh yeah?" The ring box snapped shut on its garish and likely nonreturnable contents. "Who's been there for you, every day, no matter what, for months? Whose shoulder have you cried on when some stupid song on the radio, or a guy walking down the street reminded you of good ol' Stan?"

Ramey's arms crossed at her belly, as though she'd been kicked. Her chin jerked toward the vestibule. "Get out."

Instantly contrite, Don reached toward her. "Hey, I'm

sorry. Forget I said that. I didn't mean to… It's just that after I tried so hard to make everything perfect for us—"

"There is no us."

"There could be." Don grasped her arms and shook her. "Listen to me. Stan's dead. From what I hear, he wasn't a saint. Hell, he was a motorcycle mechanic. Probably all he'd have ever been. When are you gonna stop acting like you wished you'd jumped in the casket with him?"

Tears scalded her eyes. How a marriage proposal turned into an assault, she couldn't comprehend. "Take your hands off me."

Backing away, he said, "I'm just trying to shake some sense into—"

"Get out, Don, and don't ever come back."

"But—"

"If I have to, I'll call Ed and Archie in here."

His eyes cut to the door. Head tilted and palms aloft, he sneered, "If that's the way you want it, babe. Fine by me."

Pausing at the vestibule, his finger stabbed the air. "You need me, Ramey. Next time something goes wrong, who's gonna bail you out? Who's gonna come running? You think those freeloaders give two shits about you?"

Don's bitter laugh reverberated in the hall long after the front door slammed behind him.

6

Seldom did a Monday outshine the weekend, but this one certainly did.

Ramey still felt as if she'd been cranked through Grandma Ava's old laundry mangle in the cellar. Saturday night's crying jag, writing alternately bereft and seething pages in her journal, supervising the toolshed's clean-out on Sunday and a couple of lousy nights' sleep weren't exactly invigorating, but a sense of calm was gaining momentum.

Inventorying the supply room adjacent to her office was always kind of fun, too. Clients were continually amazed at the minuscule amounts Ramey charged for bed and bath linens, curtains and hardware and color-coordinated accessories, such as vases, table settings, candles and holders, lamps, lampshades and wall decor.

"That's a trade secret," she told them, as though she belonged to the Magician's Union, instead of the International Association of Home Staging Professionals.

As yet, no one had guessed that her bargain-basement source was the local dollar store, whose prices she doubled and often tripled. Flea markets, garage sales, discount store clearance aisles and sales bins were mined, as well.

With her finger dragging down the clipboard's printed shopping list, she checked the box beside canister lights, which she used in shadowy corners to showcase architectural features. The Leonardo job had depleted her stock of ivory sheers. Several sizes of basic black-and-white lamp shades had vanished from the shelves.

She was on her way downstairs to ask if Melba Jane wanted to go shopping with her when somebody with a doorbell phobia pounded on the door.

"Hey!" Ed clomped down behind her. A hammer and two screwdrivers flew from his tool belt in the process. "Don't answer that."

Thinking it was Don, whose remorseful phone calls she'd screened since late Sunday night, Ramey crouched to peer between the balusters and out the front window. "I don't know anybody that drives a blue pickup."

"Probably a Watkins salesman," Ed said. "Or Fuller Brush. Ignore him and he'll mosey off."

The first, once renowned for the flavorings and syrups they peddled door to door, and the latter, a general household products vendor, had gone the way of the dinosaurs when full-time homemaking became most women's night job.

To spare her uncle a reminder of his kinship to Rip Van Winkle, Ramey said, "Sales resistance is my middle name. My backbone's so stiff, I can barely bend to tie my tennis shoes."

Ed's woolly eyebrows hiked a notch. "Izzat so?"

"Uh-huh." She hurried on down the stairs. "That's why I'm not buying what *you're* trying to sell me, Ed."

The man on the other side of the screen door was in his late thirties, perhaps early forties, but could have played second-string tackle for the Chiefs. Affirming that she was the Ramey Burke he sought, he introduced himself as Gordon Sweeney.

"Are Edsel, Archibald and Melba Jane Dillinger also in residence at this address?" he asked.

Having supposed her elder uncle's Christian name was Edward or Edwin, *Edsel* threw her for a second. A name like that could predestine a life of crime, unless your father had founded Ford Motor Company.

From behind the door, a raspy falsetto trilled, "Never heard of 'em, mister. Goodbye."

Sweeney's head and torso canted from vertical to horizontal. To the crack between the jamb and door, he said, "I'm disappointed in you, Ed. Less than a week on the outside and you've already violated parole. I figured you'd at least behave for a month or so."

Ed wriggled from his hiding place and stepped into the vestibule. He glared at Ramey. "Seeing as how you just had to answer the dadblasted door, I reckon you might as well let him through it."

The parole officer declined a seat in the living room, but surveyed it, the billiard room opposite and the corridor leading to the kitchen. "Nice house, ma'am."

"Might could say it's a step up from the Samaritan Mission." Ed grunted. "Lucy Curtis ratted us out, huh?"

Sweeney shook his head. "I received an anonymous tip to your whereabouts this morning."

"A tip? From who?"

"I don't know, Ed. That's where the anonymous part comes in. But I can tell you it wasn't Lucy Curtis that called."

"Okay, that's it," Ramey said. "What's this all about? And while you're at it, please explain how my uncles and aunt violated parole without stepping foot off the property since they arrived."

Sweeney informed her that six months prior to release, a prisoner must submit a plan to the probation office in the district where the parolee will reside. Included are any home offers from relatives, friends, or a shelter, like Lucy Curtis's Samaritan Mission. Whatever residence is provided must be deemed appropriate and approved before the parolee's release.

"Then, if I understand you correctly, the Dillingers put down the Mission on their release plan, but came here instead." Ramey turned on Ed, along with Archie and Melba Jane, who'd respectively shuffled and limped in from the kitchen. "Care to tell me why?"

Ed splayed his hands. "'Cause you were a little girl last you saw of us. If you'd scotched the idea, we'd have wound up at Lucy's."

Archie said, "Now, to move from the mission to here, we'd have had to write up another release plan, then cool our heels for a month or better, before Sweeney gave it the green light."

Ramey admitted, had they nominated hers as their home-away-from-prison, she'd have probably refused. Who wouldn't? If she'd actually had a game plan for the rest of her life, signing on as camp counselor for three elderly ex-cons wouldn't have made the cut. Guilt might have eventually caused her to change her mind, especially knowing the alternative was a homeless shelter, but she couldn't blame the Dillingers for their backdoor ambush, so to speak.

Yeah, well, she did a little, but hindsight took a lot of the steam out of it.

Ed couldn't have looked sadder unless he tipped over on all fours and bayed at a blue moon. "Living here with our niece has been the happiest few days of our mostly wasted lives." He held out his wrists. "But we can't say we didn't know the rules before we bent 'em."

"They're under arrest?" Ramey leaped in front of him, feet planted and arms outstretched. "You'll have to go through me to do it," she said, despite the fact that Sweeney could probably tuck her and the Dillingers under a bulging bicep and tote the whole lot of them off to jail.

"I went to high school with the editor of the newspaper," Ramey lied. "I can just see tomorrow's headline: Senior Citizens Forced From Family Home, Placed In Shelter for Indigents."

Sweeney rolled his eyes. To the Dillingers, he said, "Can I trust y'all to let me have a private word with Ms. Burke?"

"Well, we ain't gonna make a break for it, if that's what you're askin'," Ed said. "I flat forgot to pack my track shoes when they sprung me."

Sweeney watched them retreat to the kitchen.

"Characters." His glance at Ramey inferred, *present company included.*

"They've been punished enough. There must be a way to let them stay with me." She thrust out her jaw. "If there isn't, make one up."

"I can approve it at my discretion, but are you aware

of the responsibility you're taking on? They're hale and hearty now, but like you said, they're senior citizens. Medicare, they can apply for, but they don't qualify for Social Security benefits. The government won't give pensions to folks who never paid into it. And finding work is tough for parolees half their age."

Ramey had not taken the financial considerations into account. The conversion from a one-person household to four had been a bit abrupt, not to mention unforeseen. Particularly for somebody who'd decided that adopting a cat wasn't in her best emotional interest.

Factor in the Leonardos' tight deadline, then Don unfurling his bizarre true colors and, well…

"I appreciate your candor, Mr. Sweeney. It's true, I hadn't thought about any of those things you just talked about." Pausing while the ego third of her brain shrieked warnings at her compassionate superego, she continued, "But if I have to sell the house to support us, I will."

"You're sure about that?"

"As sure as I've ever been about anything."

Archie, Melba Jane and Ed weren't just family. Her obligation to them was no longer in homage to her mother. Even after this short time, she found that she'd come to love the old coots. Respected them. Admired their will to survive, their loyalty to each other and in Archie and Melba Jane's case, the love they'd sustained for over three decades through letters and occasional long-distance phone calls.

Sweeney studied Ramey's face, as though the level of her commitment was proportional to the tiny freckles fanned across her nose and cheeks. "All right, then." He smiled. "I hope they appreciate what you're giving them."

"It works both ways, Mr. Sweeney. Which is something I hadn't realized myself until now."

Before he left, he informed her and reminded the Dillingers of their terms of parole. Some future visits would be unannounced and he must be alerted immediately of any change in status or problems.

The Dillingers had one strike against them. It was Ramey's job to ensure they didn't rack up a second.

As the parole officer ambled down the sidewalk to his truck, Ramey told Ed, "Trust me. If you guys don't behave yourselves, Gordon Sweeney's the least of your worries."

"Yep. Just thinking about it's got me shaking in my boots." He favored her with a sly grin. "Did you really know the newspaper editor?"

Ramey chuckled. "I wouldn't recognize the guy if he passed me on the street."

"Well, hooray and hallelujah," Ed cackled and pumped a bony arm. "And here I was beginning to think your blood was pure Patterson. By golly, there's a dollop o' Dillinger floating around in there, after all."

7

Age had rusted the spring in Ed's step, but stealth was as predisposed as the birthmark on his thigh. He moved like a draft through the sleeping house. No trick to it, really. All a man had to do was memorize which floor-boards and stair treads squeaked, and oil every door-knob and hinge.

Piece of cake.

The second floor's layout was almost the same as when he and Archie were boys. There was a bedroom at each of the four corners with a lavatory between the two on the north side. Behind the centered stairwell, the former servants' quarters was now Ramey's office. The neighboring bedroom to the south was packed with file cabinets, swatch books, catalog, bolts of fab-ric and all manner of claptrap for her business—the na-ture of which Ed couldn't savvy, no matter how many times she explained it.

She worked her fanny off, though. She seemed to

enjoy it, too, except there were easier ways to dispose of property the owners didn't want anymore. Ed's old cellie, Jimmy "The Torch" Kubitschek, raked in ten Gs a pop for his kind of interior redecorating.

He continued along the hallway, his fingertips grazing the smooth wall. Only someone who remembered Ava Dillinger's sewing room was opposite the stairway's landing would notice the door had been plastered over.

Sylvie and Bill had removed the wall between the sewing room and the front-facing bedroom to allow for a new, private bath and a walk-in closet—a master suite, as Ramey called it. It was big enough to bunk twenty lifers, Ed thought. Twenty-five, counting the closet. A lot of real estate for one young widow to try and fill all by her lonesome.

He'd expected the house to seem smaller, as places were apt to grow in memory, then shrink when next you saw them. Instead, he felt as if he'd shrunk and the old house had doubled in size, especially at night. He wasn't fearful of the dark, as much as he'd forgotten what it was. Lights-out in prison was gray, not pitch-black, and quiet didn't exist, aside from a word guards yelled at fractious inmates.

The only place that gave Ed ease was the front porch. Maybe he could sweet-talk Ramey into buying a new porch swing. She'd said the one he'd loved as a youngster had been taken down when she accidentally bopped Portia upside the head with it when they were kids.

"I was playing airplane pilot," she'd told him, "and Portia barged in and said I had to let her be the stewardess and her stupid dolls be our passengers."

Ed smiled as he eased her bedroom door open and pressed an ear to the narrow gap he created. Thunder rumbled in the distance. Archie's snores racked from the room he shared with Melba Jane. Ed tuned them out. For a full half minute, he listened to the *tick, tick, tick* of the Big Ben clock on the table beside Ramey's bed.

As was her custom, she'd pulled the drapes closed, but the bathroom's night-light cast a feeble glow over the room. The room smelled faintly of oranges and was silent, apart from the clock and her slow, rhythmic breathing. Lying on her side with a hand tucked under her chin and her hair tangled on the pillow, she looked not a day over twelve.

Ed repressed the urge to kiss her cheek, then retreated as wraithlike as he'd entered. The past two nights, she'd tossed and churned the covers into a frightful wad. She'd slept, but scarcely rested.

Melba Jane had wanted to take a breakfast tray to her the morning after the spat with that gomer of a mailman. Ed vetoed it. Pampering was fine; Ramey'd had little of it, the last several years. What she'd needed most was a slap of cold water to her face, a yank on her bootstraps and for them all to act like Sunday was just the day after Saturday and nothing had happened to coo and cluck about.

Blevins had phoned a half-dozen times since he flew off the handle and out the front door. Ed guessed she'd told Romeo to go fly a kite. Leastwise, he hoped she had, except it meant she'd be alone again when he, Archie and Melba Jane got what they came for and hit the road.

I'll sure miss that girl, he thought. It'll be like leaving Sylvie all over again, without the hugs and tears and a chance to say goodbye.

He crossed the vestibule, then stepped out onto the porch, gently closing the front door behind him. The brewing storm had sunk the temperature ten degrees since he'd last ventured out for a smoke. Shoulder hiked to deflect the wind, he cupped a hand at his mouth to prevent the match from fizzling before his cigarette caught fire.

Bracing a tennis shoe on the low, stone parapet surrounding the porch, he scanned the sidewalk, then the street. Not a soul afoot, four-legged or two.

Thunderheads amassing above the horizon inched closer, thickening the air with the loamy scent of rain. The wind stung Ed's ears and the cold seeped into his bones. These were gifts, not aggravations, to a man whose window of the world had been a foot squared and higher than his head for half his life.

As smoke whorled from his lips, a sudden drowsiness leadened his eyelids. He was glad that sleep had begun to find him, but it sure put the kibosh on another spin around town in Ramey's van.

He'd borrowed it that first night home, after everybody slogged up to bed, their bellies full to busting with Melba Jane's home cooking. Believing it morally reprehensible to lift Ramey's key chain from her purse, Ed borrowed the spare set he'd found in her desk drawer.

Taking his leave without rousing the house was a matter of jumping the gearshift into neutral, coasting down the drive, then on to the corner before firing up the engine. The van not only looked like a guard shack with tires, it drove like one. But it was pure bliss to ramble up this street and down that avenue, as carefree as the orange tabby he saw. A voice in a dark cubby of his mind dared him to point the hood ornament southwest and follow it until a sign read, Buenos Dias, Muchacho. Gripping the steering wheel, he'd turned around and headed home at the next corner.

Wisdom is said to be its own reward, yet sometimes good fortune hitches a ride. Ed happened upon a store the size of an airplane hangar. The building's walls and parking lot were lit up brighter than a prison yard when a bed check came up an inmate short of a full house.

Fifteen minutes later, he exited those tall, pneumatic glass doors two dollars and fifty-seven cents poorer with a duplicate set of keys jingling in a plastic sack. It was a thieves' paradise, he'd thought in utter amazement. In his day, shady locksmiths pocketed fifty bucks or better to reproduce a key from a soap, clay, or wax mold.

Average home builders and owners now chose from six to ten types of doorknob and dead bolt sets and used the keys packaged with them, rather than hire a locksmith to alter the tumblers and refit the keys. Odds were, a thief with a fair collection of standards could gain entry to two or more houses on any given block.

To Ed's further astonishment, the store's chatty key-making machine operator said that every tenth or twelfth vehicle off the assembly line also had identical key patterns. Newer models featured both keyless entry pods and good old-fashioned keyholes, in the event the pod's battery failed.

"It's cheaper for the manufacturers," the operator said, and a never-ending Christmas present for professional car thieves, Ed thought.

Pondering the lessons learned from that first moonlight drive and another on Thursday night had Ed itching like Columbus for new worlds to discover. Except

Ramey's bedroom windows overlooked the driveway and front yard. One loud clap of thunder and she'd be up for a gander outside, then wonder where her van had disappeared to.

His gaze lowered from the sky to the junk from the toolshed and garbage that was piled at the curb for the garbageman. Top-heavy as that van was with the ladders on top, it'd be just his luck to crash into the trash on the way out.

Tomorrow night was soon enough for another lookie-loo, Ed decided. His mother always told him Tuesday was the best day of the week to do business. He didn't hold to such notions, but he'd touch wood on the way upstairs, anyhow.

If it rained most of the day like the weatherman predicted, he and Archie would take another poke through the attic and the cellar. Being female, Melba Jane could conjure an excuse to get Ramey out of the house awhile. A grocery run, or…Christ, anybody with eyes could see Melba Jane needed a trip to the beauty parlor, like King Kong needed a bulletproof vest.

Lightning flashed in the distance. Ed took a final drag off his Camel, then flipped the butt toward the driveway. Starting back inside, he paused, then looked back at the van. From the corner of his eye, he'd spied something moving.

An empty sack, probably. Or a paint rag. After her

errands that afternoon, Ramey'd lugged bagfuls of plunder from the van to her storeroom. But he hadn't noticed anything before, and he'd smoked a half a pack of cigarettes since then, to calm his nerves.

Just to be on the safe side, he hurried from the porch and walked across the lawn.

It wasn't a sack he'd seen whip on the wind. Rooted in place, he watched the tail of a khaki trench coat flap up, then fall back again, like a small, triangular flag. Its owner, sprawled on his back near the driveway, was beyond caring about the storm blowing in.

Ed crouched alongside the corpse, listening hard for footsteps or sirens, panicking at every shadow, every skittering leaf. He peered up at Ramey's window, expecting to see the curtains pulled wide, her horrified face staring down at him. He imagined himself running into the night, as far and as fast as his lungs and legs would take him.

Archie lay as still as a stone, eyes squinched shut, his breath slow and steady. He knew without looking at the clock that it was 2 a.m. Nature called about then every damned night, and again around five. He was convinced that if he played possum, he'd eventually show his body who was boss and drift back to sleep.

Forty-five seconds later, he peeled back the covers. Careful not to waken Melba Jane, he padded from the bedroom to the lavatory, musing that the only advantage to prison was the relative proximity of the commode.

Forgoing the blinding bathroom light, he relied on familiarity to guide him. Destination reached and purpose underway, Archie rested a forearm on the high windowsill and looked out the window.

Absently, he watched the tree branches swinging to and fro, his older brother dragging a body through the grassy slough along the house, a skeletal TV antenna waving at him from the peak of the next-door neighbor's roof.

Any minute now, the fat, purple-black clouds roiling overhead were going to cut loose a gullywasher....

Scowling, he cast his eyes downward again. No Ed. No corpse.

Humph. Must've been that chili Melba Jane fixed for supper. It'd played hell with his digestion and now, his mind. He tried to tell her that spicy food didn't agree with him. The woman never listened to a word he said.

He washed up at the sink, then backtracked to the window again. When they got down south, Lord knew what the food was going to do to him. He'd probably see spaceships and little green men running around outside every time he got up to take a leak.

Out in the hallway, Archie hesitated and looked left,

where a few more hours' sleep was mere steps away. Against his will, defying common sense, logic and literal cold feet, he hung a right and scuffled to Ed's room.

The bed was rumpled, but empty. Hardly unusual. His brother hadn't logged more than three or four hours a night since they were kids. Fact was, Ed's cellmates begged their relatives to send books of any kind, as long as they had lots of pages, to keep him from pacing the floor all night.

That's where he was, Archie wanted to believe. Roaming around for something to read, or for a piece of pie. Could be he was parked in front of an old John Wayne movie on TV with the sound off. For years, graveyard-shift guards allowed Ed the privilege so his chronic insomnia wouldn't incite a small-scale riot.

Archie returned to his room, scratching his head. Longingly, he gazed at the bed. On the side nearer the wall, his beloved wife's broad contours brought to mind the Great Smoky Mountains humped on the horizon near Knoxville, Tennessee.

He trusted Ed with his life, and would sacrifice his own to save his brother's. But trusting him out of his sight for two seconds? Well, now that was something else entirely.

Tiptoeing to the upholstered chair near the closet,

he retrieved the coat he'd flung over the back and picked up his shoes.

"Where you goin', Arch?"

A sneaker thumped the floor. Unfurling his tongue, which had dived for cover behind his uvula, he stammered, "I—uh, um, downstairs. To the kitchen. For a glass of milk." Backpedaling, he added, "You know, to help me sleep."

"Okay…" Then, "How come you need a coat to fetch a glass of milk?"

It was true what his mama always said. Women *did* have eyes in the back of their heads. "I—ya, well, these pajamas Lucy give me are awful thin. I don't wanna catch a chill."

"Hmm." Melba Jane rooted around, burrowing deeper under the covers. "While you're down there, check and see if I switched off the coffeemaker."

"Will do, honey bunch. Now go on back to sleep."

Taking the flashlight from a kitchen drawer as he passed through, Archie continued out to the back porch. Reluctant to announce his presence, he didn't turn on the flashlight, but clutched its barrel like a billy club. If it *was* his brother he'd seen and if the man he was dragging wasn't dead, but unconscious, or faking it, Ed might be in dire need of assistance.

Archie didn't hear a thing, other than creaking branches, bushes rustling in the wind and the thunder overhead. Couldn't see bupkes, either, besides the out-line of the garage, the toolshed and the distant hedgerow along the back property line.

Feeling eminently visible in a light gray coat and baby blue pajama bottoms, Archie lowered himself into a crouch. Zigzagging behind shrubs and trees, careful not to stumble into one of the holes he'd dug earlier, he cut between the outbuildings, then peered around their respective corners.

Nothing. Nobody, living or dead.

Sweating despite the needling wind, Archie scuttled on, nearly swallowing his heart when a rabbit flushed up from behind a clump of iris shoots. Approaching the brush pile he hadn't gotten around to burning, his motile heart plummeted when he saw something par-tially hidden by leaves on the pile's far side.

In the same instant the flashlight's beam allayed his worst fear, it identified the corpse he'd seen Ed drag-ging through the side yard.

Time alters anyone's appearance to some extent, but it hadn't erased the pockmarks that ravaged Oren, aka "Shifty" Falcone's sunken cheeks. His mop of sandy hair had thinned to silvery wisps, but there was no mistaking that crook-neck squash of a nose.

The nickname for the Other Dillinger Gang's get-away driver derived from his habit of grinding the trans-mission whenever he shifted from second gear to third.

It hadn't affected the wheelman's zero-to-haul-ass capability, but the moniker stuck. Truth be known, Shifty preferred it to Oren, much less Oren*thal*.

A brownish splotch on his shirt indicated he hadn't croaked from natural causes. Archie passed a hand across his sweaty forehead. He couldn't, for the life of him, imagine why Ed would kill Shifty.

Maybe it was self-defense. Like a lot of fellas that stopped growing about the time their friends started, Shifty packed a helluva chip on his shoulder. The Dillinger brothers weren't what anybody'd call strapping, but compared to Shifty Falcone, they were athletes.

'Twas more likely an accident, Archie thought. Ed was the excitable type. Thirty-five years of watching your back in prison hardly taught a man how to relax, either. If Shifty appeared from nowhere while Ed was out having a smoke, he'd have jumped first and asked questions later.

After he chucked Shifty into the burn pile, Ed must have hightailed it around front, just as Archie came out the back. Ten bucks said he was in his room catching a few z's before the do-it-himself cremation, as soon as weather permitted. Which wouldn't be until well after dawn. That slicked-up weasel on the TV said it might rain all blessed day. Even if the wind did let up and the sky cleared, a pyre of wet limbs and leaves wouldn't burn worth spit.

"Brains of the operation, my ass." Archie extinguished the flashlight. Coshing Ed upside the skull with it might shake his gears loose, but the satisfaction wasn't worth it. And if Archie traipsed into the house after him, he'd surely wake Ramey and Melba Jane. He'd rather tangle with the devil himself than explain all this to either one of them.

With all due respect for the departed, Archie set himself to the grisly task of better hiding Shifty's remains. Come morning, he'd divine an excuse for Melba Jane to divine an excuse to get Ramey out of the house for a while.

Then he and Ed would somehow transport the corpse to an alley near the Samaritan Mission. They'd leave Falcone's billfold nearby—after taking his money and anything with his name on it. The cops would assume a bum had rolled him.

You ain't going back to prison on a homicide rap, Archie would tell his brother, Dr. Einstein. *And neither are me and Melba Jane.*

Melba Jane couldn't fall asleep without Archie beside her.

It was pure foolishness, she admitted. They'd slept in separate bunks, in separate prisons, in different towns for most of their married life. But when the mattress bowed beneath Archie's weight, his body warm and soft against hers, she didn't feel like the saggy, baggy old crone she'd become.

No, in those precious moments just before weariness overtook her, she was a young, buxom, beautiful bride and he was as handsome as Clark Gable. And as soon as they hit that big score, they'd settle down in a nice house and start a family. A boy and a girl—maybe two of each, Lord willing.

One of those long-ago, pillow-talk dreams had come true, but only for a few hours. Poor, sweet Archie knew nothing about it and never would. Better for Melba Jane to grieve alone than break his heart, too.

She'd named their daughter Pearl Anne. A shock of dark hair had covered her tiny head like a silk cap. Although her eyes hadn't opened, she'd puckered that little rosebud mouth of hers, as if blowing kisses to her momma, one right after another.

Melba Jane had counted each finger and toe, marveling at the miracle she and Archie created…then the woman from the county took Pearl Ann away and gave her to a couple who couldn't have a baby of their own.

Wherever their daughter was now, whatever name those people called her by, Pearl Anne Dillinger was four years younger than Ramey, but her spitting image, nonetheless. Melba Jane had the pictures to prove it.

Sylvie had kept her promise to Ed not to visit her brothers or Melba Jane in prison. It wasn't their pride

Ed wanted to protect, but Sylvie herself, as well as Bill, Ramey and Portia. The Dillingers had caused them enough pain and embarrassment.

They'd treasured Sylvie's letters and cards—they'd received hundreds of them over the years. When she sent school photos or snapshots of Ramey, Melba Jane had shown them around the cell block, bragging that the little girl was hers and Archie's. She'd say that her name was Pearl Anne, and she was growing up strong and smart and respectable.

Deep, ragged breaths dulled the blades inside Melba Jane's chest. *You've still got Ramey to love. Keep pretending she's your own, same as you did with her pictures. Take what comfort's in that and go on.*

Lightning strobed outside the windows as she wiped her eyes again. A flickering, ethereal glow illuminated the room. Melba Jane chanted, one Mississippi, two Mississippi, three—before the thunder rolled down.

Pushing herself up on an elbow, she plucked at her nightgown, the flannel taut across her breasts and belly. "What on earth is taking that man so long?"

Sharing a bed was different for him. The same sounds and sensations that sweetened her dreams intruded on his sleep, let alone the restless legs and torments a man his age endured.

She'd heard footsteps on the stairs a while ago, but they'd trailed down the hall to Ed's room. Normally her brother-in-law crept the house as quiet as a cat in velvet overshoes. Maybe he was too tired to bother, Melba Jane presumed. He and Archie worked Sunday on the toolshed, with Preston hovering at their heels. They'd cleaned the garage yesterday, then stacked the junk from it at the curb.

But if Ed had skulked back to bed, where in blue blazes was Archie? He could've lassoed a whole cow and milked her dry by now.

Melba Jane jerked back the covers. The leopard print house shoes Ramey bought her were toasty and wide enough to accommodate her sore toe and the corn plaster adhered to it.

Careful not to stumble over her own feet, she hobbled downstairs, rehearsing her shame-on-you-for-making-me-worry speech. She expected to find him in the billiards room snoring in front of the TV, like his sneaky-Pete bachelor of a brother usually was.

But Archie wasn't there. Melba Jane searched the living room, dining room and the breakfast nook. There was no empty milk glass on the table. No dishes of any kind left for her to pick up.

On the counter beside the refrigerator, the coffeemaker's indicator light glowed like Satan's left eye. Scorched coffee bubbled on the bottom of the carafe. Another five, ten minutes and the glass would have busted six ways to Sunday.

It was her fault for leaving it on in the first place. And it was her fault again for asking her husband of all people to do her the simple favor of checking to see if she had.

Setting the carafe on a trivet, Melba Jane cocked her head toward the cellar door. So that's where Archie had snuck off to. Had to be. Even Ed couldn't roam around the attic this time of night, lest those creaky old ceiling joists gave him away.

She pictured Archie down there rooted in place, staring up at the floorboards that had just as surely tracked her footfalls through the front rooms and the kitchen. What would he do if she marched down there and caught him? Stick out his arms and pretend he was sleepwalking?

Hah. There was more than one way for a man to cheat on his wife. And Mrs. Archibald DeWayne Dillinger wasn't born butt first and brains later.

Toeing off her house shoes to walk barefoot to the cellar door, she paused at a thumping noise from outside. Hands flattened on the counter, she leaned over the sink, peering left out the window, then right, and then she blinked and looked again.

That round-shouldered codger pushing a wheelbarrow was Archie, all right. He glanced at the house, as though sensing a pair of eyes boring holes in him.

Melba Jane ducked and sidled away from the window. Suspicion licked her breastbone like a bad case of indigestion. Whatever that man was up to, it wasn't moonlight gardening.

For a fat old prison cook with a bum toe and a thrift shop nightgown drooping around her ankles, Melba Jane charged upstairs as if bloodhounds were baying at her back trail.

She hadn't quite caught her breath before Archie entered the bedroom. As intent as he was on shucking his shoes and coat, then sliding into bed, he probably wouldn't notice if she'd drawn her last.

The musty stink of dirt and body odor tainted the air. Melba Jane lay there and waited for Archie to fall asleep. Rain pattered the roof. Soon, Archie's lusty snoring upstaged the thunder. Carefully, warily, Melba Jane skootched and wriggled off the mattress. He snuffled a time or two, but didn't waken.

In the kitchen, she fashioned a hooded slicker from a heavy-duty garbage bag. Desperation being the mother of invention, after bunching her gown around her waist, she pulled on two more bags, like footed waders, and belted the ensemble with duct tape.

Armed with the flashlight from the drawer—which Archie had also used, judging by its dirty lens and case—Melba Jane goose-stepped out into the rain and across the yard.

Archie's energetic hole digging simplified her search. Oh, he'd graded the trench with leaves where his mother's rose garden used to be, but an X might as well have marked the spot.

"Sweet baby Jesus." The flashlight's beam swept the end of the exposed trench. Melba Jane faltered, clutching the shovel's handle to keep from toppling into Shifty Falcone's makeshift grave.

Archie, a murderer? A thief he'd been since he was tall enough to reach the candy jars at Cheney's Five & Dime. Later, he could open a cash register's till faster than its owner could unlock it with a key. But never, not even once, had he ever harmed a single hair on anyone's head.

Until now. The why of it, Melba Jane couldn't imagine for the life of her. But there was no doubt about it. Shifty—God love and rest him—was dead. And Archie had buried him…*in Ramey's backyard.*

The clang of a barred, steel door slamming shut was so loud inside Melba Jane's head, she fell to her knees in the soft, damp dirt. Images of Archie being led away in handcuffs and shackles ran through her mind. Tears mixed with the raindrops coursing down her face.

8

The windshield wipers beat like a tom-tom. Becky Taylor's chin hovered above the steering wheel. She switched the headlights to high beam. The slate curtain of rain pelting her car repelled light, bouncing it back at her.

Gutters had become rivers. Intersections resembled square ponds. You had to be a school bus driver or an idiot to be out this early in the morning, in this kind of weather. Or, Becky fumed, a pharmaceutical company's sales rep whose regional manager held meetings at 6 a.m.

A passing sedan's rooster tail swamped her windshield. Water tattooed the side windows, spraying the length of her car like gunfire. Becky flinched as though the sound and fury might shatter the glass.

The dashboard clock read five-forty. About now, the early-bird brownnosers—every sales force had a few—were grazing the conference room's continental breakfast spread. When her boss elevatored down from his suite, they'd greet him with a smile, a weepy Danish and a foam cup of lousy coffee in hand. If you missed the opening presentation, you weren't a team player. Which was a euphemism for a hash mark away from a pink slip.

Becky's foot plied the accelerator. Nudging along at twenty miles an hour had a negligible effect on the minimal visibility. It'd be close, but the main drag was six blocks away. Catch two or three righteous green lights and she'd plop in a swivel chair just as her boss stepped behind the lectern.

Just in case, she thought it wise to let someone know she was running late. Pulling her cell phone from her coat pocket, Becky dialed her mentor, Audra Stacy.

"You'd better not be calling in sick," Audra warned.

"I'm almost at the hotel. I may need you to run interference, though, if the traffic gods don't smile on me."

A pause. "I'll try, but hurry, okay?"

"I *am* hurrying." Yes, she should have left her condo a little earlier. Better yet, she should have checked into the hotel last night as the boss and Audra had.

Becky frowned. Sheesh, if I had three kids and a mother-in-law with a heart condition living with me as Audra does, I'd *move* to a hotel, she thought.

"Rumor of the day is," Audra said, "there's gonna

be territory reassignments. Meaning, the rich get richer and the rest of us get the podiatrist trade."

A garbage truck loomed ahead like a mutant predator. Becky swerved away from the truck, shouting, "How are we supposed to meet sales quotas, if the suits—"

"Don't bitch at me. You know…"

A grayish elongated object flumed into Becky's path. Startled, she slammed on the brakes.

"…the drill. If you're third-and-long…"

Rear tires hydroplaning, Becky's car slewed toward the curb. "Oh, *shit*." The impact was like hitting a speed bump on the diagonal.

The sedan fishtailed, rocked, then stabilized. Audra cried in her ear, "Hey! What's wrong? Becky? *Becky?*"

Her eyes locked on the rearview mirror. Behind her, whatever she'd run over, now lay parallel to the curb. The waterlogged wrapping had fallen open. The scarlet glow of her taillights outlined a hand, the fingers bent as though they were clenching an invisible stress ball.

Becky's cell phone banged off the dashboard. Her throat clamped shut on her scream. Reflex jerked her foot off the brake pedal and tromped the accelerator.

Ramey wakened and sat up as though sleep were a switch and someone had flipped it off. Rather than groggy, she was alert and well rested, just as the over-the-counter sleeping pill had advertised. She was almost cheerful, except for sensing a noise had awakened her. The alarm clock hadn't gone off. Besides, she wouldn't have set it for five-freakin'-fifty-one in the morning.

Eyes roaming the darkened bedroom, she wasn't sure what she was listening for, but had an instinctive certainty it wasn't a smoke alarm beeping for a fresh battery, a Dillinger brother stubbing a toe in the attic, or a shorn branch skittering down the shingles.

The drapes skirred open on a wet, dark, gloomy Tuesday. Nobody afoot outside, nor as she subsequently discovered, in the second floor hallway.

The *whoosh-ahh* of a garbage truck's air brakes drew Ramey back to the windows. At the curb sat a flying buttress of lumpy trash bags. She knew she'd pay additional freighting charges for her extra trash. "Money well spent," she said.

A figure hopped from the truck's cab. The rain was slackening from cloudburst to heavy drizzle, but water poured off the bright orange hooded slicker that brushed the tops of his rubber boots.

He rounded the front of the vehicle, then halted—appalled, Ramey assumed, by the heap of garbage bags. She hadn't noticed what resembled a giant burrito lying between the truck and the curb until he nudged it with his boot.

Stumbling backward, his arms pinwheeled for balance. The hood of his slicker swiveled toward the house, then he trotted to the truck and clambered back into the cab.

Pressing her nose to the glass and squinting failed to bring the burrito into focus. The distance was too great and the mist too thick to see through. Judging by its shape and size, the filthy, rolled-up carpet scrap her uncles had disposed of yesterday had probably floated into the street.

Luckily nobody driving by had hit it. Or veered to miss it, oversteered and plowed into a tree. If acts of God and Mother Nature were a viable defense against personal injury lawsuits, Preston Carruthers's annual income would plummet exponentially.

Since the garbage truck hadn't moved, the driver was likely radioing his dispatcher to authorize tacking a couple of zeroes onto Ramey's bill for removing the excess junk.

"Money well spent," she repeated with slightly less enthusiasm. Reclosing her curtains for privacy, she headed to the bathroom for a quick shower.

Detective-Sergeant Mike Constantine's shoulders hunched against the rain. He looked down at the weatherproof tarp covering the corpse.

Beyond that legendary shadow of a doubt, he knew

he shouldn't have given his six-day, five-night singles-only cruise ticket that his sisters bought for his birthday to Major Loomis's secretary.

Not that Mike would have used it. Contrary to his sisters' opinion, middle-aged bachelorhood wasn't a disease in need of a cure. Had he played it smart, he'd have put in for vacation time, booked a week's worth of appointments at a tanning salon and be happily holed up in his house right now. Instead, he had a homicide case that was already giving him a headache. And experience promised the pain was destined to slide south before he closed the file.

At 5:56 a.m., the Plainfield P.D.'s E-911 dispatcher fielded a garbage truck driver's cell-phoned report of a corpse rolled up in a rug, lying in the street. In succession, a newspaper carrier provided corroboration, as did an account from a neighbor who'd been fetching the day's edition of the *News-Messenger* from the bushes. The skeptical first officer to arrive at the scene had said, "From what dispatch told me, I figured a cat had climbed in one end to get out of the rain and drowned itself."

The fourth E-911 caller lent an interesting twist. A sobbing woman confessed to a pedestrian hit-and-run at this address. She'd hung up without disclosing her name, or phone number. Caller ID promptly supplied both.

Mike noted the fresh skid marks and the tire treads that bisected the carpet the body was wrapped in. Ms. Rebecca A. Taylor most definitely had hit it with her car. But at the moment of impact, the vic was horizontal, unrecognizable as human, and already seriously deceased.

"Care to hazard a guess on time of death?"

From the shelter of his black silk umbrella, John Slayer, the unfortunately named county coroner, aimed a bemused look at Mike. "Pick a number between last night and early this morning."

Slayer was a funeral home director, not a certified medical examiner. Determining a time of death wasn't as simple or finite as it was portrayed on TV. Weather conditions, time of day, season, location—all skewed the findings of textbook science.

Death was, however, the coroner's trade, politically and professionally. Slayer's educated guesses often proved as accurate as the M.E.'s findings following an autopsy.

"Rigor mortis is well established," he said. "I'd say the man is in his early seventies and wouldn't tip the scale past one-thirty-five, sopping wet." He grimaced. "No pun intended."

Mike allowed it wasn't. Humor was a coping mechanism, though. Just because undertakers and cops dealt with violent death on a regular basis didn't mean they were immune to its shock value.

As for the facts of the matter, rigor seldom presents in the morbidly obese. Conversely, the thinner and older the vic, the faster the muscles become rigid.

"The dead don't bleed," Slayer went on. "Those scratches on his face, neck and hands all occurred postmortem. Lividity is fixed along his back and extremities."

"Great. Between the rain, drop in air temp and exposure, that doesn't narrow things down a whole lot."

Creases striped the coroner's forehead. "I don't know what to think about the dry dirt in his ears, nostrils and mouth and what appears to be grass stains on his coat and pant legs."

Mike couldn't explain them, either. Classic signs of a struggle, they weren't. They did fit the overall scheme of an enigma in progress.

Slayer balanced his umbrella's wooden shaft on his shoulder to peel off his latex gloves. "I'll notify the Greene County M.E.'s office from the hearse. Let me know when you're ready to transport."

It wouldn't be long. The street wasn't the primary crime scene. Mike would take photographs, perform a cursory examination and commit those findings to film, check pockets for an ID, then have Slayer deliver the body to the morgue, rug and all.

Protecting the victim with a vinyl tarp both preserved and contaminated evidence. The covering wasn't sterile. It was impossible to avoid transferring particles already present on it—trace fibers, hair, etc. Equally impossible was not taking away evidence when the tarp was removed.

A microscopic examination of the vinyl surface was doable. Proving which traces fell into which category was a defense attorney's dream and the prosecutor's nightmare.

Mike saw Ryan Rickenbacher, the vertically challenged detective-in-training assigned to him, hustling up the street.

"About time you showed up," Mike said. "Still having trouble tying your tie? Or is this your day to shave?"

In truth, Rickenbacher had the makings of an excellent crime scene investigator. A little too eager, easy to intimidate and a touch too jumpy conclusion-wise, but he'd grow out of it, eventually.

Ignoring a superior officer's smart-ass remarks was a sign that the rookie's skin was thickening. "I'll start canvassing the neighbors," he said. "No, better take photographs, first." He glanced around. "Gotta measure, triangulate—"

"Heel, dog." Mike chuckled. "I realize you haven't worked a homicide before, but this one's got more exceptions than rules."

He lifted the tarp and pointed at the man's upper chest. "See that puncture wound?"

"Uh-huh."

"Very neat, very quiet, very fatal. We don't need an autopsy to know he bled out fast and internally."

Ryan nodded. "Chances are the rain has washed away any blood trails"

"Naked-eye traces, maybe," Mike agreed. "Luminol might raise some, but chemicals can't fluoresce what isn't there."

"Especially when we don't have a trunk to spray it in." Ryan knuckled raindrops from his glasses, then grunted and pushed them up on his head. "Strange place to dump a body."

As if Mike had voiced opposition, he added, "Then again, it's a quiet, older neighborhood. Houses spaced far apart and set back a ways from the street. Not much traffic, either."

"Except for a garbage truck driver and the others that called 911."

Ryan glanced at the curb, then shifted his weight. "Why do I get the feeling you don't think he was brought here and dumped?"

Common sense was the simplest answer. *Not much traffic* applied to just about anywhere on a stormy early-Tuesday morning. A killer with a d.b. in the trunk that was destined for the landfill had hundreds of commercial Dumpsters to pick from. It didn't make sense to just leave a body out in the open by the curb. A perp strong enough to wrestle a corpse into a vehicle could conceivably hoist one into a commercial trash container. Aiding the process would be the adrenaline rush at the thought of life in prison for murder, if a jury balked at recommending the death penalty.

Anyone who'd seen one emptied knew a gargantuan garbage truck equipped with hydraulic crane arms hoisted the huge bin and tipped it into the hopper. Inside the cab, the driver stayed high, dry and blind to the gravity-fed avalanche of trash.

Mike perused the slope of the nearest driveway. A swath of silt, gravel, twigs and flattened grass curved and contracted where the lawn met the sidewalk. But the concrete surface of the driveway was washed clean, as was the curb and gutter.

His attention returned to the body. "The coroner put this guy's weight at about one-thirty. Even if he weighed twice that, six inches of moving water can float a car."

Mike sucked his teeth. "Not that we know enough to speculate on anything, yet."

"So where do you want me to start?" the rookie asked.

Mike hated to tell him. Until proven otherwise, it was logical to assume the killer disposed of the murder weapon in close proximity to the victim.

"If it were me," he said, "I'd take it a hundred miles away from here, bury it ten feet deep and roll a big rock on top of it, but smarts is one of many things that separates us good guys from the bad guys."

Disbelief, then disgust animated the rookie's expression. Spreading his hands, he looked down at his knife-creased slacks and mirror-shined shoes. "Aw, c'mon. You want me to paw through all this trash for a murder weapon?"

Rank had privilege, as well Ryan knew. Mike had dug through, sunk himself into worse-smelling garbage more times than he cared to recall. "Kinda knocks the glamour down a notch, huh?"

Municipal law enforcement personnel, from the chief to meter maids, once wore uniforms. Just as progress and politics had phased out local parking meters, the department's brass mothballed their dress blues in favor of banker-style business suits.

Precisely when the investigative division's fashion consciousness was raised, Mike wasn't sure. If he ever decided to moonlight as a car salesman, he had the wardrobe for it. In some respects, resembling a visiting preacher had its advantages. In others, it was as absurd as a plumber wearing his Sunday best to fix a leaky sewer pipe.

Mike nodded at the crime-scene tape that cordoned off the block. The weather had driven a majority of the morbidly curious back inside to watch from their windows—the media, of course, excepted.

"Recruit a couple of patrol officers to help you search. Oh, and start with the garbage truck. Once it's cleared, tell the driver he can circle back later and pick up the rest of his route."

"Anything else…sir?" Ryan's tone suggested the title was a last-minute substitute for an insubordinate noun.

Mike didn't blame him, but empathy had its limits. Nobody forced either of them to become cops, much less crime scene investigators.

"Yeah, there is, kid. While you're up to your elbows in orange peels and eggshells, think about this old gent with the hole in his chest. Nothing we do will bring him back. Everything we do is a step closer to catching whoever did this to him."

Telephone receiver gripped tight to her ear, Ramey sat down hard on the kitchen's three-step stool. "Who told you that?"

Mrs. Gruening, her neighbor from across the street, trilled, "Zeke Phelkins, next door. He said the policeman down on the corner told him the homicide detective said the rain must've whooshed that poor, murdered old man lickety-split straight out of your driveway." She gasped. "Can you imagine?"

No, Ramey couldn't. Not with "murdered old man" echoing like "hello" shouted inside a cave.

No wonder the house was so quiet. Sometime after she went to bed, Ed must have killed Archie and dumped the body for the garbage man.

Or Archie killed Ed.

Or Melba Jane, up to here with her brother-in-law's insults, had done the deed and Archie, ever the loyal, protective husband, helped her dispose of the body.

As if Melba Jane needed his assistance. She'd slung hash by the institutional-sized pot-load for decades. Grandmotherly plumpness aside, she could bench press Ed—or Archie, for that matter—as easily as others her age lifted a window sash.

Mrs. Gruening said, "Didn't you hear the si-reen a while ago?"

"I must have been in the shower." Afterward, Ramey hadn't checked to see if the garbage truck had left any of her trash behind. Aggravation was best delayed until she'd had her coffee, and the kitchen was at the back of the house.

Mrs. Gruening said, "Strangest goings-on, I ever did see. The coroner sacked up the dead fella, rug and all, then the cops—well, one young man's in a coat and tie—they rooted around in the garbage truck and sent it on its way and now a bunch of 'em's digging through every can and sack on both sides of the street."

Pausing for breath, which Mrs. Gruening got more mileage from than anyone Ramey knew, she made a squeaky sound and said, "You don't think they're look-ing for more bodies do you? Or parts? Heavenly days, I saw a show on cable just yesterday, or was it last week?—could've been a month ago, same as the days string together—but there was this serial killer that cut people up like Bob's-your-butcher and scattered the parts here and yon."

Looking up at the ceiling, Ramey stammered, "No. No freakin' *way* did Ed…did Archie…. Uh-uh. It's just not possible. they wouldn't hurt each other…."

But if it wasn't a Dillinger in the coroner's hearse, who was it?

"I'm telling you what I saw with my own two eyes, Ramey. I surely didn't intend to keep you this long. It's just that there weren't no lights over your way and knowing you aren't an early riser, I thought I'd best call before the police come a-knocking at your door."

Ramey said, "Do you think they will?"

A dumb question for the former police chief's daughter to ask. It was answered, not by the one-woman Neighborhood Watch committee across the street, but by the doorbell's feeble squawk.

Ramey mumbled something that might be construed as *goodbye* and cradled the phone. Presence of mind switched off the stove burners under the pot of oatmeal and sizzling ham steaks. She exited the kitchen like a con-demned mutineer walking an exceptionally long plank.

* * *

The significance of this particular street address advanced from vaguely familiar to "I'll be damned," a second before Mike thumbed the doorbell a second time.

Chief Bill Patterson had hounded Mike to take the requisite college classes, training and exams necessary to qualify for a detective's shield. "The pay's not much better, the hours can be worse and it's hell on your family life," Patterson had said, "but you've got what it takes."

"Such as?"

"Criminalistics can be learned. You either have a sixth sense or you don't." Patterson's clap on the shoulder had nearly buckled Mike's knees. "That's why I'm the chief of police, not Chief of Detectives."

Whoever now owned his house hadn't shirked on maintaining it. The storm had sheared off branches and twigs and the lawn needed mowing, but the place had been painted within the past year or so. Between yards of shiplap siding, fascia, gables and trim, a guy could spend all summer here with a brush in one hand and a paint bucket in the other.

The woman who answered the door had the biggest, saddest brown eyes Mike had ever seen, in contrast to the laugh lines at their corners. The hair falling loose and wild below her shoulders would have a beautician reaching for the shears. Any man who secretly loathed the plastic feel of mousse, gels and sundry sprays would want to touch it, ruffle it, just for the sensory novelty.

Gorgeous, she wasn't. In Hollywood, she'd be a character actress whose name might not rate instant recognition, but that indefinable *something* pulled back Mike's shoulders. He wished he'd dabbed on that aftershave his niece bought him last Christmas.

After he displayed his ID and names were exchanged, she sighed and said, "Come in, Sergeant. I just made a pot of coffee, if you'd like some."

Not Detective Constantine, or simply Detective, but *Sergeant*. Burke might be her married name, but addressing him by rank signaled a cop in the family.

Mike and his original partner, Gary Smith, had been in Washington State on a suspected serial killer's trail when Bill Patterson was laid to rest. Recalling a family photo he'd seen on Patterson's desk, Mike said, "You're the chief's daughter."

"One of them." She smiled. "And you sold a fixer-upper bungalow several years ago that you never got around to fixing up."

Closing the door behind him, Mike followed her down a hallway and into a kitchen his mother would describe as farmhouse-size. "Are you psychic, or just a real lucky guesser?"

"Neither." She filled a stoneware mug from the cupboard with coffee and topped off her own. "I'm a home-stager. I finished what you started and made the place fit for human habitation."

"Hey, it wasn't that bad." He hitched a shoulder. "Okay, so I'm not Bob Vila, but the real estate agent—"

"Who's the chief's other daughter," she interrupted, "hired me to do the dirty work, while you were at a seminar somewhere."

She put the second mug beside the notebook he'd placed on the counter. A vintage sugar decanter, a smaller one of creamer and a spoon joined them. "Small world, huh?"

"Small town." Mike sipped the black coffee to get his bearings, thus regain control of the situation, which he wasn't sure how he'd lost. The smell of cinnamon and ham steaks wafting from the stove sure didn't help.

Breakfast was a meal eaten out of a sack at your desk, or behind a steering wheel. Kind of like lunch. And dinner, as often as not. He cleared his throat. "So, uh, Portia Carruthers is your sister?"

"Yep." Her expression telegraphed, *Brilliant deduction, Colombo,* then her lips flattened. "And I'm the one, according to my nosy neighbor across the street, with a homicide victim on my doorstep."

There it was again. The faint note of dread and fear

he'd heard when she invited him in. Taking charge and staying cool under pressure by putting an aggressor off balance was her father's political modus operandi.

Mike said, "You weren't aware of it until a neighbor told you?"

"Ethel Gruening." She watched him log the name at the top of a clean page of his notebook. "I saw the carpet roll in the street when the garbage truck pulled up next door. I didn't think much about it, other than hoping the driver hauled it away along with the rest of the junk."

"What time was this?"

"Six. Maybe a little before."

"What did you do after that?"

"I showered, dressed, came downstairs to cook breakfast for my aunt and uncles…" Her hands tightened to fists. The knuckles and back of the left one were scraped from the base of her pinky to her thumb. "And made the mistake of answering Ethel's call."

"That's a wicked abrasion on your hand, there. Bet it stung like fire when it happened."

"Clumsy is as clumsy does, Sergeant. Jute-backed carpet doesn't slip through your fingers when you drop it."

If she was baiting him to ask whether it contained a corpse at the time, he demurred.

Four plates, bowls, utensils and napkins were

stacked near the stove. No dirty dishes in the sink implied that a Mr. Burke wasn't in residence, as did an absence of a ring on her left hand.

"My husband died in a traffic accident almost three years ago."

"I'm sorry." Mike winced, accustomed to being the microscope's lens, not the slide.

"For making a perfectly logical assumption?" Her thumb rubbed the finger where a wedding band once rested. "It's okay, especially now that I'm not furious with him anymore."

"Excuse me?"

"For dying. Grief has stages. I was numb for a while, then lost, then felt guilty for everything I'd ever done or not done. Last came angry and resentful for promising me forever then welshing on the deal."

Mike didn't know what to say. It wasn't an explanation she volunteered at the drop of a dime. Not her style, though how he was certain of it wasn't clear. Yet. Reverting to the subject of the current deceased, he asked, "Your aunt and uncles. They're visiting from California?"

"No, they were just—" However the sentence might have finished, she amended to, "Why California?"

"The victim had a one-way bus ticket from Encino. His name was Orenthal Falcone. Does that name mean anything to you?"

She shook her head, then frowned, as people do when a first impulse impels a second thought. "Jeez, it'd be hard to forget meeting somebody named Orenthal."

A chord had been struck—tenuous, but perturbing. Mike let it percolate, reminding himself that Mrs. Burke wasn't a garden-variety civilian. Her stock nonanswers would shine brighter than the counter's ceramic tiles.

It was intriguing to play dodgeball with a knowledgeable opponent. She'd probably look at Mike cockeyed if he said as much, but cops couldn't help bringing cases home with them. Their kids absorbed a lot, whether they actively listened, or tuned out the old man's shoptalk.

"The victim had ID in the name Orenthal Falcone," he said, "but we're awaiting confirmation." The plastic bag he drew from his coat pocket contained a rumpled sheet of paper. "We also found this in the same pocket as the bus ticket."

She didn't touch the bag, but leaned closer to read the address and telephone number written in pencil on the paper.

Mike said, "The coroner puts the time of death sometime between late last night and early this morning. Where were you around then? Any visitors come or go that you know of?"

Straightening like an invisible hand chopped her between the shoulder blades, her lovely, dark eyes raised ceilingward. Whatever she saw there leached the color from her face.

From the far side of the kitchen, an eerie groan, like a ghost with a toothache, stood the hairs on the back of Mike's neck at attention. He looked around for the source. The sound changed to a rattle, then ceased.

"Water pipes." She sighed as if the weight of the world were squeezing the air from her lungs. "My uncle Ed replaced the washers in the upstairs bathroom sink."

That explained the noise, Mike supposed, but not her inward battle for composure he'd sensed from the moment she'd answered the door.

"What's going on, Mrs. Burke, and I don't mean the—"

"Ms. Burke." Her features were rigid, the jawline a carbon copy of an angry Bulldog Bill Patterson's. "Ramey, preferably."

Moving to the cupboard, she yanked more mugs from the shelf. "As for what's going on, damned if I know."

Mike sincerely hoped he'd never be the object of the scorched-earth glare she was leveling at the innocent automatic coffeemaker.

She added, "But there are three people on their way downstairs who just might be able to tell us both why a dead man had my unlisted phone number and address."

9

Funny thing about anger. Once it elbows through the emotional fracas, clarity follows close behind.

Orenthal Falcone, Ramey repeated to herself. Latent memory deleted the first name and emphasized the last. Falcone. Falcone. Fal... Holy shit on a stick. Make that *Shifty* Falcone and you've got something.

Specifically, the fourth and forgotten member of the Other Dillinger Gang.

For the Patterson family, Shifty Falcone had been as synonymous with a lead-footed, corner-cutting, rubber-burning driving style as NASCAR legend Richard Petty.

Ramey's style, too, according to her father, who'd sicced the Plainfield P.D.'s traffic division on her the day she passed her licence test. The cop that issued her a warning, instead of a citation for speeding had been busted down to a desk-assignment for a month.

The same no excuses kind of tough-love would soon

be exacted on Ed, Archie, and Melba Jane. They were loud, crabby, unrepentently larcenous and a few feathers short of a whole bird. But killers?

A partner in past crimes lying dead in the street alluded to that possibility. Ramey refused to believe it. Freedom was too new and precious to them, the prospect of dying in prison too terrifying. If one of them had offed their wheelman, by accident, self-defense, or on purpose, all three would have vanished into the night long before the body was discovered.

House noise filtered down from the second floor. By the sounds, all were present and accounted for. They brought to mind three trapped mice conjuring an exit strategy—like cousin Johnnie Dillinger the night Melvin Purvis and eight FBI agents converged on a roadhouse in Little Bohemia, Wisconsin. As predictably as a winter snowstorm, Bill Patterson would retell the story with the alacrity of a city cop with scant love for his federal brethren.

Ramey had researched the "Battle of Little Bohemia" for a high school paper and discovered that her father hadn't embellished history. Just as he'd told her, in 1934, three carloads full of G-men armed with submachine guns couldn't capture five gangsters holed up in a remote, snow-blanketed, two-story cabin on a dead-end road. What they did manage to do was kill one civilian, wound another and lose an agent and a local constable in the gunfight. The awful truth almost got J. Edgar Hoover fired and his fledgling Bureau of Investigation disbanded.

At this very moment, Ed and Archie Dillinger could be toying with the idea of tying bedsheets together and rappelling down the roof. With Melba Jane's shrill opposition, they'd eventually conclude the odds favored coming downstairs and lying their hearts out to Sergeant Mike Constantine.

"They won't be much longer," Ramey told him, allotting her relatives another five minutes before she flushed them out herself. "In the meantime, you can flip back a page and change my answer regarding Orenthal Falcone."

"Then you did know him."

"Only by nickname and reputation."

Feeling like a traitor, but knowing Constantine was a computerized records search away from finding out himself, she explained, "I was a little kid when my aunt and uncles went to prison for bank robbery. Shifty Falcone was their wheelman."

The detective set down his coffee mug and looked at her as if he were expecting a punch line. Comprehension brought a flat, "You aren't kidding, are you?"

"Nope. They were paroled from a life sentence a week ago and came home—here—to the house where Ed, Archie and my mother grew up."

Constantine asked for and received their full names and relationship to each other. Ramey went on, "The Patterson side of my family was your basic, salt of the earth type. Carpenters, storekeepers, railroad men, a couple of ministers—"

"And a cop." Mike's eyebrows arched. "But not just any cop. The finest chief of police I've ever had the honor to work for."

This wasn't a ploy from an investigator's bag of psychological tricks. The expression on Constantine's face was genuine. Ramey swallowed before the walls of her throat became paralyzed. "Who fell head over heels in love with Sylvia Dillinger the night he caught her burglarizing a drugstore."

She moved to the stove to stir the oatmeal. It had thickened to the consistency of curing cement. Avoiding eye contact reduced the detective to an appliance, albeit a tall one, like her refrigerator that occasionally served as a neutral sounding board.

"I'm not making excuses, but if Ed and Archie's favorite pastime had been baseball, Mom would have played catcher for hours and never gotten mad if they didn't let her bat. That fateful robbery was her first and only crime. She did it to prove to her brothers that just because she was female didn't mean she was a bush-league Dillinger."

Ramey removed a plastic container from the cupboard. As she forked the partly cooked ham steaks into it, she continued, "The Dillinger clan included her father, a bootlegger and from some ledgers I found in a trunk, a part-time bookie. My mother's grandfather was a horse thief, but he was hanged for cheating at poker. The far more famous John Dillinger was either a cousin or a bragging right, like the scofflaw's version of the D.A.R."

A chuckle warranted a peek in Constantine's direction. "Believe it or not," he said, "there's a good chance my great-grandpa brought the rope to your great-grandpa's necktie party. If there's one thing a cardsharp can't abide, it's another cardsharp at the table."

Whether it was fact or fable, Ramey laughed and immediately felt lighter, as though ten pounds of ugly secrets had melted away. If they weighed heavier on the soul than a box of eclairs on the hips, she should have divulged them years ago.

Her guard wasn't completely down, but the man seated at the counter seemed less like an adversary. Delete the sidearm and badge from the picture and you had an average guy in his early to midfifties. Five-eleven, maybe six feet tall. Medium build, brownish-gray hair, brown eyes, and smart in ways an IQ test couldn't quantify. If he'd ever worked undercover, he'd out himself. Dress Stan Burke in a suit and tie and he looked like a churchgoing mechanic. Put Mike Constantine in greasy coveralls, and anyone would be able to tell he was a moonlighting cop.

Like her husband, the exterior was unremarkable, yet the foundation was solid; he was the type of man you'd be fortunate to have as a friend and wouldn't want for an enemy.

Adding the plastic container to those Melba Jane had already stowed in the fridge tested Ramey's geometry skills and manual dexterity. "So," she said, "are you gonna cuff and stuff my aunt and uncles the minute you lay eyes on them?"

Constantine shook his head. His mouth pulled into—well, not exactly a smile or a grin. It was the best of both, Ramey decided. A *smin*.

"I could take up a hobby," he said, "or maybe have one of those—whaddaya call 'em?—social lives, if all I needed to close a case was a person with a rap sheet and association with a homicide victim."

Just then, the sound of footsteps came from the stairway. A three Dillinger pileup occurred as Ed screeched to a halt in the archway. Melba Jane slammed into him, followed by her dearly beloved.

Ramey's taut smile expressed the mixed affection and fury common to parents whose teenagers have finally arrived safe, sound and hours past curfew. "Allow me to introduce Sergeant Constantine of the Plainfield Police Department. He's understandably curious about

Shifty Falcone's body turning up in the street in front of the house."

Ed's complexion turned the color and texture of Carrera marble.

Archie cocked an ear. "Did you say, in *front* of the house?"

An extremely owl-eyed Melba Jane clutched at her sweater and moaned.

Ramey distributed the coffee she'd poured for them, then topped hers and Constantine's. "If you don't mind, Sergeant, let's adjourn to the living room, where we'll be more comfortable."

The Dillingers seated themselves on the sofa just as they had the day they arrived, except now they stared straight ahead, their backs as rigid as scarecrows.

Ramey resumed her position on the opposite sofa. Before Constantine's nicely rounded behind met the cushion on the far end, she said, "Okay, Ed. When and why did you give Shifty my phone number and address?"

"Wha'? I… Are you… Jesus criminy, girl, what are you trying to—"

"Save time," she answered. "I know you guys didn't have anything to do with Falcone's death. If you had, you'd be long gone. But somebody killed him and the faster you tell the sergeant what he wants to hear, the faster your names are scratched off the suspect list."

"Ms. Burke, I'd—"

"Ramey." She smiled. "And from here on out, you're Mike—also a time-saver. Sergeant Constantine is a mouthful."

In smooth, deliberate order, the mug levitated from her hand and was placed beside his on the table. Mike's fingers circled her wrist, indicating his desire for a private discussion.

"Excuse us," he told the Dillingers and led Ramey to the vestibule like a parent tugging a child through a crowded stadium.

She didn't balk, attempt to pull away, didn't so much as yelp something rude. A tingling sensation zipping up her arm distracted her.

"Here's the deal, Little Chief," Mike said. "I'm the one with the badge—"

"Little Chief?" Her stance projected, *watch it, buster,* even though she kind of liked the nickname.

Which must have shown on her face. Whatever lecture he'd been about to deliver suddenly evaporated. A low-wattage variation of his *smin* reappeared. "It wasn't meant as an insult."

"None taken." Her eyes flicked to the wrist he still held. It wasn't a cue for him to let go, but naturally he interpreted it as such. His arm fell to his side and he stepped back, as though he'd committed the dual sins of unlawful restraint and invading a woman's personal space. He hadn't done either, but there was no way to tell him without looking like the blushing moron she'd suddenly become.

"I'm investigating a homicide," he muttered, as if reminding himself and perhaps, her.

"Yes. You are." The cell phone ringing in his pocket startled her for a second. "I'm not trying to interfere. Falcone's tie to my relatives and ending up dead a few yards from my front door isn't a coincidence," she told him.

"I don't believe in them," Mike said.

Neither did she. "I'm asking two things of you. Trust me, and cut me some slack."

While he answered his phone, she returned to the couch with no assurance of either. As if it mattered. After months—years, really—of going along to get along, because it was easier and her own two feet weren't sturdy enough to stand on, a quiet hum of dissatisfaction had elevated to a roar that wouldn't be denied.

The impromptu conference in the vestibule had quelled Ed's earlier apoplexy. However, if looks could kill, the detective division would have a fresher homicide to solve, indoors.

A visual chicken game ensued. Ramey's eyes would shrivel and fall out before she'd blink. Presently, Ed coughed into his fist and feigned fascination with the ceiling's nonexistent water stain. Archie and Melba Jane remained as motionless as wax mannequins.

When Mike rejoined the merry group, he asked Ed about Shifty. Ed then admitted they'd stayed in touch during Shifty's incarceration and after his parole, seventeen years ago. Falcone's sentence might have been shorter, if he hadn't been in the habit of borrowing the gang's getaway cars. So many counts, so much time.

Once his term of parole expired, Shifty moved to California, where his elderly parents had retired. He'd married and divorced twice, but, "kept his nose cleaner'n an elephant with a garden hose."

If he hadn't, Ramey knew the National Crime Information Center database would kick out any outstanding wants and warrants for Falcone.

Mike repeated Ramey's earlier question about the paper in Shifty's pocket.

"Oh, that." Ed's tone implied that murder victims who happened to have her phone number and address were as common as lint. "Being as how he's second to blood-kin and we haven't seen him in a coon's age, I called him when we got to town and invited him to visit."

"All of which you neglected to tell me," Ramey said.

"I didn't? Humph. Coulda sworn I did."

Archie offered, "Probably you had one of them senior moments. And it wasn't like we'd know exactly when he'd be here… him traveling cross-country on a bus."

"You can't set your calendar by their schedules," Ed said. "Much less a watch."

"If it'd been me, I'd have hopped a plane," Archie added. "Shifty's done pretty good for himself driving a cab. The way he figured it, if God wanted us to fly, He'd have glued wings to us."

"Bus or airline," Mike said, "a round trip fare is cheaper. I wonder why your friend bought a one-way ticket."

The silence in the room was broken by another question. "What time did Falcone call to say he'd arrived?"

Ed tensed. "He didn't."

"He just showed up, huh?"

"He was…"

"He was what, Mr. Dillinger?"

Ed's fingers tightened around his coffee mug. "Supposed to call from the bus station."

"But he didn't."

"No, sir."

"You're sure of that?"

"Sure, I'm sure. I reckon his bus must've pulled into town real late."

"Meaning?"

"I dunno. Maybe Shifty was afraid the phone'd wake everybody up."

Archie almost snarled, "If you want the exact time, trot yourself down to the depot and ask 'em."

"I will." His attention focussed on Ed, Mike continued, "Falcone didn't want to disturb anyone, but thought nothing of coming from the bus station to the house."

Ed shrugged.

"When did you last speak with him, Mr. Dillinger?"

"I already told ya that."

"Tell me again."

"'Twas last Tuesday, okay?" Archie broke in. "Soon as we got to town."

"Shut up," Ed warned under his breath.

Ramey started. Something was off. The welcome-home dinner was Wednesday night—wasn't it? It must have been. Don's sacred Dart Club met every Tuesday at six. She was equally certain, when the Dillingers hit her door Wednesday morning, they said they'd come straight from the bus depot.

Gordon Sweeney, the parole officer, corroborated that. Hadn't he? No, she thought, Sweeney had met with the Dillingers at the Samaritan Mission. It wasn't clear when.

"If you haven't talked to Mr. Falcone since last Tuesday, why are you so certain that his bus got in late last night?" Mike asked.

Ed squirmed. He looked at Ramey. The coffee table. His younger brother. Archie's head bowed. Melba Jane's jab to his ribs was as blatant as its intent.

The silence was like a vacuum, sucking every molecule of oxygen from the room. Ramey's towering confidence in Ed's innocence began to sink. To her left, Mike Constantine's piercing brown eyes stayed riveted on Ed.

"Go on," Archie said. "Tell him. He's gonna find out, sooner or later."

"You want *me* to tell him?" Ed's hand raised, as though swearing in court to be truthful. "Uh-uhhh. I never flipped once in my life and I ain't starting now."

"Whaddaya mean, *flip?*" Archie pointed at his chest. "You think *I* killed Shifty?"

"Well, I damn sure didn't." Ed's coffee mug missed the edge of the table and landed on the area rug. A dark stain pooled around the leg of the table. "Why, you rock-brained lowlife. You thought *I* did it?"

"What else was I supposed to think when I saw you dragging him across the yard in the middle of the night?"

Ed's face resembled a shriveled tomato. "If I was inclined toward killing somebody, I'd have taken first crack at you in your crib, sixty-two goldanged miserable years ago."

"Oh yeah? Well, maybe you killed Shifty, maybe you didn't, but shoving him in the burn pile was about the stupidest move you ever did make." Archie shook his fist. "And by Jehovah, you've made a-plenty, your ownself."

Ed shot back, "For all I knew, *you* killed him, you jackass. Be just like you to leave him sprawled upside the front porch, in plain sight."

Mike Constantine's jaw sagged. It was fairly evident the interview had taken a steep, unexpected swerve into Bizarro World.

Archie sneered, "Not leaving him in plain sight's why I pulled him out of the brush and buried him in the backyard."

Ed fell back against the sofa. "You *buried* him?"

"I most assuredly did."

"Where?"

"In that big hole I dug up where Mama's rose garden used to be."

"When?"

Flustered now, Archie said, "Hey, what's with you givin' me the third degree?"

To which Ed demanded in common, contradictory fashion, "Just shut up and tell me."

"All right, all right. Probably ten or fifteen minutes after I saw you out the lavatory window."

Ed folded his arms and looked at Ramey. "Didn't you say that poor devil wound up out in the street?"

She deferred to Mike, who nodded in the affirmative.

"Well, then, that's a tin-plated puzzlement if ever I heard one." Ed's brow furrowed. "I know it rained to beat sixty last night, but how did Shifty wash outta the trench Archie plunked him in, juke around the house, down the driveway and onto the pavement?"

"Oh, that's not all," Ramey said. "At some point he was also wrapped in that piece of carpet you guys took to the curb yesterday afternoon."

Four pairs of eyes averted to the only person who had yet to utter a word. Melba Jane sighed, knocked back the dregs of her coffee, nudged forward a coaster on the lamp table beside her and daintily set her mug on it.

Hands folded in her lap, she said, "I'd rather die myself than see Archie sent back to prison."

The arm he'd started to slide around her shoulders recoiled, as if a cane had snagged it. "You thought I killed Shifty, too?"

"What else was I supposed to think when I saw you from the kitchen window pushing a wheelbarrow full of garden tools back to the shed?" She knuckled a tear from her eye. "And damn your hide, you didn't even turn off the coffeepot like I asked you to."

"Do you really think any of these people could have shot somebody?" Ramey asked the detective. "The alternative is believing they lured Falcone all the way from California so they could shoot him, then spend half the night playing 'drop the handkerchief' with his corpse."

"Yeah," Archie said. "If 'twas us that did it, we'd—"

This time, elbows impaled him from both sides. "Ow, jeez, I was just—"

"Shut up, Arch," his wife, brother and niece said, in stereo.

Mike seemed delighted as the muffled chirrup of his cell phone—a link to the relatively sane outside world—silenced everyone. "Constantine," he said, without a glance at the phone's digital ID.

Most people talking on a cell phone graced everyone in a ten-foot radius with both sides of a conversation. Mike did not. Nor was his series of uh-huhs particularly enlightening.

"Sometimes you get lucky," he told whoever he was talking to. "Usually you don't. Go ahead and reel in the tape, but keep the traffic moving. I'll be out in a few."

Ramey untucked her foot from beneath her leg, which now felt like a phantom limb from the knee down. "The interview is over I take it?" she asked.

"Not quite." Mike's head angled toward her, but kept the Dillingers in his peripheral sight. "What makes you think Falcone was shot?"

The question took her aback. Obviously that wasn't the cause of death, or he'd have asked, "How did you *know* he was shot?"

"I just assumed he was," she said. "My stats are a

little dated, but I remember Dad saying that guns are the weapons of choice in seventy-five percent of all homicides and nearly as many suicides."

"And most bank robberies."

If only the implication were true. The Dillingers' gun phobia was a minus in this instance. Ramey preferred not to believe that Melba Jane was secretly packing heat again.

"Falcone died of a stab wound," Mike said. "A bull's-eye to the heart inflicted by something other than a knife."

Criminal investigation was theater of sorts. From Ramey's observations, Mike Constantine was adept at timing and subtext. His voice and body language were casual, even friendly, as if he was commenting on Missouri's chance of making the Final Four.

"Not many things leave that type of puncture wound," he said. "An awl, an ice pick. Possibly a Phillips head screwdriver. Could've been a metal knitting needle. Or, now that I think about it, a shank."

Ed sprang up from the sofa. "You're crazy!" He appealed to Ramey. "He's crazy, I'm telling ya. Plenty of cons whittle spoons and toothbrushes into shanks, but what kind of a numbskull lunatic would smuggle one *out* of prison?"

Ramey deliberated a moment. "Good point."

"I hope to shout, it is," he shouted. "Hell, even Archie ain't *that* stupid."

"Hey!"

"And it still doesn't jibe with inviting Falcone here for the express purpose of killing him," Ramey said.

"He was dead when I found him," Ed insisted. "I knew if I called the cops we'd get pinned for it, same as you're trying to do now."

He fell, rather than sat back down. Elbows propped on his knees, he cradled his head in his hands. "Shifty was my friend. The best a man could hope to have. All I could think to do was hide him, till…I dunno. I reckon that's where the thinkin' stopped."

"Same for me," Archie said.

Tears wobbled down Melba Jane's grief-stricken face. "His mouth was all dirty and so cold when I kissed him goodbye."

It was a struggle for Ramey to hold her emotions in check. Judging by Mike's expression, he was moved, too. The job must have jaded him as surely as it had her father. Rare is the cop who isn't prejudiced against the most likely suspect.

She'd thoroughly despised her father's walks-like-a-duck, quacks-like-a-duck attitude. Whether applied to her boyfriends or a mysteriously broken lamp, its accuracy rate hovered at an infuriating ninety-eight-point-four percent.

Mike opened his jacket and removed a folded sheet of paper from an inner pocket. "You realize we'll have to search the house and grounds."

Ramey scanned the boilerplate form. Consent to Search was printed in bold at the top of it. Followed by multiple lines of text voluntarily relinquishing her Fourth Amendment rights.

She inwardly cringed at the idea of strangers—male strangers, at that—pawing through her underwear drawer, her bathroom, chortling at the candy tucked behind the diet books in her office. With or without her permission, the search would happen now or an hour from now, when a judge deemed Mike had sufficient probable cause to issue a search warrant.

"I'll sign this," she told the detective, "if you'll give your personal guarantee that when you're finished my house won't look like Auntie Em's farm after the tornado blew through it."

"Glory be," Melba Jane wailed. "Here I've worked my fingers to the bone for nigh onto a week, neatening things up and they'll wreck it, sure as the world."

"Shifty never once set foot inside this house," Ed said. "Not back in the old days, not last night. *Never.*"

The Greek chorus, Mike, and Ramey all jumped when footsteps thundered on the porch. An anxious,

GQ-askew Preston Carruthers rushed physically and vocally into the living room. "Ramey, good God, are you all right? I was on the way to the office when it came over the radio about the dead man, and, well, you can't imagine how shocked I was."

Actually, his breathless speech and flailing arms left little to the imagination.

"I'm fine, Preston. We all are."

He introduced himself to Mike Constantine as the family's attorney.

"Portia's husband," Ramey said. "The attorney in the family."

The distinction wasn't lost on her brother-in-law, judging by the look Preston slanted at her. "You'd better call her. She and Chase didn't feel well last night and were asleep when I left the house. I'd hate for them to hear about this from someone else." His inference being, *Like I did.*

Well, ain't life a bitch? Ramey thought. If I'd known my home would be ground zero in a homicide investigation this morning, I'd have set up a telephone tree yesterday afternoon.

"Who was the man? A neighbor?"

"No, a friend of the Dillingers, named Shifty—"

"That ID hasn't been verified," Mike said, "and the next-of-kin hasn't been notified."

"A friend?" Preston repeated. "You mean he followed you here from prison?" He didn't smite his forehead, but gave the impression. "It's a miracle you weren't all murdered in your sleep."

He strode over behind the Dillingers and commenced a group hug—or as close an approximation as the sofa they sat on allowed. "Don't worry. Criminal law isn't my forte, but I have numerous colleagues who'd represent you as a favor to me."

Ed shrugged off the hand Preston pressed against his shoulder. "Thanks a heap, bub, but nobody's arrested us yet."

"I guess you could say that's *my* forte, Mr. Carruthers," Mike said. "But before I arrest somebody, I like to have a little evidence to back it up."

"Oh. Well." Preston straightened. "Of course you do." He smoothed back the hair at his temples, which swaths of hair gel had jutting out like Bozo the Clown's. "I just wanted them to know I was there for them if they needed me."

His eyes slid to the form in Ramey's lap. "Tell me you aren't going to sign that."

"Okay." She wiggled her fingers at Mike, who gave her his pen.

"Ramey." In two strides, Preston was beside her and snatched the pen from her hand. "As family attorney, or attorney in the family, I strongly advise you not to consent to a search."

"We told her the exact same thing," Ed said, "but she wouldn't listen to us."

"I might add that my wife co-owns this property."

"But she doesn't reside here," Mike said. "Are there any rooms or areas where your wife has exclusive access?"

Preston said, "No, but—"

"Then you're out of order, counselor." Mike flipped open the cover on his cell phone. "Even if you weren't, Judge Mitchell is number six on my speed-dial."

Ramey reclaimed his pen from her brother-in-law. "I have nothing to hide, Preston."

Which would be shown to be true, soon enough.

10

Sylvia Dillinger Patterson was an organized, clutter-phobic pack rat. Inheriting a Craftsman-style house with storage galore helped on all counts, but seldom were things bought on impulse, or pushed into corners and forgotten.

Bric-a-brac and pictures were rotated by season, along with dishes, china and tableware. Clothes and accessories she loved and felt good wearing never went out of style, as though the fashion gods granted special dispensation to rebels with impeccable taste.

Ramey was a teenager when her mother drew plans on a sheet of typing paper to convert the sewing room into a master bath and a walk-in closet. Bill Patterson and the contractor thought Sylvia's sketches of built-in drawers, bins and hanging spaces of varied widths and lengths for a closet no guests would ever see were silly, expensive and negotiable.

After the project was finished, she told female

friends—and not a few enemies—who trooped upstairs for a tour that she was proudest of the shoe cub-
bies that kept footwear visible, accessible and off the
floor.

They still did. Right there in plain sight were the
spike-heeled ankle-sprainers Ramey bought and hauled
home. Going shopping with Portia was akin to paying
protection money to the Mob. If she bought something
her sister liked, she'd leave Ramey to her loafers, slides
and sneakers for a while.

A couple of dozen pairs lay scattered and jumbled
on the floor. As were some sweaters and knitted tops
that had been pulled from the bins. Mingled with them
were once-folded jeans from incentive-to-diet size
sixes to mostly wearable twelves. One faded and one
"dressy" pair of fourteens gave Ramey some slack during extended willpower outages.

It was strange that the twelves she'd pulled on after
her morning shower had buttoned and zipped without
the leg-spraddling, belly-sucking, butt-crunching gy-
rations known as the tight pants tango. Could it be that
Melba Jane's glorious meals were succeeding where
strict—make that medium-strict—deprivation had
failed? The possibilities of a well-gravied life without
carrot sticks and rice cakes tempered Ramey's dismay
at the closet's dishevelment.

Who cared what the officer who'd escorted her upstairs thought? His job was to ensure that she didn't smuggle a murder weapon in, or out. The closet wouldn't have earned a Good Housekeeping Seal before Melba Jane began "cleaning" it. And she meant well, Ramey reminded herself, for the second time that day and the nine-hundred-and-twelfth in under a week.

Down on all fours and still breathing normally, she laid aside an all-weather boot. The scavenge for its mate was interrupted by Preston's, "Oh. There you are."

Startled, she rocked back, then into a sitting position. Behind him, Officer Not Friendly didn't appear thrilled by Preston's arrival, either.

"I thought you left," Ramey said.

"So did I." Preston glanced at his watch. "My car won't start. I have a meeting scheduled with an extremely important client in less than fifteen minutes."

Slipping her other foot into its corresponding boot, Ramey squelched a comment about seventy grand, plus import fees and taxes not buying much transportation these days. "You must be desperate if you're asking to borrow my van."

He grimaced, as only an upscale professional can at thoughts of being seen driving a plebian delivery vehicle with a tie-dyed paint job and ladder racks.

"I am. Portia's either still asleep or in the shower. It'd take too long for anyone at the office to pick me up. The woman at Yellow Cab said there'd be a minimum half-hour wait." An eyebrow crimped. "And you're an ex post facto witness to a crime."

Emphasis on *post facto,* Ramey thought, taking the hand he offered to help her up. "It's okay with me, but what about the police?"

"I cleared it with Constantine's partner—Rick something or other." Preston snagged her purse from the chair. "Please, Ramey. It'll be a miracle if I make the appointment in time as it is."

Willing to loan her van, but not the key ring that unlocked everything from the garage to her post office box, she tossed the purse back on the chair and led him and their uniformed escort to her office.

"I owe you one," Preston said, taking the spare set of keys from the desk drawer. "I called a tow truck for my car. I'll have your van back as soon as I can."

"No rush. I changed shoes, so I could tag along outside. I'm not leaving the house until Mike's finished the search."

Mike, is it? was as overt as Preston's disapproval. In his milieu, first name basis was reserved for family, friends, colleagues and maître d's.

Starting from the room, he turned and looked back at her. "Listen, I'm as fond of the Dillingers as you are, but if Stan were here, he wouldn't let you stay another night alone with them."

If Stan were here, I wouldn't be alone, would have

been her obvious comeback. Before she could voice it, Preston was speed-walking toward the stairs, where another patrol officer waited to accompany him out.

The desk drawer soughed shut on its track. Through the window, Ramey saw Ed, Melba Jane and Archie huddled beside the brush pile. Mike Constantine squatted at the back. A flashlight beam swept the deadfall, winking and flaring like a semaphore.

If Stan were here... Her knuckles rapped the desktop. Well, he wasn't and hadn't been for a long time. Preston presuming to speak for him was as irritating as presuming Ramey never had, and still couldn't think for herself.

Then again, his concern was misdirected, but not invalid. Believing her aunt and uncles incapable of murder wasn't enough. Shifty Falcone didn't stab himself to death. None of them would be safe until they found out who'd done it and why.

Grasping the back of her swivel chair to shove it into the desk's kneehole, she lost her balance when the seat parted company with the castored base. The lower half of the chair shot forward and whanged off the computer tower that shared legroom under the desk. The bulky upper part slipped from Ramey's fingers and slammed the hardwood floor.

"Are you all right, ma'am?" Officer Friendlier assessed the damages, then bent down and picked up four hex bolts. "These are what holds the seat to the base plate."

That they did. What he didn't say was that all four shouldn't fall out simultaneously. Had she been seated in the chair when they did, surfaces available for fracturing her skull included file cabinets, a drafting table, metal shelving and a sawed-off, retired parking meter affixed to a domed iron base.

"I put it together myself," she said, holding out her hand for the bolts. "Maybe I should have read the instructions first."

He hesitated, then chuffed, as though they'd agreed on an acceptable explanation. "Maybe you ought to give them a look before you fix it. And next time, use the washers that come with it."

Ramey laid the bolts on the desk. The manufacturer had provided quarter-size washers to distribute pressure from the bolt heads. She just hadn't seen them in the shipping carton until the chair was assembled.

"If you don't have time to do a job right," her father lectured from beyond, "where are you going to find the time to do it twice?"

Later, she thought. Right now there's a homicide investigation to horn in on.

Mike yelled into the handset radio, "What the hell do I care if Carruthers is her brother-in-law? This is a crime scene, Rickenbacher, not a rental car franchise!"

Static crackled in his ear—what interlude supervisors in any capacity called an "Oh, shit" moment. Mike's own had coincided with the sound of an engine firing and Ramey Burke's van backing down the driveway.

Reliance on a partner that processed scenes like the other lobe of Mike's brain had ended February first, when Gary Smith traded his gold shield for a pension check and a used Winnebago. Ten weeks into a nascent like-hate relationship with Ryan Rickenbacher, Mike knew Smitty hadn't been joking about rookies being the leading cause of hemorrhoids and receding hairlines among cops.

He'd left Rickenbacher in front of the house to shadow the evidence techs, oversee the garbage detail, liaison with the uniforms canvassing the neighbors and shoo away the curious and the media. Grunt work, maybe, but every Sherlock needs a Watson.

Rickenbacher said, "I didn't think—"

"No, you didn't." The spongy ground sucked at Mike's shoes as he stepped over the trench that had temporarily served as Falcone's grave site. It and the twenty-seven other holes comprising Archie's landscaping-in-progress resembled a close order carpet bombing.

The only dumb questions are the ones you don't ask

for fear you'll look dumb for asking them, said the plaque Smitty had given Mike on his first day with the detective division. Instead of passing it on to Rickenbacher, Mike should have had it surgically implanted.

Chastened, but wisely wasting no time on excuses or apologies, Rickenbacher asked, "Want me to send a patrol unit after the van?"

Like a streaming video, images of the traffic stop, one pissed-off family member-attorney and the ensuing debate over whether the voluntary consent to search extended to Ramey's vehicle projected on the wall of the toolshed.

"Too late now, kid," Mike said. "But so help me, let anybody else into or off of these premises and there won't be enough left of you to mail home to Mama."

Reclipping the radio on his belt, Mike stopped himself from wondering what might go wrong next. That was just asking for it and only two things had gone right since he arrived at the scene: Ramey Burke redefining the term *person of interest* and slits of blue sky cracking open overhead.

Reluctantly, Mike allowed the pro column to include evidence that the Dillingers' wacko story read true. The posthumous three-card monte aspect of it, anyway. Ed's involvement wasn't provable, either way.

If there'd been indications of a struggle preceding Falcone's collapse near the front porch, the rain had obliterated them. From there, intermittent drag marks and divots corroborated the body's path to the brush pile, then from it to the trench. Footprints, scuffled dirt and wheelbarrow ruts denoted Melba Jane's subsequent disinterment.

"I've been thinking about what you said in the house," Ed said.

Mike looked at him. Well, well. Nice to hear that somebody listened when he talked. "Such as?"

The ex-con tapped another cigarette from the pack in his pocket—the fourth since they came outside. The front lawn, his personal ashtray, was littered with rain-soaked Camel butts burned to their filters. Today, he'd pinched them out and deposited them in his coat pocket.

"'Twas nothing you said, exactly." Cupping the match, Ed lit his smoke. "More of a general nature type of thinking."

Not about confessing. Age and incarceration hadn't dulled Ed's wits, they'd honed them. Minus the monk's garb and pointed ears, he'd been a cell block Yoda, spouting the hype and horseshit that passed for jail-house wisdom.

"What's stuck in my craw," he said, "is how Shifty hasn't seen the lights of Plainfield for thirty-some years, and how nobody but us knew he was coming."

"As far as we know," Archie countered, "he might could've called somebody."

Smoke jetted from Ed's nostrils. "Uh-huh. That's what I'd do. Drop a dime on whoever might want to croak me and tell him which bus I'm on."

"Except for being dead, Shifty looked about the same as he ever did. Somebody at the depot could've recognized him and followed him to the house," Melba Jane offered.

"Hear that, Constantine?" Ed's head jerked at his brother and sister-in-law. "If these two were any smarter, I'd buy 'em flea collars and a soup bone to chew on."

Melba Jane yanked the cigarette from his lips and stomped it in the mud. "Stick the whole pack in your mouth and light it why don'tcha. Maybe you'll die faster."

A criminal investigator's realm of suspects included psychopaths, sociopaths, plenty who were a side order short of a full meal and the almost painfully stupid. Individually and collectively, the Dillingers defied classification. Relatives or not, it wasn't difficult to imagine why Ramey Burke had taken them in, like colicky foundlings dumped on her doorstep. Their entertainment value was worth the price of admission.

"Assuming you had a point, Ed, care to let me in on it?" Mike asked.

"I do, but this has gotta stay on the q.t. From Ramey, I mean."

Mike nodded for effect. Ed knew as well as he did that confidentiality applied to the informant, not necessarily the information.

"I hope I'm wrong, 'cause her road's been awful rocky before and since her husband passed on, but this snake-eyed mailman she's been seeing—"

"We don't like him," Archie interrupted, as if his brother wasn't capable of relaying the tale. "His name's Don Blevins. Whatever romance there might've been went kaput real fast. It's plain to see he's got it bad for her, but she says they're just friends. He's a jerk."

Any male over the age of twelve knows the refrains to the song "Let Him Down Easy" by heart. There's *Love Ya Like a Brother,* which no guy wants to hear, not even from his sister. *Lovers Are a Dime a Dozen* promises you won't be one of hers in this life. The supposed kindest cut, *It Isn't You, It's Me,* is relationship-speak for, *It's All You, Bucko, and I Must've Been Nuts to Go Out With You in the First Place.*

Mike had been like a brother, a never-lover and the accused fault guy more times than he cared to recall, but he'd swallowed his pride and moved on. Don Blevins had not and Mike sensed Ramey hadn't strung him along.

Shivering, Melba Jane bundled her sweater tighter. The air was warming, but a damp chill emanated from the saturated ground. "Most of Ramey's friends drifted away while she was caring for Sylvie, then Bill, then grieving for Stan. Like she told me, life does go on, but couples her age don't deal real good with divorcées, much less with widows."

They don't at any age. Mike hadn't been on any of those sides of the fence, but he'd qualified as one who'd sworn that a change in marital status wouldn't affect a friendship. Suddenly, eating lunch with a buddy's ex-wife looks like a test-drive, if not a fait accompli. Old hangouts feel quarantined, or like a morgue, or willful trespassing. Conversations fizzle, until somebody blurts, "Hey, remember when…" —a harbinger of the day when a retreaded past is all two friends have in common.

Archie said, "Women don't fall for their pals, except in movies. Blevins kept pushing, though. Trying to make things happen the way he wanted 'em to be."

"He pushed too hard on Saturday night." Melba Jane's jaw cocked sideward and her eyes narrowed, as if regretting that she hadn't knocked Blevins's block off when she had the chance. "And Ramey pushed back."

The mudroom's screen door opened. Ramey started outside, then hesitated at the faint *brrrring* of a phone. As she wavered between answering or ignoring it, Ed sidled closer to Mike. "The fur flew when Blevins came to pick her up for a date and she was there on the porch, gabbing with Portia, instead of primping for him."

Eyes riveted on the interior door Ramey left open, Ed went on, "The two of 'em squared off in the living room. We didn't hear much of what was said, but Blevins didn't stay to hear it twice."

"He's called and called," Melba Jane said, "but Ramey cautioned us to check the number in the green box on the phone before we answered."

Green box, aka the Caller ID. Mike had heard more obtuse descriptions. Phone-ticker, being one.

Ramey reappeared, a corduroy jacket now topping her striped Henley and jeans. Ed smiled and waved her on. Discretion being the better part of snitching, Mike thought their conversation was over, but then an atonal, disembodied voice, said, "Blevins has had two days to stew and fawnch and divine how to make her need his brand of friendship again."

One of the first survival skills an inmate learns is the art of ventriloquism. Despite rules against talking in chow lines at every meal, an eerie, mechanical drone reverberated off a mess hall's walls. Guards busted new fish and amateurs, while hundreds of master glottologists, like Ed Dillinger, fertilized the grapevine without a detectable twitch.

His lips were as motionless as the wax novelties kids love at Halloween. "That jake knows what another death in the family'd do to Ramey. Knows I go out regular to the front porch for a smoke, too."

Ramey was less than a yard away, when he tossed out a curt, "Think about it."

Mike already was. Elimination killing straddled the line between seldom and common, depending on who kept the stats. One horrific, media-frenzied example involved a young mother who staged a vehicular drowning and murdered her children because her boyfriend had no desire to be a stepfather.

Trust a con to work the angles and hone in on a plausible one. Ed, Archie and the victim were about the same age and similar in build. A nutcase intent on initiating a family funeral might mistake Falcone for a Dillinger. A premeditated ambush could explain the unorthodox murder weapon, too.

Mike nodded at the economy-size bag of M&M's in Ramey's hand. "Sorry I interrupted your breakfast."

"I'll take these over ham and oatmeal any day." She offered the sack to him, then to the Dillingers. "When I said I had nothing to hide, I sort of forget to mention the candy behind the diet books in my office."

"Like you need 'em." The flame-thrower glare she leveled at Mike triggered a hasty, "The diet books, I mean."

"Yeah, well, I won't much longer if Melba Jane's gravy keeps working."

For a moment, Mike thought he'd heard her wrong.

The Dillingers' perplexed expressions were reassuring. They didn't know what the heck she was talking about, either.

"So," she said, looking everywhere but down at the edge of the elongated hole she stood beside. "I guess you haven't found the suitcase yet."

Ed and Archie exchanged a glance. Archie asked, "What suitcase?"

Earlier, during the interview's numerous Dillinger shouting sessions, a thought bubble with "luggage" had streaked through Mike's mind, then evaporated without a written note to that effect.

No follow-through. He was as guilty as Rickenbacher. Guiltier, being the primary on the case. No excuse, either, though Mike had felt off balance, as if he'd worn a hiking boot on one foot and a sock on the other, since...

Precisely when, he wasn't sure. Best he knew, all his jellybeans were in the jar when he prelimmed the corpse and the scene and doled out assignments.

Stress must be getting to him. And he was overdue for a physical. The division commander had issued a reminder last week in the hallway. Mike looked at Ramey, then away again. A *mental* might be more apropos.

Ed said, "Maybe Shifty didn't bring a suitcase."

"Traveled light," Archie seconded. "Him taking a bus, far as he did."

Melba Jane added, "Me, I'd have stuffed the necessaries in my pockets and be done with it. Time was, when a man tied his worldlies in a kerchief, hung it from a stick and hit the road."

"Yeah, right." Ramey laughed, her wildly messy hair and entire face getting into the act, like children's do and adults do not, unless a beer or three lowers their resistance. "Score one for Little Chief."

Mike had to hand it to her, despite her being so damned smug about it. Mustering his shredded dignity, he said, "We've barely started the search. If Falcone had a suitcase with him, it'll turn up."

"Which reminds me." From her jacket pocket, she pulled out two small brass keys attached to a coiled plastic bracelet. "The toolshed hasn't been locked since Archie started working in the yard. These open the padlocks on the garage."

"Is this the only set?"

"Besides the duplicates on the key ring in my purse." Anticipating his next question, she said, "It's still there, right where I left it, when I came home Saturday afternoon."

"You haven't gone anywhere since then? The supermarket? Maybe the drugstore?"

"I did a couple of errands yesterday, but no midnight rides to the bus station." A man as infatuated as Blevins could confuse that glint in her eyes for flirtation. "And I can prove it when Preston brings back my van."

Mike's "How?" coincided with Ed's, except the old man's was louder.

"The self-employed live in terror of an IRS audit. I keep a mileage log to separate personal travel from business. I can't swear I copied the odometer reading when I finished the Leonardo staging on Saturday, but I'm positive I did on Thursday. A little addition here and subtraction there, and voila—no mileage unaccounted for."

Ed wheezed as though overtaken by bronchial spasms. Archie pounded him on the back. "You gotta cut down on the smokes, man. They ain't called coffin nails for nothin'."

11

Like other professionals, an attorney was seldom left to his own devices during business hours. Client appointments, court appearances, depositions, ringing phones and reams of time-sensitive paperwork took precedence.

For bona fide reasons, or in the spirit of established contempt, a homicide investigator who made an unscheduled office visit might be forced to cool his jets in the waiting area until after lunch, if not closing time.

Detective-Sergeant Mike Constantine was spared that aggravation. He stepped off the elevator into the corridor of the law office, just as Preston Carruthers exited the men's restroom. The lawyer pulled up short, then sighed, as though regretting he hadn't extended his routine postleak handwashing to the recommended fifteen seconds.

Timing is everything, Mike thought, repressing a grin. "I appreciate you leaving Ms. Burke's van across the street, instead of the parking garage in the basement." He presented a photocopy of the day's second, signed consent to search form. "Natural light makes my job a lot easier."

"From what I've seen, your job seems to be harassing my sister-in-law," Carruthers said.

"Is that a personal opinion, or a legal one?"

"You know as well as I do that Ramey had nothing whatsoever to do with the murder you're investigating."

Mike wadded the photocopied form and pocketed it. He'd merely shown it to the attorney out of courtesy. The vehicle was temporarily in Carruthers's possession, but his name wasn't on the registration. "Now that you mention it, what I *don't* know is where you were last night, Counselor."

Carruthers started. An incredulous smile escalated to a throaty chuckle. "You're serious, aren't you?"

Evidently, Mike's lack of response served as one. The lawyer couldn't resist the temptation to showboat. "I left the office at five-thirty, as usual, and arrived home approximately twenty-three minutes later. I changed clothes—a Ralph Lauren jogging suit, as I recall—dined on stir-fry teriyaki, egg rolls and a glass of white wine, then settled in for a typically quiet evening with my wife and my son, Chase."

"How old is your son?"

"Sixteen, going on thirty-five."

Carruthers nodded a greeting to two men strolling toward the restroom. In the taller man's hammocked fingers was a cigarette and a silver Zippo. Free hand planted squarely over the door's No Smoking sign, the smoker pushed it open, smirking at Mike, like a high school punk daring the hall monitor to bust him for contraband.

Don't tempt me…

"Anything else, Detective?"

"Yeah. The spare set of keys to Ramey's van."

"Of course." Carruthers indicated a pebbled glass door near the end of the hall. His name, numeral and Attorney-at-Law were spelled out in surprisingly petite gilt letters. "Just go in and ask my secretary for them. She'll be delighted to hear she won't have to drive that junkyard on wheels back to Ramey's house and recruit a ride back to the office."

Mike rolled his eyes. "Are you going to follow me and make sure I don't swipe a stapler off her desk when she's not looking?"

"Hardly." Carruthers jerked a thumb at an adjacent, unmarked door. "Here's the private entrance to my office. I'm sure you can find your way out, Officer."

Ah, Mike thought. Of course.

Doomp. Doomp. Doomp. "Do-wah, do-do-wah." *Crackle-thhht.*

Archie growled and looked up from the atlas spread

open on the breakfast nook's table. At the kitchen sink, Melba Jane was shelling hard-boiled eggs to Bing Crosby crooning on the radio.

Ordinarily, he could tune out a riot in progress. Not today. His nerves were as frayed as granny's tea towels since he'd come downstairs at dawn to find a homicide dick comfortably swilling coffee in the kitchen as if he owned the joint.

For hours, the house and grounds crawled with cops. They'd left, by and by. And they'd be back. No ifs, ands or buts about it and *it* had him sweating like a polar bear on a spit.

From the front of the house, he heard Ed rapping the paneling in the billiard room. *Punk. Punk. Punk.* Then *Doomp. Doomp.* And a lilting "Wah-do-wah."

Jaysus Magillicutty. Archie cradled his head in his hands, his fingers cupped around his ears like earmuffs. Now the racket sounded like the ocean in a hailstorm, but it was a short sight better sounding than before.

Melba Jane had found the map book Archie was studying in one of the living room's bookcases. It wasn't current. President Kennedy's portrait on the inside cover testified to that. Archie was relatively certain nobody'd monkeyed with the states he was interested in for quite a spell, though, so it'd do for his purposes.

His eyes followed the atlas's squiggling red, wider yellow and skinny blue lines. But using a ruler he borrowed from Ramey's office to measure the distances meant he'd have to take his hands off his ears. Instead, he dead reckoned Nuevo Leon, Mexico, was about two inches due south, an inch and a half east, and a skosh under three more to the south-southeast from Plainfield, Missouri.

Seven inches, give or take a fraction, was the distance between living in sun-drenched freedom or permanent accommodations at Hotel Hoosegow.

Sergeant Constantine hadn't seemed to be the bum's rush type, but for all Archie knew, the county prosecuting attorney was kin to the pickle-pussed yahoo that had sent him, Ed and Melba Jane off for life stretches thirty-five years ago. Back then, they were as guilty as homemade sin of the charges against them, plus another eight or nine that never came to light. But it'd be plumb foolish to chance another tour behind bars for a crime they didn't commit.

In stir, it was common knowledge that in Mexico, a man could skate by pretty easy on a dollar a day and have a couple pesos left to jingle when he strolled back to el hacienda. It stood to reason that three ex-cons might could squeak along on two-fifty. Melba Jane was a wiz at cooking nothing into a larruping something. And what did he and Ed need, besides a sombrero and a shade tree to siesta under?

If they had to, they'd pick up a little coin on the side,

doing this and that. *Legal* this and thats. All Archie had to do was convince his wife and brother to adios while the adiosing was good.

Hands still clapped over his ears, he looked up again in the hopes that Melba Jane had finished shucking that pan of hen fruit. Visions of cantinas swarming with barefoot senoritas in fancy skirts and low-cut blouses he'd seen in *Wagon Train* reruns switched to the present, with Ed standing a few feet from Melba Jane, clenching a butter knife in his hand.

Ed flexed his wrist. Nodded. Turned toward Melba Jane, her head tick-tocking along to the music, her back to him. Edging nearer, Ed's arm raised...

Archie jumped up, shouting, "Drop it, you son of a bitch!"

Melba Jane spun around. Went bug-eyed. Shrieked, *"Hii-yaa"* and karate-chopped Ed's arm like a hatchet to kindling wood.

"Yeeooow!" The knife clattered on the floor. Hugging the wounded wing to his chest, Ed roared, "Goddamn you crazy ol' bat! That *hurt!*"

Archie scooped up the knife. "Not as much as stickin' this betwixt her ribs would, you murderin' bastard."

"What?" Ed looked from Melba Jane, still squatted in a martial arts stance, to his brother. "You think I was fixin' to kill her?"

"Don't play innocent with me," Archie said. "I saw

you from over yonder, creeping up on my wife with this in your mitt." He slapped the knife on the island counter. "Poor ol' Shifty didn't have nobody watchin' his back. Or his front, for that matter."

Disbelief slackened Ed's wrinkled, ghost-gray mouth. A scarlet flush glided up his wattled neck. A finger pointed at Melba Jane, he shouted, "First you accuse me of wanting to hurt her, now you're saying I killed Shifty?" He staggered backward. "I'm your brother, for Chrissake. Why would you even think I'd do such a thing?"

Doubt nibbled the fringes of Archie's mind. An apology being equal to admitting—again—that he was the dumbest cluck in Chicken Charlie Dillinger's flock, he blustered, "Like they say, money's the root of all evil. Could be this knife had my name on it, too. Why split a take when you can keep it all for yourself?"

Now Ed did look fit to kill. "'Cept, in case you and Bruce Lee here are too mushybrained to notice, there ain't no goldanged take to split."

"Not yet, but—"

"I didn't kill Shifty. I wasn't gonna stab Melba Jane, much less you, though the idea's sounding shinier by the minute, seeing how you're both nuttier than a peanut butter factory. I'm getting sick and tired of your damfoolishness."

Ed pushed up his sleeve to show his arm. A pinkish

splotch was welting and sure to bruise. "Lookit what *you* done to *me*. All the hell I came in here for was something to loosen the screws on the doorbell box and ask if we was gonna have lunch sometime before supper."

Archie believed him. Mostly because a butter knife was a poor choice of weapon in a kitchen full of cutlery. He was about to say that very thing when Ed stormed out, muttering about honor among thieves.

Melba Jane sighed and nuzzled Archie's chest. "My hero."

He smiled, then kissed the top of her frizzy, purple-tinted head. She was a lot more woman to love than when he first fell for her. But all that meant was, the pedestal he'd put her on had to be shored up and widened a little.

"Where'd you learn that 'hii-yah' stuff?" he asked.

"Well," she said, "you know how me and a couple of the girls took turns keeping up on our soaps on the rec room TV?"

"Uh-huh." As Archie recalled from her letters, hunger strikes, fistfights and general pandemonium broke out every year during broadcasts of daytime World Series games.

"A while back on my favorite one," she went on, "the big cheese's illegitimate son wanted control of the company, so he forged a new will and hired this ninja assassin to knock off the old man, except he didn't know the butler was an ex-Navy SEAL."

Archie had no earthly idea what that had to do with karate-chopping his brother's arm and suspected he was better off. "Why don'tcha leave those eggs go and c'mon over to the table with me. There's something I want to show you before Ramey comes back."

Anyone perusing a Missouri map might assume that by its size and name, Plainfield was a flat, featureless, semiarid municipal stepchild to the larger, better known, Springfield.

To dispel the notion and give the Founder's Day committee a fund-raising project more respectable than Oktoberfest's beer, bratwurst and bad polka music extravaganza, an enormous historical monument had been erected downwind from the public restrooms in Veteran's Park.

Line upon line of fine, embossed brass script commemorated Elmo Farris Plain's vision for a progressive, utopian community where naught but buffalo may have roamed, until he hunted them and other profitable hide- and fur-bearing creatures pretty much out of existence.

By no means did all roads lead to the town Elmo Plain built from scratch and lumber from his sawmill. Manifest Destiny's east-to-west routes missed Plainfield by miles. Then, as now, Missouri sorely lacked for interstate roadways, as though the state was situated merely to shunt Iowans, Arkansans and everybody else to Kansas City, or St. Louis, whether either was well out of their way, or not.

Whether by happy accident or political bribery, the most traveled upstate and downstate routes still bent, bowed, slanted, or in some nonlinear fashion met at Plainfield. They then bent, bowed, slanted or nonlinearly meandered onward, like a bum zipper on an overstuffed sofa cushion.

From such humble, centralized beginnings, the town's economic base now included computer software development, credit card processing, and was the hub for three of the country's largest freight-hauling companies.

Visitors who read between the historical monument's final words concluded that Elmo's bachelor deathbed was attended by a clergy of sundry faiths, a coterie of grass widows and their twenty-seven children, none of them to ever be surnamed Plain.

Ramey Burke was as versed on the town's robust founder and the plaque purveying its sanitized history as any native who'd availed herself of the adjacent latrine. She gave it not the slightest pause for thought as she looked out at the park's river rock wall from the passenger seat of her sister's Escalade.

Portia was otherwise occupied, yakking on her cell phone with yet another person who'd recognized the house ringed in crime scene tape during KDGE's noon news coverage. Ramey felt as though she were trapped in a leather-appointed elevator with *The Carpenters Greatest Hits* wafting from the ceiling speakers. Pretending to be deaf as well as invisible allowed Ramey a private brood.

One purpose of the inventory receipt Mike Constantine gave her after searching the house and outbuildings was to prevent a searchee from later accusing the cops of stealing something—invariably an item of considerable value, such as a meth-cooker's platinum Cellini Rolex.

Among the items Mike had confiscated were four wooden-handled ice picks and a silver-plated one bearing the Dillinger family crest. Ramey was as surprised by the number of utensils as the crest, which Ed later said Chicken Charlie Dillinger had traced off the label of a bottle of imported Scotch.

Also carted off in brown paper evidence bags were flat-head and Phillips head screwdrivers, 80d nails, a rattail file, trammel points, gimlets, extension bits, a pipe reamer and eight pairs of mother-of-pearl inlaid chopsticks.

The gruesome implications of each long, slender, pointy implement and tool—many belonging to her father and grandparents—had Ramey sipping ginger ale to settle her stomach.

Suddenly a bullet to the chest seemed more humane than murder by antique chopsticks. Or pipe reamer, which was thicker and blunter. Until Mike's demonstration, she didn't know a trammel point was essentially a horizontal-handled ice pick to gouge pilot holes in lumber before nailing them. And speaking of nails, in the future, clients with rickety planters made from stacked railroad ties could buy their own boxes of eight-inch 80ds to repair them.

Every item in police custody would be tested for blood. Specifically, a trace amount of Shifty Falcone's blood. Even after a surface is wiped clean, a chemical compound known as Luminol reacts with the iron in hemoglobin and glows a bluish-green.

This was trivia she'd be blissfully ignorant of, had Bill Patterson pursued a career in, say, electrical engineering.

"What a mess," Portia understated, holstering her cell phone in a dashboard bracket. As though Ramey might be confused regarding which mess she was referring to, she explained, "First the Dillingers, then Don going wacko, now a dead guy for a lawn ornament."

"That's cold," she said, thinking *even for you.* "Shifty Falcone was the Dillingers' oldest, dearest friend. And nobody deserves to die like he did, regardless of where."

"You cope your way, I'll cope mine." Portia glanced at her. "I'm sorry he's dead, but be honest. It'd be different if it was somebody we knew, instead of knew *of* and if he'd been killed in California, not in your yard."

To an extent, Ramey agreed. Portia wasn't heartless, but Shifty's murder was above all, an embarrassment. Without the Monty Python overtones, Portia'd be hard-pressed to explain to friends and neighbors how a convicted felon was stabbed to death, wrapped in a rug and floated into the street in front of her sister's house.

The Escalade slowed in anticipation of a traffic light's wink from green to yellow. Aside from being a snob, Portia also drove like a paranoid insurance agent. Their crosstown jaunt to Preston's office to collect Ramey's van shouldn't take longer than it would have to walk.

"Gee, and I thought yesterday sucked, even for a Monday," Portia said.

"Why? What happened?"

"The Scanlon deal tanked. My buyers' eyes were about twenty-five thou bigger than they could finance." She muttered an obscenity. "Hardly worth mentioning, compared to today's events, but I've hustled my butt off for months trying to unload that overpriced monstrosity."

Ramey sympathized. The ultramodern, multilevel house built of smoked glass, stainless steel and stone, exuded the coziness and warmth of an upscale plastic surgery clinic.

Portia went on, "No wonder I had a world-class migraine before dinner last night. Naturally Tripp called from college upset about something and I couldn't even talk to him."

Ramey needn't ask if she was feeling better. Portia's migraine attacks were so excruciating, she ceased to function. Medication helped, but she had to lie still in a cool, dark, quiet room until the pain subsided enough for her to sleep. If a second tablet was necessary, Portia was down and out for a day or more.

"Chase came home from school yesterday with one of those twenty-four-hour chills, fever, scratchy throat things," she added. "At first I thought I was catching it, then whammo. Railroad spike to the temple."

She appeared to be her usual put-together self, but signs of what she dubbed a "migraine hangover" were visible: A hint of pallor, residual light sensitivity and lethargy. The medication she'd taken further explained her attitude about the homicide. Sumatriptan succinate had a lingering, somewhat tranquilizing effect.

"Just because your head's not hurting," Ramey said, "I know you don't necessarily feel that great. Typical of Preston to ask me for a favor, then somehow get you involved."

The SUV glided forward again. "I'm fine. Really."

A snippy *beep* preceded a new Volkswagen Bug's swerve to the inside lane and around them. Portia looked down on it, literally and figuratively. "For once it isn't Preston's fault and it's no big deal taking you downtown. He'd arranged to bring the van back before that wiseass detective showed him the search warrant for it."

"Wiseass?" Ramey chuckled, remembering how Mike Constantine called Preston's bluff on the consent-to-search warrant. "Maybe that's why I like him. It's been a while since anybody's taken Preston's crap and thrown it right back at him."

"You do. Every chance you get."

"Yeah, well, so did Daddy, but it's a very small club. My buddy, Chase, is showing promise, but Tripp will never pass the membership requirements."

Nor would her sister, by inference. If elder children were born with bullshit detectors, they must wither from disuse at an early age. But Portia wasn't a doormat and her sons were almost adults. Why she'd threatened divorce after Preston's latest fling then reconciled didn't make sense.

Portia sniffed and said, "Dad wasn't that fond of Stan, either, you know. The Prince of Wales wouldn't have been good enough for Chief Patterson's daughters." Her tone changed from defensive to critical. "And what's there to like about a guy that barges into your house suspecting everybody of murder?"

Ramey fumbled for a response, as though she'd been asked something existential, like if bullets bounce off Superman, why does he duck when bad guys throw their empty guns at him?

"Mike didn't barge in," she said. "He rang the bell, wiped his feet on the mat and everything. And 'like' is subjective."

This was also baffling and disconcerting to Ramey, but she was loath to admit it to her sister. "Most impressive was that he didn't see three paroled bank robbers, think 'case closed' and reach for his handcuffs."

Turning at the corner, they traveled almost a block before Portia spoke. "I want you to stay with us until this is resolved. Tripp's old room is Jock Central, but it has its own bathroom. Forward your office number to your cell phone and clients won't know the difference, unless you tell them."

"No." A "Thanks, anyway" followed.

"Then the Dillingers have to check into a motel."

"Nobody's going anywhere."

Portia's fingers wrapped the steering wheel so tightly, her knuckles blanched. "Here's an idea. Think about somebody besides yourself for a change."

Ramey's jaw descended a couple of inches. "Excuse me?"

"I'm your big sister and I love you very much, but God, I'm so tired of worrying about you, especially since Stan died. You tried so hard to convince me that you were fine when it was obvious you weren't."

The Escalade angled into the left-turn lane. On the right side of the street was the entrance to the office complex where Preston leased space on the fourth floor. Reflecting in the building's windows were mare's-tail clouds that hovered like ethereal Peeping Toms.

Portia's voice achieved a pitch-perfect imitation of their mother's when laying on guilt with a trowel. "Preston is enough of a cross to bear. Is it too much to ask for you to let me have a couple of nights' sleep while Constantine figures out who murdered a man in our front yard?"

Not our, *damn it*. Mine.

The floorboard's plush carpet absorbed the irritable pitter-patter of Ramey's shoes. She'd run away from home three times when she was a kid. Not because she was mistreated, neglected, or unloved. Like a landlubbing Magellan in scooter shorts, the world beyond her block simply begged to be explored. Now that home was her sanctuary, the place she felt safest and most wanted to be, everyone was pushing her to run away from it.

As usual, her sister was defending Preston in one breath and alluding to trouble in paradise with the other. The solution to that problem was simple, oft-stated and might alleviate Portia's migraines to boot. Divorce the jerk and get on with your life. Nobody handed out endurance medals at the Pearly Gates.

The SUV pulled alongside Ramey's van, parked in a vacant discount suit store's lot between a Midas muffler shop and an Applebee's. Portia switched off the engine, then the cell phone singing in its holster.

"Yes, it is too much to ask," Ramey said. "And I wish you hadn't, because I can't turn you down without looking selfish, stubborn and probably stupid."

Portia sighed, her head falling back against the headrest. "Some things you never outgrow."

Ramey smiled. "That works both ways."

"Can you blame me for trying?"

"Nope. Do you blame me for not giving in?"

"Sure, but now you owe me. Next time I ask you for something, you're obligated."

"Something *else*. No encores allowed." Ramey dug her keys from her shoulder bag. "Go home, stick a straw in a bottle of wine and take a long soak in the tub. I'll call you later."

The van's cargo bay appeared untouched by human hands, other than Ramey's own. At the house and here, Mike had kept his promise to not wreak havoc on her possessions. Still, it was creepy to think a professional search could be quite so covert.

On the passenger seat, in place of the clipboard with her mileage log, lay another property receipt, turned facedown. Along with her business records, he'd confiscated six more screwdrivers and extension drill bits she used to mix paint.

A fresh smudge on the receipt led to the corresponding one on the heel of her hand and forearm, then the source on the window ledge. "Well, hell," she muttered.

An average of once a week, her mother resorted to a potato brush and borax to scrub the fingerprint powder off her father's shirt cuffs and the dark ring above his belt line. "I swear, Bill," she'd say, "you can't walk past a jar of that stuff without getting it all over you."

Like father, like daughter, only Ramey didn't think fast enough to realize the van's interior and exterior door handles and ledges—every surface Falcone might have touched en route from the bus depot—would be dusted for his latents.

Ripping a paper towel from the roll behind the seat, she spied residue on the steering wheel, along with the headlight, turn signal and gearshift knobs. Leaning over to examine the glove box, she yelped at a sharp rap at the driver's side window.

A stone-faced Don Blevins palmed the quarter he'd

clamped between his knuckles. He motioned for her to roll down the glass.

Instantly furious at having the crap scared out of her, the urge to swing open the door and knock him into the middle of next week was almost too sweet to resist. Expending some of her agitation on the window crank, she yelled, "What did you do? Stake out my van?"

"We need to talk." Don's fingers hooked the ledge of the car window, as though obstructing any attempt to reraise the glass. "You won't take my calls. It's all over the news what happened to the last guy that came to your house."

"Is that supposed to be funny?" Ramey thumbed the door-lock button. The mechanical *thunk* sounded like cannon fire to her. Tires screeching on the street behind him must have absorbed the external noise.

"No, I— Look, I'm sorry, okay?" He shook his head. "Jesus. All of a sudden, everything I say or do is wrong."

Reluctant to take her eyes off Don, she groped for the key ring she'd dropped on the passenger seat. "I have to go. Portia's expecting me to meet her at a new listing."

"I knew it was too soon to propose, but for that kind of—" Don swallowed, then licked his lips. "Hey, let's just forget Saturday night ever happened. We're still friends, right? There's no reason we can't grab a burger now and then, have a few laughs...."

Ramey's fingers closed around the key chain. She jammed the key in the ignition.

The engine rumbled to life. A gorgeous spew of noxious fumes billowed from the exhaust pipe. "Back off, Don, and I don't mean just from my van."

Gravel pinged off the undercarriage as she wheeled a reverse forty-five. Peeling out from the lot, she nearly threw herself into the windshield when she trounced the brakes to yield to oncoming traffic.

I am not afraid of Don Blevins. But it was easy to think that, watching him gradually shrink to a blurred, vertical line in the rearview mirror.

What had happened to that good judgment she prided herself on? Love is blind, which would be a fantastic excuse, if she'd ever loved him. Even *liking* him hadn't been exactly effortless.

Gaze diverting from a boat-size Chrysler Sunday-driving on a Tuesday afternoon, she checked the mirrors for a pursuing, postal service LLV—governmentspeak for a Long Life Vehicle.

A white truck striped in red and blue in her van's side-view mirror sucked the moisture from her mouth. Her eyes flicked to the lumbering sedan ahead, then the passenger-side mirror.

Oh, for— Get a grip, Ramey Jo. Unless Don hijacked a Liberty Uniform & Linens truck, he's still back at the parking lot, brushing your dust off his jacket.

Dust. The elbow she was about to prop on the smudged window ledge winged the opposite direction. Don's cheap shot about the murder was the only mention he'd made of it. Which, as her father would say, was passing strange. Homicides didn't happen in Plainfield that often. You'd think even an egocentric asshole like Don would have been more curious. Had the situation been reversed, Ramey would have practically interrogated him.

The slo-mo Chrysler hauled rubber through a red light. Rolling to a stop well behind the pedestrian crosswalk, Ramey hesitated, then took out her cell phone. From her wallet, she removed a business card with a number handwritten on the back.

"Constantine," boomed out the receiver end.

She rolled her eyes. Telephone etiquette was not his strong suit. "Burke."

"Wha—Oh." A chuckle dwindled to a concerned, "No trouble out your way, I hope."

"Not that I know of. I've been AWOL for a while, picking up my van." She snorted. "You know, the one with ten pounds of fingerprint powder sprinkled over everything. Including me."

Mike's grimace was audible. "Oops. Guess I should have warned you."

"You lost points from the overall neat and unintrusive score, but this isn't a complaint call." A deep breath didn't trigger second thoughts. "Have you found the murder weapon yet?"

"No."

"Okay. Assuming you lifted prints off my van's door, if somebody left another set since you dusted it, can they be lifted?"

"It's possible," he said, "if they aren't disturbed in the meantime." Another phone rang in the background. "Does this somebody have a name?"

"Yes, but—" She raked back the hair tickling across her face. In cop parlance, Don was a potential lead. If today wasn't his first stalking attempt since their fight Saturday night, he might have seen something, whether he realized it or not.

"Don Blevins," she said. "He's a mail carrier. We used to be friends."

Mike's pause lasted four beats. It wasn't, Ramey speculated, the first time he'd heard of Don. Out of the mouths of ex-cons...

"Be straight with me, Little Chief. Anything else I need to know right now?"

Again she consulted each mirror to see if Don was following her. Squares of generic sheet metal roofs rowed behind her like color swatches on a sample card. "If there were, I'd tell you."

"Then how's this for a plan. I was going to come by the house later, anyway, with some follow-up questions. Instead of you trying to drive and talk, I'll bring along my Ace SuperCop Fingerprint Kit. We can discuss the particulars when I get there."

A wonderful serenity eased both her mind and her hold on the cell phone. It was an odd reaction for someone to have at the prospect of a second interview with a homicide investigator, but there it was.

"Thanks, Mike," she said, but he'd already disconnected. Maybe it was a cop thing. Her dad was never big on good-byes, either.

Mike tossed his cell phone on a stack of file folders on his desk. Shoving backward in his swivel chair provided a few extra cubic feet of breathing room. A man needed air to think, even if it smelled of scorched coffee, a dozen aftershave preferences and sport coats marinated in old sweat and cigarette smoke.

The cubicle whose number matched his extension in the P.D. phone system was as spacious as a library study carrel. Three walls were shingled in Polaroid snapshots, sticky notes, interdepartmental memos, crude cartoons and BOLO bulletins, as if perps they were to be on the lookout for ever resembled their mug shots.

The bridged shelving and his desktop were crammed with files, books, manuals, notebooks, crime scene photos, electronic paraphernalia and strewn paper. Under the desk, more of the same was twined with electrical cords and cables. In under thirty seconds, Mike could and had unearthed a note jotted on a restaurant napkin from a case he'd worked months ago.

The aisle of open space between the row of cubicles and the scuffed pale blue wall was known as The Chute. Practically at Mike's elbow, a grinning Ryan Rickenbacher juked side to side in his chair. "Guess I don't have to ask who that was."

Mike's conversation with Ramey was brief. He hadn't mentioned her name.

"Feeling a tug on your chain, Sarge?" Ryan unwrapped a sour apple Jolly Rancher. The kid was addicted to them. "First clue, your voice slides down a register when a female's on the line." He popped the candy in his mouth. "From what I've seen, Ms. Burke isn't your type, but this dumb dog look comes over your face when she's in the vicinity." The balled cellophane wrapper scored Mike's trash can. "Or on the phone."

Bait, pure and simple. No way was Mike going to take it. "What do you mean by not my type?"

"For one, she's about your age. Not that you go for teenyboppers, but—"

"As a matter of fact, I'm seven years older than her."

"No shit?" Frowning, Ryan did the mental math. "You're holding your own pretty well."

"Thanks. I'll let you know when I start needing help to get out of the car."

Chugging along in his own train of thought, the rookie went on, "The lady does have a lot of smarts going for her—other than that retirement home for ex-cons she's running. She's got a nice face and she doesn't go overboard with the makeup, but compared to your last squeeze, her figure's kinda broad in the beam."

Mike's palm taps on the armrests coincided with a ten count. Fifteen. It hit twenty-seven before he said, "Weight fluctuates. Dumb is damn near always permanent."

"Just an observation, boss. Until this morning, I thought you and me both liked 'em young, blond and on the skinny side."

Live and learn, Mike thought. Sometimes the curve takes years to plateau. "Your observations *and* mine are out of line. Ramey Burke is a material witness in an active homicide case." He looked at his watch. "That's ticking toward ten hours old."

Whether the clock started at 6:00 a.m. or 3:00 p.m., if a solid suspect wasn't identified within the first forty-eight hours, the prospects for clearing a case nose-dived fifty-percent.

The world revolves on an eight-to-five schedule, but during those initial two days, an investigation's primary detective and secondaries develop and track leads, conduct interviews and brainstorm till they're too punchy to function.

After a catnap, a hot shower, food and a cup of what'll become another day's gallon of coffee, Mike and the rookie were back in the ever-narrowing trenches.

"Burke was never a suspect." Ryan's tone suggested a question wrapped inside a statement.

"No motive," Mike said. "She never met Falcone."

"By what they told you, the Dillingers don't have a motive, either."

"I haven't ruled out anything or anybody, sport, if that's what you're asking."

Rather than further challenge Mike's objectivity, the rookie flipped through the field reports. "Too little to go on is standard operating procedure. Too little and too much at the same time is messin' with my mind."

Mike agreed. His comment at the scene about the case not playing by the rules was more prescient than he'd anticipated. "This security guard you talked to at the bus depot—he's sure Falcone was carrying an L.A. Lakers gym bag?"

"His grandson plays football for Hickman High up in Columbia. The school's colors are purple and gold, like the Lakers."

"But the cab driver that picked up Falcone at the

depot *isn't* sure he had a bag when he was dropped off at the coffee shop."

"Not a hundred percent," Ryan said. "When I told him Falcone drove a cab in Encino, he was surprised Falcone didn't mention it. "Other than giving him the street address, he kept his lip zipped, tacked on a two-dollar tip to the fare, and was still standing by the curb when the cabbie turned the corner."

By the Dillingers' statements, the cab driver was the last person to see Falcone alive. The time of death was crucial, but John Slayer's guess at the scene that morning wasn't likely to change much.

A second interview with the garbage man and Rebecca Taylor, the motorist who'd driven over Falcone's corpse, hadn't shaken loose any new information. Expanding the neighborhood canvass yielded no additional witnesses, although Mike was certain that others had dodged that roll of carpet before Ms. Taylor hit it broadside.

Within the hour, Rickenbacher would leave for the drive downstate to witness the autopsy. The Greene County Medical Examiner's office served several surrounding counties, usually on a first-in, first-out basis. In addition to the M.E.'s preliminary findings and forensic evidence, which Mike doubted they'd be blessed with, the vic's clothing would be thoroughly searched for a bus station locker key, or a rental receipt.

While the cab driver couldn't swear Falcone was carrying a gym bag, the bus depot's security guard associating it with his grandson meant a greater likelihood he'd have noticed its absence when Falcone exited the building.

Uniformed officers had scoured the area between the coffee shop and Ramey's house and came up empty. Mike hated loose ends. Every case had some. This one was like shooting confetti out of a cannon.

Mike recalled the bus station security guard's description of the Dillingers' arrival in Plainfield, early last Tuesday morning. To his warning against loitering, Ed insisted the trio was waiting for a friend to pick them up. Then at the stroke of eight, Ed stomped to Yellow Cab's courtesy phone and ordered transportation.

Approximately thirty minutes after the Dillingers left the depot, Gordon Sweeney, their parole officer, received confirmation from Lucy Curtis at the Samaritan Mission that they were on premises, as expected. Sweeney further related the Dillingers' subsequent disappearance from the Mission, his interview with Ramey and her insistence on them residing with her.

"Ed Dillinger is a born con man," Sweeney had told Mike, "but I knew right away that Ms. Burke has won more tangles in this life than she's lost. It didn't take long to decide that when those two butt heads, the smart money would be on her."

No argument, Mike thought. The smart money was also on Ed for Falcone's murder. Evidence at the scene corroborated all three Dillingers' stories, but left a critical question unanswered: Did Ed find Shifty Falcone dead and drag him to the back of the property? Or did he stab him, then drag him?

"Give me the lowdown on Falcone's stepson, again," Mike told his partner.

Ryan huffed on his glasses and wiped them on his tie. "Anthony Howard Chinn, aka Howard Chinn, forty-one, no criminal history. He was taking in Falcone's mail at his apartment when I tried the home phone. He said his stepfather was a loner. Falcone worked enough hours to pay the bills and play the ponies without screwing up his Social Security checks."

"Which couldn't have been much," Mike said. "He didn't start paying in until after he was paroled."

"Two, three hundred a month, according to Howard Chinn." Ryan looked up. "Penny-ante, same as his gambling habit."

Meaning, there was no debt worth busting Falcone's kneecaps for, much less following him halfway across the country to do it.

"Chinn and Falcone weren't buddy-buddy," Ryan said, "but they did look out for one another. It wasn't unusual for Falcone to take off for a week, or two—

Vegas, or Reno, mostly. He went on a casino cruise ship once and got sicker than a dog."

Mike nodded. "That jibes with the Dillingers saying he wouldn't fly, either."

"Chinn figured this trip was more of the same. He said he didn't have a clue Falcone was traveling to Missouri, let alone on a one-way bus ticket."

"Whether he's lying or not, it sounds like Falcone didn't plan on going back to California," Mike said.

"Or he did, but wasn't sure when."

"Or he planned on going back," Mike suggested, "but not by bus." Another unknown they'd likely never have an answer to. "How about Falcone's ex-wives?"

"No contact for several years." The rookie's brow and nose wrinkled like a rabbit's to adjust the plane of his glasses. "I left a message on his apartment manager's machine, too. If he doesn't call back, I'll try again later."

He closed the file. "I'd better be hitting the road, Sarge. I don't want the slice and dice to start without me."

Mike drummed his pen on his desk, wishing he had someone other than a rookie available to witness the autopsy. Or to interview Don Blevins and host the come-to-Jesus meeting with Ed Dillinger, freeing him to make the trip south.

In the unit were several investigators he'd feel confident delegating either assignment to, if Ryan caught the flu in the next minute or so. Aside from that, send-ing the kid home and drafting a replacement was the same as stamping *Incompetent* on his forehead for the entire department to see.

"You don't trust me, do you?"

Mike's head snapped up. He considered lying, then decided a partner with guts enough to ask deserved the truth. "No more than Gary Smith trusted me my first few months on the job. No less, though, either."

Ryan's face flushed, but he nodded, then tucked an accordion file under his arm. "I can live with that."

Good answer, Mike thought. "Tell the M.E. to pull out all the stops on this one. Unless he or the lab finds something to run with, Falcone's homicide may go colder than he is."

12

In build and appearance, Don Blevins resembled those buff, thirty-something guys jogging on treadmills in the background of a fitness center's commercial. His wary, but game, do-I-know-you smile inferred that he didn't ignore postcard reminders from his dentist for routine cleanings.

"How ya doin'?" he said, still apparently trying to pick Mike from a composite memory of his apartment complex's tenants.

After ascertaining that yes, he was Donald Alan Blevins, Mike provided his own name. "I'm with the Plainfield P.D.'s Homicide Unit. Mind if I come in?"

Refusing was within Blevins's or any citizen's constitutional rights. Few did. The guilty figured hospitality presupposed innocence and they could talk circles around a detective on their own turf. The innocent assumed shutting the door in an investigator's face made them look guilty.

Blevins split it down the middle. "No, I don't mind." He stepped back. "But see, I'm in this dart club that meets every Tuesday night and I'll have to leave in a few—"

Mike strode inside. "Everybody's got a life, Mr. Blevins. I won't take up more of yours than necessary." The subliminal message was that speed and painlessness depended on his cooperation.

The apartment's layout was the basic living room, dining area, kitchen combo. A hallway led to a bathroom and two bedrooms—a master and a shoe box with no closet space and a stellar view of the adjacent building's brick wall.

The bachelor stereotype of a giant leather recliner, Mom's discarded swaybacked couch, a big-screen TV, assorted electronic components and TV trays for lamp tables endured because in most instances, it was true.

Men recreate. Women decorate. Nothing sexist about it. Eve probably rearranged the plants and tidied the Garden while Adam reclined on a rock formation, chucking apple cores over his shoulder and keeping an eye out for snakes.

Blevins was a domestic nonconformist. Other than the Elvis painting—a bona fide oil on canvas model, not the cheesy, velvet kind—his residence had all the soul of an airport concourse: walls several shades brighter than typical rental property eggshell-white.

Silver metallic miniblinds at the windows and door to the deck. A right-angled chrome and rolled black leather couch and love seat. Chrome and glass coffee table and a side table beside a club chair. Metal modern art floor and table lamps. Enormous black lacquered entertainment center—doors closed and red tassels hanging from the knobs, for God's sake.

"Nice place," Mike said, knowing instantly that Ramey had no hand in it. "Real cozy."

Blevins grinned like a proud papa. "It isn't to some people, but it suits me." Motioning for Mike to take a seat, he said, "Want something to drink? A diet soda, or…" He glanced at a gleaming appliance hunkered on the breakfast bar like a trophy. "Say the word and that baby'll whip up an espresso, a cup o' cappuccino, or a latte in a heartbeat."

For a man in a hurry, he sure was eager to show off his toys. You'd think a criminal investigator dropping by for a chat was status quo.

Mike declined the refreshments, recorded Blevins's vital statistics in his notebook, then explained the reason for the visit. The letter carrier admitted to hearing about the homicide on the radio around noon. After the ritual expressions of shock and sorrow, Don said, "I guess you're questioning everybody that frequented the house."

Interesting choice of verb. "I understand you're a friend of the family."

"Oh, yeah?" An eyebrow peaked. "That's one way of putting it."

"How would you put it, Mr. Blevins?"

"Well, you know." Leaning back on the couch, he crossed an ankle over his knee. A socked foot jerked, then jiggled, as though scrubbing the air. "You wouldn't be here if somebody hadn't told you about me and Ramey."

Ed Dillinger's remarks suggested empathy was the tack to take. It almost always was. "It's your side I want to hear, Don."

"There's nothing much to tell, really. Me and Ramey met at a party last fall and started going out. It was fine by me to take things slow. She hadn't dated anybody since her husband kissed that Freightliner's front bumper."

The foot halted. "Everything was great until her aunt and uncles showed up." Blevin's jaw slewed sideward. The foot shifted into overdrive. "Ramey's a—whatchacallit—an introvert. Quiet, kind of shy, doesn't like to make waves. Moody, too, but if you know how to handle her, you can snap her out of it."

Cops were exposed to enough domestic disputes for a warning bell to sound when phrases like "know how to handle her" popped up in conversation. In this instance, Mike suspected mano-a-mano bullshit. His knowledge of Ramey's personality was measurable in hours, but clashed with Blevins's description.

"Then at dinner last week," he went on, "she was a completely different person. I mean, the gravy boat got more attention than I did." He snorted. "Just what every fat girl needs, right? A live-in cook."

Mike's chuckle sounded genuine. Anyone acquainted with him would liken it to a rattlesnake poised to strike.

Blevins's eyes slitted and averted to the corner of the coffee table. "It's true that you choose your friends, not your relatives. That doesn't mean it's okay to let three ex-cons move in and start calling the shots."

"Any man would get a bellyful of that, pretty fast," Mike said.

"Damn right. Ever since, she's been too busy, too tired, too *something* to give me the time of day." The violin sonata was almost audible. "That's the thanks I got for being patient. For being good ol' Don, always there for her."

Mike remained as silent and motionless as Elvis's trademark forelock. There were times to prod and times to let the subject forget you exist. This was one of the latter.

"I knew if I could just get Ramey out of that house for a while—kick back, have a few drinks—she'd realize how much she'd missed me. How great we are together and how it could be for us."

A moment crawled by, then his hands splayed.

"Didn't happen." He feigned a what-the-hell smile; that excitable foot twitched. "Maybe I jumped the gun a little. Nothing ventured, nothing gained, ya know? Now she's mad. Probably had nothing good to say about me to you, but you know how women are. She'll get over it. Sooner or later, she'll need good ol' Don again." He shrugged. "In the meantime, good ol' Don might find somebody who appreciates him."

Good luck with that, Mike thought. "This special evening you'd planned—that was Saturday, correct?"

Blevins nodded. "We always go out on Saturday."

"And Sunday is your day off."

"Sundays and Mondays." Left foot rejoining the right on the carpet, he frowned at the translucent wall clock, then the door. "Sorry, man, but I really need to get going. The guys in my dart club—"

"What were you doing last night between the hours of 6:00 p.m. and midnight?"

Finally, Don's expression belied the sixty-four-thousand-dollar question. "Driving back here from El Dorado Springs, Kansas."

Located thirty-some miles from Wichita, the town was too far away for a bedroom community but a fair slice of its population hit I-35 south every morning to earn their daily bread. As the proverbial crow flew, El Dorado was about 250 miles west of Plainfield, Missouri. Crows seldom being in charge of highway construction, a trip that should take four hours, clocked in nearer to six.

Mike said, "I bet you can prove it, too."

"Yes, sir." Blevins appeared to be prouder of his alibi than his espresso machine. "I have credit card receipts from the motel I stayed in Sunday night and the convenience stores where I stopped for gas, coming and going. The clerks in all of 'em know me by name."

"They do, huh?"

"If they don't, they'll recognize my picture. I've been a regular customer for the better part of a year— ever since the court let my ex-wife take the kids out of state." He sucked his teeth. "That bi—uh, the ex told the judge, if she didn't transfer to El Dorado, she'd lose her job. My attorney argued that visitation would be a hardship, especially since I'm already coughing up three hundred a month in child support."

Fingers flexed in a stranglehold, Don continued, "She didn't think I'd keep coming every Sunday, rain or shine. The boys spend the night with me at the motel, then I take 'em back to her Monday evening at six, on the dot. It'll be tricky when they start school, but my transfer to Wichita ought to come through before then."

The phone rang. While Blevins answered it in the kitchen, Mike made a note to check ex parte filings. The court didn't hand out orders of protection like sale bills on a street corner, but the record would show if the former Mrs. Blevins ever initiated one.

"Yeah, I know what time it is," Blevins said into the phone. "Something came up." A brief pause, then, "None of your business, bro. I'll be there in a few."

A cowhide bag similar to a shaving kit was in his hand when he reentered the living room. Serious dart players carried their own flights, tips and shafts. House equipment was strictly for John Q. Public's desecration.

Mike floated the idea of a dart's potential as a murder weapon, then ditched it, albeit reluctantly. Falcone's chest wound was too deep and too large in circumference.

A hunch of a different nature was shaped into a joke. To ensure it was received as one, Mike manufactured a laugh. "All your exes live in Kansas?"

Blevins's face blanked for a second. "Oh—yeah, I get it. Like Texas, in that country song. No, just one of 'em."

Which begged the question, "How many ex-wives do you have?"

Don waved it off. "Ancient history. Me and my first wife were married right out of high school and split a couple of years later. No kids involved, thank God, other than the two of us."

Before Mike could ask, Don continued, "She

skipped town after the divorce. We haven't stayed in touch."

The interview wasn't finished, but was almost over for now. Mike stood and eased past the coffee table. The glass edge was polished, but a false move would be regretted, possibly for life.

He asked for and received the most recent ex-wife's contact information and the receipts Blevins mentioned, which were conveniently folded together in his wallet.

"I can do the math," Mike said, "but how about just telling me what time you got home last night."

"Eleven-fifteen. I noticed, because I set the VCR to tape a dart tournament while I was gone, but I came in too late to watch it."

Plenty early to kill Shifty Falcone, Mike thought.

"Then about one, one-fifteen, the jackass and his old lady next door woke me up, screaming and bouncing each other off the walls. I called 911 and when the cops got here, I signed a complaint against them. Not that it's done any good before."

Wasn't that a happy coincidence. A domestic disturbance and a departmental incident report with your name as complainant timed approximately when Falcone breathed his last.

Reverting to a host's hail-fellow-well-met demeanor, Blevins pulled open the door, then leaned a shoulder against it. "I understand why the cops have to check everybody out, but c'mon. We both know who actually killed that guy."

Mike ventured a wild guess. "Your vote's on Ed or Archie Dillinger."

Blevins's head swayed side to side. "The two of them could've been in on it. If I had to choose, I'd go with Ed. Harmless as he looks on the outside, that old bastard's hard-core mean, through and through."

The wind flattened Mike's hair against his skull as he stepped out into the breezeway. It smelled of perfumed dryer sheets and diesel exhaust from a nearby construction site.

"Prison's a helluva way for Ramey to get the house to herself again," Blevins said from the threshold. "But that's what it'll take to get those jailbirds out of there."

The door made a sucking sound as Blevins shut it against the weatherstripping tacked around the jamb. Mike eyed its wood-grain paint job.

The M.E.'s determination of Falcone's time of death would, as always, have a *between the hours of* qualification—a wide one, in this case. As golden as Blevins's alibi might seem to him, it was as air-tight as a colander.

The Dillingers declined an invitation to watch the local evening news, so Ramey sat alone on the billiard room's leather sofa. With a click of the remote, the television's square, ebony eye winked and crackled to life from the built-in bookcase flanking the fireplace.

Chicken Charlie had lived to see the snowy miracle of television, but didn't anticipate the advance from hulking cabinet models to modular units wired for cable, auxiliary speakers, VCRs and DVDs.

Apart from a few other token nods to modernity— new fixtures in the adjacent "water closet" and discreet recessed lights in the ceiling—the room was essentially the same as when her grandfather and his band of wheeler-dealers smoked cigars, guzzled whiskey, played poker or pool and talked politics.

Walnut panels reached from the baseboards to the picture rail. Here and there, several of the planks seemed slightly askew. Ramey hadn't noticed it before, but supposed it wasn't unusual for eighty-year-old wood to warp a little. Especially when their caretaker was somewhat lax about tung oiling them every spring and fall.

Like the living room, wooden beams crosshatched the ceiling and cushioned window seats fitted alcoves in the signature, Craftsman cupboards along the exterior wall. A hefty oak mantel spanned the fieldstone fireplace, hearthed in bronze Carthage marble.

After Ava Dillinger's death—ironically, of liver failure, despite never tasting a drop of strong spirits—

Sylvia disposed of the stuffed boar's head Charlie had hung above the mantel before the house was completely finished. Nicknamed Volstead, in honor of the constitutional amendment prohibiting alcohol manufacture and consumption, the hideous snarling beast chased Sylvia in so many nightmares, she'd dragged it outside and shotgunned it to smithereens, then raked the bits into a pile and torched them.

Ramey smiled, imagining her mother dispatching her personal boogeyman with a double-barreled Winchester. As the story went, the entire police force responded to a neighbor's frantic telephone call about a massacre in progress. Bill Patterson never lived down his bride's "first degree hog slaughter."

An electronic clarion call heralded KDGE's six o'clock newscast. *FY-Eye On The Sky Weather* was the station's viewer-friendly priority. Ramey parked her loafers on the wooden steamer trunk in front of the couch, while the senior meteorologist left no adjective unturned in his quest for new ways to describe clear skies and average early-April temperatures.

Two national and three local commercial spots later, the anchor introed Mitzi Ives, who "filed this report from the scene of the city's second homicide this year."

The segment was a prerecorded stand-up in the parkway in front of Ramey's house. Undulating yellow crime scene tape strung between the trees added a menacing, gothic drear to her perfectly lovely, almost well-kempt lawn and home.

The gist of Ms. Ives's report was that the city's Homicide Unit was investigating a suspected murder that had occurred sometime before 6:00 a.m. "in a neighborhood where residents felt safe leaving their doors unlocked and walking their dogs at night, until a few hours ago."

Ramey groaned at the melodramatic spin. The image conjured by the editorializing was of panicked neighbors stacking furniture in front of their doors and windows and pets sitting up with leashes clamped in their teeth, begging to go out.

Murder was scary and ugly in any neighborhood, anywhere—a fact that needed no embellishment.

The coverage segued to Ms. Ives seated in a wing chair in—Ramey shot bolt upright—*Ethel Gruening's living room?*

Now live and wired for sound via a button mic clipped to her lapel, Ms. Ives said, "For one resident, to waken on this rainy, Tuesday morning and find out a man had been killed mere yards from her doorstep was a horrifying experience."

The camera angle receded and widened to include Mrs. Gruening, who was perched on a matching wing chair. Her bedazzled smile and the sparkle in her bird-like, trifocaled eyes better resembled the aftermath of

Lady's Night at Sinatra's Place than post-traumatic stress.

Mitzi Ives inquired, "How did you feel when you saw your normally peaceful street teeming with police and homicide investigators?"

"Oh, my goodness." The hand Ethel clapped to her bosom punished the mic hidden in her knitted shawl. "It was—well, at first I thought some Hollywood director was making a movie. You know, on location, I think they call it. Then I realized of all—"

"Terrifying," Ives interrupted, as if Ethel had deviated from her scripted response. "Were you, as an innocent bystander to a tragedy, subsequently questioned by the police?"

Ethel puckered her lips and sniffed in disgust. "All *they* wanted to know is if I saw or heard anything out of the ordinary last night. I couldn't say as I did, so off they went without so much as a—"

"Thank you, Mrs. Gruening," said Mitzi Ives through a rictus smile. "Now back to the KDGE newsroom for an update on this continuing story."

Lloyd Acton, the funereal anchor, reported, "A spokesman for the Plainfield Police Department refused to release any details regarding Orenthal "Shifty" Falcone's untimely death, or the ongoing investigation, pending notification of his next of kin and results of an autopsy. However, a source outside the depart-

ment speculated that the victim's death, which occurred within hours of his arrival in Plainfield, may
have some connection to his past criminal activities."

Acton's swift transformation from somber to ami-
able, preceded, "On a lighter note—"

With the press of a button, Ramey remanded him to
broadcast oblivion. A peek through the room's plaid
curtains revealed a KDGE van bristling with antennae
and satellite dishes parked in Ethel Gruening's driveway.

Throughout the day, every media outlet in town had
called—in a few instances, knocked on the door—de-
manding information, an interview, one teensy little
quote, for Cronkite's sake.

The Dillingers were under strict orders not to answer the door or the phone. Ed and Archie never had,
or would. It was Melba Jane, who adored chatting up
telemarketers and wrong numbers, that couldn't be
trusted. Luckily, Ed's constant tinkering with the doorbell that wasn't broken had rendered it mostly mute.

Technology had pretty well disabled the phone, as
well. Ramey had simply forwarded the house number
to her office number, then forwarded it to the cell
phone. Outgoing calls could still be made, but Melba
Jane didn't know that.

Combining the private and business lines clogged
her cell's voice mailbox with messages. A smug sense

of triumph resulted in deleting them en masse every hour or so.

Ramey reclosed the drapes and returned to the sofa to fume about the sorry state of TV journalism. A swig of icy-cold beer from the longneck bottle on the trunk should have sizzled on contact with her tongue.

"A source outside the department my ass," she told the blank TV screen. "Try a senile source right across the street."

But how did they know Falcone was an ex-con? And how did they know his name *and* nickname, for that matter? No restrictions against fraternizing with the neighbors—Ethel, in particular—had been necessary. In that regard, Ed, Archie and Melba Jane made hermits look like party animals.

Had the police leaked Shifty's name and background information, the news anchor would have taken credit for the scoop, and wouldn't have played coy with the specifics. Acton, having seniority, would have served up Falcone's rap sheet with the gravity afforded a freshly indicted Mafia don.

Of course, a surname like Falcone and the allusion to "past criminal activities" had probably planted the Mob hit scenario in numerous viewers' minds already.

13

One look at Mike Constantine averred that stressed, bleary-eyed criminal investigators possessed the power to rejuvenate themselves after a case is resolved.

The conclusion was drawn from his neat, medium-starched, cleanly shaved appearance that morning, which had dwindled to the weary, rumpled Detective-Sergeant who'd knocked at Ramey's front door thirty minutes ago.

If every investigation aged him a century or so, he'd have started the day looking like King Tut late of the tomb, not your average, slender late-fortyish guy with a holstered .38 clipped to his belt.

Ramey recognized a hungry public servant when she saw one. While he nattered about the alleged huge lunch he'd eaten and the sandwich he'd pick up on the way back to the office, she microwaved one, then a second plateful of leftover Tater-Tot casserole.

Melba Jane had called the evening's entrée an

"in-cell specialty of the big house." How she'd acquired frozen potatoes, summer sausage, salsa and cheese spread in prison, Ramey didn't ask and her aunt hadn't volunteered.

Dinner, in fact, had a rollicking interlude of "Ramey, tell Ed he don't own the butter tub"; "Ramey, if Archie's finished with the pepper, I'd like some, *please*" and "Hey, hon, tell that pucker-pussed old battle-ax to go easy on the goldanged cheese next time."

Afterward, they'd scattered upstairs for private sulks. "I don't know why they aren't speaking to each other," she'd told Mike. "But it won't last long. They enjoy zinging each other too much."

She sent Mike to the billiard room to relax while she waited for a fresh pot of coffee to brew. When she entered the room, he was caressing the antique pool table's mahogany rail. The longing in his eyes would be heart-stopping, if it was directed at something other than the furniture.

"Woven leather pockets," he said. "Mother-of-pearl sights. Carved legs and ends." Whistling backward, he snatched his hand away like a small boy discovering why a stove burner shouldn't be touched. "This beauty belongs in a museum."

"Not until I'm too decrepit to play," Ramey said.

She set a tray with mugs and a thermal carafe on the liquor cabinet, now stocked with Preston's brand of

Scotch, Portia's Chardonnay Sbragia and a few bottles of her grandfather's domestic moonshine, which by now could fuel a 747.

"Do you mean that?" Mike said incredulously. "You'd actually get rid of the pool table?"

"Let's put it this way. The toughest part of staging a house is convincing the owners that heirlooms stuck in boxes, cedar chests and sitting around gathering dust are clutter."

"Then you'd better hope my folks never decide to sell their house. Mom isn't just hoarding a couple of generations' worth of crud. She pitched a hissy when one of my sisters dug through the attic for her old Barbie dolls to sell on eBay."

Ramey handed him a mug of coffee. "At least your sister may someday cash in on the craze. I was so mad the year Santa brought me three Barbie dolls, instead of a G.I. Joe, I dismembered them and threw the parts, wardrobe, boxes and all into the fireplace. The house smelled like fried plastic for days."

Mike took a swig from the mug and smacked his lips. "Aah. Full strength, high-octane caffeine. My kind of woman, even if you are a serial Barbie killer."

A flutter akin to a staging project's prereveal jitters, ricocheted in Ramey's midsection. Was Mike Constantine flirting with her? And was she flirting back?

Mike went on, "Believing that the same thing that

starts my engine in the morning has no effect on me after sundown makes no sense, but when I want coffee, I want coffee."

"Uh-huh. Me, too." As a finale for that scintillating bit of repartee, she added, "Decaf is for sissies. And pointless, if you think about it."

His nod was reflexive—a human bobble-head responding to audio stimulation. The change in his expression was subtle, familiar—probably imperceptible to those who were oblivious to the physical reactions of others during conversation. Especially throwaway gestures of listening when you could tell the person had stopped doing so five minutes ago.

It hurt Portia's feelings whenever Bill Patterson left a conversation without moving a muscle. Ramey's, too, until she realized his disconnects were optimum opportunities to ask for advances on her allowance, to borrow the car, or casually mention a letter grade's descent to the lower end of the alphabetical spectrum.

"So, Sergeant Constantine, let's move on to those follow-up questions you mentioned on the phone, shall we?"

He started, as though she'd sprouted whiskers and prehensile claws. "Hey, what'd I say? And what's with the demotion from Mike?"

"It isn't a demotion. It was presumptuous of me to undermine your authority and interfere with the interrogation this morning."

"Huh?" He glanced over his shoulder. "Is the governor here?"

Ramey selected a rock maple pool cue from a wall-hung cabinet. Whacking him upside the head with it for his silly remark might be a bit extreme. Instead, she chalked the tip and drew a bead on the cue ball. Billiards was her tranquilizer. Cheaper than a prescription and zero side effects.

"Okay, Little Chief. I don't normally apologize on spec, but whatever I did to trip your temper, I'm sorry."

Well, hell. Nothing like a blank check apology to spoil a nice, irrational snit. In truth, Ramey hadn't felt so small since she'd clopped around in her mom's pink lace peignoir and high heels pretending to be a bridesmaid.

Naturally, Portia always got dibs on being the bride.

"It isn't you," she said. The cue ball broke the pyramid, pocketing the four and the eight. "It's me."

And it was, but the leap from banter to bitchy surprised her as much as it had him. She hardly knew Mike Constantine. This wasn't a social call. He wouldn't be here if the Other Dillinger Gang's wheelman had picked someplace else to get himself murdered.

"No, it's me." He set the mug on the tray and helped himself to a cue stick. "First off, I'm a guy." Blue chalk dust twirled in the light from the overhead fixture. "It's a statistical cinch that any misunderstandings are my fault."

It was a sexist remark, but who was she to argue?

He also knew his way around a pool table. The five ball kissed the nine and thunked in a side pocket. "Numero dos, you being a cop's daughter means a lifetime of the freeze-out in action."

A sizzling bank shot nailed the ten ball. "On one level, you know it's unintentional." A sweet, eleven-thirteen combo. "But you resent it, because seeing somebody's eyes glaze over is more insulting and disrespectful than the person just walking out of the room."

Ramey stepped back, sputtering, "I—You—How'd—" then slammed her mouth shut.

"Something tells me I'm on a roll." Mike's tone suggested he wasn't referring to billiards and that psychic invasions of privacy were a good thing.

"Do you read Tarot cards, too, Sergeant?"

"Nah. Just faces and body language." Rubbing a hand over his stubbled chin hid a grin, but not the tease in his eyes. "My, oh my, Ms. Burke. Once upon a time, those vibes you're sending out would've gotten your mouth washed out with soap."

Ramey couldn't contain her laughter. He was a wise-ass, all right, along with cocky, smart and intuitive. And at least twice during one of the most stressful days of her life, he'd made her laugh in spite of herself.

Unfortunately, he was also a cop. The job always comes first and they're never, ever off duty, not even in their sleep. It takes a special kind of woman to endure solitary anniversaries, birthdays, holidays, dead-of-night departures and arrivals. Sylvia Dillinger Patterson was one of them. Her younger daughter had lain awake too many times, praying and listening for her daddy's tread on the stairs, to let herself fall for a man with a badge.

Instead, she'd clean Mike's clock playing eight ball.

"Much as I'd like to keep playing," he said, "I can't spare the time. Unless talking between shots won't mess up your aim."

It might, but the level of distraction would be equal. If only her fallow hormones could simmer down. Honestly, how pathetic was it to ogle him like a *Men's Health* cover hottie while he shrugged off his sport coat?

Muscle-bound, he wasn't. His shoulders were broad and his waist narrow, but little of the trapezius or deltoid persuasion rippled between them. No biceps bulged as he draped the coat over the back of a leather recliner, whose armrests were dotted and dashed with cigarette burns from her father's Pall Mall cigarettes.

He loosened his collar and tie, tucking the ends inside his shirt placket. With his pocket bristling with pens and slips of paper, and a service weapon riding behind his hip, he resembled an armed and dangerous computer tech.

Who picked that instant to glance up and catch her staring at him. As a blush burned across her face, she focused on spotting the pyramid, then lifted away the triangle. Rather than lag for break, she conceded it to Mike to offset her home table advantage. And, she confessed to her inner hussy, scope out his glutes. After all, guys didn't watch Women's Professional Billiard Association tournaments on TV for the trick shots. Just because Ramey was on a cop-free diet didn't mean she couldn't peruse the menu.

Placing the cue ball behind the foot marks, Mike took a few practice strokes, saying, "Don't let me forget to return the spare keys to the van before I go."

She nodded, acknowledging the manifold reminder to himself, as well as to her. The investigation eclipsed everything. A friendly game of billiards included. "Those keys were in a desk drawer in your office, according to Corporal Maris's report. Is that where you always keep them?"

"Yes."

"And you haven't had duplicates made from them recently?"

"From the spares? No. If I needed another set, I'd have them copied from the originals."

His break was proficient, counting the three in a corner pocket. Now Ramey must sink the striped balls in numeric order before he dropped the remaining solids, starting with the one. Whoever counted the eight in a predesignated pocket was the winner.

He prowled the table's far end, assessing his next shot. "The reason I went into the zone a minute ago was word associating coffee to Bean Me Up, Scotty over on Virginia Avenue."

From van keys to gourmet coffeehouses. A person could get dizzy from his line of questioning. She said, "I practically keep them in business. That full-strength high octane we aren't drinking is Scotty's house blend."

"Did you buy it yourself, or did you send one of the Dillingers to get it?"

"I bought it. I seriously doubt they know that whole block's given over to antique stores, tearooms and boutiques."

Mike feathered the cue at the one ball, which was nudged against the jaw of a side pocket. Close, but no cigar. He didn't elaborate on his interest in Bean Me Up, Scotty, either.

Ramey eyed the yellow-girded nine ball, picketed by three others. *You don't win by planning one shot at a time,* her father's voice whispered in her ear. *The leave is as important as the make.*

A kick shot off the cushion dispatched the nine. As if immune to physics, the cue ball's reverse English sent it down the table toward the ten.

"Nice," Mike said.

She grinned. "I had a hustler for a father."

At pocketing the ten and eleven, she waggled her eyebrows at him, thinking how impressed and irritated he'd be when she cleared the table in a single inning.

On that arrogant note, she scratched like a freakin' *girl* on the twelve. Minnesota Fats probably never sneered, "I'm still two up on you" to an opponent, either.

"Not for long, Ms. Burke."

Plainfield Slim's corner hook and a perfectly executed clean bank evened the score. Balls four through seven were easy pickin's. The biggest obstacle between him and victory was the eight. On modern tables, a ball hugging the cushion should be a money shot. This relic's down-filled cushions were so sensitive, they didn't guide a ball to a pocket, they repelled it—the crux of Ramey's advantage.

In her experience, when informed of this nineteenth-century anomaly, men often regarded it as a dare. She was about to test Mike's testosterone over matter quotient when he laid his cue on the table. "Sorry, but I'll have to ask for a rain check. I can't do justice to Mr. Falcone with my mind spinning off in two other directions."

"Of all people, I should know a cop's priorities." Catching an unintended edge in her voice, she forced a chuckle. "Besides, I'm used to guys throwing in the stick. Usually I'm ahead when they do, though."

"Guys like Don Blevins?"

The jack-in-the-box she'd wound up with her impulsive cell phone call that afternoon had finally sprung. "Forget redusting the van for his prints."

"No need to," Mike said. "Being a government employee, they're already on file."

"Then let's leave it at me being too dumb to realize sooner that Don wanted a lot more than friendship. One of those forest for the trees things everybody saw except me."

She shook her head. "No. I did see it. Thinking if I ignored it, it'd go away was the problem." A concise review of Don's proposal, the nasty repercussions, and the scare he gave her when she picked up the van followed.

"He's hurt," she said. "His pride, more than anything, but he'd never hurt *me*. I guess there's something about starting the day with a murder that makes everyone a potential boogeyman."

"Somebody is," Mike said.

"True, but—"

"Be honest, Ramey. When you called me, you thought Blevins was stalking you. Watching your vehicle was a short hop backward from him watching the house, hoping you'd go somewhere so he could get you alone to make up."

Mike lagged the cue ball off the cushion. "I don't have to read minds to know that's the other reason you called me. If Blevins was hanging around and saw something, or someone last night, no way would he come forward on his own."

"Better a stalker than a homicide suspect." Ramey sighed, ashamed of herself for jumping to that conclusion and siccing Mike on Don. "He's just a letter carrier who believes the solution to things beyond his control is controlling everything else. That's another thing I can't blame him for."

She splayed her hands on the varnished mahogany rail. "His little sister, Amy, was born severely retarded. Their parents died eight or nine years ago. Since then, every weekend, Don drives to Kansas to visit Amy in the institution where she lives, so he wasn't even—"

"He told you that?" Mike slapped his forehead. "You have *got* to be…" His voice trailed off to a strangling noise. "Blevins is one sick puppy. One seriously sick puppy."

Moving beside her, his hand hovered an inch above hers, then fell away. "It's not my place to tell you this, but you have a right to know. Blevins mentioned Amy when I questioned him this afternoon. She does live in

El Dorado, Kansas. Only she's his ex-wife, not his little sister."

The pounding at Ramey's temples was like an echo chamber. *He lied. He lied. He lied.*

"It's their two kids he visits every weekend. By his own admission and an earful over the phone from Amy Blevins, he does it more to aggravate her than to earn a father-of-the-year award."

A moment—a very long moment—passed before the drums receded, the information was digested, the nauseating taste in her throat subsided. "I think I knew all along. Not the extent of his deceit, but how hard he worked to make me feel sorry for him."

It was all she could do not to beat the edge of the table with her cue stick or snatch up a ball and hurl it at the wall. "I buried my parents, then my husband. A divorced father can't compete, but a devoted brother of a mentally handicapped young woman? Now *there's* a tragedy that'll tug the ol' heartstrings and make a saint out of you all at the same time."

A sudden, crushing exhaustion flooded through her. She pushed away from the table. The couch seemed miles away, but damned if she'd make a bigger fool of herself, crumpling up like a rag doll on the rug.

The cool, leather cushions wheezed under her weight, then Mike's. Bless him for sitting quietly, letting her catch her emotional breath.

In a way, her increasing unease around Don and the vicious things he'd said about Stan last Saturday night buffered these new and sickening revelations. Oh, he thought he was master manipulator, but when they met, she'd been too numb and vulnerable to care about much of anything. She wasn't fair prey.

The other day, she'd asked Mark Mason why a handsome, heterosexual guy would spend platonic time with a chubby, middle-aged widow, when he could be out with a possible future-making girlfriend. Mark hadn't answered, because she already had: he wouldn't, unless he was after a different type of gratification.

Maybe she'd understand the Dons of the world someday. The kind of ego—or perhaps the lack thereof—that mocked those who sincerely cared about them.

Presently, she said, "There was this boy, back in elementary school named Erlin Hayes. He was a typical fifth grader—not the class clown, troublemaker, genius, or the dummy. Just Erlin, like I was just Ramey."

Mike nodded. "Along with twenty-some other *justs.* His mom's cupcakes weren't scorched on the bottom, or store-bought, but no sprinkles or gumdrops on top, either."

"Exactly." Ramey smiled at his voice of experience. "Erlin didn't want to be another invisible kid, though.

First he started limping, then he'd come to school with bloody cotton balls stuck to his arm with a Band-Aid, hinting about this awful, probably fatal disease the doctor thought he had."

"Which got your and the other kids' attention," Mike said. "And the teacher's."

"Especially the teacher's. Terrified that she'd call his mother, Erlin forged a note to Mrs. White, saying their phone had been disconnected because his medicine cost so much, they couldn't afford to pay the bill."

Remembering the candy necklaces she'd emptied her piggy bank to buy for her terminal classmate and the magic pen she gave him that wrote in red, green *and* purple ink, opened old wounds almost as tender as the new one Don had caused.

"When everybody found out the lyin' little creep had been scamming us, the Hayeses moved to another school district. For all I know, they changed their last name to Blevins."

Anger welled up inside and she welcomed it. "Erlin trapped himself before he had time to get bored with the Heathcliff schtick. Don took his so far, he couldn't figure out how to stop."

Her heels tapped the floor like castanets. "If I'd said yes when he proposed, I bet sister Amy would have passed away in her sleep before the month was out."

Mike winked in that proud, supportive way people do when saying "Atta, girl" would sound patronizing. "By my impression of Mr. Blevins, that poor girl wouldn't have survived the weekend."

Between his drawl and images of Don delivering the sad news and details of the expedited memorial service, Ramey laughed until her eyes watered. A crying shame, as it were, that the scene would never play out for real. For her, anyway.

"You might as well swear out a warrant in advance," she said, "because if I ever see Don Blevins, again, I'll punch his lights out."

"Like the saying goes, revenge is better served cold, Little Chief." Mike set the coffee tray on the steamer trunk. Having emptied the mugs in the half bath's sink, he refilled them from the carafe. "Coffee, not so much."

Little Chief. The more Ramey heard it, the more it seemed like a pet name, not a nickname. There was intimacy in the homage it paid to Bill Patterson, and to the female "chip off the old block" she'd been since birth, despite strenuous denials to the contrary. In retrospect, she couldn't imagine why no one had called her that before. Not even her father.

And, she thought, Mike connecting those oh so obvious dots wasn't some spiritual, transcendental phenomenon often experienced by devotees of certain wild mushroom species. Had her father supervised the high school football team, Mike would have tagged her Little Coach. Yes, there was an attraction and it was mutual. And mutually inappropriate for different reasons. His, professional. Hers, personal. His were subject to change. Hers were not.

The investigation providing terra firma for them both, she said, "We've established that Don Blevins is a narcissistic bastard. How that relates to Shifty Falcone's death, I'm not clear on."

"A problem that applies to everything about this case, so far." Mike pulled a folded sheet of notebook paper from the leather pouch he'd left beside the trunk. "For instance, like you said this morning, you neglected to write down your odometer reading on Saturday night. If the van didn't move from then, until Carruthers borrowed it this morning, the mileage doesn't add up."

"It did, though. I told you I did a few errands yesterday."

"How many miles do you think you drove? And don't be conservative."

A mental review prompted, "Six or seven. Definitely less than ten."

"That still leaves a chunk of miles unaccounted for."

"How many?"

"Seventeen."

Without having the original log to use as a reference, Ramey couldn't check his math, but she trusted him.

"Carruthers told me he drove straight to his office. His secretary's phone records corroborate that. I clocked the mileage between there and here and subtracted it from the reading. Without your ten, the discrepancy was twenty-seven miles."

Ramey shook her head. "Barring a mechanical glitch, I can't account for it, either. Between Thursday and Saturday, if any of my subcontractors on the Leonardo house borrowed it, I don't remember it."

"I asked when I print-carded them for elimination purposes on the prints lifted off your van. Beatty Frick said he'd knocked it into neutral and pushed it about ten feet back from the garage door, but that's it."

The mystery mileage reminded her of a question he'd asked earlier. She held out her hand. "Now's as good a time as any to remind you."

Retrieved from his trousers' pocket, the set of spare keys were warm to the touch; the sensual implications of which, she refused to contemplate.

Although the ring had seldom left the desk drawer, oxidation had dulled the keys' patina. By contrast, the serrated edges and shoulders beneath the bows were as silvery bright as a mint dime. Or brass-plated metal used for a template in a duplicating machine.

"Were Shifty's fingerprints found in or on my van?"

Mike hedged. "A cab driver positively IDed him as

the fare he picked up at the bus station around midnight last night."

"Was he carrying a suitcase?"

No answer at all translated to a yes.

Ramey laid the key ring on the sofa's armrest. "Somebody made copies of those fairly recently. Just tell me, you don't seriously believe that whoever duplicated them drove my van seventeen miles to ditch the murder weapon and Shifty's suitcase, but left his corpse out on the curb."

Mike slipped his tie free of his shirt placket and tightened the knot. "No comment."

"Oh, for— Listen to me. I don't always miss the trees for the forest. Ed's at the top of your suspect list because he admitted to discovering the body. That happens to be why I believe he didn't kill Shifty. If he did, implicating himself is as stupid as disposing of the evidence without disposing of the victim."

Mike feigned rapt fascination with the tops of his shoes to avoid looking at her. As if that would stop Ramey from pleading her uncle's case.

"You think I'm afraid you'll find evidence of Ed's guilt. Well, I'm not, because there isn't any. What scares me is the prosecuting attorney building a circumstantial case against a career criminal who can't prove he *isn't* a murderer."

Bill Patterson's faith in the justice system was unshakable. From what Ramey knew of Mike Constantine, he shared that faith. Yet neither would swear that judges and juries were infallible. That the guilty were never acquitted and the innocent never convicted.

Mike took a sip of coffee, then rested the mug on his knee, layering a new stain atop this morning's ink trail. "Here's where I could and should lay a department approved line of mumbo jumbo on you."

Neck retracted to deepen her voice, Ramey said, "Never fear, Ms. Burke. It's only a matter of time before we bring the perpetrator to justice."

"Eh-h-h. That's sort of Dudley Do-Right meets *Law and Order,* but the general drift."

"Save it, Mike. Better yet, I wish the department had mumbo jumboed to KDGE. Whoever tipped them to Shifty's name and criminal record has Mrs. Gruening, across the street, glued to her windows watching for Eliot Ness."

"I heard about her serial killer theory." Mike chuckled. "But you're mistaken about a departmental tip to the TV station. There wasn't anything in the press release concerning Falcone specifically. His ID was definite by then, but I chose not to include it."

"Somebody must have added it, then. Where else could they have gotten the information?"

"Not from us. And I ought to know since I wrote the release and gave it to our Public Information Officer."

Twirling strands of hair around her finger, she wondered if an enterprising reporter had shadowed the cops, then questioned that cab driver. If so, more of Falcone's bio would lead KDGE's ten o'clock broadcast. Spilling all their beans earlier would have given the *News-Messenger* plenty of time to research and develop its own in-depth story before tomorrow's edition went to bed at midnight.

"I appreciate the hospitality and your help," Mike said, his voice as impassive as his expression. "But…"

"You're taking Ed in for questioning."

"He knows more than he's telling."

Protesting was senseless. Ramey'd planned to corner Ed herself, after Mike left. No great loss. She'd bide her time and pounce later, when he came home.

She excused herself to summon Ed from his bedroom. Midway upstairs, she took the cell phone from her pocket, which she'd switched from ring to vibrate, while Mike was chowing down on his second plate of leftovers.

Ed Dillinger's right to legal representation would be arranged before he and Mike arrived at the police station. She chuckled, anticipating her brother-in-law's enthusiasm at climbing back into a suit and tie for some pro bono overtime.

"A personal injury attorney, he works from sun to

sun," she said, the autodialer tweedling in her ear. "But a family lawyer's work is never done."

Or a niece's with two other relatives to interrogate while their fearless leader was out of the picture.

14

Ed Dillinger's head swiveled toward his learned counsel. "You ain't gonna object to that, either?"

"On what grounds? Constantine assured you that charges of driving without a license and unauthorized use of a motor vehicle won't be pursued."

Mike cast his eyes downward at his notes to keep a straight face.

It wasn't amusement he'd felt, or projected when Preston Carruthers strolled into the interrogation room, trailing a slipstream of cologne and peppermint mouthwash. All Mike wanted from Ed was the truth. The purpose of a defense attorney—public or private—was to obfuscate, if not suppress it.

Luckily, Carruther's area of expertise was civil, not criminal law. That difference was made marvelously apparent when he declined a private consultation with Ed.

Joining the party with an elevated blood alcohol content probably aided his client as much as the breath mints he noshed to mask the liquor on his breath. Dollars to Glenfiddich, a fan of courtroom dramas would have a better shot at wasting Mike's time and trying his patience.

And for that, he could kiss Ms. Little Chief Burke smack on those sweet, full lips.

No, no, no, Sergeant Lover Boy. She's a material witness in a homicide investigation. Nothing hearts and flowery about it.

Ed said, "So what if I borrowed the van a time or two, last week. No harm meant or done in gettin' the lay of the land again."

He further admitted that he'd duplicated Ramey's spare keys to simplify his moonlight joyriding. Yes, he'd considered a spin on Monday night, then decided against it, for fear the storm would waken Ramey and she'd notice her vehicle was gone, or hear him pulling back into the driveway.

Having established that he, Archie and Melba Jane had used the coffee shop on Virginia Avenue for a cab stand, Mike asked, "When did you instruct Mr. Falcone to taxi from the bus depot to Bean Me Up, Scotty?"

"Same time I gave him Ramey's phone number and the street address."

"It seems kind of odd that he wrote all those down for future reference, but not the shop's address."

"Naw, t'ain't. Ramey's private line's unlisted. If

Shifty forgot that coffee joint's name or address, he could look 'em up in the phone book at the bus station."

"But Ramey's business phone and address *are* listed," Preston said, helpfully, although not to his client. "In the commercial pages, under Home Design and Interior Design Consultants."

"Did I know that?" Ed snapped.

"Oh. Well." Preston squirmed in the uncushioned metal chair. "Perhaps you didn't, at that particular time."

For the next several minutes, Mike went at those subjects from varied directions. Ed didn't expand on his answers, or deviate from them.

"When you moved Mr. Falcone's body to the back-yard, why didn't you take his ID?"

"Didn't think to, I reckon." Ed's eyes narrowed. "Didn't figure on that jackass brother and sister-in-law of mine dragging him from there to yonder, neither."

One by one, Mike laid out enlarged crime scene photos of the deceased. They weren't as gruesome as previous cases he'd worked, but bad enough to rate a flinch from Ed and Preston Carruthers. "Mr. Falcone was your oldest, most trusted friend."

"Yes, sir."

"And he was as much a brother to you as Archie is— or so you said this morning."

"That he was. Closer in some respects, on account

of I didn't have to put up with him day in and day out my whole life."

Mike leaned on his forearms, his voice as malevolent as a corpse for breakfast and a nonstop sixteen-hour workday could muster. "But you were going to strike a match and watch that best, dearest friend burn down to nothing but a pile of ashes."

Nostrils flaring, the old man's eyes locked on Mike's, his hatred as visible as the dark flecks orbiting his pupils.

Preston cleared his throat. "I don't think you have to answer that."

"Shut up, boy." Arteries that braced Ed's wattled neck darkened and distended. The tremors Mike noticed that morning were more pronounced now, mocking his grizzled tough-guy image. "Yeah," he said. "That's exactly what I had in mind when I pulled that brush o'er the top of him. Not because I killed him. 'Cause nobody'd believe I didn't. Me, or all three of us dying in prison wasn't gonna bring 'im back."

Knobbed hands flattening on the table, Ed levered slowly from his chair. One by one, he turned over the photos, then bent at the waist, his face halted inches from Mike's. "I swear to Jesus, if you don't believe nary a word I've said, I could no more have gone through with lighting that fire than I could if it was Ramey or Portia in that brush pile."

Mike gestured a command for him to retake his seat. Dillinger was a convicted felon. A consummate survivor and self-preservationist. But given the opportunity, whatever lengths he might have gone to in disposing of Shifty Falcone's remains… No. He wouldn't have struck that match.

Unfortunately for Ed, the moral constraints of desecrating a corpse, as opposed to creating one, weren't as refined.

Mike flipped back several pages in his notebook. "You said this morning that you had no idea what day or time Mr. Falcone would arrive in Plainfield."

"No, sir."

"Buses stop for meals. Stop to take on passengers or drop them off. Do you truly expect me to believe that Mr. Falcone didn't once contact you en route?"

"Expect whatever you care to, bub. I already said a dozen times I thought he might call. He didn't. Simple as that."

"Maybe he tried," Preston suggested, "but the line was busy."

"Could be, I s'pose," Ed allowed.

Preston brightened. "Or if he did and Melba Jane answered, he might have hung up, thinking it was Ramey."

His client graced him with a look that should have deepened Carruthers's salon tan. "Ain't there someplace else you need to be about now?"

Mike amended the adage about an attorney representing himself having a fool for a client. In this instance, the joke was on Dillinger, though there was some veracity to Preston's last remark.

Telephone activity records indicated three long-distance pay phone calls to Ramey's home phone number. The duration of each call was one minute—the minimum allotted to a complete connection. It was impossible to determine whether they netted a couple of unanswered "Hello-hellos?" then a hang-up, or as much as a fifty-nine-second conversation.

The report also confirmed multiple calls to the house from Don Blevins. Two originated from his home phone late Saturday, after the argument with Ramey. Fifteen were from his cell phone on Sunday and Monday. Several coincided with his time-dated receipts for food and fuel.

If Mike were in his cubicle, he'd pop in a Beatles CD, punch up "Nowhere Man" and brood. Everyone identified with John Lennon and Paul McCartney's lyrics at one stage of life or another. They were particularly apropos for a frustrated detective who, right about now, could be soused to the gills on piña coladas from a cruise ship's cantina.

Or, more likely, chilled out in his cabin, sipping a brewski and catching up on his reading.

He forced his train of thought back to where it belonged. "After you dragged Falcone to the brush pile, where did you dispose of his gym bag?"

Ed started. "His what?"

Lying being the purview of cops, not suspects, Mike said, "The cab driver that dropped Falcone at the coffeehouse swears he was carrying a gym bag when he exited the car."

Ed's eyes skittered in their sockets, as though flashing back to the crime scene and its surrounds. Or feverishly manufacturing an explanation.

"You're strong for a man your age," Mike said, "but deadweight's deadweight. You couldn't cart him off in the van by yourself and you chose not to involve your brother. But Falcone's bag and the murder weapon? Those joyrides you took were to scout dump sites in advance, weren't they?"

"The hell they were." Ed's fist hammered the table. "There wasn't no bag. I told you that this morning, when Ramey asked after it. You gotta listen to me. Either that hack's lying, or Shifty ditched it himself somewheres. Why, I dunno, but in all this time, I coulda come up with a better story than that bushwah you're layin' on me."

In an uncustomary show of boldness, Preston said, "Is that why you brought Ed down here? To ask him the same questions over and over again?"

Fuckin' A, sport, Mike thought. Welcome to Nowhere Land.

The attorney raised the lid of his briefcase and chucked in the legal pad he'd doodled on. "Either arrest him, or this ridiculous discussion is finished."

Mike's pager buzzed before he could educate Carruthers on the twenty-hour hold pending charges provision of the law. The LED readout's 10-06 was Ryan Rickenbacher's numeric code for "Honey, I'm home."

Gathering his notes and files, Mike said, "Sit tight, gentlemen."

He reluctantly switched off the videocamera before walking out of the room. Tempting though it was to electronically eavesdrop, in his absence, conversations between a suspect and counsel were privileged. Mike sensed nothing germane to the investigation would transpire. Ed was too savvy to spill his guts at the cop shop. It was the reaming he'd give his nephew-in-law that Mike hated to miss.

He heard Rickenbacher's assault on a vending machine before he witnessed the tantrum in progress. Clenching the chrome frame, the rookie rocked the cabinet snarling, "Gimme my dollar back, you greedy son of a bitch!"

Mike picked up a hand-lettered Out of Order sign from the floor. Reaching over Ryan's arm, he retaped the paper to the front of the machine.

"Aw, come *on*." Ryan's sweaty palms squealed down the bowed, Plexiglas panel. "I saw the route guy working on it this morning."

"He had to order a part. Repairmen always have to order parts."

Mike staked his partner to the break room's liquid burned offerings, rumored to be coffee. Stir in lumps of powdered milk substitute and two packets of chemical sweetener and it tasted like crème de battery acid.

"Getting anything out of old man Dillinger?" Ryan asked.

"A headache." Mike rubbed his temple, as if it would quiet the whine in his ears. He was running on fumes and knew it.

Twice tonight an inference had clicked, like an electrical spark. The flash, he remembered. The impetus shimmered a tantalizing inch out of recall range.

Ryan said, "The M.E.—"

"Not yet." Mike virtually toured his house, sorting the laundry hamper, composing a grocery list, power-washing the deck. Memory couldn't be forced. Mental sleight of hand tricks didn't always work. Beating his head on the table never did. "Howard Chinn," he said, grasping at a vague cognitive association. "Tell me again how you contacted him."

"Huh?" Ryan blinked. "Oh—the vic's stepson. He

answered the phone when I called Falcone's house. Said he was there bringing in the mail when the phone rang."

Phone. That was the nexus; the flashpoint. "How was the connection? Clear? Staticky? Did you hear anything in the background? Music, traffic, voices?"

"Nothing out of the ordinary. Why?"

The break room's vinyl sling-back chairs were chiropractic torture devices. Mike fidgeted around to find a comfortable position, saying, "When I talked to Ramey tonight, she'd forwarded all incoming calls to her cell phone. Chinn happening to be at Falcone's house when you called is as convenient as Don Blevins's documented trip to Kansas and noise complaint against his neighbors. I'm wondering if Chinn might be intercepting Falcone's calls."

No bells were ringing in the rookie's belfry. He had a lot fewer candles on his birthday cake, but his day hadn't been any shorter or easier than Mike's.

"First thing tomorrow," Mike said, "contact the Encino P.D. Verify Howard Chinn's whereabouts now and for the past week. Also, find out whether Falcone subscribed to call-forwarding. Sometimes it's bundled with discounted rate promotions."

"Gotcha." Even right side up, Ryan's notes to himself resembled Sanskrit written during a psychedelic episode. "So you think the stepson's involved?"

"Just covering all the bases. Falcone's disappearing

gym bag bugs me. Ed Dillinger swears he never saw it and the searches turned up zip."

"An answer for that came to me while I was driving to Springfield," Ryan said. "Isn't it possible that some punk out cruising saw an old man walking down the street and jumped him? The Dillingers hauling the corpse all over the place may have just complicated a mugging gone bad."

Mike admitted he'd considered that scenario. "But why would anybody jump Falcone, take the bag and leave his wallet unless he had prior knowledge that something more valuable than clean underwear was inside the bag?"

"Like Howard Chinn." Ryan shrugged. "That does make a strange sort of sense."

"Everything about this one's strange." Mike snapped his fingers. "Have California check whether Falcone had life insurance, too. How much and who's the beneficiary."

"Anything else?"

A slug of tepid, milky sweet coffee tripped Mike's gag reflex. There ought to be a law. And it ought to be a hanging offense. He crumpled the foam cup and threw it at the trash barrel.

"Your turn, kid. What are the M.E.'s preliminary findings?"

"About what we expected, with an interesting twist

or two. No surprise that time of death can't be refined much, unless you take the weather into consideration. Dry dirt in Falcone's ear canals, mouth and nostrils suggest he was buried, then protected by the carpet before the storm hit."

Mike's contact at the National Weather Service said the rain started at the Plainfield airport 1:47 a.m., Tuesday. When it began falling in Ramey Burke's backyard wasn't as precise.

Ryan quoted the M.E.'s standard form. "Death was due to internal exsanguination, due to puncture of the aortic artery." He put the report aside. "But from the condition of Falcone's heart, he was overdue for a massive, probably fatal coronary."

Everyone dies of heart failure, hence all the underlying "due to" clauses in a death certificate.

"Unofficially," Ryan went on, "judging by the diameter and length of the wound, Doc likes an ice pick for the murder weapon. He loved your knitting needle idea, though. Psycho homicidal granny on the loose would make a great story for the next M.E. national convention, but the diameter and depth don't jibe. Plus it'd take a sharper tip to breach the sternum."

"Our lab's results scored a zero on the ice picks and tools we took from the house. Not a speck of blood on any of them," Mike said.

"All that means is, the killer didn't give it a rinse and

drop it back in the drawer. It doesn't rule out a shank, either."

Except for the credibility in Ed's remark about smuggling handmade weapons out of prison. Mike blew out a breath. His gut told him the homicide wasn't premeditated. The weapon contradicted that. People don't wander around with ice picks in their pockets.

Leads were fizzling fast. They had to find that ice pick and ID its owner. Until then, they had nothing but tangents to go on. Forty pieces of circumstantial evidence equaled one piece of direct evidence, such as a fingerprint. At last count, Mike had a tubful of disconnected circumstantial and a dead man for the direct variety.

Ryan said, "Remember saying Doc should pull out all the stops on this one? One thing that got him curious was some spots he found on Falcone's shirt."

"What kind of spots? Blood drops?"

"No." Ryan took his set of crime scene photos from the accordion file. "I didn't notice them, either, until Doc pointed them out. See them there, around the placket, near the wound?"

The pictures' resolution and gritty, tired eyes didn't help, but the fabric did appear dappled with something.

"It looks like one of my shirts, when I'm trying to drive and eat a burger at the same time," Ryan said. "Doc doesn't know what it is, but he was interested enough to wave a magnifying glass over Falcone's chest, then shave a patch of his chest hair. Damned if there weren't some tiny pinkish spots on his skin."

Mike squinted at a close-up shot of Falcone's shirt. "What kind of spots?"

"Speculation isn't in Doc's vocabulary. His assistant guessed a premortem rash, a caustic substance and didn't rule out Whattaburger grease. Doc excised pieces of the shirt for a gas chromotography test, stat."

Great. A new paradox to keep Mike from falling into a peaceful short night's sleep. Telling himself the stains derived from a food source and the skin rash was precisely that wouldn't satisfy a mind howling for answers.

Particularly when *stat* to an overworked, underpaid lab tech was Latin for, "I'll get back to you a month from next Friday."

"If you've got any questions for Ed Dillinger," he said, "be my guest. Carruthers is babysitting and he's the worst excuse for a defense attorney I've ever seen, but I'm out of bullets."

Ryan sagged in the chair. "I'm beat, Sarge. If it's all the same to you, I'd rather use what steam I've got left to make that call to California."

"Then I'm cutting him and Perry Mason loose."

Ryan chuckled. "Might as well. He'd be a bad influence on the guys in lockup, anyhow."

Joints crackled and popped like distant fireworks as

Mike stretched his arms over his head. He wondered what Ramey was doing, besides pacing the floor with her checkbook in hand in the event she had to make bail for her uncle. Preston, no doubt, had left his at home.

"I'll be late coming in tomorrow. Page me if California has anything interesting to say." A softer medley of aches and pains accompanied Mike's groaning, "I have a couple of hunches I didn't have time to chase down today." He looked at his watch. "Make that yesterday."

"What kind of hunches?"

"No way, kid." Mike walked to the trash can and picked up the foam cup he'd bricked off the rim. "Like my old partner Smitty always said, 'Keep the woo-woo shit to yourself, unless it pans out. If it does, everybody'll think you're a genius. If it doesn't, you won't have to hear about it for the rest of your natural life.'"

15

Clangety-clang. Whap. Clang. BANG...bangbang.

The epicenter of the earthquake—the noise-intensive portion—struck just as Ramey reached the back stairs' landing.

In the breakfast nook, Ed bellowing, "What the hell was that?" was seconded by Melba Jane's slightly more distant wail from the kitchen, "Archie! Oh, dear Lord! Something's happened to Archie!"

Ed led the frantic exodus outside. Ramey, close on his heels, salivated at a passing whiff of hickory-smoked bacon sizzling on the stove. Behind her, Melba Jane gimp-jogged along, yelping, "Ow, ow, ow," from the toll her running exacted on the pinky toe jutting out the hole in her sneaker and the backache she'd complained of since shifting Shifty's corpse to the curb.

The three-member rescue party hung a right and almost immediately skidded to an abrupt, goggle-eyed halt. Archie, as inert as a tipped tombstone, was prostrated in the grassy slough between the driveway's concrete tracks, pinned by the extension ladders that were normally secured to the rack atop Ramey's van.

With his face protruding between the two upper rungs of the ladder and his feet sticking up from the lower ones, he resembled a framed, three-dimensional work of abstract art. A yard or so away, a hatchling robin flailed its wings, cheeping for its mother.

Archie's lids fluttered open. His field of vision adjusted from the clear blue stratosphere to his brother, wife and niece standing gape-jawed before him. "What, you think I'm Houdini?" he croaked. "Get this thing off'n me."

As Ed and Ramey scrambled to hoist off the ladder, she said, "Melba Jane, go call 911. Tell them we need an ambulance."

"No we don't," Archie said, though he seemed reluctant to test that opinion by moving anything other than his eyeballs and mouth. "Just got the wind knocked out of me, is all."

"I'd reckon," Ed said. "You blew that poor li'l baby bird clean outa its nest."

Melba Jane "Aww-w-wed" and shuffled over to the other, now-motionless accident victim. Mother Robin swooped from branch to branch, chattering threats in vain. Melba Jane's fingertip gently nudged the tiny ball of down. She sniffed and shook her head. "It wasn't as lucky as you, Arch."

"Trying to save that consarned bird was what nigh-on got my neck broke, woman." He gingerly pushed up into a sitting position. "'Twas flappin' around on the ladders when I come out to fetch the newspaper. I thought I could plunk it back in the nest before its mama flew home."

Ramey surveyed twigs and straw cradled in the fork of a limb overhanging the van. Balanced on one edge, the mother bird's head craned, then bowed, masticating breakfast to feed her surviving offspring.

Ed pulled Archie to his feet. "Be as brave as you care to for the womenfolk. If something's paining you, I want to know about it."

Chin buckled in stubborn denial, Archie brushed dirt and grass clippings from his dungarees. "I suspect I'll be black-and-blue afore the day's out, but nothing serious. Woulda been different if I'd smacked the cement instead of the ground."

Different, as in a skull fracture, Ramey thought, stretching up to examine the ladder rack. "Were you taking off the ladders to reach the bird's nest when you fell?"

"Never got that far." Archie moved to the rear of the van. "I stepped up on the bumper to snag the bird, then grabbed ahold of the ladders to boost up a little. The next I knew, ziggety-zing, the whole shebang slid down on top of me." He scowled at the rack, then the ground several yards behind the van. "How'd those gizmos get flung to hell and gone?"

Ramey had already noticed the gizmos, officially known as ladder clamps, scattered in the grass as though they'd been fired from a catapult. All four clamps had been bolted to the rack for safety and to deter theft. In the holes below their handles were the still-fastened padlocks to further discourage ladder thieves.

Melba Jane harrumphed. "Looks to me like somebody was trying to steal those ladders during the night and got scared off."

Ed struck a match to light his cigarette. "Amateurs."

"Kids'd be my guess," Archie said. "All piss and no vinegar." He flinched. "I mean, all balls and— Aw, jeez, never mind."

Ramey's thumb rubbed a clamp's enameled aluminum handle. Exposure to the elements had pitted and chipped the once glossy surface. She thought back to Early Dawes's reaction when she showed off the snazzy new replacements for her worn-out strap-and-winch system.

"You give seventy-five smackers apiece for these?" Early whistled through the gap in his teeth. "Land sakes, girl. Jack Hugh Prout down to the hardware must've seen you comin' and mourned your leavin'."

The electrician ushered her to his truck, a retired telephone company service vehicle. "That's all the riggings you need. They're hog-tight, gooseproof and didn't cost more'n ten bucks total, including sales tax and a sodie pop from the cooler."

A web of sun-blistered bungee cords twined his ladders' upper and lower rungs and hooked the rack's support posts. Giant cowbells were welded to each ladder's top and foot. "I double-dog dare any sumbitch to get a ladder off'n my truck without me and sixteen others hearing him do it."

Unimpressed and stung from his disparagement of her shiny, new contractor-grade clamps, Ramey slipped a hand into a cowbell's craw. A yank on the clapper sliced the string that attached it to the bell. She dangled the now-detached clapper in front of Early's nose.

He snatched it away, bellowing, "What in Sam Hill did you do that for?"

"My dad taught me that it's always logical to start with the simplest answer to a question," she said. "If I was the sumbitch that wanted your ladders, breaking the bells is the easiest way to keep you from hearing me take them."

The fancy shmancy clamp she now held didn't fail due to a design flaw. It simply wasn't possible that four devices, bolted to the ladder rack with padlocks inserted in their handles gave way simultaneously. The three-hundred-dollar set of clamps were worth as much as the extension ladders they were intended to protect, too. A fact any self-respecting tool thief would be aware of.

Ramey was toeing the grass in search of the bolts that had once held the clamps in place, when Archie hugged her shoulders. "No reason to look like your dog just died, sweetheart. I'm fit as Beelzebub's fiddle, save a knock and a scratch or two. It coulda been worse, but it wasn't."

Worse? The possibilities gave her cold chills. What if the clamps had held, until she'd wheeled around a corner? The sideward lurch could have slewed the already top-heavy van into oncoming traffic, a jaywalker, a light pole, a parked car.

Hit the brakes too hard and momentum would have speared them through another vehicle's rear window—or backward, through somebody's windshield.

Archie said, "There's all manner of screws and bolts in the garage. Me and Ed'll set those ladders to rights, after breakfast. It won't take fifteen minutes and we'll tighten 'em till they squeal for mercy."

"Thanks, but I don't trust these clamps to hold them anymore." Ramey picked up the other three and handed them to him. "The ladders can stay in the garage until I find something safer." She added to herself, *and tamper-proof.*

Melba Jane started for the back porch. "I done left

breakfast cookin' on the stove." Over her shoulder, she called, "If it's not burned to cinders, how many eggs do y'all want?"

Ed ordered three sunny side up, then changed it to scrambled, "since you can't fry rooster bullets over easy to save yourself."

"None for me," Ramey said, having lost what appetite she'd brought with her downstairs.

Even then, she hadn't been hungry, but would have eaten to pass the time, before putting the day's plan in motion. Regardless of whether she'd ferret out answers to questions her aunt and uncles refused to supply, she was too restless to stay home and storyboard the next staging job.

The aluminum ladders lying on the grass resembled train tracks. Ramey chafed the arm she'd slathered with skin lotion after she was burned the other day in the shower. In her tiny office where she'd kept the spare keys to the van, Ed had repaired the breakaway desk chair, but she'd pushed it aside in favor of an uncomfortable, but trustier bar stool.

Household accidents injured thousands every year. Some were of the looking-to-happen kind, like a Plainfield man's idea to rid his yard of moles by filling the runs with kerosene and dropping a match in the hole. But three incidents and a murder in the week since the Dillingers moved in?

"Wherever you're off to this morning, I'm riding shotgun," Ed informed her.

Ramey jumped, shrank back. *"No."*

Ed looked surprised, hurt, irritated. "Ain't no need to yell."

She forced a smile to lighten her tone. "What makes you think I'm going anywhere?"

"For one, the nice britches and sweater you're wearin' instead of jeans and a T-shirt. Coming downstairs dressed, combed and made up before you've had your coffee's another."

"Maybe I'm turning into Portia."

He chuckled. "Like you ever could, or'd want to. Don't take me wrong, now. She's a fine gal. She just frets too much about things that don't matter and not enough about those that do."

Ramey studied the face she'd come to love. Was he a Judas? Or was she, for thinking, even for a moment, that he'd do anything to hurt her?

Before the day ended, she hoped to have answers to that and a dozen other questions. In the meantime, a Dillinger of any persuasion tagging along would be a hindrance.

"While I'm out shopping," she fibbed, "promise you'll keep an eye on Archie. Anything that seems out of the ordinary, call an ambulance, then call me on the cell phone."

Ed took a drag off his cigarette, then dropped the butt and ground it under his heel. "I thought you fixed the phones so calls can't come in, nor go out."

Ramey cursed to herself. "Okay, you got me. You can dial out, but I'd rather you didn't, unless it's an emergency."

He grunted. "Make whatever you want outa this, hon, but it takes a better con than you're working to con a con man."

The block-wide building's towering granite walls, arched windows, crested roofline and broad staircase rising majestically from the sidewalk harked back to an era when municipal libraries resembled castles—at least to young patrons once enthralled by Merlin, Mordred and King Arthur's Knights of the Round Table.

As an adult, Mike Constantine voted in favor of every tax increase earmarked for Plainfield Public Library, then secretly hoped the measures failed. He acknowledged the need for a new, spacious, twenty-first-century facility, but couldn't abide that old Carnegie castle falling to ruin or being crushed by a wrecking ball for a parking lot, or another taco palace.

Showing my age, Mike supposed, trudging up the steps to the main entrance. Feeling it this morning, too.

As predicted, the Falcone case had haunted his

dreams. A faceless figure chased Ramey, an ice pick gripped in his fist. An enormous silver dollar moon rose over the treetops, the ethereal light glistening off her body lying in a shallow trench. A roaring wall of flames ravaged a mountainous, crackling pyre of limbs and branches.

That one had bolted Mike upright in bed, sweat plastering the sheet to his chest, and his mouth so dry, he could scarcely swallow.

Orenthal "Shifty" Falcone hadn't rated a cameo in those technicolor nightmares. Mike's interpretation of them wavered between premonitions to a hideous composite of a homicide and a relentless, disorienting attraction to Ramey Jo Patterson Burke.

His fingers hooked the library door's serpentine brass handle. Could be he was the one in danger of being demolished by another kind of wrecking ball.

He wasn't a loner by nature. He'd come close—very close a few times—to talking himself down the aisle, then backed off, realizing the difference between hoping for forever and promising it.

"Love starts between your ears," his father said. "When I met your mother, it felt like I'd been lost and finally found my way home. Four kids and fifty-four years later, it still does."

Until yesterday morning, Mike hadn't understood what he'd meant: that home wasn't a place with a roof and walls, and feeling found could happen without knowing you'd ever been lost.

Breathing in that imposing, musty smell peculiar to libraries of a bygone age reminded him of the reason behind this potential goose chase Ramey had inspired.

Indirectly, Mike allowed, but her doubts and the inconsistencies she'd remarked on had piqued his interest and curiosity. About a lot of things.

Shifting the leather pouch to his other hand, Mike eyed the carved walnut staircase to the building's upper stories. With nothing to prove to his pride or a younger partner, he headed for the elevator alcoved in a reading room.

The third floor was given over to administrative offices, storage and historical and genealogical research. The space allotted to the latter was in stark, almost blinding contrast to the first level, due to the whitewashed plaster walls and dysfunctional venetian blinds.

Mike nodded "Good morning" to the bearded librarian at the information desk and continued to an adjacent room. Along a side wall, a row of microfilm readers was semibarricaded by soaring metal shelving units. All but one patron churning the machines' hand cranks were senior citizens.

The exception, a wild-haired brunette in a royal purple sweater and cream wool slacks, sent a zing straight to Mike's belly, like a low-voltage hit from a stun gun.

He must have grunted, or groaned, or made some sort of Neanderthal-like noise, because seven elderly researchers and Ramey all swiveled around and stared, as if determining whether the newcomer in their midst might require emergency CPR.

"Great minds, huh," he said, to his audience's junior member. "Why am I not surprised you're here?"

"Same goes for me." Ramey grinned and motioned for him to drag up a chair beside her. "Interesting reading, these newspaper archives."

"Sshhh," cautioned the lady at the neighboring machine. "If you *must* talk, do so in whispers."

"Yes, ma'am," Mike whispered, then scooted his chair closer to Ramey's. His thigh touched hers. She didn't move away. "Sorry to crowd you, Little Chief, but you heard the lady."

"I don't mind." A rosy glow bathed her cheeks. A deft, light touch with a mascara wand further defined those amazing dark eyes, as did a wash of pale blue shadow.

And it was for him. He knew it, as surely as he'd lathered and shaved twice that morning, selected a shirt and tie, instead of grabbing the first he'd seen in the closet. He'd even given his shoes a buff before tying them.

Her breath was moist and warm on his skin, when she said, "Are you thinking, what I'm thinking?"

God, I hope so. The tension between them was palpable, expectant, glorious, agonizing. "You tell me."

Her shoulders turned, her chin tipping upward, her eyes closing, as if spellbound, then...

It broke. Almost audibly and certainly physically. She jerked away, stammering, "The past. History repeating itself. No, not repeating itself exactly, but linked to it."

"The past," he agreed, lamenting the so-near-present, yet cognizant enough to swing his leather pouch up from the floor and across his lap.

"The Dillingers reminisce a lot about prison and growing up in Plainfield." A quaver in her voice suggested that her recovery from awkwardness was also a work-in-progress. "They duck and run from questions about the bank robberies."

He nodded, stalling a few seconds, while reverse polarity rerouted his blood supply. "You're their niece. I doubt they're real proud of being convicted felons."

"Oh, so sharing prison anecdotes and recipes is fine, but talking about how they wound up there isn't?"

She had a point. She usually did. "You think they're intentionally hiding something?"

"Someone, is my guess. Another accomplice, or a victim with a thirty-five-year-old grudge against them and Shifty Falcone."

Mike picked up an empty microfilm carton and

scanned the yellowed label. "Don't get mad, but that's a helluva reach, isn't it?"

"Sure, it is. But that's why you're here, too."

His hunch involved the oldest, most popular motive for murder, not a person or persons unknown. For her sake, he hoped hers panned out.

She shrugged. "I just can't stop obsessing about the news coverage last night on the TV and the story in this morning's paper. Somebody tipped the media to Shifty's membership in the Other Dillinger Gang—as the 'wheelman,' no less. Whoever did must have had prior knowledge."

"And an ax to grind," Mike said. "Otherwise, the source would be credited."

"Absolutely. Local history buffs love to be quoted as experts, and why not? Human interest angles sell newspapers and have friends and relatives setting their VCRs for those fifteen seconds of televised fame."

Mike returned the carton to the table. "What if the source wasn't an expert? What if he, or she, just came down here to do what you're doing?"

"Based on what? Falcone's name and a goofy allusion to his nonillustrious past? That's pretty much all anyone had to go on yesterday, and that wasn't publicized until the 5:00 p.m. newscast. I missed the ten o'clock segment, but KDGE's Web site only repeated earlier info, with a sidebar about prisons rescinding life sentences because of overcrowding."

Defiance and a trace of smugness flashed across her eyes. "I Googled Orenthal Falcone first thing this morning and got nothing. The Internet is a terrific resource, but it hasn't replaced old-fashioned hands-on snooping. Plus, if a reporter had cherry-picked these archives, the newspaper would have cited itself as the source."

Back when the Dillingers regularly withdrew cash from banks without benefit of an account, the staunchly conservative *Plainfield News* published a morning edition, in competition with the moderate-mannered *Evening Messenger.* In the early eighties, their respective owners realized that funneling the town's advertising revenue into one pot, rather than two smaller ones and halving the staff and overhead was a capital idea.

Mike's parents still complained that the consolidated *News-Messenger* was the ugly stepchild of both its forebears. Its subsequent sale to an Eastern newspaper chain was tacitly ignored.

Ramey said, "Since you're not keen on my theory, what's yours?"

"Nothing specific. Just general background on the Dillingers' criminal activities."

That was ninety-nine percent truthful. Money being

the root to a myriad evils, it was also a possible explanation for Falcone's cross-country bus ride that had nagged Mike like a thorn in his thumb.

Anticipating Ramey's next question, Mike said, "One of these years, all our closed case files will be scanned into a database. Since the clerks are still stuck in the fifties, I assigned a uniform to plow through the boxes in the basement, while I did some digging here."

Her eyebrow lifted. "Impatient, huh?"

"No, ma'am. When I know what I want, I go after it."

The remark and its implications suspended time for a few seconds. Mike thought he heard a door softly close and the bolt snick home—an emotional defense mechanism anyone who'd utilized it would recognize. Someday, if he gave in to impulse, he might slip through those barriers before she shut him out.

Ramey pressed the heels of her hands against the table's edge, and maneuvered her chair backward. "He who's on official business and on the clock should have the driver's seat. I'll watch from the bleachers and let you know if I see something interesting."

Long-stemmed roses, candlelight, champagne and Delta blues on the stereo were supposed to be romantic. For Mike, it was the scent of her hair, the warmth of her hands resting lightly on his shoulders, a cramped, airless corner of the library and the drone of a microfilm machine's cooling fan.

"Are you memorizing that old sports page, or do you want me to turn the crank thing?" she whispered.

Resigned to his status as a hopeless unromantic, he sighed and gave the crank thing a whirl.

Lithographic columns streaked by on the screen like a film noir bridge cues a flash forward in time. The sensory and physical effects of the movement rivaled a roller-coaster ride.

Robbery reports hopscotched the area. The news of the first heist at a savings and loan forty miles from Plainfield received less ink than an obituary. By the third robbery, city, county and state law enforcements had begun to connect the crimes and communicate with each other.

The Other Dillinger Gang's MO varied, but not much. A few minutes before noon on a Friday, a well-dressed couple would arrive for a prescheduled meeting with the bank president. This being the late sixties, before the advent of drive-through service, ATMs, direct deposit, debit and credit cards, the timing ensured a flush vault, in anticipation of customers, or their wives, with paychecks to cash.

Security cameras were also as rare as a second bank officer's security code to access the vault. After Mr. and Mrs. Respectable ushered the president to the vault, a farmer dressed in his Sunday-best overalls and toting a paper shopping bag joined the queue at the tellers' counter.

What happened next was brilliant, in Mike's opinion. He had no difficulty visualizing the bedlam that ensued when the farmer uncovered the hole in his sack. A hoard of mice scurried from it and darted between customers' feet, skated across on the floor and clambered up to the counter.

Ramey shuddered. "I'm not afraid of mice," she assured him. "Every spring and fall, I send plenty to that big cheese factory in the sky. It's seeing the little bastards zoom across the room that freaks me out."

"I beg your pardon, young lady," said the woman beside them. "This is a library, not a cocktail lounge."

Without hesitation, Ramey said, "You're absolutely right and I do apologize. It won't happen again."

"See that it doesn't." The woman's glare strafed Mike, as though pegging him as a bad influence. She'd fall to a dead faint if she knew how bad an influence he'd like to be.

His attention returning to the task at hand, the newspaper article described in tongue-in-cheek fashion the panicked reactions of employees and customers who'd made their eventual descent from the desks, chairs and kiosks where they'd taken refuge. In one instance, an hour passed before a teller finally found the bank president hog-tied and gagged in the vault and its assets significantly depleted.

The farmer's and Mr. and Mrs. Respectable's getaway vehicles were invariably stolen and ditched in a parking lot, along with the clothing they'd worn. A second string of boosted cars transported the gang to yet another prearranged location. Where they went from there and in what make, model, or number of vehicles, nobody knew.

A glimpsed banner headline, then a rewind yielded a smudgy photograph of a perp walk starring Ed, Archie and Melba Jane Dillinger. The caption identified a fourth, rougher-looking character as Orenthal Falcone.

"Wow," Ramey breathed alongside Mike's ear, which triggered a brief bout of dizziness not ascribable to the motion on-screen. "There's some old snapshots of Melba Jane in the family album, but they're either out of focus or she's sitting at the table."

Once Mike's vision cleared, he released a mental wolf whistle. Other than losing a little huskiness and hair, Ed and Archie hadn't changed much, but thirty-five years and seventy-some pounds ago, Melba Jane had been a dead ringer for the lush and luscious Ava Gardner.

Mike reversed the machine's crank to previous stories relating to the crime spree. His finger tapped the screen beneath each pertinent sentence containing a bank official's description of Mr. and Mrs. Respectable.

Laughing, Ramey said, "Five-eleven to six feet two? Archie wouldn't be that tall if he stood on a box. And nobody then, or now, would call Melba Jane average looking."

Mike figured Ed, the shorter of the brothers, for Mr. Respectable and Archie for the farmer. In any event, "That's why cops don't fully trust eyewitness descriptions. Fear and hindsighted machismo almost always turn a runty perp into a fullback for the Rams."

"Yeah, well, I'd say what most of these people remembered about Melba Jane wasn't her height."

"Not if she was wearing a dress like the one in that photo. Oochie-*mama.*"

Ramey's cuff to the top of his head earned another scathing look from their neighbor. The one Mike returned suggested she wouldn't be as easily distracted or perturbed if she paid more attention to her research than to theirs.

The mood turned somber as they reviewed accounts of the brazen fourth and fifth robberies at banks on opposite ends of Plainfield. This time, the heists were pulled two hours apart on a Wednesday, the week's second-busiest shopping and banking day.

Two well-dressed gentlemen carrying briefcases emptied the vault, while someone—undoubtedly a drabbed down Melba Jane—loosed the rodents. Security guards statewide had been alerted to the gang's modus operandi, but didn't expect a midweek hit. Even if they had, they were woefully disadvantaged by fleeing mice, customers, employees, three wily thieves and their wheelman.

The audacity of the double heist pushed the Other Dillinger Gang's luck too far. The suspects' vehicle—a pickup truck—was captured within hours of the robberies, just beyond the north side of town and not far from Bill and Sylvia Patterson's home.

Unfortunately, then-Lieutenant Patterson, the officer in charge of the manhunt's largest search team, had ordered his squad to cover the city's east and west perimeters, and to pay particular attention to unoccupied cars.

An *Evening-Messenger* editorial decried the Dillingers' familial relationship and all but accused Bill Patterson of trying to aid and abet his in-laws' escape:

Malfeasance is the ten-dollar word for accusations leveled at Lt. William F. Patterson by concerned city council members and the public at large. Chief Nathan Blount adamantly denies the charge against Lt. Patterson. Although expected, Blount's response fails to address whom Lt. Patterson served and protected by diverting the city-wide manhunt for a gang of bank robbers.

Blount's belief in Patterson's integrity is admirable. Perhaps, as Blount maintains, the gang's ringleaders being the brothers of Lt. Patterson's wife had no effect whatsoever on the execution of his sworn duty as a municipal law enforcement officer.

If true, an impartial investigation of the incident will silence the outcry. Until then, the citizens of this community will rightfully aver that "Blood is thicker than water."

Ramey's hands left Mike's shoulders. Sitting down hard in the chair beside him, she stared at the screen as if the text would read differently a second time, or from a different visual perspective.

"How could anybody even *think* that?" she asked. "Daddy wanted to be a cop from the time he was a little boy. His blood ran midnight blue, for God's sake."

"Appearances deceive, Ramey."

"And like it says, blood's thicker than water. So what? Ed and Archie were his brothers-in-law, not his brothers. My father would have done anything to help them go straight, but even if Mom begged him to look the other way, he wouldn't have."

He had for Ramey's mother, Mike thought. While Sylvia put back the loot she'd burgled from that drugstore. Did he run interference for Ed, Archie and Melba Jane, too?

He laid his hand over Ramey's. "If it's any consolation, I can't believe he would, either. Not in a million years."

She didn't pull her hand away, but her smile diminished before it was fully formed. "Jerome Goodnight." Grabbing the crank, she twirled it backward to the edition's front page. "Here it is.

Jerome H.D. Goodnight, president of the First National Bank of Plainfield, collapsed shortly after his secretary found him bound and gagged inside the vault. Goodnight was transported by private car to the hospital for treatment of a mild heart attack."

Mike nodded, acknowledging that the quote held significance for her, but had no idea why.

"Jerome H. D. Goodnight? That old—" she glanced over her shoulder, then mouthed *bastard*. "Goodnight and a couple of his cronies on the city council were furious when Dad was promoted to assistant chief of police. Later, when the council recommended appointing him chief, Goodnight tried to block it."

"Now that you mention it, I vaguely remember that," Mike said. "I was a green bean, right out of the academy.

Department politics wasn't my forte—they still aren't—but I do recall the prediction of a major outbreak of 'blue flu' if the council voted down Patterson's appointment."

Mike's pager vibrated as Ramey continued reeling the microfilm onto its spool. Freeing her hand, she pushed a strand of hair behind her ear. "Kinda sounds like a grudge, doesn't it?"

Not really. Not in the way she inferred. Lingering doubts about Bill Patterson's integrity aside, if Goodnight wasn't pushing up daisies by now, he was pushing 112.

The ET911 message on Mike's pager translated to *phone home, now, Sarge.* Rickenbacher had probably first tried Mike's cell phone, which he'd switched off, as per library rules. The building's thick stone walls blocked the signal, but not the ring tones, and no end of patrons were eager to snitch on violators.

"Walk outside with me so I can call the office," Mike said. "If I don't have to rush back there, I'll spring for a late breakfast or an early lunch."

Ramey hesitated long enough to raise his hopes, then shook her head. "Thanks, but I want to read the *Plainfield Daily News*'s side of the story."

A cop would have to be heartless to not sympathize with a niece desperate to acquit a loved one of a crime. "I'll do some more checking, too."

That was also the truth. Reviewing the old case files

had a tangential relationship to her Jerome H. D. Goodnight theory, in the manner of a strong money motive for Ed to cancel Shifty Falcone's membership in the Other Dillinger Gang.

The *Evening Messenger*'s editorial had vilified the wrong man, but blood really was thicker than water.

"Hey," Ramey said, as Mike retrieved the leather pouch from the floor. "What time did you bring Uncle Ed home last night from—uh, after your meeting?"

The woman beside Ramey appeared oblivious to another noise infraction. Eavesdropping on them must have won out over genealogical statistics.

Relying on Ramey to catch the distinction, Mike replied, "You might say we parted company around one-thirty."

By their interested listener's rigid backbone, curiosity was about to blow her gaskets. As Mike left the room, he heard Ms. Nosy Parker inquire, "Are you Chief Patterson's daughter? Why, years ago, gosh, it may have been before you were ever born, your mother and I…"

Mike rolled his eyes, tempted to turn around and reinvite Ramey to lunch. But she could hold her own, he decided. And Rickenbacher's page probably forecast another tasteless vending machine ham sandwich and a bag of chips for his midday meal.

16

"Anybody down there?"

Melba Jane shrieked. Her arms snapped above her head in classic surrender position. The flashlight toppled from her hand, clunked on the hard-packed dirt, flickered and died. Darkness enveloped her, oppressive and impenetrable, like the inside of a cow.

As the Almighty's deep, disembodied voice echoed off the subterranean stone walls, she cringed in terror. Judgment Day was upon her…except her heart was thumping wildly. What little she remembered of Sunday School classes lent a relative certainty that the wages of sin were supposed to be paid *after* a body departed the mortal coil, not while it was still sucking air and perspiring heavily.

And if the Lord was fixing to cast her into the lake of fire, you'd think He'd specify Melba Jane Dillinger, not just "anybody" who happened to be snooping around Chicken Charlie's old hootch hideout.

A concerned and considerably less condemnatory, "Ms. Burke, are you all right?" clinched it.

Light shafted from a rectangular hatch twenty feet or so afar and well above her head. The rays had a celestial quality, but the iron ladder they illuminated could hardly be confused with a stairway to heaven.

"Who's there?" she yelled. "What do you want?"

There was a three-beat pause. "It's Gordon Sweeney, Mrs. Dillinger. I'd advise you and anyone else with you to come out."

Dread as chill and dank as the underground grotto she was in spiked the hair at Melba Jane's nape. Why hadn't she thought of Charlie's storehouse *before* Ed and Archie had taken off in that taxi?

No, by gum, her being trapped like a hare in a hold was *their* fault. They'd grown up here, for pity's sake. They should've recollected the cellar their papa bored out 'neath the garage, in case revenue agents caught wind of his bootlegging business.

If Charlie Dillinger's numbskull sons had spent as much time using their brains as they did sitting on them, she wouldn't be in this fine mess of a predicament.

"I'm a-comin'" she said, this alternate kind of Judgment Day suddenly not sounding quite as direful.

Squinting against the sunlight, she grudgingly clasped the parole officer's helping hand. "I was down there by my lonesome. Take a gander for yourself if you don't believe me."

Sweeney's gaze swept the trap door, the dirt and pea gravel she'd shoveled away to expose it. Bracketed on the walls of the garage and on shelves were chairs, picture frames, lamps and assorted flea market plunder Ramey collected for her business.

"What's down there, anyway?" he asked.

As though having the fear of God put in her wasn't unnerving enough, Melba Jane couldn't, for the life of her, recall the story she'd divined to tell Ramey if she came home unexpectedly and found her down there.

Never break a law you don't have to was a rule Shifty Falcone ignored once too often. Don't lie for sport was another. The truth was seldom as frolicsome to tell, but less likely to trip you up in the long run.

She said, "Spiders, slugs, dirt and busted glass is about all I saw before you scared my vitals up between my ears. Way back when, my father-in-law peddled booze to speakeasies all over Missouri. Down there's where he hid the barrels between shipments."

Sweeney didn't appear surprised. Then again, before and after Prohibition, whiskey stills were as common in Ozark hills and hollers as methamphetamine labs were now. About as prone to explode, too, by what she read in the newspaper.

The parole officer gave her muumuu, grimy socks

and sneakers the up-and-down. "So, you thought it was such a nice day, why not dig out the old trapdoor and look around?"

"You might could say that. The idea struck me while I was listening to the radio. Haven't you heard songs that send you back, make you feel like you're there again?"

His smile allowed that he had, except his sentimental journeys hadn't extended to spelunking a manmade cavern.

"You're right, Officer Sweeney. It wasn't smart for an old lady like myself to wander down there by my lonesome." Melba Jane dabbed her brow and temples with a tissue from her muumuu pocket. "I could've taken a tumble, wrenched an ankle—"

"That doesn't explain why no one answered the door. I noticed Ms. Burke's van was gone, but when I saw the garage wide open, I thought the three of you were pretending no one was home."

She knuckled her hips, a bona fide, hundred-and-eighty pound mass of indignation. "Shame on you for thinking such a terrible thing about people you barely know."

It was a silly thing to say to a parole officer, but she'd been cordial, almost completely honest, and if his mama hadn't taught him to respect his elders, he was due for a comportment lesson.

"I'm in no mood for games, Mrs. Dillinger. Where are Ed and Archie?"

"I don't know." The compulsion to avert her gaze was so intense, Melba Jane's eyelids twitched. In prison, maintaining eye contact could be construed as contempt, defiance, a threat. On the outside, to avoid, or break it, indicated deceit.

She reeled from an awful homesickness for the place where rules of conduct and behavior were as precise as the punishment for infractions. There was safety in them, and a peculiar sort of freedom. Bars, high walls and concertina wire that separated her from the world at large also protected her from it.

"Don't lie to me, Melba Jane."

"I'm not. Ramey said she might be gone till late afternoon, maybe evening. Believe it or don't, after she left this morning, the boys jawed here in the yard a bit, then called a cab and told me not to worry, they'd be back soon."

Sweeney had the look of a man poised to jump without asking how high. It had also crossed Melba Jane's mind that Ed and Archie had run off without her.

Archie loved her, but Ed was his brother. If he wasn't arrested for murder before Wednesday's end, tomorrow was a sure bet.

Melba Jane and Archie had their doubts about Ed's innocence, but guilt didn't much matter. Once a judge swore out that warrant, Ed was done for. He could plead not guilty, be bound over for trial and wither in city lockup for upward of a year, or plead guilty and board the next prison bus.

Oh, sure, if he pled not guilty, Ramey could and probably would post his bond—ten percent of the untold thousands she'd forfeit if he then skipped town to avoid prosecution.

He'd never do that, even with the means to repay her finally in hand. That left bailing before a warrant was issued. Rather than let Ed strike out alone, Archie would promise himself to send for Melba Jane when they felt it safe to do so—as if such a refuge existed for two ex-con fugitives.

"Archie will be back any minute now. They both will." Just saying these words slackened the bands crushing Melba Jane's chest. "You'll see. That taxi's gonna pull up at the curb, then Ed'll raise Cain with the driver over the fare."

Sweeney's eyes expressed the pity folks show for a Christmas puppy dumped by the side of a country road before Valentine's Day. "I hope you're right, Mrs. Dillinger."

He moved to kick the trapdoor shut with his foot. "But a half hour's benefit of the doubt is all I can afford to give them."

* * *

The glare off a truck's chrome bumper was like getting pasted by a prison Kleig light. Blinking at the dots that frolicked across his field of vision, Ed used his hand for an awning and leaned forward as far as the cab's seat belt allowed.

"That's him." Voice rising to a screech, he yelled at the driver, "Hey—stop—pull over—there—in *there*."

Slowing to a crawl, the cabbie looked where Ed pointed. "I can't, mister. That's a hamburger joint's drive-through lane."

The meter read thirty dollars and a quarter. Ed peeled a ten off his roll and threw it at him. "Then drive through the son of a bitch and buy something, you idiot." He yanked up the door handle. "Wait for us somewhere close, or that's all you'll get outa this trip."

Slamming the door behind him, Ed hurried down the sidewalk. He didn't care whether his brother followed, or waited in the cab.

As shaken as Archie was after that ladder knocked the whey out of him, Ed had tried to leave him home. Archie'd have none of that. No-sir-ree Bob. He didn't trust Ed out of his sight was the why of it. Ed might resent it more if a general lack of trust didn't hold as true for him as his brother and that mouthy tub of lard he'd married.

There was just no telling what those two might've

cooked up besides lunch while Ed cruised around town in a jitney. Melba Jane was as good at rolling out schemes as piecrust. And it'd be a frosty day in August before Ed forgave her for that polt she kung fued on his goldanged arm.

Thank Almighty God, she threw him over for Archie at that Fourth of July lawn party the folks had invited the whole town to. Melba Jane was a beauty back then, her hair like a coal-black waterfall and a figure finer than the risqué pictures on that deck of French playing cards his dad hid in the liquor cabinet.

Ed was over her before the fireworks blasted the stars clean out of the sky. He'd never looked back or wondered what might have been, either. Not more'n ten thousand times.

Somebody'd been looking out for him. Crazy in love as he was, if Melba Jane had been *his* wife when they got busted at that roadblock, he might have gone for the sheriff's revolver. If a deputy didn't kill him outright, he'd have had a chair reserved for him at the gas chamber.

Slow-witted Archie cried as the cops cuffed her and shoved her into the backseat of that county car. So had Ed, but not on the outside.

"What the—" He halted in front of a print shop. Now he did look back. And forward again. Then at the passing traffic. Every which-a-way save up, but his quarry had vanished.

Jehosophat and criminitlies. Wouldn't you know, just *thinking* about Archie and Melba Jane was enough to sprag a man's wheel?

"Where'd he go?" Archie said, huffing up behind him.

"If I knew that, would I be standing here like one o' them cement petunia planters?"

Ed regretted the remark even before Archie winced. Bruises darkened his brother's hairline and below his left eye socket. That scrape on his jaw and under an ear might blossom purple before suppertime.

The external wounds would heal. Archie's expression mirrored a little boy who'd always tried his best to follow in his father's and older brother's footsteps, but stumbled and went splat, as often as not. He was a finer man than Charlie Dillinger was, or Ed would ever be. Someday, Archie would conjure the words to tell him so.

"I can handle this, Arch. You go back and talk up that hack driver, lest he decides to leave us stranded."

"Nah, let's both of us vamoose on home. Trouble we've got a-plenty of. Stirring up more won't fix a thing."

"It will for Ramey. She's the one's gotta live here after we're gone."

Ed coughed and moved away from the print shop's noise and chemical fumes. They still had the sidewalk to themselves, curse his lousy luck. He lit the last Camel in his pack, took a drag, then exhaled. "It's simple as this. We can't watch out for Ramey from way down south of the border. Gotta tighten it up afore we hit the bricks."

"Not today, we don't." Archie swatted at a fly hectoring his nose. "Not with Ramey refusing to be gone from the house for longer'n a minute or ten since last weekend."

True enough. With few and brief exceptions, that girl'd stuck closer to home than a cat with a new litter of kittens. Absent a watch, Ed tipped back his head to squint at the sun. By that reckoning, his temper had overruled common sense nigh onto two hours ago.

"Ah, well," he said, "seeing as you're in no shape for traipsing around, I suspect we'd—"

Ed's cigarette butt arced toward the gutter. He balled his fists and strode toward the splayfooted jake with the leather pouch swinging from a shoulder strap.

"Hold up, boy. You and me need to talk."

Whether he recognized the voice or just its pure contempt, Don Blevins stopped, spun around and went sheet-white—by order of appearance, if not sequentially.

"Ed?" He stared at Archie's banged-up phiz and swallowed, hard.

Archie sneered, "Didn't your mama tell you to never walk under ladders?"

Blevins hesitated, as though testing for quicksand before committing himself. "Yeah. Doesn't everybody's?"

"Lucky for ol' Don, here," Ed said, "he didn't need to walk under the one that sent you sprawling. Even with the clamps unscrewed, it sat snug as a bug on top of Ramey's van, till you grabbed the end of it."

Archie stepped closer. "Good thing I happened along. She might've been hurt real bad. Like the burn in the shower she got. And the bashed-in skull she could've got from that jerry-rigged desk chair."

The mail clutched in Blevins's hand bent double. The rubber band bundling it drooped an inch beneath the fold. "What ladder? What are you talking about?"

Ed rocked back on his heels, chuckling. "Brings to mind a new cellie that come on our block. Highway, we called him, 'cause he got riled when everything didn't go like he thought it ought to."

The rocking ceased. Ed sucked his teeth. "Highway was a sly one, I'll give 'im that, but he picked the wrong road to venture down. Wasn't long till somebody broke both his axles and carved a hole clean through his radiator."

Ed smiled. "You savvy what I'm sayin', Blevins?"

The postman licked his lips. He glanced over his shoulder, as though expecting the cavalry to come 'round the corner. He blustered, "It's a felony to threaten a federal employee and—"

"What we're makin' you is a promise, Donny boy," Archie said.

Ed chucked Don on the arm, real friendly like, as men do, then said, "Good to see you, bub. Stop by the house for a beer sometime." Ed's closing remark popped fresh beads of sweat on Blevins's forehead.

"If I were you, I'd be finding a church and praying fervent that our niece doesn't get so much as a hang-nail, anytime soon."

A leisurely browse through flea markets usually re-laxed Ramey. Plainfield's revitalizing downtown was becoming a tourist mecca for collectors of all stripes, eBay merchandisers, trend speculators and lovers of all things funky, retro, kitchy, cheap, or dear to their im-pulsive hearts.

In the old brick warehouse where women once crouched over industrial sewing machines to stitch trouser seams and shirt plackets, a wide, center aisle now divided stalls framed with two-by-fours cladded in chicken wire. The spaces varied from narrow niches to room-size, and the merchandise from overpriced junk to elegant antiques imported from European estate sales.

For over two hours, Ramey had fingered and hoisted and scrutinized thousands of dollars worth of tchotchkes, fabric, furniture and artwork that might wend their way into a future staging job.

A new vendor's booth cleverly signed By the Yard specialized in lace and embroidered trims, and shelves of leather-bound classics. Ramey's violent opposition to books strictly as room decoration didn't stop her from cadging onto bargains for her reading pleasure.

The jacketless copy of Thomas Wolfe's, *Look Homeward, Angel* was a 1929 first edition and marked accordingly. It smelled mildewed and dust-steeped, the paper brittle and brown at the edges. Skimming the first page, the phrase *dark miracle of chance* jumped out, then *rugged young widow.*

Thoroughly spooked, she jammed the novel back in place and hurried from the booth to the neighboring one. She should be home, not dawdling the afternoon away, creeping herself out reading passages in a musty old book like a gypsy does tea leaves.

Sips of springwater from the bottle she'd smuggled in her shoulder bag swept the cotton from her mouth and hopefully doused her overactive imagination.

You can't go home again. Can't go home and twiddle your thumbs while a murder investigation grinds to a halt. Since opening those Pandora's boxes disguised as microfilm spool cartons, she'd reviewed, transposed, realigned and discarded clues pertaining to Shifty Falcone's death.

Mike hadn't disclosed everything he knew. It was an advantage, perhaps, to be less informed than the cops, but have an insider's knowledge of the suspects. Time would tell whether Mike's contradictory findings fit her deductive who, why and how scenario. Or, she admitted, were as superfluous as the rhinestones and feathers hot-glued to that perfectly lovely silk lampshade.

Left to its own devices, Ramey's finger would punch up Mike's phone number. Instead, the tip dusted the handle of an art nouveau standing ashtray. If she asked Ed to bring down a similar one from the attic, would he actually use it, or would he keep flicking his nasty cigarette butts into the shrubbery?

No thought required for that answer. People don't change. Intentions might be honorable in the extreme and behaviors might reflect them, but a leopard fed a vegan diet is still a spotted carnivore.

It was a goofy analogy, she allowed, but quintessentially *her,* which somewhat validated the point. As surely as speckled brown filters would continue to flock the boughs like bagworms, Ed was a thief and a conniver—whether he ever stole another nickel, or not.

Archie was Ed's eternal foil and sidekick, and Melba Jane was their camp follower, just as Portia would forever be the angel child and Ramey the sad-eyed beagle.

With a touch of bulldog and bloodhound on your father's side, she thought, delving again into her shoulder bag for her cell phone.

Mike had called four times since leaving her with Chatty Cathy's great-grandma at the library. The impulse to alert him to her evening plans diminished before she unlocked the cell's keypad. He'd listen, but couldn't act on accusations based on old newspaper stories, observations, educated guesses and womanly intuition.

Besides, what if she was wrong? No harm, no foul, if her amateur cloak-and-daggering failed to trap a killer. And there'd be hell to pay if it didn't.

Neither call she was about to make would be answered by Detective-Sergeant Mike Constantine. As she held the cell to her ear, a sinking sensation in her belly promised there'd be hell to pay, if she was right, too.

Mike pushed the stack of yellowed files on his desk aside to make room for a legal pad. Switching the phone receiver to his other hand, he said, "Tell me again, Mr. Blevins. Slower, this time."

"At about one, one-thirty, I was working my route, minding my own business, when those crazy old bastards jumped out and started threatening me. They said if anything else happened to Ramey, they'd come after me."

Mike's fingers tightened on the phone's receiver. "What do you mean by 'anything else'?"

Blevins described the household accidents the Dillinger brothers accused him of causing. As Blevins explained the horror of being accosted by two pissed-off geriatric ex-cons, Mike half listened while he consulted the Falcone case's field reports.

The morning of the murder, Corporal Maris, the uniform who'd escorted Ramey upstairs, had noted the broken office chair. After Ramey went outside, Maris went back to reexamine the chair, thinking that a murder weapon or something pertinent to the crime might have been shoved inside the seat or the support post.

Blevins said he didn't know when the alleged shower incident had occurred. By the bruises he'd seen on Archie Dillinger's face, the ladder accident must have happened that morning.

"Was Ramey there?" Mike asked.

Blevins bellowed, "How the hell do I know! I haven't talked to her since the big blowup on Saturday night."

"Oh, yeah?" Mike's pen tattooed the tablet. *Gotcha, ass wipe.* "What about that conversation you two had in the parking lot when she picked up her van?"

An extended silence funneled over the phone line. "Okay, so I forgot about that, but—"

"How did you know her van was there?"

"I saw it while I was on my route." Another pause. "Look, I didn't call you to get the third degree. Ed and Archie are criminals. They *threatened* me."

Abject terror must have paralyzed him, considering how long it had taken him to report the altercation. "Then I'd advise you to come down to the front desk and file a complaint against them," Mike said.

"I just did, didn't I?"

"A formal complaint requires a signature, Mr. Blevins. You know—like the one against your neighbors, the night Falcone was killed."

"The front— Aw, hell, forget it. Thanks, Constantine, for all your help."

Mike moved the receiver away from his ear an instant before Blevins slammed down his. "Another day, another satisfied customer."

Rickenbacher snickered. "What's up with our favorite mailman?"

"I don't know for sure." Mike repeated the gist of the nonformal complaint. "I can't decide if he's trying to lead me down the bunny trail or if the Dillinger brothers are."

"Just what we need. Another wascally wabbit."

The rookie was referring to Howard Chinn, Falcone's elusive stepson. Blevins's complaint had interrupted the rookie's updates, courtesy of the Encino, California P.D.

Mike had guessed right. Calls to Falcone's home telephone had been forwarded to Chinn's cell phone and were now going unanswered. Direct calls to

Chinn's cell tripped a "customer out of the area, or has switched off the unit" recording.

Chinn had been heard from but not seen for several days by any of his friends, neighbors or patrons of his favorite dives. By and large, his known associates weren't Rotary Club members. They could be lying, hungover, high, or simply reluctant to admit that they, like Howard Chinn and thousands like them, could beam up to Pluto without a ripple in the ozone layer.

Mike knocked back the dregs of a flat, lukewarm can of soda. He couldn't remember when a hunch proving right had ever felt so wrong. Or as frustrating as Ramey's communications blackout.

A sweep of the library's parking lot wasn't necessary to know she'd left the building. Squinting at a microfilm reader for hours on end would be an effective torture device the CIA should implement.

Wherever she'd wandered to, the outbound message on her cell phone indicated calls to the house were still in forwarding mode, and she was screening his.

There was too much Bill Patterson in that woman, along with a fair contribution of Dillinger, to sit idly by while a homicide investigation churned around her. Where she was and what was simmering in that canny mind had Mike wishing he'd cuffed her to him when he had the chance.

Falcone's stabbing didn't read as premeditated.

Rather than mitigate, that escalated the danger. Seasoned killers don't sweat the small stuff. Nancy Drew Burke fit that category, except to a murderer who'd had thirty hours and counting to think about life in prison, or syringes loaded with sodium thiopental, pavulon and potassium chloride

"I can't win for losing," the rookie groused.

Somewhat grateful for the diversion, Mike asked, "What makes you say that?"

"First, Ed Dillinger isn't quite good enough for a homicide charge. Then Blevins's alibi seems too tight for coincidence. Last night, you liked Howard Chinn. Today, after I spent all morning and half the friggin' afternoon on the phone, it's pretty obvious you're not liking him for it so much, either."

"Yeah, I do." The voices in Mike's head were like schoolkids yammering, "Pick me, pick me!" Another under-the-radar possibility lurked in the shadows, taunting him. Who could think straight with that kind of racket rattling in his brain?

He chafed his face, knowing the Greek chorus could all sit down and shut up and solid answers would still hover beyond his reach.

"Based on your info," he said, "Chinn had a stronger motive than Ed Dillinger."

"Twenty-five-thousand bucks stronger. Falcone's life insurance broker hasn't returned my call yet, but if the policy carries a double indemnity clause, Chinn stands to collect fifty Gs."

Mike snorted, "In California, that'll buy him maybe a year's rent on a halfway decent condo."

"People kill for less than that every day, Sarge. A pizza delivery kid in St. Louis got his throat slit yesterday for eighteen dollars and change."

Mike eyed the files from the basement's morgue. Pages were missing; others nearly illegible from coffee stains, water damage, typewriter ribbons unchanged since the Coolidge administration.

From what he had gathered, upon their arrest for multiple bank robberies, the Other Dillinger Gang had $2,763 on them. The amount of money from the original five heists they were suspected of was between $125,000 and $200,000. A plea bargain reduced the robbery counts to three, but the heavy sentences imposed reflected President Johnson's declared war on crime. What was absent from the records was an explanation for the discrepancy in the amount reported stolen, or whether it was recovered.

"Sorry, kid," Mike said, pushing back his chair. "I've gotta get out of here for a while. Clear my head before it explodes."

"And maybe swing by Ms. Burke's to get the skinny on those accidents she's been having?"

"Among other things." The answer was ripe for

misinterpretation, judging by the grin on Rickenbacher's kisser. Let him think what he wanted. It'd
give him something to do until that insurance broker
called back.

Sport coat slung over his shoulder, Mike kicked the
desk chair into the kneehole, then cursed when his
phone rang.

"Go on, I'll take it." Rickenbacher punched the
lighted extension button. "Hey, Doc. Yeah, yeah, Sir
Speedy, I owe you a steak dinner." He grabbed a pencil. "The lab test said it's what?"

Mike watched the rookie write glycols, glycol ethers
and polyglocols on the back of an envelope.

"Excellent," Rickenbacher said. "Now give it to me
again in English."

While the showboating county M.E. clarified that
chemical composition for his partner, Mike grabbed the
phone book off the shelf. He flipped through the Yellow Pages like a man possessed.

Sometimes the pieces meshed as neatly as a chain
on a cog. At others, an absent, unquantified element
was the cotter pin. Without it, the facts refused to link
in an orderly fashion.

His finger tabbed the franchise auto repair shop's
bold-printed telephone number. That damned linchpin
was smeared on Shifty Falcone's shirt all along. What
a genius criminal investigator who considered himself

a skilled shade-tree mechanic had missed, a gas chronograph-mass spectrometer had identified.

Glycols. Glycol ethers. Polyglocol.

Chemistryspeak for a spot or two of common, ordinary brake fluid.

17

Hernando's Hideaway was as secluded as the song it was named for. Hungry tourists who negotiated the twisty two-lane south from Plainfield often cruised past the unmarked drive that led to the restaurant's parking lot.

Over a decade ago, annexation for an electrical generating plant had brought the landmark eatery into the municipal fold. Residential development would follow eventually. For now, the burned-out shell of the old Macklin place marked where the suburbs petered out and rural began.

Hernando's brown stucco facade and tiled roof blended into the wooded hillside like a rectangular rock formation, albeit one with arched, stained glass windows and doors.

A placard on the locked front entrance advised customers to knock three times and whisper, "Joe sent me," when Ernie Schmidt, the restaurant's owner, slid open the hatch. Regulars assumed they'd be welcomed inside with or without the password. The aroma of authentic Tex-Mex cuisine wafting out was too mouth-watering to chance it.

Around the side, a solid inset door led directly to the bar. Rumor had it that the secret to Ernie Schmidt's success wasn't the food or ambience. His after-hours, high-stakes poker games were held by invitation only. Supposedly, from the day the annexation proposal garnered approval, the mayor's luck improved and the sheriff couldn't buy a pot.

That aura of skullduggery had an odd appeeal to Ramey. Where better than Hernando's to lay a trap for a killer, or prove her hunch wrong.

Preston had arrived moments after the hostess showed Ramey to a table in the main dining room. Spying her sister and husband from the foyer, Portia made her way to them, sans escort.

"I thought I'd be the first one here," she said in lieu of hello.

"That'll be the day." Preston's tone was teasing, but earned him a sour look. Portia dodged the kiss he attempted to plant on her cheek.

For her sister to not keep up appearances in public was a first.

"Love that sweater," she told Ramey. "You should wear purple more often. And did I catch a glimpse of slacks instead of blue jeans under the tablecloth?"

Like a nougat inside a chocolate shell, a compliment was in there somewhere. Ramey was almost sure of it.

Her sister's green eyes flicked to the fourth place setting. "Is a certain someone joining us?"

Preston started. "Like who? Chase?"

"If you ever listened to anything our son said, you'd know he's interviewing for a summer job at the arcade in the mall. The 'who' I had in mind is the guy Ramey's been spending a lot of time with lately. Officially, of course."

The dining room's lighting was as subtle as the murals painted on the walls, but Ramey felt a blush, whether it showed on the outside, or not. A warning was implicit in her glare at Portia. Thankfully the waiter's offer to bring something from the bar was of greater import.

"I'll retain water for days," Portia told him, "but you can't come to Hernando's and not have a margarita."

"I can." Preston ordered his usual Scotch, no rocks. Two upraised fingers signaled a double.

"Iced tea for me," Ramey said, "and the check's mine, too." Before her guests could argue, she said, "I mean it. It's the least I can do after calling and asking you both to drop everything and meet me for an early dinner."

Portia flapped a hand. "An excuse not to write copy for Sunday's open house ads was a real sacrifice."

"I have to go back to the office tonight," Preston

said. "I wish you'd picked someplace not so far out in the boondocks to have dinner."

A dig for an appetizer. How typical. Maybe she'd stick him with the tab after all. "Gee, I don't know why we don't do this more often."

"Don't start, you two." Portia nibbled a tortilla chip from the table's glazed pottery bowl. "Especially not here. I have lots of fond memories of this place and I won't let you spoil them."

Hernando's had been their parents' favorite restaurant and a proving ground for their daughters' lessons in table manners. Ramey's mouth quirked at the iced tea glass the waiter set in front of her, wishing she'd ordered a Shirley Temple in their honor.

Impulsively, she hoisted her glass and said, "To Bill and Sylvia."

"Why, Ramey, aren't you forgetting someone?" Preston's glass clinked hers a second time. "And to Stan Burke, without whom no family toast would be complete."

Mike tapped his steering wheel with the heel of his hand. A fender-bender had backed traffic up for blocks. To his right, a parking lot beckoned.

Screw procedure. He kicked up the unmarked's grill lights and the gumball on the dashboard. Catching the flash in the rearview mirror, the driver ahead of him eased forward enough for Mike to crank a sharp ninety into the lot.

"Hernando's Hideaway" drummed in his ears. Another call to Ramey's house had connected to her voicemail. When Melba Jane finally answered Mike's pounding at the front door, she'd said Ramey had pulled into the driveway just long enough to holler to Archie that she was meeting Preston and Portia at Hernando's for dinner.

And you couldn't ask for a finer, more remote, potentially fatal location to stage another accident.

Whipping onto a side street, then left down another, Mike invented a shortcut the long way, slowing, then gunning through four-way intersections with the impunity of a cop answering a bona fide call.

Circling back to the main drag, the roadway narrowed from four to two lanes. Glitzy commercial development and apartment complexes devolved to increasingly woebegone houses. Burglar bars secured windows where dope was the tenants' most valuable possession. Every third house had a Beware of Dog sign tacked to the porch pillar and a chained pit bull to back it up.

Farther on, a billboard staked in a rolling, former cow pasture boasted of a future industrial park. Its nearest neighbor was a salvage yard enclosed by a post and sheet-metal fence.

Mike shot around a motorhome lugging up the grade. The speedometer wagged at seventy—nearly twice the legal limit on this stretch. Still, not an inch of pavement or the weedy verge escaped his scrutiny.

Dozens of skid marks blackened the asphalt like lazy, double parentheses. Dented, sagging guardrails hugged the shoulder, or what was left of them, anyway. Tow truck drivers made their mortgage payments winching up vehicles that sailed off this particular edge into the steep ravines.

Fear sketched images of Ramey's van upended and flames licking the undercarriage in Mike's mind. Even without sabotage, she'd racked up almost as many speeding tickets as birthdays. Driving under the influence of complacency was as dangerous as alcohol consumption.

But not this time, Mike thought, spotting the break in the leafy hedgerow surrounding the restaurant. Letting up on the accelerator, he doused the emergency lights. The muscles at the back of his neck and across his shoulders and gut began to relax. It was only a reprieve. A temporary one at that.

Shaded by the branches of a century oak tree, the empty ladder rack on Ramey's van itself resembled shiny, horizontal rungs. Several spaces over was a silver Mercedes, parked slantwise—a precaution certain drivers took to protect their vehicles from door dings, often reprised with a wicked key scratch. Farther down, a pearl-white Escalade with a Boulevard Realty decal on the rear window established that this dinner party for three wasn't into carpooling.

Mike backed into a space between a conversion van and a mud-plastered Jeep and killed the engine. Rickenbacher answered his cell on the first ring. "What's your twenty?" Mike said.

"I batted oh-for-three on those search warrants you wanted. The judge said there isn't sufficient probable cause on the Burke house, the Carruthers', or the car."

It was a long shot, Mike admitted, but worth a swing.

"The good news is Encino picked up Howard Chinn. It'll be a while before they can verify his alibi."

Mike said, "In the meantime, I want you to surveil Ramey's house. Don't get too close. Ed Dillinger smokes out on the porch. If he doesn't make you, that old busybody across the street will."

"What are you going to be doing?"

"Playing it by ear." Almost ending the call, he shouted, "Hey," then, "Unless all three Dillingers take off somewhere in a cab, stay put. I wouldn't put it past Ed to decoy you for the hell of it."

When Mike entered Hernando's bar by the side entrance, a Travis Tritt ballad was playing on the sound system. Something about a storm in search of thunder.

Mike related on several levels. One of them named Ramey Burke.

Narrow pass-throughs in the mirrored back bar allowed service to the dining room. Finding the best observation post from the stools along the carved, rosewood bar would be interesting. The opening directly opposite the Carruthers' and Ramey's table was too risky. Choice number two, a right-angled perspective, was already occupied by a city councilman and a stunning redhead, who might not be his wife. The leftward position Mike took by default was in Preston Carruthers's line of sight, whenever he turned his head toward Ramey.

The bartender, a lanky fellow who needed a haircut worse than Mike did, set down a bowl of Chex mix and a napkin with flamenco dancers printed on it. "What'll ya have?"

"Bourbon and water with a twist." Mike laid a five on the bar. "Hold the bourbon."

"Funny guy, eh?" The bartender's gaze lowered to the badge Mike revealed on his inner jacket pocket. "Comin' right up, sir. And it's on the house."

In the dining room, a waiter served salad plates and removed empty glassware. Whatever he said to Carruthers received an affirmative nod. Portia shook her head, spoke to the waiter, then smiled and nodded.

The soles of Mike's wingtips scraped back and forth

on the brass rail they rested on. My, oh, my, what he wouldn't give for a button microphone hidden in the table's floral centerpiece.

"The Dillingers had to know," Ramey said. "During the hearing, the same reporter who broke the story about their arrest all but slandered Daddy. The reporter accused him of everything from accessory before the fact to obstructing justice."

Portia's fork batted at a cherry tomato. "Yes, but as insulting as it must have been for him, what about Mom? Talk about divided loyalties. And guilt? You know she must have blamed herself for everything. Like it was her fault that her brothers robbed banks for a living."

"That's just it. It infuriated me so much, I didn't go home after I left the library for fear I'd slap the crap out of Ed, Archie and Melba Jane."

The waiter reappeared with Preston's fresh drink, Portia's cup of decaf and a pitcher to refill Ramey's glass. The presweetened, icy-cold tea tasted wonderful, but didn't slake her thirst. Anxiety and lying were like standing in front of a box fan with your mouth open.

"It should have occurred to me long before now," she went on, "but of all the banks in this state—in the whole freakin' country—why did the Other Dillinger

Gang hit two in a town where their brother-in-law was a cop?"

Derision edged Preston's chuckle. "History repeating itself somewhat, I suppose." The tines of his fork stacked bits of arugula, red onion and peppers. "I read somewhere that John Dillinger's first robbery was stealing coal by the ton from railroad gondolas in his hometown."

"Or," Portia said, "the Dillingers truly believed Dad *would* intervene for them. Not out-and-out aid and abet, but..."

"Let some other cop in some other town make the arrest," Ramey finished for her. "It makes a lousy kind of sense for them to think he'd choose to spare Mom a little pain and embarrassment."

"Fat chance of that happening," Portia argued, around a chunk of cucumber. "Dad was color-blind. Saw everything in black-and-white. No gray areas, not even for her."

Despite the element of truth in that, Ramey bristled. Portraying their father as a stiff-necked ogre wasn't fair. Some boundaries he set were rigid; others were negotiable—particularly, she admitted, for the baby of the family.

And they wouldn't be having this conversation at all if Bill Patterson hadn't fallen in love with and married a never-charged burglar by the name of Sylvia Dillinger.

Ramey choked down a few bites of salad, then pushed the plate aside. Stress usually amped her appetite. Breathing usually amped her appetite. Just thinking about the barbecued brisket, new potatoes and asparagus she'd ordered provoked her gag reflex.

Preston looked at the discards, then at her. "Are you on a diet or something?"

"No," she said, at least to the front half of his question. It was the *or something* that turned her stomach inside out. Wringing the napkin in her lap, she blew out a sigh. "I intended to wait until dessert, but I might as well fess up and get on with the favor I have to ask."

Amusement, then concern rived Portia's expression, as though realizing whatever curtailed her sister's caloric intake must be serious.

Preston sipped from his highball glass, his attention not on Ramey, but on something beyond her shoulder—in all likelihood, a panoramic view of the hostess's cleavage.

Leaning forward, Ramey rested her arms on the table to block the provocative scenery and imply earnestness. "You guys were right. I shouldn't have let the Dillingers barge in and take over the house."

Preston grunted. "In addition to myself and Portia, that apology is a week late for Mr. Falcone."

"If they killed him, which I honestly don't believe they did," Ramey said. "Let Mike Constantine figure that out. What I can't forgive, forget, or *live with* is them almost costing Daddy his career."

Portia's hand clasped Ramey's wrist. "That was thirty-five years ago. Letting it tear you apart now won't change a thing."

Ramey summoned every ounce of wounded pride she could fake. "Maybe it's silly, but I can't stand the thought of going home as long as they're there, much less pretending we're one big, happy family."

The waiter's arrival with their entrées couldn't have been timed better had Ramey conspired with him in advance. His fussing and fawning and tipcentric eagerness raised a planned dramatic pause to an intermission.

When he finally retreated, Ramey plastered on a brave smile. "Let's relax and have a nice dinner, all right? Talk about the real estate market, the weather—anything as long as it isn't Ed, Archie and Melba Jane."

Preston said, "But what did you mean—"

"Then afterward," she continued, "I'm taking the Dillingers back to the Samaritan Mission. If your invitation still stands, I'll lock up the house and run away to yours for a few days."

"Of course it still stands," Preston blurted. "In fact, I'll drive the Dillingers downtown while you're packing."

"Thanks, but I want the satisfaction of telling them exactly what I think of them, then showing them the door."

Anticipating his rebuttal, she added, "If they refuse to leave, a call to their parole officer will take care of it."

He nodded, chuckling. "I'm sure Gordon Sweeney would be more than happy to oblige."

The brisket Ramey ordered was slow-cooked to perfection. On one side, new potatoes swam in melted butter, their skins sprinkled with parsley. On the other were steamed asparagus spears drizzled with lemon. How she'd swallow a bite of it now, she couldn't imagine.

"Just promise you won't change your mind." Portia's green eyes bored into hers. "You have no idea how much I want you to come stay with me."

Ramey shook her head, then bowed it, afraid her own eyes would deceive her. "No," she said, "it's too late for that." Then wished with all her heart that she could.

"Sure thing, Mike. I can set up a checkpoint in ten or fifteen minutes." Captain Bynum belly-laughed. "Son, whatever you're smokin', save some of it for me."

"I don't have time to explain." But Mike did, as concisely as he could, and gave details of the location he'd chosen. "It's my only chance, Cap. I guarantee, if that evidence is there, it won't be an hour or two from now."

A pause, then, "Hang on a sec."

Sixty or more ticked by as Mike sat in the car, his pulse skittering whenever the restaurant door opened.

"Lucky for you, it's a slow night," Bynum said. "A tow truck and four units are en route. Two were patrolling close enough to get the ball rollin' pretty quick."

Mike took a moment to exhale. "I owe you, Cap. *Huge.*"

"Ten-four on that." Bynum cleared his throat. "Gotta ask, though, if you hook this lunker you're fishing for, what about entrapment? Homicide requesting a Traffic Division checkpoint at a specified location smells pretty hinky to me."

Mike had considered this moments after Preston Carruthers looked in his direction at the restaurant. "I didn't buy the booze for him, or pour it down his throat. It doesn't seem any different than netting a couple of shit-faced bubbas at a scheduled stop."

"Works for me." Bynum laughed again. "If the wife wasn't putting supper on the table, I'd mosey down there to watch myself."

"I'll let you know what happens, Cap."

"See that you do."

The next call terminated Rickbacher's surveillance and invited him to join the party south of town. Assuming there'd be anything to celebrate.

By the beam of a penlight, Mike copied pertinent information on a half-dozen sheets of notebook paper.

The exercise muffled but didn't mute the captain's question that resounded in his head. If, by legal definition, his strategy was determined to be entrapment, the odds were high that a judge would throw out any evidence confiscated as a result of the stop.

"No guts, no prayer of an indictment." Keying the ignition, he stifled the urge to get out of there before any certain someones exited the building and recognized his car.

True to Bynum's word, two patrol units, light bars flashing, were parked diagonally from each other on the road's respective shoulders. Uniforms pulled boxes of flares, blaze-orange cones and sawhorses from their trunks.

Another unit pulled in from the south. As Mike strode toward the first two, a fourth blue-and-white nosed in behind his unmarked car. After introductions and handshakes all around, Mike distributed the sheets of paper from his notebook.

"If it's all the same to you guys, how about Ellery and Jenks take northbound and O'Hara and Skaggs on the south."

Ellery, a sergeant by rank and power lifter by bulk, needn't be told the assignments weren't arbitrary. He grinned, as if to say, *Let the good times roll.*

Mike dictated the make, model and tag number he'd circled on the papers. "That doesn't mean everyone else gets a by. This is a legitimate checkpoint. I suspect this individual in particular will reek of probable cause and flunk the Breathalyzer."

"What if he does?" Jenks asked, then partially answered his own question with another. "Will he be alone in the vehicle?"

"Should be." Damn well better be.

All bets were off if Carruthers decided he was too drunk to drive and hitched a ride home with his wife. Or, Mike realized, Carruthers could leave the restaurant first, get busted for DUI, then tell Portia to repark her SUV in Hernando's lot to take him home in his car.

O'Hara said, "A tow from out here's gonna cost this dude a hundred bucks, easy."

"If we're lucky," Mike said, "the price he pays will be a lot higher than that."

Ellery waggled his flashlight at an oncoming sedan. "Let's open up this pop stand, fellas. We've got customers lining up on aisle two."

Returning to his car, Mike rolled down the window and slumped down in the seat, the headrest even with the crown of his head. Revolving light bars, butting headlights and silver and orange reflectors brought to mind a scene from a sci-fi flick. Strange how a road with relatively sparse traffic became gridlocked when both lanes were blocked.

The stops seldom lasted longer than a couple of minutes. Most motorists drove off with a smile and a wave. A teenage driver with three other passengers sneered, "Trying to make your quota early this month?"

Mike laughed into his fist when Ellery drawled, "How'd ya guess, kid? Two more tickets and my wife wins a toaster oven." Elbow propped on the window ledge, he added, "Care to knock that down to one?"

"I was just—uh, no, sir. No insult meant, Officer."

A northbound white SUV eased around the curve, a blonde behind the wheel. Behind it, a cargo van with technicolor starbursts was tinged red by the Escalade's taillights.

The unmarked unit on the shoulder didn't rate a glance from Portia Carruthers as she glided past. Before Ramey's front bumper drew even with Mike's rear one, his cell phone rang. "We've got to stop meeting like this, Little Chief."

"Were you busted down to traffic?" she asked. "Or are you moonlighting?"

"Neither." He looked up at her through her passenger window. "Take care driving home."

She scowled. "I want to know what's going on, Mike."

"Negatory." A minivan he didn't remember seeing at the restaurant came into view. "I'll give you a call, later. It'll be nice if you answer it. For now, just face forward and keep moving."

"But—"

"Do it, Ramey. Please." He pressed the disconnect.

Several eternities elapsed before the minivan, then a blue Ford pickup advanced enough for a silver Mercedes to appear in Mike's side mirror. Portia's SUV had vanished around the next bend. Another few yards and Ramey's van would, as well.

It was Officer Jenks who initiated the "Hi, how are you, sir, would you mind showing me your license and proof of insurance?" His casual thumbs-up indicated that the attorney was about to participate in the night's first field sobriety test.

Slapping the sportscar's roof with his palm, Carruthers mouthed off about law degrees and rights and golfing buddies in high places. Jenks calmly explained that a Breathalyzer would resolve any difference of opinion regarding Carruthers's level of impairment.

As Mike approached, the attorney shoved Jenks and yanked his ID from the cop's hand. Chuckling, Mike shook his head. "Counselor, I know it's April, but I swear it feels like Santa just came to town."

"What the— Where did you—"

Ellery snapped a cuff on Carruthers's wrist and spun him around none too gently to shackle the other. "Sir, you're under arrest for assaulting an officer, driving while intoxicated, drunk and disorderly…" Grinding an elbow into the squirming attorney's back, he added,

"And if you don't stop fighting me, I'll tack on resisting arrest."

"I'll have your badge, Constantine. I'll have *all* your badges."

"Promises, promises." Ellery recited Miranda as he assisted Carruthers to his patrol unit for transport to the drunk tank. By the obscenities scorching the air, the attorney had no use for the right to remain silent.

A caravan from the checkpoint to the city's impound lot was led by a flatbed tow truck. Mike tagged behind, his gaze focused on the sparkling Mercedes, swaying gently like a hula dancer on an elevated stage.

Bringing up the rear was a frustrated Rickenbacher, who thought he'd missed out on all the fun.

"Carruthers losing his cool was pretty comical," Mike had told him. "The joke will be on us, though, if all we wind up nailing him for is a few misdemeanors."

18

Cellar windows to attic, the house was lit up like an airport control tower when Ramey slowed for the turn into the driveway.

With a quick shift to reverse, both literally and figuratively, she angled the van into the curb in front of her neighbor's house. Nobody in the whole freakin' family played fair. Why should she?

Mike Constantine didn't, either. Whatever he was up to with that DUI checkpoint had demolished her carefully laid plan.

Entering through the kitchen, she plopped her shoulder bag on the island, toed off her shoes and helped herself to a cup of coffee. Melba Jane had left on the radio—an orchestral arrangement of "The Point of No Return" from *Phantom of the Opera* was playing.

Irony certainly wasn't in short supply these days.

Ear pressed to the cracked cellar door, the hum of the water heater's burner unit was the only detectable sound Ramey heard. Living room, empty. A sitcom on TV entertained the furniture in the billiard room.

Hugging the stairway wall—the secret to Ed's stealthiness—Ramey paused midway up. No voices reached her, but the pitter-patter of smallish felons' feet echoed down from the attic.

She almost felt sorry for them. Ponce de Leon searched in vain for the Fountain of Youth. It had taken her a week to figure out what Mr. Green Jeans, Mr. Fix-it and Mrs. Clean were up to, but they'd had the same success at finding their Fountain of Ill-Gotten Swag.

Unless one of them *had* found it and rehidden it from the other two. Or two of them, specifically Archie and Melba Jane, were pulling a fast one on Ed, until the homicide heat cooled off.

The Three Musketeers, they weren't, but they did maintain a screwball sense of loyalty. Maybe that was a tenet behind "honor among thieves." Steal from everybody else, but don't rat out or rip off your own.

That semicomforting thought propelled Ramey to the second-floor landing. The attic's creaks and groans eclipsed proximate noises. Light spilled out of every doorway. Ed and Archie were in the attic. Melba Jane was "cleaning" somewhere on this floor.

Ramey chalked up her blindness to their search to a hundred distractions. The newspaper archives tipped her off to the never-found loot. It was still missing, apparently. She gulped down her coffee, ostensibly to calm her nerves and as a precaution against an accidental burn, in the event she and her aunt startled the bejesus out of each other.

For the first time, she identified with her father, sock footing through the house, hoping against hope that Ramey and her boyfriend-of-the-month were behaving themselves on the couch.

If Melba Jane's hearing was as acute as a horny teenager's, she'd have heard the *cri-i-ck* of the floorboard in the hall outside her and Archie's bedroom.

Ramey stood in the doorway, her mouth open, her brain not quite registering the visual signals it was receiving. When all synapses finally did fire, all she could manage was, "Oh. My. God."

Her aunt sat on the area rug beside the bed. At its foot were feather pillows, a stack of folded sheets, their matching cases and a thermal blanket. She wrenched sideward. A banded stack of hundreds toppled from a gash in the mattress and joined the others in her lap.

The two women gawked at each other, stunned dumb for what seemed like several minutes. Melba Jane said, "Oh, hi, I—uh, didn't know you were home," then wriggled in front of the mattress and crossed her arms over the money.

"Wish I could say 'nice try.'" Ramey set her mug on the dresser and stalked to the new residential branch of the Bank of Plainfield. "But you're not even close." She motioned for her aunt to move aside.

Flattened against the bed, Melba Jane's chin receded and her lower lip pooched. "You got no right sneaking up on an old lady that way."

Ramey bent to grip the rug's fringed hem.

"Could've affrighted me into a heart attack or a stroke or something."

It was a strain, but with a slick hardwood floor and leverage, Ramey pulled the rug and her aunt away from the mattress. A veritable avalanche of cash tumbled from its innerspring vault.

Melba Jane gasped and clapped her cheek. "Merciful heavens. Will you lookee there? Hallelujah, it's a *miracle*. The Lord has provided!"

"Oh, for— Will you give it up, already?"

Paper bands cinched around each half-inch thick bundle were stamped $10,000. Counting the piles in her aunt's lap, fanned on the floor and the rest scooped from the mattress, God's largesse amounted to 180,000, mint-condition dollars.

Melba Jane grunted and huffed as she laboriously gained her feet. "Stuffed in there like they were, they put kinks in Archie's back, then mine after we traded sides. They sure are pretty, though, all heaped together. Willie McKinley looks so real, he might could pucker up and whistle 'The Star-Spangled Banner.'"

Bereft of an appropriate rejoinder, Ramey examined the rent in the mattress's welted edge. Tiny hand-sewn stitches extended six or seven inches on each side of the gap, then intersected with the manufacturer's machine-sewn seam.

"Is that how you found the money? Because of the lumps in the mattress?"

"Eh, kinda-sorta. I never dreamed what the lumps were. I was fixing to make up the bed when it struck me that if I jabbed a wooden spoon or something in from the side, I could maybe jigger the batting a mite."

Melba Jane's chuckle was more bemused than amused. "Truth be told, I done poked one of your grandma's hat pins into every mattress in the house. Guess I never skewered the right spot." She clucked her tongue, her hands rubbing up and down her bare arms. "Lawsy, the boys are gonna chew me up, spit me out and stomp the wet spot when they hear about this."

The knot rising in Ramey's throat wouldn't soften, no matter how hard she swallowed. "All three of you go downstairs and stay there. I'll be down in a little while."

Her expression must have convinced her aunt that this wasn't the time to argue. "All right, hon. If that's what you want."

Hesitating at the door, she said, "Beg pardon for asking, but Ed and Archie'll want to know what you're gonna do with the money."

"I don't know."

"But—"

"Go *on*, Melba Jane. And shut the door behind you."

The moment it did, the tears Ramey struggled to hold back streamed down her cheeks. Falling over on the bed, she buried her head in her arms and cried, just as Sylvia Patterson surely had whenever her secret became too painful to endure.

The mattress Ramey sprawled on was the third her parents had bought over the years. Her mother must have hollowed out each replacement, cached the money, then resown the slit.

You made your bed, now lie in it. Sylvia said it so many times that Ramey swore, she'd wash her own mouth out with soap if she ever repeated it to her children.

If only she'd known...

It wasn't just a hoary old heirloom of a phrase mothers have annoyed their kids with since time immemorial. For her mother, placed in the impossible position of betraying her brothers, or betraying her husband, it represented a self-imposed life sentence with no possibility of parole.

With Ramey's realization came a certainty that from first mattress to last, Sylvia always hid the money in the same place. Never at the head, cushioned by a pillow. Not near the foot, well beyond the reach of a petite woman's toes. Always on the side. *Her* side.

"I can't bear the thought of your daddy sleeping on this mattress after I'm gone," she'd said the day before she died. "Promise you'll take it to the attic. Don't breathe a word about it to anyone and that darlin' man'll never know the difference."

Odd as the request was, Ramey fulfilled it—with one minor exception. Rather than wrestle the mattress up the attic stairs, she'd exchanged it for the one in the seldom-used guest room. The guest room where Melba Jane and Archie had slept for a week.

There's no such thing as coincidence was another favorite saying of her mother's. *Just because we can't divine a reason, doesn't mean there isn't one.*

"Okay, Mom," she whispered at the ceiling. "If sometimes I walk into a room and catch a faint whiff of lily of the valley, maybe you inspired Melba Jane's idea to fix the mattress. I hope you understand that I can't let them keep this money."

Wiping her eyes and face, she blew her nose on the pillowcase, then exhaled a deep, ragged breath. She felt wrung-out. Wretched. And absolved of and perhaps forgiven for her growing bitterness toward her mother for protecting her brothers instead of her husband.

It was impossible to know for sure, but she sensed the choice hadn't been that simple. The allegations about Bill Patterson's collusion with the Dillinger brothers almost coincided with their capture. Even if

Sylvia *wanted* to return the money, she was trapped. Everybody would believe Bill Patterson was involved from the beginning.

Ramey tossed aside the grotty pillowcase and began filling its twin with the loot. "The hundred-and-eighty-thousand-dollar question is, what am I going to do with it?"

Her disposal problem was similar to her mother's. The statute of limitations on the robberies had probably expired, but Ramey couldn't just hand the money over to Mike.

Sylvia Patterson made her bed and lay in it for thirty years to protect her husband's integrity. For her daughter to now do the presumed *right thing* would resurrect all the accusations and innuendos against an honorable, honest cop who could no longer defend himself.

Currency was paper. Paper burned. Destroying government property was a felony, but the Feds had to catch her first.

She hoisted the bulging pillowcase over her shoulder, like a hobo who'd cashed in his trust fund. Strike a match to it and Ed and Archie will throw themselves on the fire like a stop, drop and roll in reverse.

Coach Vince Lombardi once said, "A good defense is the best offense." Or was it, "A good offense is the best defense"?

Now that Mike thought about it, he was pretty sure the latter was correct. Oh, well. From a legal standpoint, the former suited his purposes—hence the patrol unit parked outside the tall, chain-link fence topped with razor wire.

Standard procedure was to inventory the contents of an impounded vehicle—glove box, console and trunk included. The written record minimized the chance an owner would accuse a tow truck driver or the police of stealing the gazillion-dollar tiara allegedly stuffed under the seat of a '67 rust bucket Plymouth.

There being two sides to every statute, procedure also discouraged tow truck drivers or rogue cops from lifting bona fide valuables from vehicles in temporary police custody.

Impoundees were far more prone to whine, "I've been robbed," than tow operators and cops were to surrender to petit larceny. The best insurance against liability was to cover your ass in advance.

Mike stepped from the unmarked unit and strode toward Preston's Mercedes thinking, and if you're a criminal investigator about to make a damn fool of yourself, you might as well have a civilian, a uniform and your partner as witnesses.

Phil Thames, the tow company's driver, squinted at the sportscar, which had been deposited like an island in a sea of clunkers. "She's a beauty, ain't she?" He handed Mike the keys. "I don't haul many of these, as a rule."

Mike's ears pricked. "Generally speaking? Or this vehicle in particular?"

"Second trip this week. Picked 'er up at a house, oh, along about Monday or Tuesday."

"Tuesday," Mike said. "Where did you take it?"

Phil pointed in the general direction of downtown Plainfield. "About a half block from that private parking garage on Mt. Vernon Avenue. She fired right up after I eased 'er down at the curb. The owner said he must've flooded it when he tried to start 'er."

"I need a copy of that trip ticket," Mike said. "ASAP."

"Sure thing."

Carruthers's luck was running out. Mike could taste it. Catching stupid perps was like shooting fish in the proverbial barrel. Sometimes the smart ones got away; sometimes they outsmarted themselves.

But not always, he cautioned the chirpy little bird in the back of his mind. Just *sometimes*.

The sportscar's two-seater cabin, illuminated from opposing sides by Mike's and Rickenbacher's Maglite beams, was as bright and nearly as immaculate as an operating theater.

"By the book," he reminded the rookie and himself. They'd gloved up to prevent destroying any forensic evidence that might be present, but couldn't be collected, even if a blood smear waved and hollered, "Yo, dudes, here I am."

A trace of new car smell mingled with a men's cologne and a noxious floral perfume. The solid, goosenecked console between the seats was devoted to navigational, communications and climate-control equipment. A sweet ride, but shy of places to chuck spare change and candy bar wrappers.

The doors' cargo pockets and minuscule glove box yielded the usual junk—a mini atlas, pens, a cell phone charger, various receipts, Trojan condoms, breath mints, a CD's plastic jewel box.

"Sarah McLachlan?" Mike ejected the disc from the CD player and popped it in its case. "There must be a warm, fuzzy side to Carruthers that I missed."

Rickenbacher rolled his eyes. "A wise man plays his lady's tunes when she's in the car."

"Is that a fact? I knew I'd been doing something wrong all these years. I couldn't quite put my finger on it."

The outside air temp hovered in the high forties. Sweat glistened on Mike's forehead and glued his shirt to his shoulder blades as they moved to the rear of the vehicle. The lid's chrome trefoil taunted him. Feelin' lucky, Mike?

"Careful with the buttons on that keyless gizmo," Phil said. "Smush the wrong 'un and the trunk opens backward and the roof retracts."

"It does?" Rickenbacher whistled softly.

"Lemme tell ya, it's somethin' to see. The back window swivels 'round and the top folds up lickety-split."

The uniform's utility belt creaked as he shifted his weight. "Can we get this over with, Sarge? With four units at the checkpoint, I need to go back out on patrol."

Mike sighed, closed his eyes and depressed the button under his thumb.

Rickenbacher's flashlight beam splashed across a leather CD keeper and a briefcase, both sitting upright. Draped lengthwise across them was Carruthers's suit-coat, folded lining side out. A set of golf clubs lay on the diagonal, the bag's butt-end snugged into a rounded, rear corner.

"Skimpy on luggage space, huh," the uniform said. "I guess if you can afford the wheels, you buy what you want to wear on vacation when you get there."

Mike switched his Maglite to his left hand. He bent at the waist, stretching to reach into the triangular-shaped space behind the golf bag. What he pulled out was a rumpled set of coveralls. The price tag still clipped at the armpit seam twirled in the breeze.

"Carhartt, extra large." Holding them up by the collar, he resisted the urge to grab a sleeve and tango across the impound lot. "And under them, sports fans, is what appears to be a fine-lookin', yellow and purple L.A. Lakers gym bag."

If Rickenbacher's jaw fell any farther, the retractable top of the Mercedes would fit between his molars.

Adrenaline flooded Mike's system like mainlined grain alcohol. "A hundred bucks says there's an ice pick with blood and brake fluid on it inside that bag." His thumb strummed across his fingertips. "What do you say? Any takers?"

The Dillingers greeted Ramey's entrance to the kitchen with wide, goofy smiles commonly associated with small children and ice-cream cones.

Ed patted the bench beside him. "Take a load off, honeybunch."

"I'll fetch you a fresh cup of coffee," Archie said.

Melba Jane trilled, "Cinnamon rolls. A baker's dozen is warming in the oven."

Ramey laughed in spite of herself. "Do you guys really think I'm that easy?" Sliding in beside Ed, she pinned the pillowcase between her feet. "The coffee, I'll take, since I left mine upstairs. But a pass on the cinnamon rolls."

Melba Jane looked crushed. "Are you sure?"

"She ain't hungry," Ed said. "Quit acting like she just kicked your damned dog."

Chastened, Melba Jane waddled sideways across the opposite booth, leaving the end for Archie. In front of Ramey he placed a handled, ceramic bowl with a maraca motif. It was shaped like a coffee cup, but was actually designed to serve chili. Archie, the master brownnoser, might as well have brought the entire carafe. And a straw.

"Here's the deal," she said. "You guys answer a few questions for me, then I'll tell you what I plan to do with the money." Hopefully she'd think of something by then.

"Shoot," Ed said.

"Why did you rob two banks here in town where your brother-in-law was on the police force?"

"Humph." The look Ed gave her was askance and then some. "Same reason we hit them others upstate. You see, hon, banks have vaults and vaults are inclined to have a fair pile of money in them."

"And there's cops in every town," Archie told her. "The secret to pulling a heist is staying outa handcuff range of any of 'em."

Ed added, "I know what you're really asking. The point you're missing is, our intention was to get away clean. If'n we had, nobody would've batted an eyelash about Bill."

Ramey sincerely doubted that. They'd have been arrested, eventually. The hue and cry might not have been as vicious, but the press and the public loved airing dirty laundry, particularly when cops are involved.

"So how did you get caught? From what I read in

the newspaper archives, your modus operandi was pretty slick."

"Oh, it was." Melba Jane snorted. "Until Mr. Brains of the Outfit over there got too big for his britches. He figured after we hit one bank, the police would be so busy that the other heist would be a pushover."

"And it was, by God," Ed said. "We had them flat-foots flat-footed."

"Except for the two working a wreck right where Shifty parked our first string of getaway cars." Archie ran his fingers through his hair. "Whew, boy. Thinking back on that still has my heart bouncing off my tonsils."

"We hightailed it to our second string," Ed said, "and wouldn'tcha know, cops were nosing around them, too. They took a squint at the Buick we were in, then at us and zip bang, the chase was on."

Voice rising an octave, Archie went on, "Shifty lost 'em. Mercy, how that boy could drive. We knew we had to ditch that Buick before they got onto us again.

"He dropped Melba Jane and me here at the house with the money. Him and Ed went to snatch two cars so's we could split up and vamoose. What they come back with was a junker pickup truck they stole from an old boy 'bout six blocks over."

"It's all we could *find,* fool. It was broad daylight. Every third jake we saw had a badge pinned to his shirt."

Ramey's fingertip circled the rim of the coffee vat. "Come on, Ed. Admit it. You knew you were as good as caught. That's why you left the money with Mom."

"Bullsh—oney. 'Twasn't room in the truck for it and the four of us. We trusted Sylvie to keep it till we could come back for it."

"And she did," Melba Jane said, quietly. "Whilst we paid our debt to society."

"Except it wasn't her money to keep. And it isn't yours, either." The answer to its disposal was as obvious as the lie Ed just told to save face. "It's the bank's money."

Archie looked at Melba Jane. Melba Jane looked at Ed.

Ed looked nauseous. "'T'ain't neither. I'll grant it was when we took it, but insurance paid it all back."

A valid contention. The logic, however, had a fatal flaw. "Unless your initials are F.D.I.C., the money still isn't yours."

Ramey reached into the pillowcase and flopped a stack on the table. "Remember upstairs when you said President McKinley's portrait on the bills was lifelike?"

Melba Jane blanched. "Sweet Mary Magdalene. Is that why we can't have it? 'Cause it's counterfeit?"

"Oh, it's real all right. Absolutely genuine, uncirculated, United States currency. The problem is, the

Treasury Department redesigned bills of every denomination several years ago."

Archie laughed. "By what we've seen of 'em, a kid with a box of crayons woulda done a better job. The picture's antigoggled and the ink's greener'n corn stalks in July."

Ed started. Howled profanities. Pummeled the table-top with his fists. "Of all the *snake-bit, egg-rotten, lousy goddamn luck.*"

His brother and sister-in-law recoiled, as actors in werewolf movies do when clouds shrouding the moon dissipate and the village's eccentric but beloved physician sprouts fangs, fur and a bestial disposition.

"What he's trying to say," Ramey interpreted, "is that this money might as well be counterfeit, because you can't spend it."

"We can't?" Archie's frown lines deepened. "How come? You said it's the genuine article."

"Because, you knuckle-dragging, granite-brained idiot," Ed snapped, "how in the hell can we explain where we latched onto a bagful of brand-spankin'-new, thirty-five-year-old hundred-dollar bills?"

Three aged, dyspeptic walruses wouldn't look as morose as the felons sagging into the breakfast room's benches.

Before the shock wore off and they hatched a scheme to have their loot and spend it, too, Ramey slid from the booth, crammed the pillowcase under her arm and skulked away.

Once outside, her clever idea of parking on the street instead of in the driveway, seemed like a death wish. Speed-walking alone in the dark carrying almost two-hundred-thousand dollars in cash evoked the creepy feeling that an underworld version of Gotham City's Bat signal had paged every mugger and miscreant in a ten-mile radius.

While juggling a purse and the loot, Ramey's eyes, as wide and unblinking as Ping-Pong balls, flickered from bush to tree to the shadowy pools they cast. Ears peeled for footsteps not her own, she initiated a silent negotiation with God, vowing an immediate and major improvement in church attendance, vocabulary and behavior, if He'd hold the boogeymen at bay.

It either worked, or the bad guys were at a lodge meeting elsewhere. Key rammed in the lock, she wrenched open the van's door, scrambled up in the seat and locked herself inside.

Safe smelled like paint, turpentine, musty drop cloths, Murphy Oil Soap, ammonia, spools of garbage bags, glue sticks, sawdust and the Mickey Mouse air freshener swinging from the rearview mirror.

As the panting, trembling, cold sweats abated, a keen annoyance with herself bubbled up and spilled over. Phase Two of Plan B-in-progress wasn't doable in the winter-white slacks and purple sweater she still wore. Neglecting to grab a coat on the way out, she was also freezing her ass off in them.

The solution to her wardrobe crisis was as near as the local, never-closed, monolithic discount store.

Except lugging the bulging pillowcase inside might arouse significant curiosity on the part of the store's grandfatherly greeter. So would dashing in to buy a purse big enough for the swag, then going back in again, bleating, "Silly me. I forgot to buy bread and milk for the kids' breakfast."

Hair flapped up off her neck and wadded in twin bunches, Ramey gazed yearningly at those so close, yet so faraway sliding pneumatic doors. She couldn't leave the cash behind in the van.

Or could she? It wasn't exactly the cream of the lot's vehicular crop. Equally unlikely was that a thief trolling for boostable contents, or a morally ambiguous passerby, would peek through one of her windows and say, "Smells like a hundred-and-eighty-grand in that fat ol' pillowslip. I think I'll break out the window and check."

The deciding factor was the infinitesimal yet rapturous possibility that burglars would solve the disposal problem for her while she was inside the store.

The swag was still there when she returned with six

plastic shopping bags and fifty-six dollars and seventy-seven cents less in her checking account.

A detour into Creekside Meadows, a future tract house development on an arid, limestone plateau afforded Ramey the privacy to change into her purchases. Minutes later, she wheeled into the parking lot of the Bank of Plainfield's southside branch.

Giant sodium lights forced permanent insomnia on the landscaping's boxwoods and hollies. As Ramey nosed the van into a parking spot, shivers of fear and exhilaration zipped up her spine.

Several months ago, the commercial loan manager warned her about a purse snatcher who'd robbed a customer on the sidewalk outside the bank's entrance. It happened so fast that all the victim saw was a white male wearing a jean jacket. Because security cameras installed on the front of the building are aimed at the door, the robbery wasn't captured on videotape.

The manager explained that industry surveys showed that customers expect cameras inside the bank, at the drive-through windows and ATM. They didn't appreciate being in Big Brother's crosshairs while waiting in the parking lot for Aunt Lulu to deposit her Social Security check.

At the time, Ramey filed away that factoid in a mental drawer labeled Trivia That Might Come In Handy Watching *Jeopardy*. She perused the bank's facade and roofline. If a new poll had given the nod to full frontal surveillance, they'd done a primo job of hiding the cameras.

"Okay," she said, with a sigh. "Initiate Phase Three." Leaping from the van, she jogged down the sidewalk and around the corner of the building. Its blank brick wall equaled no cameras on point, as if it mattered.

Without a doubt, at the back of the building, cameras were trained on the night deposit bin near the corner of the main drive-through lane, the auxiliary lanes and adjacent ATM.

Thursday morning, when employees discovered the windfall mixed with the usual zippered vinyl bank bags, they'd rush to review that videotaped footage.

The heavy steel night repository box had a narrow slot at the top and a larger, hinged drawer that commercial customers, like Ramey, could access with a key. It was considerably more difficult and slower to stuff the strapped bundles into the skinnier, shorter slot than dumping them in the drawer. However, even if the list of key-issued patrons was long enough to circle Earth, Ramey's name was on it. Under B, for Born Smarter Than That.

The pillowcase lightened as she popped one ten-thousand-dollar brick after another through the slot. What a hoot it would be to see the expression on everyone's face when the video was replayed. Better still, to eavesdrop on the discussion of whether the anonymous benefactor in a hoodie, 3-X sweatpants puddled over corduroy men's house shoes, yellow Playtex gloves, a bandanna tied around the mouth and wraparound sunglasses was male or female.

Or, she thought, chuckling softly, a walking wardrobe malfunction from Planet Zerkon.

Back in the van, she whipped off the waist-up portion of her disguise and the house shoes and stuffed them back into the shopping bags. No harm leaving the sweatpants over her slacks for a while until she warmed up, or the van did.

By the clock on the dash, her subsequent round-trip to a fast-food joint for a cup of coffee took about eight minutes. "Perfect," she said, pulling around to the back of the bank and halting beside the night depository. Inserting her official key, she dropped her personalized, zippered, vinyl bank bag in the drawer, as she had countless times before.

Tomorrow, if anyone who might have driven by earlier reported her van parked in front of the bank, she'd say she was filling out a deposit slip. As for whether she'd happened to observe any Zerkonian fashion disasters in the vicinity…

The mere thought had her laughing all the way from the bank.

19

Mike placed the gym bag and the ice pick on the interrogation room's table. Plastic evidence bags protected the items destined to become Exhibit A and Exhibit B.

Though his face was pale and clammy, the area around Preston Carruthers's mouth and eyes was as green as the paint on the walls. His hypertensive attorney, Aaron Hoag, was flushed as pink as a newborn.

Despite the human color palette, it wasn't looking a lot like Christmas. Not for them, anyway.

Mike flipped around a chair and straddled it. "Care to explain how those items wound up in the trunk of your car?"

"Don't answer that, Preston. The search Sergeant Constantine conducted was illegal."

"Not a search. An inventory. And it was so textbook-legal, the prosecuting attorney's buying my lunch tomorrow."

Addressing the videocamera's cyclops lens, Mike said, "For the record, a subsequent Breathalyzer shows Mr. Carruthers is no longer legally intoxicated." His eyes lowered. "You're aware of that fact, right, Mr. Hoag?"

"That a second test was administered, yes. That the results are indicative of my client's level of impairment?" He shook his head.

Here we go, Mike thought. Let the games begin and may the best man win. "I understand your concern, but it's a shame you feel that way." He shrugged. "Guess it's back to the drunk tank for you, Carruthers. Another oh, fourteen, sixteen hours and you ought to be dried out to your hired gun's satisfaction."

"What? Fourteen— No—*wait*." Carruthers glared at Hoag, his new persecutor and appealed to Mike, the savior—a role reversal provoked by the defense attorney's specious pissing contest.

"What's it gonna be?" Mike checked his watch. "The pizza delivery I chipped in on will be here anytime now."

Hoag's mouth worked, as if a poppy seed was stuck between his teeth, then declared his client competent to answer questions.

Mike bestowed a congratulatory smile on Carruthers for sparing himself further bonding with the inebriated lowlifes downstairs. Before Godfather's brought that thin crust mushroom pizza, Preston Carruthers would wish his attorney had won the first round.

From a file folder, Mike pulled out a photocopy of the towing company's bill for transporting the Mercedes to his law office the morning of the murder. Next came the adjacent muffler shop's invoice for repairing Ramey's punctured brake lines.

"Proof his car broke down," Hoag said. "And that Preston took it upon himself to repair his widowed sister-in-law's van."

"That's plausible, except for this." Mike read from the mechanic's statement that Carruthers was informed that the damage to the van was the result of tampering, not normal wear and tear.

"Tampering," Mike repeated. "A fact, along with the repair itself, he failed to mention to Ms. Burke. Now, I ask you, why wouldn't a responsible, caring Eagle Scout warn his widowed sister-in-law that someone had intentionally sabotaged her vehicle?"

Hoag flapped a hand. "Why worry her over a petty act of vandalism?"

"Uh-huh. Dispatch gets lots of complaints about punks throwing themselves under cargo vans to puncture the brake lines."

"It was an oversight, then. The poor woman's home was already a crime scene. I'd go so far as to call it a kindness."

"You would." Mike chuckled. "I'd call it his fourth, maybe fifth mistake."

Carruthers's eyes widened, then pinched at the corners, as though replaying the crime and its aftermath. Not the reaction of an innocent man.

"The funny thing is, if he'd told Ms. Burke that the brakes were on the fritz and he'd taken it in for repairs, it would have diverted suspicion *from* him."

A similar point had been made to Rickenbacher at the impound yard. The rookie had screwed up big-time when he allowed Carruthers to take the van. Except in the manner of clouds and silver linings, had Rickenbacher refused, they'd have been aware of the tampering sooner, but less likely to suspect Carruthers of causing it.

Truth was, the cleverest move Carruthers should have made would have been to immediately alert Rickenbacher about the faulty brakes. The clandestine repair was a huge, panic-driven error in judgment. Having given Carruthers several seconds to call himself a dumb-ass in six languages, the lab's report determining that brake fluid was the substance on Falcone's shirt skimmed across the table.

"Getting the drift, gentlemen?"

Joining the report was a copy of the fingerprint-ident card from the booking process for Carruthers's DUI. Last, but so beautifully not least, were the matching prints lifted from the ice pick's handle and the gym bag's. Both belonged to Carruthers.

Mike said, "It'll be a day or so before the lab confirms the spots on the coveralls in your trunk as brake fluid. But I honestly can't thank you enough for leaving the time-dated credit card receipt for them in your car."

He sat back in the chair, his palms polishing the armrests. "I'd guess about now, you're wishing you'd bought gloves to wear with that new outfit."

"Circumstantial," Hoag said.

"Forensics don't lie."

"They can be misinterpreted." It was a bluff, and a dismal one. Hoag's tone inferred that conjuring a convincing, believable explanation for a jury would require major league prestidigitation.

Carruthers heard it, too. He wasn't a stupid man, although keeping direct evidence of a homicide in his trunk might allude to that.

Once a crime was committed, paranoia, self-preservation and a need to regain control often overruled common sense. It was astonishing how often the fear of being seen disposing of damning evidence precluded the instinctive impulse to get rid of it.

Control was key. Hide it in a secure location accessible solely to you, then at some opportune time in the future, ditch it as far away and disconnected from you as possible.

Istanbul, if you can manage it. Roadside trash bins in a couple of different states would also suffice.

Mike cupped his ear. "Hear that whisper on the wind, Carruthers? It's saying give it up, sport. You're toast."

"That's for a jury to decide," Hoag said. "The prosecution must convince twelve people beyond a reasonable doubt. I need only to convince one that such doubt exists."

"A hung jury isn't an acquittal."

Hoag's face darkened a shade. "Nor is it a conviction."

"Fine. Don't let him talk, but have the decency to tell him your advice has nothing to do with his right to remain silent and *everything* to do with padding your fee."

Mike addressed Carruthers directly. "The choice is yours. Make things easier on your conscience and your wallet, or don't say a word. Either way, we've got you."

He pictured Rickenbacher and other plainclothes in a room down the hall huddled around a black and white monitor. For investigators, watching and listening to a live, video feed was as mesmerizing as the World Series of Poker.

Like no-limit Texas Hold 'Em, interrogation was an art, a science and improvisational theater. Read your opponent correctly, alter your game and "tells" accordingly, lie and bluff with impunity, and God willing, the perp will confess.

Switching again from hard-ass investigator to sympathetic, what-a-friend-you-have-in-me, Mike leaned forward, arms extended and splayed on the table. Careful to depersonalize and mitigate the circumstances, he said, "Look, Preston. I know this wasn't premeditated. It just happened and you'd give anything in this world to change it."

Tears filmed Carruthers's bloodshot eyes. "Oh God, yes. I didn't mean—"

Hoag barked, "Shut up!"

"Of course you didn't mean to." Mike stopped short of calling the homicide an accident. "Everything was fine, then all of a sudden…"

"It wasn't my fault. He was just *there* and—"

Hoag clamped Carruthers's wrist and yanked it. "Stop it! I can't help you if you don't keep your mouth shut."

"It was pitch-black," Mike said. "A storm moving in, not a soul in sight. It scared the hell out of you when Falcone materialized out of nowhere, didn't it?"

"Questioning," Hoag warned. "That's what my client is here for, not to be subjected to idle speculation."

"It's eaten at you ever since, hasn't it, Preston? You can't sleep, can't concentrate…." Mike sucked his teeth. "Booze takes the edge off, but it's only temporary."

Before Hoag broke the spell, Mike pressed, "That face. You can't forget it, can you? Seeing that old man's face when you rammed that ice pick into his heart."

"It was—I didn't realize what I'd done till he…he *fell.*"

Hoag groaned and slouched in his chair. Nearly audible were his mental gears grinding the prospects of a successful temporary insanity defense versus a plea bargain to involuntary manslaughter.

"It wasn't a stranger you intended to kill, though, was it?" Mike asked. "It was Ramey Burke."

"Ramey? Why would I— No, no, you've got it all wrong."

"That's why you were jabbing holes in her brake lines with that ice pick. You wanted her dead. Wanted your wife to have sole ownership of the house. But it had to appear accidental."

Just saying it made Mike's stomach clutch. It was impossible to predict where or when those brakes might have failed.

"You were sweating bullets before you ever got to the house, weren't you? Your wife's afraid of storms. What if the thunder wakened her while you were gone? Or your son? What if Ed Dillinger went out on the front porch for a smoke?"

Carruthers's tongue swiped his upper lip.

"Homicide, plus the attempted homicide of your poor widowed sister-in-law?" Mike sneered. "By the time the prosecution's through with you, the jury'll beg to execute you, *personally.*"

"I wasn't trying to kill her!" Carruthers shouted. "I just wanted her out of the house for a few days."

"Like on a ventilator in ICU?" Struggling for composure, Mike reached for a legal pad and positioned it in front of him. Turning to a clean sheet, he took up a pen, the barrel rolling between his fingers, a civilized substitute for Carruthers's throat.

"Take it from the top and save the bullshit 'wasn't my faults' and 'didn't mean tos,' for the courtroom."

Carruthers sighed, visibly affronted. "If Ramey had just accepted Don's proposal, no one would have been hurt."

"Blevins was your accomplice?"

"Of course not. A means to an end, which he failed at miserably."

"A means to—" Mike interrupted himself. "Start over, in chronological order."

Another poor-me sigh. "Last Wednesday, when Ramey invited us to dinner, I checked into the Dillingers' background. Between that, remarks made that evening and an unannounced visit the next morning, I surmised that the missing money from their robbery spree must be hidden in or near the house."

"But you couldn't look for it with Ramey around. Not to mention, her aunt and uncles," Mike completed Preston's reasoning.

The Dillingers would have been evicted, Carruthers explained, the instant Don and Ramey left for the airport. While the happy couple honeymooned—paid for by Preston, along with the cubit zirconium engagement ring and a five-thousand-dollar postnuptial bonus to Blevins—Preston would have been free to treasure hunt.

"This alleged stash," Mike said. "How did you know the Dillingers hadn't already found it?"

"By the holes Archie kept digging in the yard, it was obvious the senile fools had forgotten where they'd buried it."

Also obvious was his ignorance of the in-house search. So was Mike, until the monetary discrepancy in the old case files and Ramey's jokes about Archie's landscaping, Melba Jane's scrubathon and Ed's all-thumbs repairs jelled into a money motive for Falcone's murder.

Mike had theorized the wheelman had either demanded a bigger cut, Ed had second thoughts about a four-way split, or when Ed told Falcone they couldn't find the money, Falcone called Ed a liar and went ballistic.

Right motive, wrong killer. A rabidly curious medical examiner and a phone call to the franchise repair shop across the street from Carruthers's office exonerated a paroled career criminal and trapped a pillar of the community.

Carruthers whined, "Do you know how many attorneys have flocked here straight out of law school in the past few years? They can afford to work cheap. They don't have spoiled, shopaholic wives with hobby jobs. They don't have one son at Yale and an insolent, tree-hugging liberal addicted to videogames at home. Chase has no ambition and Portia coddles him shamefully. He'll still be living in the basement when he's forty."

To Mike's disgust, Preston's woe-is-me rationale for beating the robbers to their loot continued. Violins should have keened in the background as Carruthers described his valiant battle against depression following the deaths of Sylvia and Bill Patterson and Stan Burke. Extramarital affairs and a shiny new sportscar made him feel all better, until Portia got a bellyful and filed for divorce.

"You've met my wife," he said. "Stunningly beautiful though a bit high-maintenance, but I do love her. We reconciled for our sons' sake, then last week, after a heart-to-heart, we agreed it was senseless to postpone the inevitable any longer than necessary. I'd planned to move to a pied-à-terre by the end of the month."

Apartments were where the lower class laid their heads. Wait'll he got a load of the cot-style accommodations he'd soon call home.

"Did Ramey know about the split?" Mike asked.

Carruthers shook his head. "Neither do our boys. Chase suspects it, as does Tripp, but it isn't the type of news parents break on the phone. I was flying to New Haven this weekend to tell him."

And, Mike thought, ditch an incriminating ice pick and gym bag en route. "Portia's entitled to at least half of your marital assets. You figured the cash from the robberies would prevent a downward spiral to a used Ford sedan and cheap Scotch."

Carruthers snorted. "Actually, I saw it as a refund on the taxes I've paid to feed, clothe and cage the Dillingers all these years. *They* certainly didn't deserve it. None of them has ever held an honest job, much less paid a nickel in property tax on that monstrosity of a house their father built."

As motives went, that was among the squirreliest Mike had ever heard. By his expression, Aaron Hoag couldn't quite wrap his mind around it, either. It added a whole new paragraph to Webster's definition of *entitlement.*

From there, the events leading up to Falcone's murder and the crime itself were almost anticlimactic. After Ramey told Blevins to take a hike, Carruthers was forced to do his own dirty work, again. Ramey's continued good health triggered the brake line tampering. Time was the enemy. Any minute, a deadbeat Dillinger might strike pay dirt.

His breath quickening, Carruthers said, "I'm not a grease monkey. A diagram of the van's brake system was on the Internet, but it was so dark that night, I couldn't see what I was doing. Then somebody kicked my shoe. A voice said, 'Who are you? What are you doing under there?'"

He buried his face in his hands. "I was terrified. Thought it was Ed, at first. The man started off—toward the porch. I grabbed him. Spun him around."

Tears oozed from the cracks between his fingers. "I had to stop him. I couldn't let him tell anyone. My arm jerked up...to hit him, keep him quiet, until I could get to my car and get away. The ice pick. I forgot it was still in my hand." He looked up at Mike, his features flushed and contorted. "You've got to believe me. I didn't mean to kill him."

"That doesn't make Falcone any less dead."

"It just happened. I swear."

Contempt leavened Mike's voice. "You blubbering sack of slime. 'I didn't mean to. It just happened.' You don't even have the guts now to admit you killed a defenseless old man."

"I didn't— He was a *thief*, for God's sake. He didn't deserve that money."

Mike pushed backward off the chair. A cocked fist ached to exact a little old-fashioned justice.

Fingers splayed and flexing, he strode to the door and beckoned the uniform waiting outside. "I need a break. Get him a box of tissues, then tell Rickenbacher to take over."

He glanced back over his shoulder. Loudly enough for Carruthers to hear, he said, "Make that one tissue, fussy as he is about how his goddamn tax dollars are spent."

Cookie-cutter usually defined tract houses as unique as game pieces on a Monopoly board. Though the homes in Oak Haven ranged in style from pared-down Italianate villas to Tudors to bloated Provençal cottages, the aura of nouveau riche sameness prevailed. Each plot of weedless lawn was untouched by paws, or human feet, save the guy who mowed it precisely on the diagonal twice weekly.

Spotlights tucked in the professionally landscaped and maintained shrubbery washed the blue-gray brick and stone facade of the Carruthers' home. Corkscrew yews in concrete urns flanked the recessed entry. On one side, the requisite fountain splattered into a meandering rivulet banked by sword grass, Japanese maples, barberries trimmed into maroon mushroom caps and flowering plants Ramey couldn't identify, or smell.

That merrily gurgling fountain, however, was having its usual suggestive effect. The sound was a Pavlovian downside for anyone whose potty training involved a trickling bathroom faucet.

Ramey's finger was poised to jab the doorbell again when one of the carved, walnut double doors swung open. Portia looked tired, miffed and a little tipsy.

Her long-stemmed wineglass motioned Ramey inside. "I was beginning to think you weren't coming." Her eyes lowered to Ramey's empty hands. "And just as I guessed, you aren't staying."

She turned, the hem of her aquamarine silk robe rippling over the circular foyer's polished slate floor. Ramey closed the door and followed her into the morning room.

It was her favorite in a house too magazine perfect to feel like a home. The white carpet was so thick, it was like walking on freshly fallen snow, but her sister had furnished the room with family pieces she'd loved when she was growing up.

Once upon a time, she and Ramey draped quilts over the boxy, caned Jacobean sofa and pretended they were camping at Roaring River State Park. Sylvia's platform rocker and her father's massive club chair and ottoman had been reupholstered in complementary patterned chenille.

In a corner by the bow window, the brass trumpet

and needle arm of a victrola shone like old gold, as did the fittings to Ava Dillinger's treadle sewing machine cabinet.

Ramey caressed the wide library table her father had used as a desk. Above it hung a pewter-framed enlargement of his and Sylvia's wedding photograph—one of the few of him in a coat and tie instead of a uniform. Being the dad, thus the family shutterbug, snapshots glued in photo albums seldom included him.

"Care for something to drink?" Portia asked. "I can make a pot of coffee if you like. You know, since you're driving."

Ramey sighed. "I'm sorry. I really am."

Her sister kicked off her mules and curled up in the club chair. A lopsided smile conveyed forgiveness. "I figured you wouldn't have much luck kicking out the Dillingers. It was three against one. And they have their act down cold."

"Do you honestly dislike them that much?" The rocker tipped forward as Ramey sank down in the plump seat.

It was a magic chair. Countless scrapes, bruises and hurt feelings had been tenderly, lovingly cared for by nestling in her mother's lap and letting her warmth and the gentle motion of the chair soothe whatever ailed her.

Portia said, "That's what's so aggravating. The

Dillingers are impossible to ignore and much as I wanted to dislike them, they do grow on you after a while."

Her eyes narrowed to a nearsighted squint. "Good grief. What's that black stuff all over your slacks?"

Glancing down, Ramey brushed at the fleecy lint from the sweatpants she'd pulled on over them at the bank. "I—uh, something flying around in the van, I guess." The dratted fibers clung to the off-white wool as though they'd been glued on.

Ramey's heart began to beat in sync with the rap music coming from the stereo speakers in Chase's basement bedroom. "Is Preston home?"

"He's still at the office." Portia's lips tightened to a moue. "What a dedicated officer of the court I married."

Braced for the impossible to avoid, Ramey asked, "Are you sure he's there?"

"I haven't checked up on him, if that's what you're asking. Confronting him, then pretending to believe his lies, or calling him on them isn't worth the effort. It hasn't been for a long time."

Noting the morning room's open French doors, her voice softened to a murmur, as though Chase might be lurking on the outside. "That's why I'm filing for divorce, as soon as he has a sit-down with Tripp at school and I talk to Chase." Correctly interpreting Ramey's expression, she said, "No reconciliations this time, Sis."

She drank down her wine and set the glass on the magazine table beside the chair. "The thing about watching what you wish for, 'cause you just might get it? Well, I did and God, I can't wait till it's gone. My unfaithful husband, this three-thousand-square-foot igloo in Yuppyville mortgaged to the chimney caps...."

She laughed. "I'm dying to tell the neighbors what a bunch of self-centered phonies they are. I can't, though, unfortunately. I tried to be them for too long and these properties come on the market too often to blow a commission for me, or the agency."

Ramey ached to believe her ears. It wasn't the wine, a mood, the residue of another quarrel talking. Portia had finally realized that losing battles were those you can't win, no matter how hard you fight.

"Trust me, there's no backing down," Portia said. "Actually, I didn't last time. During our so-called reconciliation, I hired an attorney outside Plainfield's legal good ol' boy network."

News of the impending divorce had no bearing on what Ramey had to tell her—other than kicking Portia while she was down, but trying to be up. Preston was a certified jerk, but he'd been *her* jerk and the father of her children for almost twenty-two years. Marriages of that duration can be dissolved legally and financially, but the emotional binding ties are seldom completely severed.

"I didn't expect you to break into a happy dance," Portia said, sitting straighter in her chair, "but something's wrong, isn't it? That's why you came by to tell me you'd changed your mind about staying here instead of taking the chicken's way out and calling."

Now or never, Ramey thought. And never wasn't an option. "I never intended to stay. Almost everything I said tonight at dinner was a lie."

Portia's eyebrow crimped, as if she were reviewing the conversation at the restaurant.

"I wanted Preston to believe the house would be empty. Which it would have been, after I checked the Dillingers into a hotel. Then I'd have left the van parked a couple of streets over and walked home."

Before Portia could ask why, Ramey went on, "I was laying a trap for Preston. According to old newspaper stories about the Other Dillinger Gang's string of bank robberies, the tens of thousands of dollars they stole was never found. At least, that's how it appeared.

"There's no doubt in my mind that Preston knew about it and thought it was hidden in the house somewhere. He's been looking for it, every chance he could, since the day after the homecoming dinner." She paused. "Or was, until the morning Shifty Falcone's body was discovered."

Whether her sister had consumed one generous glass of wine, or a full bottle, the alcohol's effect was dissipating. Her blood-red nails dug into the club chair's rolled armrest. "What are you trying to say?"

They both started when the telephone rang. Portia hesitated, then scooped the cordless handset from its dock. Frowning at the Caller-ID screen, her head turned toward Ramey as she answered it.

"Hello? Aaron who? Oh—oh, yes, of course, I remember you. Hoag, Petrie and Warren. Your offices are a floor above Preston's." Her features relaxed as she said, "I'm sorry, Mr. Hoag, but Preston isn't home—"

Eyes widening and fixed on Ramey's, her bare feet slowly eased from under her, as though invisible wires were pulling them to the floor. "The police have charged him with *what?*"

20

Ramey was too tired to sleep. Too wired for office work, to read or watch TV. Talking would be good, but required someone to talk to and it was 2:15 a.m., Central Standard Time and she didn't know a soul in London. Or Seoul, for that matter.

That left making cookies. Specifically, therapeutic chocolate-intensive, no-bake cookies. With the recipe calling for three cups of rolled oats, they were almost healthy. Breakfastlike, even.

Cooking relaxed her. Solitary, middle of the night, comfort food cooking, in particular. There was a wondrous reassurance and orderliness and predictability in following instructions that stated precisely how much of what, stirred in when, virtually guaranteed the desired result.

If only life worked that way....

Unconditional love was like fission—both a conqueror and a divider. And fusion? Well, from what she recalled from physics class, that explained how both subtle and enormous differences in opinions, personalities and appearances strangely emphasized the similarities.

"And therein lies the difference between cooking and life." Her laughter echoing off the kitchen walls sounded a tad delirious, even to her. "A list of ingredients, you're born with. A general idea of the recipe, you learn from your parents."

In accordance with the one she was following, the apportioned sugar, milk, cocoa and dash of salt were added to the melted butter. She eyed the dark brown glop at the bottom of the pan. "And boy does that look like what life turns to way too freakin' often."

Adjusting the stove burner from low to high, she laid the spoon on its rest and leaned a hip against the cabinet front. No-bakes were truly a snap to make, but timing was everything.

Languid bubbles burbled at the goo's outer edges. Tiny volcanoes erupted in the middle. She set the timer and checked her watch. Second hand at two twenty-two and twelve seconds. Mark-set-go.

Rap-rap-rap.

Startled, her head wrenched sideward, then tipped. Knocking. Somebody was at the door? At two twenty-two and twenty-two seconds in the technical morning?

Assuming the prodigal and repentant Dillingers had

returned, she hurried to let them in. Throwing the door open, she said, "Ed, you old—"

Mike Constantine looked slightly jaundiced in the glow of the porch fixture's bug light.

"Oh. Hi," she stammered, then, "Yikes, my cookies," and sprinted for the kitchen.

Switching off the burner, she grabbed the pan by its thankfully heat-resistant handles and set it on the island's tiled countertop. "Jeez, that was close. Sixty seconds to the, er, second."

Mike entered the kitchen, as though uncertain whether he was invited to come inside. "I was driving by and saw all the downstairs lights on."

"I'm glad you did." And she was. She'd even expected him to, though she wouldn't admit it to him. That somebody she needed to talk to was him. Considering the circumstances, why she'd felt immediately comfortable around him made no sense at all, but there it was.

She smiled, observing the just-a-guyness inferred by his unbuttoned collar and unholstered belt. "Insomniacs don't get a lot of company."

He pointed at the ceiling. "Why'd you think it was Ed at the door?"

The trouble with cops is much and everything. They didn't miss much and were suspicious of everything.

"Because," she began, frantically consolidating honesty as the best policy and brevity's soul of discretion. "After dinner at Hernando's, the Dillingers and I had a difference of opinion about who's the boss around here. Later, when I got home from Portia's, I found a note saying they'd packed up their toys and moved back to the mission."

Mike chuckled. "They'll be back ringing your doorbell by tomorrow afternoon. Suppertime at the latest."

"Maybe, except they put the *born* in stubborn. And they'll have to knock, like you did. Ed short-circuited the chime the other day trying to fix it with a butter knife."

"My fault. I took away his screwdrivers." Peering over her shoulder, Mike sniffed the still foamy chocolate sauce. "If that's what I think it is, my mom used to make them by the ton."

"Did you like them?"

"Are you serious? I'd eat them till I almost hurled."

Grimacing, she reached for the vanilla bottle and a teaspoon. "Me, too, but that comes under the heading of a little too much information."

"You have one sister. With three, you learn the concept of feast or famine at a very young age. You also learn why girls have long fingernails."

Ramey glanced at her blunt, unpolished ones. Portia's talons had drawn blood when they were kids. Words were now her weapon of choice. The razor-honed barrage she'd unleashed a few hours ago had hit the mark, too. It'd be hard to miss an indefensible target.

"Hey." Mike's fingertip gently pressed her jaw, turning her face toward his. "A minute ago, I half expected you to slam the door in my face. You didn't, but you don't have to act like everything's fine for my benefit."

"It isn't." Ramey attempted a smile. "You know what they say. When the going gets tough, the not-so-tough eat chocolate and fake it."

"Not unless they have to."

"I do, though. I'm afraid of what'll happen if I let my guard down."

"You don't need it with me." His eyes promised he'd catch her if she'd let herself fall. "Know how I know? My guard went down a few days ago, and for the first time in my life, I couldn't put it back if I tried."

His lips were as soft and warm as she'd imagined, his tenderness intensifying the sense of empty spaces filling, spilling over, eclipsing the world and all its heartbreaks. Pulling back, her eyes too heavy-lidded to open, she said, "I wish you hadn't done that."

"Why?"

"Because it was just a fantasy, but now it's reality and I want you to do it again."

He grinned. "That's a problem for you?"

"A huge problem. My dad was a cop. You're a cop. I don't date cops, let alone, well…"

"Too bad, Little Chief. I'm not quitting my job and I'm not quitting you, so I guess you'll just have to get over it."

He kissed her again, a brief, powerful closing to an argument she'd already lost with herself. "For now, though," he said, "we're going to finish those cookies and talk."

"But—"

He handed her the premeasured half cup of peanut butter and a spatula to scrape it out with. That was another thing wrong with cops. They weren't very often.

Apparently discontent to sit down and watch, Mike hovered at her elbow—the one winged above the pan, jockeying for leverage. "Want me to stir that in for you? Or are you waiting to pour in the oats?"

Rather than say something rude, such as, "Keep your mitts out of my batter, Detective," she suggested he spread the waxed paper on the counter for the cookies to cool on.

The box had a built-in tear strip, but Mike fetched the kitchen shears from the knife block. Someone, presumably his mother, taught him that cutting waxed paper sharpened the blades at the same time.

Impressive. And, Ramey allowed, a weird habit to be impressed by unless you favored practicality over supposed convenience.

The quietude elongated to an awkward silence. Paper rattled. The stove's finicky timer dinged a belated sixty-second warning. Her wooden spoon thumped the bottom of the pan.

Mike's palms ironed the waxed sheet's curled ends, then anchored them flat. "Hard to know where to start, huh."

"Yeah. It's supposed to hit seventy-five degrees this afternoon is the best I'd come up with."

"Then you know about Preston."

The plastic pull ring on the oatmeal carton zipped off as easily as advertised. "I was at Portia's when Aaron Hoag called from the police station."

"That's why I was surprised to see your van in the driveway. I figured you'd be at her house."

"I should be. Would be, except after Portia hung up the phone, she told me she hated me and kicked me out."

A third cup of oats thickened the mixture to the consistency of drywall compound. "She's scared and angry and needed an enemy to take it out on. With Preston in jail, that left me."

The spoon handle banged the pan's rim. Specks of dough splattered the tile counter. "Telling Chase his father has been arrested for murder will be only a warm-up for meeting Tripp's plane when he flies home from college."

She took two tablespoons from the drawer. Laying his aside, Mike pulled over a bar stool and sat down. Intuitive man that he was, he realized that while she focused on scooping dough from the pan and sliding it onto the paper with a fingertip, she could speak freely, as though she were alone.

"I won't insult my sister by saying I know how she feels. Nobody can. The boys are her greatest concern. How they'll handle this. Whether their friends will rally around them or ostracize them. Or rally, then disappear without a trace, which is worse."

"The real ones will stick by them."

"Sure, but when you're hurting, you tend to notice the ones who aren't there that you trusted and believed you could count on, no matter what."

"Which," Mike cleared his throat, "should include you, shouldn't it? Why she pushed you away when she needs you most, I don't understand."

"Because I'm a traitor." Ramey crowned a skimpy cookie with a smidgen more dough. "Portia thinks you and I conspired to trap her husband." She looked at Mike. "She's only half wrong. I absolutely did ask them to dinner to set a trap for him."

She explained the empty house scheme that should have proven irresistible to her greedy brother-in-law. "Except your traffic stop thoroughly screwed up my chance to play amateur detective."

"How'd you know—" Elbow planted on the counter, his jaw came to rest on the heel of his hand. "Keep talking. Believe me. I'm all ears."

The cookies mounding the waxed paper resembled a giant domino—the pattern neat, aligned and progressively logical. The conclusion drawn about Preston was composed of disparate, nonsequential, seemingly inconsequential fragments.

And still was. Relating the fragments in a connect-the-dots fashion would be as messy as unsandwiching peanut butter from two slices of bread. "Who killed Shifty?" she said. "A question that drove me nuts, until I realized it was the wrong one."

"Great." Mike rolled his eyes. "Two sentences and you've lost me."

"Dwelling on *who* defied an answer. Nobody appeared to have a motive. Aside from the Dillingers, nobody knew Shifty was coming to town and they didn't know when. Add an ice pick for a murder weapon— an almost obsolete utensil more people use to punch new holes in belts than to chop ice."

With the last tablespoon of dough, the batch yielded twenty-seven cookies. Mike's waggling fingers called dibs on the pan and the crumbs clinging to the bottom and sides.

Ramey took two cans of soda from the fridge, then

sat down beside him. "Scratching the who and the ice pick left *why* was Shifty killed."

Mike's tongue snagged an oat flake stuck in the corner of his mouth. "Keep talking. I'm kind of busy reliving my childhood."

"Things came together when I read about the missing money from the bank robberies."

As she'd begun to tell Portia before Aaron Hoag's telephone call intervened, the loot was the key to random comments and incongruities dating back to the homecoming dinner. In combination, an arrow pointed exclusively at Preston Carruthers, III.

"Preston said something about the Dillingers robbing seven banks, but being prosecuted for three—a fact he couldn't have known without a hasty background check that afternoon. By the next day," she said, "he's suddenly Ed and Archie's mascot, helping with yard work, cleaning out the toolshed, the garage. Trust me, clean is what my brother-in-law stays, not what he does.

"Then Monday, Gordon Sweeney is at my door, following up an anonymous tip that the Dillingers had moved in here and violated the terms of their parole."

Mike carried the empty pan to the sink and turned on the faucet. "A couple of details you neglected to tell me."

Ramey frowned, thought a moment, then said,

"Why would I? At the time, I figured Don Blevins called Sweeney to get back at me. And might have, if he'd known the parole officer's name." She snapped her fingers. "Besides, I didn't meet you until the morning after."

Shutting off the water, Mike paused alongside the island counter, deep in deliberation. "Nope. Sorry. That falls within the twenty-four-hour, prior to incident rule."

"The what?"

"Ignorance of the law is no excuse, ma'am. The penalty for a witness withholding information pertinent to a homicide investigation is a whole cookie."

The cop face and tone threw her for a second, then she burst out laughing. "Then you may as well take a dozen, because I also didn't mention nearly frying myself in the shower, my desk chair falling apart and the van's ladder clamps mysterious unbolting."

Mike's blissful expression and mouth noises translated to Oh man, these taste just like the ones Mama used to make. Between bites, he said, "Those I heard about. Thank God you weren't hurt, but Preston hoped you'd blame Ed and kick them out so he could search the house. Different intent, same result."

"I did wonder," she said. "The ladder tampering almost convinced me. I was asleep on the couch when he brought Ed home from the police station. That gave them both opportunity, except, like you said, our screw-drivers are still in police custody."

Mike snorted, grinned, then shook his head. "Good thinking. Real good thinking, as a matter of fact."

"Awfully slow on the uptake, though. I should have realized sooner that Preston tipped Sweeney before the murder and KDGE and the newspapers afterward to divert suspicion."

"Partly," Mike said. "I think he hoped the Dillingers would panic under pressure and leave town." He un-spooled two paper towels. "What slid past me was him saying he'd heard about the homicide on the radio on the way to his office. None of the stations broadcast that until about an hour after Preston's Lawyer Boun-tiful routine."

Ramey broke off a chunk of cookie and popped it in her mouth. "Okay, but *way* before that, I should have guessed that Ed, Archie and Melba Jane weren't trying to set a record for triathlon hole digging, closet cleaning and general disrepairs."

"They're slick and you were busy earning a living."

"True." Another chocolate and peanut butter infu-sion preceded, "Funny, though, I thought once the 'why' revealed the 'who,' I'd also know how the ice pick fit in."

Mike nodded. "Another dirty trick in progress. Pres-ton was under your van puncturing the brake lines with it when Falcone surprised him. He stabbed him, stashed the weapon and Falcone's gym bag in the trunk of his Mercedes, then the next morning, faked car trouble to have the damage repaired before you noticed it."

Ramey's mental *click* was almost as audible as it was painful. Contrary to conventional wisdom, money wasn't the root of all evil. In fact, blaming an inanimate commodity deflected responsibility from those, like her brother-in-law, who were willing to kill for it. Money doesn't kill people. People kill people. Poor old Shifty was just in the wrong place at the wrong time.

Mike took her hand in his. "Once Portia knows the extent of what Preston did—what he tried to do—she and those boys are going to need you like they've never needed you before."

Ramey smiled. "I'll be there. So will Ed, Archie and Melba Jane, whether Portia wants them, or not." She hitched a shoulder. "Just because they're bossy and cranky and maybe a little bit crazy, they're family."

Gaze averting to a place far in the distance, Mike sighed and said quietly, "Which brings us back to the missing money."

The possible responses pinged in Ramey's mind like BBs in a tin can. They ranged from a sincerely stupid, "What money?" to the truth she couldn't divulge for much the same reason her mother carried the guilty secret to her grave.

Secrets and lies. Cops and robbers. Destined to be forever at odds, yet entwined, by some freaky force of nature.

Maybe that inevitability inspired her, or perhaps another nudge from Sylvia had her saying, with perfect and absolute honesty, "There is no money, Mike."

"No money?" he repeated. "Then—"

Careful to maintain her verb tenses and tone, she added, "If the money was here, do you think the Dillingers would have left in a huff and moved back to the mission?"

After a long moment, but not long enough to completely overcome skepticism, he said, "After turning the house and the yard upside down for a week, I suppose you're right."

Head angled to deliver a kiss designed to blow the Detective Sergeant-side of his mind, Ramey scowled when he got his breath back and said, "What do you think happened to it?"

She looked him straight in the eye and with no hesitation at all answered, "Well, Mike, after all these years, I'd say there's just no telling."

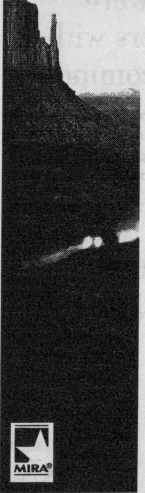

They were twin sisters with nothing in common…

Until they teamed up on a cross-country
adventure to find their younger sibling.
And ended up figuring out that, despite
buried secrets and wrong turns, all roads
lead back to family.

Sisters

by Nancy Robards Thompson

SUZANN LEDBETTER

32068   AHEAD OF THE GAME   ___ $6.50 U.S. ___ $7.99 CAN.
                    (limited quantities available)

TOTAL AMOUNT $ _____
POSTAGE & HANDLING $ _____
($1.00 FOR 1 BOOK, 50¢ for each additional)
APPLICABLE TAXES* $ _____
TOTAL PAYABLE $ _____
            (check or money order—please do not send cash)

To order, complete this form and send it, along with a check or money
order for the total above, payable to MIRA Books, to: **In the U.S.:**
3010 Walden Avenue, P.O. Box 9077, Buffalo, NY 14269-9077;
In Canada: P.O. Box 636, Fort Erie, Ontario, L2A 5X3.

Name: _____
Address: _____ City: _____
State/Prov.: _____ Zip/Postal Code: _____
Account Number (if applicable): _____

075 CSAS

*New York residents remit applicable sales taxes.
*Canadian residents remit applicable GST and provincial taxes.

MIRA®

www.MIRABooks.com   MSLE0506BL